BLOOD KISS

"Awaken child," Lizabet whispered, passing her left hand up and over the spellbound girl's eyes.

Chloe did not flinch as she opened her eyes and looked into the vampire's face, only inches from her own.

"Behold your czarina, young one," Lizabet purred. "My word shall be your will. You have been chosen to be my apostle." Lizabet moved in closer, pressing her body snug against the girl's, feeling the youngster's heat, the delicate curves and swells of her lithe body as she slipped her arms around her waist like a familiar lover. "You are mine now. Now and forever."

With that, she cocked her head and sank her fangs deep into the soft flesh of Chloe's neck. . . .

BOOK YOUR PLACE ON OUR WEBSITE AND MAKE THE READING CONNECTION!

We've created a customized website just for our very special readers, where you can get the inside scoop on everything that's going on with Zebra, Pinnacle and Kensington books.

When you come online, you'll have the exciting opportunity to:

- View covers of upcoming books
- Read sample chapters
- Learn about our future publishing schedule (listed by publication month *and author*)
- Find out when your favorite authors will be visiting a city near you
- Search for and order backlist books from our online catalog
- Check out author bios and background information
- Send e-mail to your favorite authors
- Meet the Kensington staff online
- Join us in weekly chats with authors, readers and other guests
- Get writing guidelines
- AND MUCH MORE!

**Visit our website at
http://www.pinnaclebooks.com**

DAUGHTERS OF THE MOON

Joseph Curtin

PINNACLE BOOKS
Kensington Publishing Corp.
http://www.pinnaclebooks.com

PINNACLE BOOKS are published by

Kensington Publishing Corp.
850 Third Avenue
New York, NY 10022

Pinnacle and the P logo Reg. U.S. Pat. & TM Off.

First Printing: November, 2000
10 9 8 7 6 5 4 3 2 1

Printed in the United States of America

*This book is dedicated to the memory of
my brother Larry and my mother, Jean.
Wish you could have read it.*

ACKNOWLEDGMENTS

A first novel is never easy to write. It takes a toll on the author and takes time away from those closest to him. I would like to thank my beautiful wife, Karen, first and foremost, for her patience and support throughout this endeavor. Without her, there is only darkness. Thanks also to Dawn Kotapish for the early punctuation edits, and a special and sincere thank-you to Lori Perkins for guiding me to John Scognamiglio. Thanks, John, for giving me a shot.

Prologue

Hungary, 1610

She thought at first the distant pounding was in her head, the onset of another one of her spells. The countess cursed and rose slowly to her feet, bracing herself for the wave of vertigo that always preceded the blackouts. The thumping stopped as suddenly as it had begun, and she paused for a long moment, taking stock of herself before turning her attention once more to the girl.

"Oh, I would not forget this, pretty one," the countess said, bending down and pulling the ankle restraint tight. "Not for one as spirited as you."

The girl, a sixteen-year-old peasant named Doricza Szalaiova from the neighboring town of Rednek, had been employed at the castle for little more than a month. Her stay had been relatively uneventful until last night when she had been brought before the countess and had naively declined her sexual advances, unaware that it was not a matter of choice. Large and powerfully built, she had already weathered a beating that would have left most women—or men, for that matter—dead. All her resistance, however, along with any hope she may have harbored of ever leaving Castle Cachtice alive, lay puddling in the thick blood pooling around her bare feet on the cold flagstones. Doricza opened one swollen eyelid and groaned, a final, barely audible plea of abject and total surrender.

"What was that, miserable whore?" the countess asked, rising up just inches from Doricza's face. "I could not hear you. Did you ask for another kiss?"

Doricza could feel the countess's warm breath on her face. She squeezed her eyes shut in anticipation of another bite when the door at the top of the stairs exploded in a splintery shower of wood and mortar.

Count Gyorgy Thurzo, Lord Palatine of Hungary, emerged from the band of raiders that spilled down the dark stairwell into the torch-lit bowels of the castle. A crusader and veteran of countless bloody campaigns, he stared, wide-eyed and repulsed, at the human carnage strewn about the torture chamber.

"So, it is true . . . ," he said, finally finding his voice. "Accursed woman, you have brought shame upon the nobility and disgrace to the family name. These atrocities will not go unpunished. The people demand justice."

"Do not speak to me of the family name, Cousin," the countess scowled. "You know it means nothing without my money."

Count Thurzo could scarcely believe his ears. The woman's arrogance was forever a source of amazement. "You shall have to answer for this, Erzsebet," he said, as if talking to a child. "To the people of Hungary, and ultimately to God."

"I answer to a higher power than your God!" the countess spat, reaching into the folds of her gown. "And as for the people . . ." She whirled and brought the knife around in a deadly arc across Doricza's jugular vein, barely able to contain her glee as the blood poured and splashed the tangle of soldiers struggling to pull her away.

* * *

The Blood Countess of Europe was tried in absentia on January 7, 1611, a mere eight days after her arrest. Fearing intervention from King Matthias II, a Catholic, Count Thurzo moved quickly. He staged the trial in Bytca, his own village, before the Hungarian Parliament could reconvene and lay claim to the vast Nadasdy-Bathory landholdings.

Twenty handpicked jurists listened as thirteen witnesses spun grisly tales of cannibalism, black magic, and vampirism before returning with the predetermined verdict. Citing the esteemed war record of the countess's deceased husband, the Black Knight, Ferenc Nadasdy, Count Thurzo sentenced Erzsebet Bathory to lifelong imprisonment inside the walls of her own castle.

The countess languished for three long years entombed in the north tower of Castle Cachtice before slipping from this world and crossing over into the waiting arms of the Dark Master on August 21, 1614.

The peasants danced in the streets upon learning of her passing, but that night they sealed their windows and doors with garlic and wolf bane, refusing to believe that something so evil could ever truly die.

Part One

Part One

One

Chloe Covington sat silently, motionless save for her blond hair dancing in the slipstream that poured over the windshield of the big convertible. She heard the words of the tall man sitting next to her as they roared down the narrow strip of North Carolina blacktop, but they meant nothing. Her brain was unwilling to recognize his utterances as anything more than a jumbled collection of random syllables lacking any cohesion or syntax.

The man shifted, settling back into the plush interior of the Eldorado Biarritz, still speaking for no one's benefit but his own.

"I think we can do without the radio for a while, sis," he said, dialing the knob back with an abrupt click. "The signal from WDUR is just about crapped out and I can't find anything except gospel music. You don't mind, do you?"

She stared straight ahead, the wind blowing her shoulder-length hair away from her face, fully exposing her delicate features. Nondescript at first glance, her looks drew the envy of other women and the attention of men who had the intelligence to look twice. A slight ridge added a touch of character to an otherwise perfect nose, and her sad eyes looked out pensively beneath long, thick lashes, dominating and defining a face still rooted in the innocence of childhood at the age of seventeen.

"No, I didn't think so," he said, a trace of exasperation creeping into his voice. As he studied her in profile like this, it struck him for the first time just how much she looked like their mother.

Their mother.

His stomach hitched into a slow roll as the surreal events of the last two weeks crashed through his head, reminding him just how quickly the tide of his charmed existence had turned.

Up until this point, Clinton Covington's life had been a carefree lope into the waiting arms of wealth and power. He was the firstborn and only son of Cornelius Covington, founder and president of Covington Tobacco Company, Norfolk, Virginia, one of the top three tobacco producers in the United States. Clinton was well built and handsome, almost to a fault, with a thick crown of wavy brown hair that always fell with a determined, jaunty flip across his forehead, whether he was seated at a board meeting or breaking in a new girl from the typing pool. His mouth was hard edged and carried about it an underlying sneer that was apparent even when he tried to smile. Thick, arched brows framed dusky brown eyes that had always viewed the world as his very own, and the grandeur of the Covington plantation, bedecked with manicured lawns and surrounded by oceans of bright-yellow Virginia tobacco, was the only world he had ever *really* known.

The mansion, one of the great houses of the old South, rested like a crown jewel some 150 yards from the main gate. A full domestic staff of no less than twelve was employed to maintain its upkeep and to see to the creature comforts of Cornelius Covington and his family. Clinton had grown quite accustomed to his lot in life early on, subconsciously acknowledging that he existed on a higher plane than everyone else, without ever giving much thought in his twenty-three years on the planet as to why. In fact, he never really gave much thought to anything until that sunny afternoon two weeks ago, when the idyllic splendor of life on the Covington plantation was shattered.

It was a Saturday, and with most of the house staff off for the weekend, Clinton had the luxury of the main garage all to himself. He was applying a serious coat of wax to the Eldorado, and taking his sweet time. He walked around the car slowly, pausing to admire his wavy reflection in the hood's vast expanse of sheet steel. Chammy and wax in hand, he lovingly worked his way toward the trunk and the tail fins. He was rubbing a circular layer of wax into the left tail fin, being careful not to smear any of the pasty substance on the twin-bullet taillights, when he heard Parselle frantically calling his name.

Clinton had known Parselle all his life. She was as much a part of the Covington plantation as the tobacco fields and the distinctive Doric columns that adorned the main entrance to the mansion. Starting on the house staff as a teenager and working for his father long before he was born, she now oversaw the entire staff and was almost considered family. She was out of breath and in tears when he met her at the bay door. The look of sorrow and shock on her face alarmed him more than the words he could barely decipher through her sobs. She choked back her tears, looked him straight in the eye, and said, "It's your mother, boy. There's been an accident."

She had not called him "boy" since he was a child and it only served to quicken his flight down the grassy hill and up the long driveway to the house, his heart racing and his mind swimming with all the awful possibilities of the unknown. He braced himself for the worst as he bounded up the steps two at a time, but nothing could have prepared him for the bizarre spectacle that greeted him as he burst through the oak doors and into the vestibule.

His mother lay in a crumpled heap at the bottom of

the main stairwell, her head twisted at an impossible angle, her eyes wide open but seeing nothing. A small trickle of blood had found its way out of her open mouth, landing in two dark red blots on the perfect starched collar of her white blouse.

His father stood on the stairwell, inches above her, his arms hanging limply at his sides like unfamiliar appendages attached only moments ago. Finally noticing Clinton standing in the foyer, Cornelius Covington looked up into the eyes of his son, his face twisted with despair. Something else was there, too, under the surface—suppressed, difficult to pinpoint, but as apparent as a child hiding under a bedsheet.

Chloe stood at the edge of the scene, robotic and mute, paralyzed with fear, unable to move. Her face was emotionless, and her eyes, an unusual and striking pale brown flecked with gold, were faraway and empty.

He would learn later that his mother had taken a violent fall down the sweeping marble staircase, breaking her neck in two places—the third and fifth cervical vertebrae to be exact—and died instantly. Chloe had apparently witnessed the whole incident—although no one could be sure, since she hadn't spoken a word from that point on.

The ensuing pathos of the wake and funeral was made all the more woeful by Chloe's inability to acknowledge the hugs and tears of family and friends or the soft-spoken condolences of acquaintances.

By his own admission, Dr. Mackof, their family physician, was completely baffled by the complexities of Chloe's condition. Her initial state of numbness was similar to the shell shock suffered by soldiers who had undergone some traumatic experience in battle, but her ability to retain basic knowledge of social customs and language led him to believe it was a classic case of hysterical amnesia. A condition, he explained, that occurs when a person faces an event so horrible or overwhelming that he or she is unable to face reality and the parts of the brain dealing with that event simply shut down.

He did, however, know of a specialist, a psychotherapist out of Duke Hospital in North Carolina, who was reputed to be doing some groundbreaking research in the study of stress-related memory loss. His methods, considered somewhat unorthodox for 1959, involved a combination of sedative drugs and psychotherapeutic sessions using free-association and suggestion in an attempt to prod and jog the memory of the patient. As Dr. Mackof carefully explained all of this, Cornelius Covington listened with a quiet stoicism. Slumped in his thronelike leather chair behind the massive desk in his study, with seemingly endless fields of tobacco visible through the picture window behind him, he looked like the most miserable man in the world. Satisfied he had heard all he needed to hear, the old man suddenly hoisted himself out of the imposing chair with a squeak and leaned forward, his fingertips spread out on the dark oak of his desk. Clinton knew from watching his father for so many years that this gesture was an indication that the business at hand was over and there would be no further discussion.

"See Elaine and make whatever arrangements are necessary, Ted. Chloe will see this man immediately. My daughter will not spend another night walking through this house like a mindless zombie. Nothing else is of consequence. Not anymore."

His father's clout had always been a source of inspiration for Clinton. He had known early on from lessons learned at his father's knee that power, money, and influence comprised the holy trinity for the real world. Within two hours of his secretary, Elaine, working the phones, Dr. Kianpronanz of Duke University had cleared his *booked-solid* agenda and agreed to see Chloe the very next morning. Clinton couldn't help but smile as he piloted the big Caddy through the North Carolina backwoods, knowing his father's impromptu and generous grant to the new psychology wing at Duke might have had something to do with the expedient clearing of the good doctor's slate.

He stepped on the gas as they came out of a sweeping right-hand corner and roared down the winding asphalt ribbon into the Appalachian foothills, the setting sun glinting white-hot off the Eldorado's polished chrome. He stole a quick peek at the Biarritz's inlaid dash clock: 6:35 P.M. and less than a hundred miles to Durham. He figured he could cover that in an hour and a half, plus another half hour to find the hospital and register his sister.

Chloe would be given a complete physical upon arrival and then held for observation overnight before her first session with Dr. *Can't-pronounce* in the morning. The man had his work cut out for him. The bond that had existed between Chloe and their mother bordered on symbiotic, and when she died, it seemed that a part of Chloe had died, too.

A chemistry had existed between the two of them that was almost scary at times, almost as if they knew what the other was thinking. When Chloe had been just a toddler and learning how to talk, his mother would sit with her for hours talking in silly elaborate rhymes that made sense to no one but themselves. She would accompany her mother on the piano and they would sing, making up their own songs as they went along. His mother had a great voice, a lovely and versatile soprano with a three-octave range.

A voice he would never hear again.

Chloe started up suddenly, an abrupt, excited movement that was a marked departure from her near catatonic state of the last two weeks. He followed her gaze and found himself looking at the most spectacular sunset he had ever seen.

"Yes, Chloe," he said with mock encouragement. "It is beautiful, isn't it?"

He didn't realize that for very different reasons it was the last sunset either of them would ever see.

Two

The sun dropped behind the Blue Ridge Mountains, setting the horizon ablaze in a brilliant, almost violent concession to the wan full moon looming in the sky over the eastern seaboard. Across the wooded floor of the inner coastal plains, the mounting, incessant song of the crickets gave rise to the nocturnal inhabitants of the forests, which covered the high land before sinking into the marshy tidewater and surrendering to the sea.

On a rolling crest overlooking the banks of the Roanoke River, a white-tailed buck paused suddenly in midstride, its soft brown eyes wide with alarm. Its keen nose worked the lazy April breeze wafting through the pines, searching for the telltale scent of a predator, but finding only a slight tang of increased electricity in the air currents. Bending to finish its meal before the inevitable storm, the fluted ears picked up a faint rumble, growing ever louder, drowning out the hushed roar of the rapids upstream. The buck bolted into the woods just as the migration of toads swarmed over the crest and poured through the underbrush.

Local legend held that the glen was haunted ever since Jefferson Davis Henshaw had disappeared without a trace some eleven years ago. No one seemed to know exactly when it had happened, but sometime in March of 1948 the old moonshiner simply vanished from the face of the earth, leaving his cabin door ajar and an unfinished meal on the table. His truck had been parked out back, topped off with fuel and loaded with a fresh batch of corn-squeezin's ready for delivery. An exhaustive search of the area had turned up nothing out of the ordinary aside from the very peculiar discovery of a large wildcat hanging upside down from a tree, its throat ripped out and drained of blood.

That summer, the high grass surrounding the cabin had withered and died, never to grow again, refusing to renew itself with every subsequent spring. A heavy stillness permeated the air, owing more to dread than calm, welling up from an unseen doom that was as inevitable as tears at a funeral. Man and the more noble beasts of the earth steered clear. Only the lowest forms of the animal kingdom, those that crawled on their bellies or wallowed in filth, shying away from the light of day, would tread there. And now with the moon at its apex, the horde of toads circled the dilapidated cabin jutting from the barren earth like a lone tombstone and waited for the resurrection of the thing that lay beneath it.

The beast had lain so long in the dank, sandy soil that she had almost become as one with it. The subterranean network of rootstock and plant growth that had enveloped her limbs rotted and withered, weakening the infrastructure of the immediate terra firma, producing a slight sinkhole effect around the cabin. More than a decade had passed since she had gone under, slowly corrupting the soil as she pulled the vital nutrients from the fertile earth, harnessing energy, gathering strength, and waiting. There had been times throughout the long sleep when she would dream. Dream of the days she had walked the earth in human form. Some of the dreams were troublesome: the storming of the castle and the discovery, the betrayal by Dorka and the others at the trial, the endless days and nights in the tower. Some dreams would bring what might be called a smile to the remnants of her crumbling face:

the perpetual parade of the peasant whores, their unbelieving screams reverberating off the stone walls and blending with the gales of her own uncontrollable laughter. And the blood. Absolute rivers of it during the good times.

The dreams had no beginning and seemingly no end, although at times they would awaken her, full of anticipation, hazily wondering at her surroundings before settling back into the healing foundation of Mother Earth. On this night, though, she had dreamed of the girl with the golden eyes and had awakened, instantly cognizant, as one would awaken in the middle of the night knowing there was an intruder in the house.

It was time.

Three

Being very careful not to disturb the woman sleeping next to him, Cornelius Covington eased his arm out from underneath her and slipped silently from the gigantic bed. Elaine had an affinity for falling asleep immediately after sex, due no doubt to the ferocious abandon with which she performed, but she was a notoriously light sleeper. He draped a robe over his shoulders, still well muscled and broad as he neared fifty-five, and picked his way through the mottled darkness, fearing she would demand another go-round if awakened. With the deliberate step of a cat burglar he slipped into the hallway and closed the doors behind him with a soft, careful click.

Self-loathing clung to him as tenaciously as the long shadow that followed him across the carpet and into his study. Having Elaine in the same bed that he and Grace had shared for twenty-five years—there was no excuse for that—none at all. He had never in any of his past indiscretions been that bold, and the fact that she was dead and in the ground barely two weeks made it all the more reprehensible.

Unable to face his own reflection, he averted his gaze from the inlaid glass of the French doors as he elbowed his way into the study. For all the rooms that made up Covington Manor, the study was the only one that was his and his alone. It was a reflection of the man, spacious and well appointed, suggesting a substantial elegance, void of frills and pretense. A floor-to-ceiling bookcase dominated the north wall, packed with treasures, mostly unread: Joyce, Hemingway, Faulkner, Steinbeck, and Fitzgerald. He looked wistfully at the titles in their handsome leather bindings as he passed and wondered where all the time had gone. He lingered at the window, rolling the fine braided cord of the vertical blinds between his paddlelike fingers before drawing it down with a quick yank. The slats turned out with a snappy about-face, exposing the southeastern fields stretching gallantly to meet the horizon for a fuzzy kiss under the last fading light of day. A somber chime rang out from the grandfather clock behind him, as if to herald the onset of nightfall. Cornelius eased into his chair as the seventh and final peal sounded and he hefted a bottle of Scotch from the recesses of the desk drawer.

He reached across the desk and pulled the gold chain dangling from his reading lamp, adjusting the green shade so that the light it threw his way was minimal. He preferred, of late, to sit in the dark. He very nearly reached for the phone before bringing his hand back to the tumbler of Scotch where his finger resumed its lazy circle around the rim of the glass. It would be folly to call the hospital now. The children were not due to arrive for at least another hour. Besides, Clinton would certainly have the good sense to call as soon as they had arrived safely.

He allowed himself the briefest of smiles as he finished that thought.

Good sense and Clinton didn't always go hand in hand. Oh, the boy was smart enough, there was no question about that. Although he showed little patience for the mundane, day-to-day idiosyncrasies of business, he could at times be brilliant.

Cornelius poured himself two generous fingers of the Scotch and reflected on that day just a few months ago, when Clinton, in one singular, shining moment, had laid to rest any doubts he may have had in his son's ability to spearhead Covington Tobacco.

It had been the quarterly closeout meeting, and the entire board of directors had been on hand along with the majority stockholders to review and assess the 1958 fiscal year. The news was not good.

Kingsbury Tobacco, of Kingsport, Tennessee, was taking a big bite out of the market with their new brand, Dominica Gold. It was a good cigarette, mixing the sweet, flue-cured Virginia tobacco with the mild, air-cured burley tobacco that was so difficult and unprofitable to grow on the seaboard. The blend resulted in a mellow but satisfying taste that most smokers, especially new smokers, found very appealing. In just eight months after its debut, Dominica Gold accounted for a whopping seventeen percent of the total market share, knocking Covington's signature brand, Cheyenne, out of the top spot into a distant second at eight percent.

The floor was opened for suggestions, but none were forthcoming, until Clinton rose silently from his chair and looked carefully into the eyes of every man in the room.

"Gentlemen," he began, satisfied with what he saw, "I think each and every one of us can agree that this is indeed a very grave situation that affects the livelihood and financial well-being of all concerned. Given the popularity of Dominica Gold and our inability to produce a similar blend to compete on a level playing ground, the only solution I can see is to make Dominica Gold less appealing to the American smoking public. The quickest and most efficient way to do this is to undermine their confidence in a product that they are sticking into their mouths at an average rate of seventy-two times a day."

He let that statement sink in as he strode to the front of the room and pulled the various histograms, run charts, and check sheets from the presentation wall, exposing the large map of the continental United States underneath.

"My proposal is simple," he continued. "We will dispatch operatives to every major city in the country whose sole purpose will be to discuss in crowded public places the questionable hiring practices of Kingsbury Tobacco; in particular, the *lepers* they have working for next to nothing in their processing plants. Taverns and restaurants will be targeted, of course, but our focal point should be the subway systems during peak capacity, specifically the morning and evening rush hours. Four operatives will work each train. Two will start at the lead car and two at the end car. Blending in with the daily commuters, they will, during the course of their idle patter, enter into a lengthy discussion regarding operative A's decision to switch from Dominica Gold to Cheyenne cigarettes. Terrible thing, did you know they have lepers working for room and board at the Kingsbury processing plant? It's true! My cousin so-and-so worked there last summer and he quit because he thought he would catch it—and so on and so forth. By the end of the commute, each team will have worked its way to the middle of the train so that every car has been saturated with the story. As people get off the train they will take the story to work with them in the morning and home with them at night. Once the rumor has spread sufficiently in the major metropolitan districts, it will only be a matter of time before it carries into the outlying rural areas. If we start immediately, we should be able to launch this operation full scale in no less than two weeks, and I predict we will begin to see results as early as one month after that."

Clinton stepped away from the map and looked at the stony expressions of the men sitting at the long conference table. Slowly, as the simple beauty of the concept sunk in, their stares of disbelief turned into wide grins. A smattering of applause broke out amid hearty laughter.

It was, of course, a brilliant plan and Cornelius could not have been more proud of Clinton if he had just scored the winning touchdown in the Rose Bowl. Within seven weeks of launching Operation Leprosy, Kingsbury Tobacco sales had dropped thirteen percent and were continuing to fall. He gave Clinton a full seat on the board and threw in a brand-new 1959 Eldorado Biarritz convertible as a bonus just to show the boy how proud he really was.

As underhanded and crafty as Clinton could be at times, Cornelius couldn't help but think that his daughter, Chloe, had a better head for the business end of it. Despite the special preparation and schooling they lavished on Clinton, she was, if truth be told, the smarter and more driven of the two. She excelled at everything she did, not like Clinton, who seemed to get by on charm and dumb luck.

No, Chloe was different. She always seemed to have her nose in a book, whether it was Tolstoy's *Anna Karenina* or a dog-eared issue of *Popular Mechanics* she happened to pick up in the waiting room at the dentist's office. The child was blessed with an inborn thirst for knowledge that no school could teach or no parent instill. When she was as young as eight years old, they would find her in the manor library, a stack of encyclopedias at her elbow, meticulously going through each volume and absorbing information off the pages. As a small child she had regarded school as a wondrous gift, thrilled at the concept that people were there for the sole purpose of teaching her! She had gone through seven years of grammar school (double promoted in sixth grade) never receiving a grade lower than an A and had just graduated valedictorian of her high school class. Offers from colleges were pouring in from all across the country. If there were any drawbacks to her all-around academic excellence, it was that her interests were so wide and varied she had yet to declare a major course of study. Cornelius was taken aback, but not totally surprised, when she walked into his office last winter and told him she wanted to pursue a career in the theater as a writer and director! Where she got such nonsense from, he couldn't be sure, but he had a pretty good idea it had come from her mother.

Grace had always been an ardent patron of the arts and had been actively pursuing a singing career when they met in New York back in '36, giving it all up to marry him. Bad choice, Grace, he thought as he looked out the window into the night sky, wondering if she was looking down at him and frowning. There were worse marriages, he supposed, but she had certainly deserved better. All the wealth and opulence of Covington Manor couldn't absolve his infidelity or make him a better husband, but he could always look in the mirror and say he had done a pretty good job of raising his children.

Until now.

He took a long sip from the generous tumbler of Scotch he had poured, savoring the burn as it trickled down his throat. He thought of Clinton and Chloe driving out through the gates that afternoon, his daughter sitting like a robot in that big Cadillac, unable to respond to the kiss he had laid on her cheek or acknowledge his sad good-bye.

He knew he had lost her forever.

Never again would he see that unequivocal love a daughter reserves for her father shining in her eyes when he looked into her face. Emptiness maybe, or fear—or God forbid—stone-cold hate. No matter what happened at Duke Hospital, whether this specialist could help her or not, he had lost his daughter forever—there was no escaping that. He could only shudder when he thought of the horrors that lay ahead for him if and when Chloe regained her memory. He deserved whatever punishment the law could exact, although he would probably never see the inside of a penitentiary, not with his lawyers and connections. But the thought of Chloe seeing, *knowing*, what he had done, that was too much for him to bear.

They had been fighting that morning, Grace and he, and it was starting to get ugly. Grace knew all about him and Elaine, and although she had seemed cool when she first confronted him about the affair, she was losing her composure and growing more agitated with each pathetic denial that he uttered.

"I can smell her all over you. It's in every room of the house!" she yelled at him, her voice dripping with disgust. "I want her out. I want her out now and you can go with her, for all I care! I've put up with your nonsense all these years for the children's sakes, but they're grown now, Cornelius, and I don't have to put on the happy society couple facade anymore—and know this as I stand here: I stopped loving you with this one. For the love of God, Neil! Right here in the house!"

She was dead serious this time, and he knew it. As she stood there trembling and emotionally drained, the most incredible thing happened. Faced with the shame of a broken marriage, a tarnished reputation, and the disintegration of his family—he smiled. He couldn't stop the muscles in his face even as he realized it was happening.

"G-G-Grace . . . ," he stammered, trying to suppress the ridiculous, shit-eating grin, "you've never been so wrong about—"

The sting of her hand across his face cut him short and put a quick and merciful end to the foolish smirk that had possessed him.

"You bastard!" she hissed. "How dare you laugh at me! I want you and your whore out of my house immediately! Personal assistant, my ass! When I'm through with you, the whole world will know she's nothing but a cheap *whore* and you won't be welcome at the doorstep of any decent home in the South!"

In twenty-four years of marriage she had never used language like that. As she brushed past him out the bedroom door into the hallway, he had no doubt she intended to destroy everything he had worked all his life to build. He only wanted another moment with her—to tell her it would never happen again, that he would fire Elaine (he could set her up in an apartment in town), and he would get some help and everything would be all right. So he bolted after her, catching her at the top of the stairs. In one horrible moment that he would give his right arm to live over again, he grabbed her before she reached the first step and spun her around, unable to believe what happened next even as it was happening.

Grace tore herself away from him and tottered backward, suspended for one frozen moment in time. She looked at him unbelieving, reaching out one last time before she tumbled backward down the long arcing marble staircase. It seemed to take forever, that fall, and he heard with horrible clarity the thud of her body bouncing down the marble steps. He did not see Chloe standing in the lobby until Grace had landed at his daughter's feet in a twisted heap, her unseeing eyes looking up toward the vaulted ceiling.

Chloe stared down at her mother's crumpled body for what seemed like a very long time. She looked up, her gaze climbing the winding staircase, step by step, until finally she was looking directly at him. Like a stone disappearing into the depths of a well, the light and vitality drained from her eyes and they went blank, leaving behind the vacuous, filmy stare of the lobotomized. He may have lost consciousness for just a second, but he couldn't be sure. Everything that immediately followed seemed fragmented and cloudy: Clinton shaking him on the stairs, Dr. Mackof shining that damn light into his eyes. If the police were suspicious at all, they didn't show it: Just a couple of quick questions, Mr. Covington, sir. We're so sorry but we have to ask . . . you say you heard the fall? Quite a shock for your daughter, I'm afraid. When she . . . eh, feels better, we might have a few questions for her—just procedure, you understand. Perhaps you could give us a call?

In the days that followed, Chloe's condition remained virtually unchanged. She did not, as many had suggested, "snap out of it." Indeed, her behavior seemed to grow more bizarre with each passing day. She had taken to wandering about the house at night, usually ending up in the exact spot she had been frozen to the morning of the accident. After some prodding and gentle persuasion, she could be led upstairs to bed, where she would sleep most of the day away. He had found her one night at three in the morning standing stark naked on her bedroom balcony staring at the moon. Twice that night he had put his daughter to bed only to find her a short time later standing again on the balcony, exposed and shameless in the chill of the spring twilight. Finally he had simply thrown a blanket around her, poured himself a drink, and watched her stare blankly into the night sky. Around five-thirty, as the sky grew lighter, Chloe abruptly turned and headed back into her bedroom. She stopped briefly at the French doors and looked over her shoulder to steal a final glance at the oncoming day, a profound and bitter sadness etched on her face. As she crawled into bed and fell immediately to sleep, Cornelius Covington knew this must stop or he would go mad.

Those next few days were the most difficult of his life: living with the horror and guilt of what had happened, dealing with funeral arrangements, relatives, praying that Chloe would snap out of it and dreading the repercussions when she did.

The most important thing, above all else, was to have Chloe back. What happened to him now was of little consequence. He called Mackof after the sleepwalking had begun, pleading with the goddamn quack to help her or at least find someone who could. If he had to sit and watch his daughter stare at the moon like an animal one more night, he might have gone completely insane.

Thank God, Elaine was there for him.

Like a drunk finding comfort in the bottle that led to his ruin, he slept with her that very same night. The fact that he couldn't even wait one night after Grace's death spoke volumes about the hold she had over him. He had been walking around in a sexual fog since that first day she had walked into his office six months ago wearing that low-cut red dress.

She had just started in a low-level administrative position in the personnel department at Covington Tobacco and was dispatched up to his office to get his signature on a memo that was to be photocopied and handed out to all the employees at the curing plant.

"Excuse me, Mr. Covington, sir," she purred in a voice as sweet and thick as honey, bending over the desk at just the right angle. "If I could just get your signature on this memo, we can . . ."

Agitated at the interruption, he peered over the top of his reading glasses and found himself looking straight down her dress at the most magnificent set of tits he had ever seen, and in his time he had seen more than his fair share. Within three months she had climbed out of personnel and was working as his personal assistant, seeing to his appointments, arranging his business calendar, and generally making his life "easier." She had proved to be so invaluable that he had had a room in the mansion converted into an office, enabling her to manage his personal as well as his business affairs, seven days a week if need be. Looking back, he knew that had been his downfall—having her in the house. Grace could overlook a lot of things, but that was just plain stupid, trying to hide her in plain sight like that. If he had been thinking clearly, he would have set her up in an apartment in town, never giving Grace a clue that she even existed. Christ, he had really fucked up.

He polished off the Scotch and hoisted himself out of the chair with a wheeze. The low rumble of distant thunder drew his attention back to the window as he turned to go.

The sky over the Atlantic had turned a sickly purple and was growing darker by the moment. The tobacco fields pulsated and billowed, bending under the sudden gale that roared in and rattled the manor windows in their panes. Off in the distance he could see two giant waterspouts rising from the sea like twin serpents to meet the churning storm clouds.

It looked like all hell was going to break loose.

Four

The movement was so subtle that you might not have noticed it at all had the toads suddenly not stopped croaking. In the perfect stillness of the eerie blue glow of dusk, the barren dirt floor of Henshaw's cabin shifted, rising and falling into itself with the erratic heartbeat of the terminally ill. With the last rise, bony fingers pushed their way through the earth. They clawed and found a hold, displacing soil as they bore down, launching the crown of the foul, shaggy head through the fresh wound in the floor. Like a diver rising up and breaking the surface on empty lungs, the beast propelled herself through the earth's crust into the world above, reveling in the liberating embrace of the cool night air. Eyes wide, she scanned her surroundings, the initial look of wonder dissolving into a triumphant leer as she threw back her skeletal head, filling the tiny cabin with guttural laughter.

She pulled herself free from the grip of the earth and stood erect, gauging the level of energy flowing from her core to her extremities.

She was still weak. The climb to the surface had been laborious but the twilight was exhilarating, and she fed off it. She shuffled, somewhat uneasily, over to the hearth, where a faint shimmer of reflected starlight had caught her eye. Seeing perfectly in the dim gloom, she looked into the remaining shards of glass dangling from the mirror's frame at the death mask staring back. The whealed skin clung tightly to the underlying bone like gristle to a bad steak, discolored and raw. The flames had taken their toll. All the nights spent in the regenerative womb of the earth nestled in corrupt soil had not healed the scars completely. They were, after all, nights without blood.

Blood.

Her eyes, dark and oddly beautiful in the ruined face, sparkled with the very thought of it. She actually started to salivate as the hunger overtook her. Once known as one of the most beautiful women in all of Europe, she regarded her cadaverous reflection with indifference—an unsightly but temporary condition at worst. Yes . . . the blood would replenish her, make her whole again.

She turned from the mirror and slipped from the shanty into the waiting twilight, the rotted gown hanging off her emaciated frame like a spiderweb. Standing in the hollow, she looked up at the billions of stars framing the luminous full moon that welcomed her back to the night. She was reminded of the golden eyes of the child from her dreams. If they were to cross paths on this night, she must move with haste, for destiny was fickle and it waited for no man or god.

She closed her eyes, letting her mind drift back centuries before, to the old days, to the beginning, to the Scholomance. Nestled deep in the heart of the Carpathian Mountains, they had gathered, the ten of them, select practitioners and scholars of the Left-Hand Path to learn the Dark Craft from the Master himself in exchange for their immortal souls. A small price to pay, she knew, for all the secrets of heaven and hell. And the things they learned! All the mysteries of nature unveiled, including the language of animals, the command of the weather, and every conceivable charm and incantation practiced since the beginning of time. The boundless energy to be tapped from the simplest things in nature, impressive enough in its own right, paled in comparison to the immeasurable power to be wrung from a single human life. The magical qualities of blood were many and varied, depending, of course, on the nature of the person and the circumstances under which it was drawn. The blood of a wicked person, for instance, would generally hold greater magical power than that of a common victim. Yet it could not match the potential for enchantment inherent in the blood of the totally innocent, such as children or truly devoted men of God.

The Left-Hand Path, she knew, must be approached with caution, as it grows more treacherous with each turn. Those who do not tread carefully may find themselves lost. Familiars, gestures, language, herbs and plants, parts of the bodies of animals: the sorcerer's armory was diverse and complex, and to master it required rigorous practice and great discipline. Ah . . . but the rewards were so grand, she thought as she opened her eyes and gazed up into the violet sky.

The child was near. She could sense her—and someone else, too. Was the child bringing a gift? In less time than it takes a mortal to blink, she scooped up one of the toads milling at her feet and sliced its head off with a flash of her barbed thumbnail. Carefully smearing the blood on the hem of her tattered dress, she tied off five knots in the stained fabric and recited the Lord's Prayer backward in homage to the Evil One. Her nose led her around back to Henshaw's well and the several inches of standing rainwater that had collected in the wooden pail at its base. Turning to the west, she dipped the bloodstained knots into the pail and paddled the surface as she said the words aloud. "Wind . . . Rain . . . Thunder . . . Lightning . . . Hail."

It was going to be one hell of a storm.

Five

Clinton Covington was not even aware of the first few warning drops that struck the windshield as he navigated the switchback curves of the twisty roadway. He was so engrossed in his own thoughts that it was not until a large angry raindrop splashed off the bridge of his nose that he actually looked up, startled, into the agitated sky.

An ominous green thunderhead was racing toward them out of the Atlantic, heading due west into the mountains. Its turbulent underside, backlit by the veiled moon, crackled with flashes of lightning like fire in the belly of a dragon. It came, seemingly out of nowhere. All the usual warning signs, the sudden drop in temperature and the turning of the sky, had crept in under the cloak of nightfall, catching him totally by surprise.

The perimeter of the cloud was just now starting to overtake the speeding Cadillac, and the rain, sporadic at first, was picking up in both tempo and intensity. His first thought, born of panic, was to try to outrun it. He surrendered to common sense and jumped on the brakes, easing the big convertible over to the shoulder and sliding to an abrupt stop with a wet crunch of gravel. Intent on saving the new-car smell of his black-and-white leather interior, he jumped into the backseat and peeled back the boot from the rear deck, freeing up the convertible top. Moving as methodically as possible, he pitched himself back into the driver's seat and hastily rolled up the windows. His manicured fingers found the switch on the door panel that powered up the roof and he pressed down hard. The rain was falling steady and hard now. The hum of the roof's electric motor was barely audible over the swelling howl of the wind as the Biarritz's convertible top began its agonizingly slow ascension from its covert perch on the rear deck. He cursed the freak storm, his rotten luck, all the saints in heaven, and anything else he could think of. His sister, Chloe, oblivious to the rain soaking her, turned toward him with the most quizzical expression on her face, which only added to his agitation.

"It's called rain, Chloe," he muttered through clenched teeth as he reached across her lap and rolled up her window. Good God, man! She just sits there! He couldn't wait to drop her off at the hospital and go into town. He'd get a good stiff drink, and see what kind of trouble he could get himself into. Durham was a college town and he was sure there were plenty of sweet young things. . . .

The humming stopped.

Clinton stared in mute disbelief at the convertible top, incomplete and stranded midway over his head, a good foot-and-a-half short of the locking clasps atop the chrome windshield trim. Rain funneled in through the gap, splashing his arms and legs. He flicked the switch on and off, his anger and frustration rising with every failed attempt to reactivate the motor. Clinton Covington, a man who was used to having things go his way, sat slack-jawed for a moment, unable to comprehend the mechanical betrayal perpetuated by his $13,000 dream machine. Out of desperation, he popped the hoodlatch under the dash and scrambled out the door into the full force of the storm, shielding his face from the blinding sheets of rain. He scurried in a half-crouch to the front of the car, his fingers groping blindly through the grill. He caught the latch and tugged, firing the heavy spring and releasing the massive hood with a relieved thunk. With more than a little effort he grunted up, hoisting the formidable hatch and ducking under it at the same time, gaining partial shelter from the rain ping-ponging off its surface. As he surveyed the shadowy internals, dimly illuminated by the tiny hoodlight, he realized he had no idea what he was looking for or what to do with it should he find it. The big V-8 with its jumbled accoutrement of wires and hoses housed a thousand mechanical secrets, of which he was privy to none. Because he could do little else, he inspected the battery terminals for a loose connection, giving each cable a hefty tug. Having tapped out all his diagnostic know-how, he slammed the hood back into place only to be startled by the apparition of Chloe's face staring through the windshield at him in the driving rain.

She looked downright creepy sitting there with the rain still pounding her and that horrid blank expression on her face. A brilliant flash of lightning strobed across the sky and cast a frightful glow on her features. He felt a chill, not brought on by the wind or the rain, run down his spine. As he made his way around to the side of the car he glanced at the convertible top, frozen in midfold, swaying precipitously in the wind. Damn her, he thought as he cracked the door open and squeezed himself inside. This was all her fault. Brushing the wet hair out of his eyes, he thumbed the switch again.

Nothing.

Sitting helplessly in the waterlogged interior of his prized convertible, with the rain continuing to pour in and no end in sight, Clinton Covington reached his breaking point and simply lost control of his senses. He lashed out at the dashboard and door panel with his clenched fists, an enraged scream pouring out from the bottom of his lungs. Her most basic survival instincts still somewhat intact, Chloe shifted away from her big brother, edging herself up against the door like a cornered animal, her eyes wide with alarm. Clinton reached up and clawed in vain at the leading edge of the failed roof in a futile attempt to force it closed, bellowing every obscenity he had ever known and inventing a few new ones in the process.

"Help me! God damn you!" he screamed into her face, his rage overtaking him completely. "Help me close the motherfu—" He stopped in midrant, aghast at the way she was looking at him.

She was petrified. His little sister was afraid of him.

The fury that had consumed him gave way to a shame that cut to his heart and filled him with remorse. In a sudden, startling moment of clarity, which could have changed the course of his life were he not destined to die horribly tonight, he realized the man he had become was a far cry from the vision held by the child he used to be. Disgrace washed over him as he hunched over the steering wheel, wrestling with the sudden realization that he actually was a bit of an asshole.

"Goddamn it . . . Goddamn son of a bitch . . . ," he said through clenched teeth. Clinton brought his head down in abject surrender on the bridge of the steering wheel, bumping it like a metronome to accentuate each word as he cursed his own wretchedness. Amazingly, he thought he heard the hum of the electric motor start up with the last bump. He looked up and saw the convertible top in motion again, unfolding and kissing the top of the windshield. He quickly reached up and fastened the clasps securely into place, locking the roof down tight before fate could somehow take it all back. He sat back in the wet leather seat and started to laugh, soaked to the bone, but suddenly safe and out of the elements. With the storm raging outside, he reached over and adjusted the heat control on the dash, trying to find a comfort level that would hasten the drying process without being stifling. Chloe flinched at the sudden movement and Clinton bit his lip, remembering the outburst that had frightened her so.

"It's okay, Chloe," he said in the gentlest tone he could

manage. "Everything is going to be fine. We're going to get you to the hospital and everything's going to be all right. Please don't be scared."

She seemed to relax ever so slightly, perhaps sensing that the real danger had passed, but the look on her face, a subdued mixture of wariness and offense, was wearing thin on his already brittle good nature.

It wasn't that emotions like compassion and regret did not exist in Clinton's psyche. They just made him feel uncomfortable and took away from his general enjoyment of life, so he relegated them to a far-off corner of his mind, to be used only in cases of extreme emergency. Emotions, his father had told him more than once, were dangerous distractions for men of purpose and were inclinations best left for women and children.

The old man hit the nail squarely on the head with that one, Clinton thought as he pulled the gearshift lever into drive and pressed his soggy loafer down on the accelerator. Wet gravel and cinder spit out from the Eldorado's tires as the big Cadillac roosted off the shoulder and squealed down the twisty two-lane into the teeth of the storm.

As it turned out, the old man had been right about a lot of things a lot of the time. Cornelius Covington had lived one hell of a life, and as Clinton grew older he learned that the old boy had been many things in his time before he had been his father. As a child Clinton had seen his father as omnipotent, and he'd been pretty sure that aside from maybe the president, his dad might have been the most important man in the world. People were always going out of their way to be extra nice to him. Some, he knew, were even afraid of him. Important men from Washington, D.C., would come to see his dad, and Clinton would sit outside the study on the thick marbled carpet, peering through the sheer white drapery, watching his dad do "business."

Clinton learned more about the stark realities of life watching his dad work than he ever could from the Le-Mans Academy (where tomorrow's leaders are made) or any book. There wasn't a prep school in the world that could teach you how to turn a donation to the National Educational Association and a roomful of hookers and drunken congressmen into a state-funded irrigation bill that would conceivably double your raw tobacco yield within the next decade.

Power, his father had told him, was not something someone could give to you. Real power has to be taken. There was no doubt about it, his father was a world-beater and an ass-kicker, but this thing with Chloe had the old man whipped like some old boot-shy mongrel hound. Seeing his father in this state he had to wonder. Was he ripe for the taking? Why should he sit around and wait for him to . . .

The initial barrage of hail that strafed across the hood and windshield startled him so much that he jumped back in his seat, an audible gasp escaping from his throat. The hail fell sudden and violent, as if fired from a cannon. He groaned aloud as it pounded relentlessly into the El-dorado's shiny exterior. It skipped off the polished finish and cascaded into the furious rhythm of the wiper blades like scattered bursts of white buckshot, blinding him completely, for seconds at a time. He slowed to a crawl and tried to gather his wits as the roar of a thousand castanets, joined by the deeper beat of the hail drumming off the fabric roof, assaulted his already frayed nerves. The surface of the road, which had been painted a glossy black by the rain, was now almost completely covered by a ghostly blanket of shifting white, luminescent and chalky in the stark path of the high-beam headlights. Clinton cut the headlight beams to their standard setting and peered over the hood, seeking a clearer view of what lay immediately ahead of him. He crept along at no more than twenty miles an hour, receiving no feedback from the Eldorado's tires on the pelleted surface. As they rounded the bend out of a descending left-hand corner, he brought the Caddy to a complete stop, unable to comprehend exactly what he was looking at.

About twenty yards directly ahead, the road simply disappeared. All immediate traces of it had been washed out, seemingly swallowed up, by the rain. A roiling membrane of hail bubbled and churned on the inky surface, inching toward them, growing larger, feeding off the onslaught of crystal destruction that hurtled into it from the green sky. Flicking the highbeams back on, he could see the road emerge again and climb from the soupy quagmire a good fifty yards away from where they now sat. Although he could not be sure, he guessed the water was at least three feet deep, maybe more. The very thought of sitting stranded in the middle of that murky ooze with the water creeping up over the windows made him shudder and he quickly jettisoned any thoughts he may have had of trying to drive through it.

Clinton wheeled the Biarritz around toward the opposite shoulder with the full intention of heading back and holing up in Williamston for the night, when he noticed the access road forking off into the woods from the eastbound lane. With his hand poised on the gearshift lever, he followed the stark beam of the headlights to the open, inviting mouth of the fire road creeping out of the hillside and weighed his options. To hell with it, he thought. It was less than twenty miles to Durham. If he stayed due west he should have no problem navigating the side roads back to the high side of Interstate 64. He stepped on the gas and barreled straight ahead, the rear end fishtailing, then hitching again, as the tires bit into the gravel.

The canopy of trees lining the road acted as interference, diminishing the maddening beat of the hail as he drove deeper into the hillside. The forest rattled and whined all around them, the hardwood and pines whipped to and fro by the gale force winds. Squinting hard into the din beyond the fringe of the Eldorado's high beams, he notched the wiper speed down a click and took note of the covert network of trails and dirt roads winding their way through the tortured trees. Probably an old moonshine run, he thought. Clinton smiled at the notion of the law chasing the hooch runners through these woods at night in some wild game of cat and mouse. After only ten minutes of picking his way along the unfamiliar terrain, he realized that his internal compass had betrayed him and he had lost any directional bearing he may have had. Peering through the darkness, he thought he saw a flicker of light appear in his peripheral vision, but in an instant it was gone. The path rose up ahead of him and, as they crested the hill, he saw it again, off to his right. A dull glimmer through the windswept trees, but it was there. He brought the Eldorado to a halt and backed up slowly. As it came into view, Chloe, who had remained expressionless throughout, turned and looked also. She stared intently and then turned slowly and gazed at her older brother. Her eyes locked on his and a faraway smile broke across her angelic face. For a moment it was his turn to be afraid.

Pulling his eyes away from that incomprehensible smile, he backed the Eldorado along the edge of the road until he saw the path, overgrown with years of vegetation, splicing off toward the light in the distance. Not realizing that he never had any choice in the matter to begin with, he pointed the Cadillac toward the flicker of blue light, sealing their fate forever.

Six

Planted squarely in the center of the cabin's dirt floor, the vampire stood unblinking, her emaciated frame frozen in a limp slouch. In all reality, her body was simply a vessel, a host for the demonic virus coursing through her veins that had assumed charge of her functions when she had crossed over centuries ago.

She had powered down her physical extremities and channeled all her remaining energy to her cerebral cortex, enhancing her telepathic and extrasensory capabilities in anticipation of the child's arrival. With the exception of the beating of her black heart, she had not moved a muscle for the better part of two hours, when suddenly she felt a pulse, an aberration, in the surrounding electrical field. In an instant she released her body from standby and glided to the shattered window, watching the violent tempest howling outside the cabin. Closing her eyes, she scanned the immediate area for the delicate electrical charges and alpha rhythms consistent with human thought processes. Her forehead wrinkled as she sifted through the interference brought on by the storm. She caught a thought and channeled in on it, her head jerking back slightly, jolted by the desperate energy of the thought transmission. She blinked, startled to find that it came from a male of the species. She suspected this child was being sent to her by the Master. Although she did not know in what capacity or what purpose she was to serve, she knew for certain it was a female.

Undaunted, she cast out once more, this time picking up a different charge, muted and incomprehensible but definitely feminine. Try as she may, she could not read a simple emotion, let alone a complete thought. Puzzled, she refocused, concentrating on the thoughts of the other, when she saw the twin headlight beams cutting through the woods. She stood at the tiny window, oblivious to the sleet blowing in around her. As the approaching headlights grew brighter and larger, she quickly untied the bloodstained knots in her tattered frock. The storm let up as each knot unraveled. By the time the Cadillac rumbled into the clearing, it was just a distant memory, leaving a crisp ambience lingering in the still air, belying the destruction it had left in its wake.

One more enchantment was requisite before the confrontation, and although it was a minor one, it would require her full concentration. The blue flames crackling in the hearth roared as she slid past and crumpled into Jefferson Davis Henshaw's only chair. It was a massive pine structure cut from the same tree as the simple table sitting beside it, where he had died screaming eleven years before. She settled in, listening to the slamming of the car doors, and waited until the knock came on the door to impose the *glamour*, a simple but effective, deception she had learned from the Moldavian gypsies centuries ago.

Before Clinton Covington could knock a second time, he heard the voice, a rusty croak, chime out from behind the weathered door. "Yes! Come in pleeease . . . warm yourselves by the fire. . . ."

Standing on the stoop, cold, wet, lost, and miserable, with his little sister shivering under his arm, Clinton had the strongest urge—for just a moment—to turn and run for his life. But that would be just plain ridiculous, what with that nice, warm fire blazing inside. And that voice! So inviting, so soothing. . . .

His fingertips barely brushed the rusted flange that

served as the handle when the door swung open as if by its own accord. The tortured squeal of the hinges tickled his ears like the jingle bells that adorned all the doors in Covington Manor at Christmastime when he was a child. He looked about in wonder at the interior of the ramshackle cabin, delighted by the unpretentious homeyness and warmth of the decor.

What a nice little place this was!

Knickknacks and metal pitchers overflowing with brightly colored wildflowers adorned the simple shelves lining the knotty-pine walls. Livestock portraits hung between the handsome exposed beams on both sides of the stone fireplace. A wooden rake hung next to a nineteenth-century pie safe with door fronts paneled in pierced tin, just like the one his grandmother used to have in her kitchen. Nestled into one corner was a small but comfortable-looking bed, crowned with a massive quilt in a bright blazing star pattern, pieced, no doubt, by the frail, little old woman seated at the table, smiling so sweetly at them.

"Come in, you poor dears. You must be chilled to the bone," she purred, staring at Chloe. "Let me put on a pot of broth before you catch your *death* of cold! You must forgive an old lady, I don't get a lot of callers out here."

"We don't want to inconvenience you any," Clinton said, tugging at Chloe who seemed just the slightest bit reluctant to cross the threshold. "But I was wondering if you could tell me the quickest way to get back to Interstate sixty-four. We were on our way to Durham and got off the highway. I thought I could make some time on the back roads through the hills, and sure enough we ended up lost. It was pure luck that we saw your—"

"Luck! Yes . . . do you think that's what it was?" she cackled, staring over his shoulder at Chloe. "This is your lucky night, then. Come closer please and close the door behind you. That draft will be the death of you! Step over here by the light of the fire, young man; let me get a look at you. This old lady, she can't see too well—growing old, it's the most terrible thing. So unfair, don't you think? Now tell me, where are you off to on such a horrible night?"

Amazing how much she looked like Grandmother Lucy, Clinton thought as he closed the door behind them. Chloe must see it, too. Was that a flash of recognition in her eyes? She was staring at the old woman as if she knew her.

"Excuse my sister, Chloe, for staring, Miss—"

"Bazore. Lizabet Bazore," the woman said proudly, smiling as if she had just said something quite clever. A middle European accent was evident, buried, but not quite yet dead.

"Yes, please excuse her. She has been rather . . . ill of late. I was taking her to the hospital at Duke University, as a matter of fact, when the storm broke and washed out the Interstate. I had no other choice but to get to higher ground on the back roads."

"Poor child," the old woman interrupted, ignoring Clinton altogether as she rose up out of the chair and approached them.

Chloe did not take her eyes off the old woman as she shuffled over, somewhat spryly, and brought her gnarled old claw of a hand up to the smooth, perfect skin of the teenager's cheek. Her fingers lingered there like a lover's.

"Ahhh . . . so tender," she leered, her eyes growing wide. "Youth and beauty, so fleeting, they are never really yours to keep—unless of course you take them. Then they are yours forever. Like *power*, wouldn't you agree, Clinton?" she asked, flashing him a wicked smile.

Couldn't have said it better myself, Clinton thought. He was really starting to like this old broad. Did he tell her his name? Backing away from the fire, he felt a sharp pain in his sinuses and a sudden wave of nausea pass through him from out of nowhere. It really was far too hot in here. That fire was much larger than necessary for such a tiny . . . He blinked and opened his eyes wide, trying to focus. The knotty-pine walls shimmered as if they were a reflection in a pool of troubled water, fluctuating and breaking apart like a television screen with poor reception. He watched, his mouth dropping open in wonder as the knickknacks dissolved into piles of mouse shit and mold and the brightly festooned bed degenerated into a heap of rags on a musty, old cot. Through it all, the old woman stood grinning at him, seeming to take a great deal of satisfaction from his bewilderment.

With the methodical cadence of a priest crossing himself after prayer, she passed her left hand down over Chloe's eyes, locking them shut and denying her the spectacle of the ensuing bloodbath. As Chloe fell into a deep trance, she turned slowly toward Clinton with a sly grin. The flesh crumbled off her rotted bones as she revoked the glamour spell completely, allowing him a look at the true face of the angel of death who would send him to hell.

"Good Christ!" he moaned, fumbling backward. He caught his balance and made a mad break for the door, but she was on him immediately and drove him into the wall, laughing maniacally as her long nails tore into the flesh of his back. Energized by his fear and the smell of blood, she flipped the big man over and straddled him, squeezing his face in her hand, drawing more blood as the talons dug into his skin. A foamy string of drool rolled off her black lips as she watched the blood pooling off his face, flowing from his broken nose.

"Sweet one, it's been so long. You really must excuse me if I take my time," she cooed, opening her mouth wide and exposing the razor canines protruding from the pink distended gums.

"Oh God . . . Oh dear God!" he cried through his split lip.

"Not even close," she whispered.

And then she began to feed.

Seven

With the satiated contentment of a glutton who had eaten to exhaustion, Lizabet Bazore rolled languidly off the emaciated carcass that used to be Clinton Covington, savoring the luscious sensations coursing through her body as her flesh replenished itself. Limp and giddy like after an intense orgasm, she lay on her back alternately giggling and moaning with pleasure as the healing blood and life force of Clinton Covington strengthened her emaciated frame and restored the suppleness and vitality to her flesh. When the tingling subsided, she rose straight up off the floor in one fluid, singular motion. She stretched her arm out before her and lightly pinched the soft pale skin on her forearm, observing the texture and elasticity. She took careful note of the restoration, smiling with self-absorbed satisfaction. Ah, yes . . . almost there, she thought, pleasantly surprised with the progress of the regenerative process after only one feeding.

Oh, but what a feed. He was so strong! She could feel the potency of his life force surge through her as she fed, nearly causing her to swoon when he at last surrendered and went limp in her arms. It had taken him close to four hours to die, even with the uncontrolled savagery of the initial attack, and in the end he had prayed to her—prayed for his own death. She had always, even as a mortal, savored the pleading and the whimpering that accompanied a long drawn-out death, believing it enhanced the vitality of the life force being drained. Besides, she liked it.

She stepped casually over the body at her feet and considered the girl. For a long time she stood there, inches from Chloe's face, coveting the sensual tenderness of her skin, reveling in it like an old woman pinching a baby's cheeks. She was so exquisite, grown up and fully formed, but possessing a delicate waiflike quality that made the vampire's mouth water.

Feeding again was the furthest thing from her mind. The girl was an enigma to her. She had seen her before, in the dreams when she had gone under for the long sleep. This was the child with the golden eyes and she knew that their destinies were intertwined, although to what end she did not know. She stood there for a moment, stroking the tender skin of the girl's cheek, and looked past her closed eyes, deep into the child's mind, searching for answers to the questions she had found. Her brow furrowed in frustration as she tried to pull a coherent thought from the jumbled cacophony of electrical impulses dancing inside the child's head. It was like trying to read a book without being able to open the cover. Although she appeared to be of sound mind, and although the abundance of electrochemical activity indicated a high level of intelligence, she could find no trace of the girl's nature, mannerisms, or psychological complexion. Amazing, she thought as she walked around the mysterious child, her mind reeling with the possibilities. She was like a prize block of Venetian marble awaiting the hand of a master sculptor. No thoughts to call her own. No will to call her own. No spirit . . .

Suddenly it all became crystal clear.

"Chloe . . . ," she said aloud, listening to the sound of the name roll off her tongue. How foolish she was not to have seen it before.

The child had been sent by the Dark One to escort her

out of the long sleep and see to her well-being and comfort. What a splendid gift! For more than a century she had been without true companionship, relying on her own wits for survival, her own cunning for food. She missed the old days as a mortal when Darvulia, Dorka, and Helena were there to attend to her every need, from drawing her bath and preparing her clothes to procuring the whores for the torture and the bloodletting. She missed the fellowship of the later coven years when the immortals would gather in the forests of the old country with their demons and familiars, imbibing in pleasures so profane no human could even imagine them. It had been a mistake making the long trek across the ocean alone, she could see that now. Even for those who walked the Path of the Left-Hand, a mere century of nights alone could seem like an eternity. This child, this blessing from the Master, would be both servant and confidante, a bridge to this New World and into the next millennium.

"Awaken, child," she whispered, passing her left hand up and over the spellbound girl's eyes. Chloe did not flinch as she opened her eyes and looked into the vampire's face, only inches from her own. Her brother's blood, still fresh and sticky, stained the creature's teeth and jaws. "Behold your czarina, young one," Lizabet purred, delighted with the look of awe on Chloe's face. "My word shall be your will. You have been chosen to be my apostle, and when my kingdom in this land is secure, you shall sit at my left hand and share in the bounty. Ah . . . the things we will do, the things I will teach you!" Lizabet moved in closer, pressing her body snug against the girl's, feeling the youngster's heat, the delicate curves and swells of her lithe body as she slipped her arms around her waist like a familiar lover. "And what are those secrets that you have locked away in your mind, child?" she asked, staring intently at her own reflection in Chloe's lustrous pale brown eyes. "No matter. You are mine now. Now and forever."

With that, she cocked her head and sank her fangs deep into the soft flesh of the girl's neck. After the slightest initial resistance Cornelius Covington's youngest child relaxed and melted into the embrace of the revenant, the distress and sorrow flowing out of her along with the lifeblood from her veins. A pleasant numbness, like the final euphoria experienced by those unfortunate enough to freeze to death, enveloped her being as the blood drained from her body and her biological system neared shutdown. Teetering on the brink between life and death, Chloe loosened her grip and felt herself falling into the abyss.

With her head swimming, drunk on the purity of the virgin's blood, Lizabet Bazore fought off the irresistible urge to keep feeding as she felt the girl nearing the point of no return. With desperate, calculated haste, she pulled out at the very last moment, leaving Chloe stranded in a dark limbo between life and death. Bleary-eyed and lightheaded, Lizabet raised her left arm to her mouth and opened her wrist. Wincing as she always did at the sight of her own blood, she pressed the wellspring of immortality to the child's gaping mouth.

Chloe sucked instinctively at the wound, casually at first, then latching on tightly as her system began to absorb the unholy venom. With the speed and destruction of a wildfire, the viruslike demonic entity roared through her body, breaking down and reassembling her genetic makeup, taking possession of her biological functions and mutating or destroying unnecessary tissues and organs. Racing up her spinal cord, it seeped into the neural chassis, triggering a brief electrical storm in the brain, similar to a grand mal seizure. With the cognitive drivers of the neocortex temporarily shut down, the virus manifested itself in the R-complex, the most ancient and primal of the neural drivers in the human brain, weaving itself intimately into the very fabric of her psyche.

Still cradling the girl with one arm, Lizabet Bazore grew weak and light-headed. She struggled to pull her wrist away from the fledgling vampire's champing mouth.

"Enough, Chloe," she whispered to the mewling child. "There will be more blood. More blood than you can drink in a human lifetime." She watched intently, still fascinated after all these years by the permutation brought on by the vampiric communion. She watched the light of humanity fade from the girl's eyes, regressing back several hundred millions of years to the dawn of time. She saw the Temple of Man crumbling against the backdrop of an angry red sky as the dragons trampled through Eden, leaving pestilence and disease in their slimy wake. Looking deeper into the unblinking eyes, she saw the Beast Himself emerge from the pools of bubbling filth, brandishing a sword of fire that He tossed into the ruins of the temple, setting the sky ablaze. Feeding off her human soul, the fire roared up from the depths, and as it splashed against the retinal walls, Chloe Covington awoke, a newborn vampire with no past life and no identity to call her own. Having crossed over while in a state of hysterical amnesia, she would walk the night with no memory of her mortal life, carrying only her most inherent personality traits and instinctive mannerisms down the Left-Hand Path.

Lizabet backed away from her, watching with childish delight as the disoriented creature looked warily around the small cabin. She was something to behold, this one. Her hair, which had been a nondescript mousy blond in her human incarnation, shimmered like spun gold. Her skin, perfect and unblemished to start with, was now a supple ivory sheath pouring over her lithesome body like frozen milk. Rings of yellow fire, bright as coronas around an eclipse, rimmed the watery depths of her eyes.

She cast those eyes warily at Lizabet now, backing away

from her in a defensive semicircle. Chloe's primal instincts were already razor-sharp, and although she could sense no immediate threat, she could smell the menace emanating from the ancient revenant. Still circling, Chloe backed herself against the wall of the cramped space like a cornered mongoose, scared and bewildered, but prepared to fight.

"You have nothing to fear from me, young one," Lizabet laughed, amused by the child's trepidation. "I am perhaps the only being in this world who would not seek to destroy you. You have been chosen by the Master himself to serve me, and in exchange for your loyalty and servitude, I have given you life immortal. You are born of my own flesh this night, nurtured by my own blood. The bond between us is eternal, total and all encompassing. I am your mother, your mistress, your present, and your past. When you are at my side, you are powerful and without equal. Without me, you are nothing but a bastard recluse walking the night on borrowed time. You are reborn now, but you will die in a fortnight without my guidance. Do you believe this to be true?"

Chloe heard the words of the powerful one in her own head before the creature's lips even began to move, almost as if she had spoken them herself.

"Yes . . . yes, I do. Believe that to be true," she answered, finding a quirky pleasure in the unintentional singsong rhyme and having no idea why.

"I will teach you the ways of the Left-Hand Path and all the secrets of heaven and hell. From me you will learn the how and the why of the blood and the power to be wrought from the fruits of Mother Earth. The forces of nature will bend to your will and the base beasts of the earth will gather to do your bidding. All this will be yours if I deem you worthy," Lizabet promised. "Assist me in reclaiming the eminence that is my birthright, swear your allegiance to me and you will sit at my left hand when I secure my kingdom on behalf of the Master. Betray me, and your suffering will be the stuff of legends told for centuries at all ends of the earth."

Cast adrift in a sea of the unknown, the thing she had become reached out for the one thing that felt familiar and stable—that intuitive desire to know, to learn, that characterized the thing she used to be.

"I want to know these things, these secrets that you speak of. Teach me these things and I will never leave your side," Chloe vowed, knowing only that she was bound to this being. For the moment, that was all she knew. And she was hungry. So hungry.

Lizabet smiled, pleased with the sincerity of the newborn's answer. She had known Chloe would awaken confused, hungry, and basically helpless. "Excellent. We begin immediately. The night is still young, but there is much to do before dawn breaks. We must cover our tracks and leave no trace of our whereabouts. There are those who would seek to destroy us under the light of the sun." With a sly grin she nodded toward the remains of Clinton Covington lying crumpled in the doorway. "Do be a dear, Chloe, and pitch that into the fire."

The transformed Chloe dutifully dragged the body of her brother across the dirt floor and rolled it indifferently into the hearth. There was no recognition. The poison coursing through her brain had extinguished any emotional attachment. She hefted it into the crackling blue fire and looked up expectantly from her half-crouch, awaiting further instructions from her mentor as the flames engulfed the body.

The old one could not have been more delighted with the way things were progressing. Just as she had reckoned, the child had no clue to her past or felt any of the pathetic emotional ties to her humanity that had been the ruination of so many of her kind. "Well done, my young lovely," Lizabet said, flashing a smile that would shame a crocodile. "Come now. I will not spend another moment in this filthy tomb." She glided out the doorway into the night, beckoning Chloe to follow.

Standing in the hollow of the glen, staring up at the dazzling, star-drenched North Carolina sky, Chloe felt a oneness, a harmonious link with all creation, and for just a moment the confusion and the uncertainty gave way to a profound feeling of bliss. But the euphoria dissolved as the words of the powerful one pulled her from her reverie.

"We will need to find proper accommodations and I am certain that we . . . Chloe! Pull your eyes from the sky, child!" Lizabet scolded. "If you wish, you can stand there and stare at the stars until the sun rises, but I can assure you that that would not be wise. Time is growing short and we must distance ourselves from this place before morning. They will be looking for you. . . ." She caught herself. She would have to watch her tongue until she had a better reading on the girl's exact state of mind. "What a grand coach!" she declared suddenly, walking around the pearl-white Eldorado.

Lizabet remembered the first night she had seen a horseless carriage rambling through that narrow cobblestone alley in Prague at the turn of the century. She had been in the middle of a feed and the contraption had so startled her that she had dropped the whore she had been feeding on right in its path before darting into the shadows. The carriage had run the prostitute over, crushing what precious little life she had left under its wheels and nearly toppling the noisy machine in the process. Although amused by the wailing of the grief-stricken driver, it was the novelty of the automobile that had held her attention as she watched the curious crowd gather below her, milling around like so much cattle. She had observed the evolution of the device over the last century with casual interest, watching it develop from rickety, wooden-wheeled carriages into powerful metal and glass fabrications that bore little or no resemblance to their predecessors. But she had never seen one as luxuriously appointed and pleasing to the eye as the Biarritz. The space-age styling and advances in technology were the stuff of science fiction when she had gone underground for the long sleep in 1948. Looking at it now as it gleamed under the light of the full moon, she was impressed with the ingenuity of mankind.

"Do you know how to operate this motorcar?" she asked Chloe, rubbing her hand along the chrome piping atop the tail fin.

Much to Chloe's surprise, she knew exactly how to operate the vehicle. She had driven it many times, sneaking it out of the garage early on Sunday mornings and cruising the plantation grounds, being very careful to park it in exactly the same spot before Clinton woke up. Slipping in behind the wheel, Chloe instinctively pumped the accelerator pedal twice and twisted the ignition key a quarter turn, firing the big V-8 to life. While the motor settled into a smooth idle, she reached over and switched on the radio as she had always done, punching the buttons until the fuzzy signal from WRAL-AM in Raleigh poured from the speakers, filling the car with the soulful wail of Dion and the Belmonts.

Lizabet opened the passenger door, laughing delightedly. "It appears there are a few things you can teach *me*, child. Ah, the things we will do together, you and I! This is but the first step in a journey of discovery and conquest, and when this century of wonder comes to a close, my reign will extend all the way to the gates of hell." She stopped just short of getting in the car and looked at the ramshackle cabin as if deep in thought.

"A memorial to my near-ruin and a monument to my rebirth," she hissed, her voice tinged with hate. "One day they will erect a statue here that would shame the Colossus of Rome! But for now . . . ," she exhorted, raising her arms theatrically, "let it burn!" With that, the shack burst into flames, obliterating the calm of the rain-cleansed night air. She slid in next to Chloe, marveling at the illuminated dash and the gadgetry throughout.

"Take us far from this place, my darling," she said, watching the flames and smoke churl into the black sky. "Deliver me from this painful memory of this wretched grave to the long warm nights of our tomorrows!"

Chloe adjusted the rearview mirror and looked into the golden eyes of the reflection staring back at her, wondering whose it was and how it came to be. At that moment she would have foregone all the long warm nights of her tomorrows for just one of her yesterdays.

Eight

Mary Gannon knew as she always did at this point that it was only a dream, although that knowledge did little to comfort her as she stumbled through the crowded E wing of Buchanan High School. Her only chance to wake up safe in her own bed was to reach the double doors at the end of the long green corridor and fling herself onto the sun-dappled lawn, free from their pointing fingers and the snide whispers. But most of all, free from the unseen terror that shuffled just out of sight behind her. It was gaining on her, she knew. The harder she ran, the heavier her legs became, until it was all she could do to drag herself along slowly, laboriously placing one foot in front of the other. She cried out in shame and anger, cursing the inability of her body to follow the simplest commands. She paused to rest for just a moment, leaning up against the seemingly endless row of lockers, when old Mrs. Schue from the bank slammed the locker shut, almost catching her hand in it.

"Ready for the history final, Mary? Mary *Gannon?*" she asked, a malicious smirk stretching across her wrinkled face. "You know it will count for half your grade!"

History! She hadn't been to history class all year. She had meant to go, but she just kept putting it off until— what period was history? My goodness, where was her schedule? She had no idea what class was next or what room she was to report to and the bell was ringing . . . if only she could find her locker.

"Yes, find your locker, Mary. I believe I left them in there," the voice called out from the shadows, the shadows that were closing in around her. He was right behind her! Pulling herself up off the floor, she dragged herself down the hall toward the crowd gathered at the mouth of the auditorium, never daring to look back until she had blended into the safety of the masses. It seemed the whole town was in the crowded gymnasium. She looked around desperately, searching for a friendly face or a reassuring word, finding only sneers and innuendo everywhere she turned. She closed her eyes, fighting back the tears—she was damned if they would see her cry. When she opened her eyes, everyone was dressed in their graduation caps and gowns filing toward the stage to accept their diplomas from Mayor Thomas and the chamber of commerce. Almost in unison they all turned to look at her, the entire town, mumbling, and shaking their heads in disgust, their eyes brimming with contempt.

"Mary! Mary Gannon!" Mayor Thomas beamed, genuinely glad to see her. He was such a sweet old man. "So glad you could make it. We have a diploma for you, too, my dear!" He reached behind the lectern and pulled out the small wiggling bundle, holding it high in the air for all to see. "Here it is, Mary!" he yelled gleefully as the baby burst into tears, frightened, and wailing at the top of his lungs, his cries meshing with the mounting laughter.

She rushed out of the auditorium, unable to control the tears any longer, rushed into the unknown gloom of the darkened hallways. She ran until her legs became heavy again, slowing her to almost a crawl.

"Mary!" the voice called from the darkness, so close she could hear the sticky wetness of his footsteps on the shiny linoleum tile. "I'm so glad you came back. We have to get to your locker, Mary, I left them in there. . . ."

She turned to run, but her legs would not move at all, and she knew in a second he would be there. She knew who it was. She had known all along.

"Oh God, Bob, please . . . please not again . . . ," she pleaded. But it was too late.

"I need them for gym next period, Mary."

Bob lumbered out of the shadows, the tattered remnants of his flannel shirt clinging to the quivering, stringy tissue hanging from the mangled shoulder sockets where his arms used to be.

"I need my arms for gym, Mary. How am I supposed to play basketball with no arms?" he demanded. The look of confusion and pain on his face gave way to anger and then hate as he advanced on her. She stepped back, clanging into the lockers, trying to avoid the blood, the blood pouring out of the yawning wounds in his torso as if from twin fountains. "I knew you would come to me, Mary," he said, his breath hot on her face, "I was so lonely waiting for you to—"

She woke up in her recliner, a scream caught on the back of her teeth, barely escaping her mouth in a short yodeling gasp. Breathing heavy and trying to get a bearing on her surroundings, Mary Gannon clutched the arms of her Strat-o-Lounger and looked around the living room of the small farmhouse. It was dark and quiet save for the light dancing along the walls from the snow-buzzing picture tube of her television.

It's never going to end, she thought as she pulled herself up out of the chair and switched on the hurricane lamp on her end table. The goddamn dreams are never going to end! It had gotten to the point where she was afraid to go to sleep, never knowing when she would wake up screaming and soaked in sweat. The dreams had been infrequent of late, sometimes coming only once or twice a week. But they were getting worse. Bob had never gotten that close to her before. She would always wake up, screaming, just as he emerged from the shadows. But this time, my God, he was right on top of her, and she knew— she knew that he was going to kill her. What would happen next time? Maybe she would just die of fright. She'd heard that if a person dies in their sleep, they have a heart attack and actually die for real. That was probably bullshit, but it didn't seem too improbable to her. In fact, maybe she would be better off dead, she thought as she padded over to the television and twisted its knob all the way around, trying in vain to find something to watch. Nothing but snow. Lord, what time was it? She checked the small brass flip-up clock, next to the lamp. Almost 4 A.M. She must have nodded off during *The Tonight Show.* Jack Paar had been talking to James Arness from *Gunsmoke,* which just so happened to be her favorite show. James Arness, now there was a man, she thought as she wandered over to the hutch. Strong, virtuous, and handsome in a rugged, almost fatherly kind of way. The kind of man Bob had been before the accident.

Her fingertips grazed the tops of the brass picture frames resting on the hutch before she gave in and wistfully picked up the largest one, a photograph of her and Bob at Myrtle Beach. Jimmy had taken it when he was just eleven years old. She felt the tears coming and choked them back, wondering if she could ever look at anything that reminded her of Bob without feeling that terrible emptiness inside.

Things had finally been going so well for them. Lord knows the first few years of their marriage were no bed of roses. She had just entered her sophomore year at Buchanan High School when she met Bob, a senior and a big man on campus to boot. Looking at his handsome face smiling up at her from the grainy black-and-white snapshot, she could see how easily she had fallen for him. She gave herself to him on their third date, losing her virginity and conceiving a child in the backseat of his father's '36 Hudson Sedan. Of course it had turned into a full-blown scandal. Nothing was a secret in Stockton, North Carolina, and the townsfolk hadn't had anything this juicy to sink their teeth into since Parker Dobbs had shot his wife and Ed O'Neil, their farmhand, both buck naked in his bed back in '33. Word is, he got right into bed with them afterward—lay down right between their two dead bodies and stuck both barrels of that Remington in his mouth before he blew his own head off.

Mary's mother had turned her back on her, diving back into the bottle she'd discovered after Mary's father died of pleurisy in 1929. Mary had left school in February when her belly grew too large to hide under frumpy blouses, and Bob grudgingly married her in March. He didn't love her then. She knew, if anything, he resented her. He had a shot at playing football at the collegiate level, instead he found himself married and living in his father's house, working the family farm he had always dreamed of getting away from.

Things got a little better when Jimmy was born in June and they almost resembled a family, the three of them, living in the cramped quarters on the second floor of the Gannon farmhouse. They lived there rent-free, under the watchful eye of Bob's father, Jonathan Gannon, a truly moral and decent man whose only concern was that his grandson grow up in a loving household, regardless of the circumstances of his birth.

Bob's father was the glue that held the family together, and after he passed away in 1945, Bob began to drift back to his old ways. Free from parental restraints, he regressed to the easygoing days and the freedoms he had lost at eighteen. He started going into town after supper, hanging out with his old high school buddies, Jeff Lawson and that skunk Bob Hayes. Oh, it had started out slowly enough. Once, maybe twice a week, and he was always home before eleven and ready to work in the morning.

It didn't take long, though, before it was four or five nights a week and he'd be out till all hours and not worth a shit when he got up in the morning, smelling of stale beer and Louise Miller's cheap perfume.

Mary had cried a lot back then, too, trying to keep a happy face on for Jimmy, who was only six years old, but knew something was wrong with Mommy and Daddy. She was at her wit's end. More than once she thought of packing up the truck and taking off with Jimmy. She was damn close to doing it, until one night Bob had one more too many and rolled the truck going around that hairpin turn where Thornridge Road splits out of Route 40. He racked it up pretty good. Rolled it over three times and landed upside down in a retention ditch with his skull halfway through the windshield. Bob had always had a pretty hard head and when he regained consciousness, he walked the seven miles home and passed out on the couch. It was a Saturday morning, and when the sheriff came by to ask Bob why his truck was in a retention ditch off Route 40, Jimmy was standing there in his cowboy jammies, carrying all the pain in the world on his six-year-old face. When the sheriff left, Bob sat there at the kitchen table, hung over, his face all cut up and bruised. Jimmy sat right across from him, eating his oatmeal and watching his daddy stare at his untouched cup of coffee. Then he asked the question.

"What happened to your face, Daddy?"

Bob pulled his hands away from his face and looked at his son sitting across the table from him, waiting for him to tell him why his face looked like hamburger and why the sheriff had come to see him and why they don't have a truck anymore. Jimmy wanted his dad to tell him that he was being chased by German spies or that he was running down a couple of cattle-rustlin' desperadoes. But Bob didn't tell him anything. He just broke down and cried. He didn't have any funny hero stories or lies left for his son, only tears. Tears of shame and self-hatred, fueled by the pathetic reflection of himself in his son's wide, innocent eyes. Loud, wailing sobs wracked her husband's body. Mary had thought for a moment that he might be having some sort of breakdown. Jimmy rushed up from his chair and hugged his dad, showing a tenderness and compassion for another's pain that was extraordinary for a six-year-old. Despite her anger and her frustration, Mary couldn't help but join in. The three of them sat there, crying and hugging each other, bathed in the stark, early morning sunlight at the tiny kitchen table.

Bob never touched another drop after that day. It was as though the velocity with which he had hit bottom was so great it had catapulted him back to some higher moral ground from which he could view the emptiness and despair that lay in the darkest depths of his soul. He quit going into town and rededicated himself to being a good husband and provider, molding himself into the type of man his son could look up to and respect.

Things grew better between the two of them, too. He grew to love her again. He found the happiness and fulfillment in her arms that had evaded him in the roadhouses, staring into a glass of beer, searching for direction in the sorry lyrics of the songs pouring from the jukebox.

They made a pretty good go of it on the farm, raising corn and soybeans on their 230 acres and selling it as livestock feed for the meatpacking industry. They managed it themselves and only had to hire outside help from town around harvest time. It was hard work, a lot of fifteen-hour days, but it was good work and it made for a good night's sleep. They had started a savings account and a retirement fund, socking away whatever money they had left at the end of the month when they were done paying the bills.

Jimmy grew up tall and strong like his father, deciding early on that he wanted to be a police officer. He joined the marines right out of high school, figuring a two-year hitch in the U.S. Marine Corps couldn't hurt his chances of getting into the police academy at Raleigh. With Jimmy gone, the two of them grew closer still, spending their nights together cuddled up, talking about the things they would do in their golden years. Sell the farm, maybe move down to Florida, maybe do a little traveling.

And then it happened.

She was in the kitchen frying up some hamburgers and home fries for Bob's lunch, daydreaming of Florida beaches and palm trees, when she heard the screen door open hard and thwack against the siding of the back porch. She whirled around, startled by the noise, her mind unable to comprehend what her eyes saw. There was Bob, eyes wide and glassy from shock, propped up against the doorjamb, trying to maintain his balance. He staggered into the kitchen and looked at her almost apologetically and mouthed her name, "Mary . . . oh . . . Mary. . . ."

He had no arms.

Through the thick blood pouring from the gaping holes in his shoulders, she could see the shredded flesh and muscle clinging wetly to the frayed remains of his shirt. Blood flowed copiously from the wounds, splashing onto the floor around his feet. She wondered for one crazy moment just how much blood a human body could hold. Bob left a trail of crimson footprints resembling some ghastly dance-step diagram on her freshly scrubbed floor as he careened about the entryway in a daze, mumbling incoherently about his sleeves being too long and the grinder, Mary, the grinder! She screamed, unable to grasp the reality of the situation, and backed away from him out of reflex as he stumbled toward her. The look of pain and distress on his face brought her back to her senses and she ran to him, catching him as his knees buckled and he began to fall. She eased him down to the floor, cradling and rocking him, telling him not to talk, that everything was going to be okay. She ran to the closet, pulling out all the white linen and bedding she could carry, and tore them into manageable pieces, packing the wounds and tying them tight, trying to stem the unending flow of blood. Struggling with his large torso, she somehow managed to pull him to his feet and get him out the door and into the truck. They were halfway down the driveway when she remembered she had left the burners on under Bob's lunch.

"Hold on, honey," she said as calmly as possible, backing the truck up the drive, "I have to turn off the gas." Bob's head rolled lazily on his shoulders and he nodded at her, a look of detached compliance on his face as they bounced back up the bumpy drive toward the house. Keep it together, Mary. Keep it together, she said to herself over and over as she ran into the house and dialed the gas off under the burning food. Duke Hospital was a good thirty miles away, she thought as she ran back out to the idling truck. Bob would never make it. Their only chance was old Doc Carrol in town, and she'd have to pray he wasn't fishing. "Hang on, baby," she said, jumping behind the wheel. "Just hang on. We'll be at Doc Carrol's in no time."

Bob slid silently toward her when she slammed the truck door, his head resting on her shoulder. He was dead.

Bob had been loading corn into the feed grinder, something he'd done a million times before, when the intake mechanism snagged his sleeves, pulling his arms into the machine. Unable to free himself, his hands, then his arms, were fed into the gearing and ground into pulp until his body, too big to fit into the opening, slammed into the mouth of the grinder. Something had to give, and it wasn't the metal teeth of the industrial gearing. With the remorseless, functional patience only a machine can possess, the feed grinder chewed Bob's arms from their sockets and spit him out like an indigestible peach pit into the dirt.

Jimmy got a three-week leave from the marines to come home and tend to the funeral arrangements and tie up the loose ends around the farm before winter set in. He had requested an early discharge so he could stay and take care of his mother, but she would have none of it. He only had eight months left of his hitch, and she told him to stick it out. Jimmy was in the shore patrol, a corporal already, and she insisted he stay and finish up strong so he could pursue his dream of going to the academy. There had been enough shattered dreams in the family, and she was damned if she was going to add her son's to the lot.

She saw Jimmy off at his train back to Camp Pendleton and drove back to the house as if in a daze, not even bothering to turn on the wipers in the heavy gray rain. The finality and horror of the whole ordeal, numbed by the flurry of activity after the accident, hit her like a cold shot when she let herself into the big empty house and stood in the kitchen surrounded by the solemn quiet that was exclusive to the truly alone. That first night alone in the house was the worst. Everywhere she looked, everything she did, somehow reminded her of Bob—that Bob was no longer there and never would be again.

Going through the mechanical charade of eating supper. Pushing the food around on her plate, trying not to look at Bob's empty chair. Sitting in the living room, watching television but seeing only the indentation in the sofa where he used to sit. She cried herself to sleep that night and many nights afterward, until the tears could no longer flush the pain and emptiness from her heart. The nightmares began soon after the crying stopped. Usually the same dream, a variation of the one she had tonight, but always ending with Bob wandering out of the shadows with no arms and that horrible, lost look on his face. She looked down again at the picture of them at Myrtle Beach, wishing she could remember him like this instead of that haunting specter that lurked in the fringes of her dreams. She realized she was doomed to take that image with her to her grave.

"DOOMED! YES, AND SOONER THAN YOU THINK!"

The voice, metallic and grainy, boomed into her head, startling her so that the picture fell from her hands and shattered on the floor at her feet. She whirled around, her eyes, wide and terrified, darting back and forth across the room. Good Lord, did she imagine it? Was she finally going insane? The voice seemed to come from everywhere and nowhere all at once, leaving a tinny hum resonating in her head, like the acrid smoke trailing off a live wire after an electrical short. Stepping carefully over the picture frame's broken glass, she made her way cautiously over to the television and switched it off, cutting off the snowy static in midbuzz as her heart regained a somewhat regular beat. She cocked her head, listening intently to the silence as she turned and looked around tentatively, eyeballing every shadow, every dark shape in the dimly lit room.

Her body relaxed, and she let out an audible sigh, convinced that all was well in the house and that her mind was playing tricks on her at this late hour.

"Storm must have really spooked you, Mary," she said aloud, much like a child whistling through a graveyard late at night, stirring up false courage to banish the unseen phantoms lurking behind every headstone. Time to turn in, she thought, the lack of sleep is really starting to take its toll on my nerves. But Christ, it had been so real. And so loud!

She bent to gather up the afghan from her recliner when the distant humming started in her head. The hum intensified, rising to an almost crippling level before gradually falling away into the distance. She stood trembling and confused in the lonely silence of her living room, unable to write this off as her imagination or lack of sleep, when the laughter started. It sounded like delicate crystal breaking at first, tinkling and harmonic in the far reaches of her mind, before rolling into a haughty, mocking giggle that reverberated through her skull. It stopped abruptly, and in the awful quiet that followed, she realized she was being watched. Her skin broke into gooseflesh, standing the fine hair all over her body on end as she struggled with the sudden and undeniable certainty that she was going to die.

"Are you frightened, Mary?" the voice asked, still inside her head, but less so, as though the source was closer, more tangible. "Oh yes, and you should be. I'm right behind you now. At the window. Turn around and look."

Her body shook uncontrollably. The fear had so completely ravaged her neuromuscular system, it was a struggle just to stay upright. But the voice, for all its unnatural affectations, carried a beguiling flirtatiousness, a persuasive undertone that she could not resist.

Calling up all her resolve, Mary Gannon turned herself around in a spastic pirouette, hanging her head low so she could see nothing but the floor, and dragged her body toward the latticed window that overlooked the rambling front lawn and the fire road that meandered past the house. Standing just inches from the window, she lifted her eyes from the floor with the somber resignation of the condemned, bracing herself for whatever horror waited there. Peering into the inky darkness, she could see nothing unusual aside from the water that had pooled up in her front lawn from the storm. The moonlight shimmering in the puddles lent a deceivingly tranquil air to the scene while she woefully searched the night for her unseen tormentor. Heart pounding, she craned her neck and pressed her cheek to the glass, checking for someone or something against the side of the house. As she turned to view the other side, she saw the tendrils of hanging hair fall into her field of vision from above. The face followed, upside down, slowly descending into view with the fluid, mechanical pace of an elevator, until finally their eyes met and the thing smiled at her. Unable to turn away from the grisly sight, she stared for a moment at the expansive row of sharp teeth pressed into the black lips straining to form the unnatural grin. She broke from the window in a full-tilt run. Her scream caught up to her halfway across the room, her momentum almost carrying her into the girl who was standing in the entryway to the dining room.

She thought at first she was looking at an angel, a savior who would deliver her from damnation and vanquish the hell spawn at the window. The girl was exquisite. A precious waif chiseled from porcelain and trimmed in gold. In her delirium Mary nearly expected to hear the blare of Gideon's trumpet calling the armies of God down to the fight. Instead, she heard the tumblers in the lock of her front door falling, and as she turned, the demon entered her home, casually locking the door behind her.

"Your thoughts of salvation are almost as amusing as your dreams, Mary Gannon," Lizabet Bazore said, the grin growing wider. "Though not nearly as enjoyable. An angel! I rather like that. In a moment you will see the irony in that, although I doubt you will appreciate it. Step away, Chloe."

The angel stepped back obediently. The demon advanced on Mary, peeling off the ragged smock it wore. The revenant stood in front of her, naked and unashamed, the smile gone from its face. Its skin was almost the same color as the angel's but the texture was cobbly and worn, like cheese in the early stages of curdling and the body bore the withered tone of beauty corrupted by neglect and abuse.

"Old whore, I shall teach you a few things about neglect and abuse," the thing hissed as it closed in, now only inches from her face. It looked at her intently, its red eyes turning dreamy, almost sleepy. Mary Gannon recognized the crazed look in the beast's eyes as desire, and she fought back the nausea that came with the realization. An uncontrollable shudder ran through Mary's body as the monster reached out and stroked her hips and buttocks through the sheer fabric of her nightgown. She was already going into the early stages of shock when Lizabet's head jackknifed down and the long fangs sank deep into Mary's breast. The vampire snapped its head back, champing and sucking on the generous mouthful of flesh and tissue it had torn from her body. Had she not fed so well earlier on the carcass of Clinton Covington, Lizabet may have very well given in to her voracious cravings and torn the woman to pieces, leaving precious little for her young protégée. Fighting off her own greedy desires, she pushed herself away with a low moan. Savoring the exquisite essence of the flesh, she paused for a moment to bask in the intimate sensations of her oral debauchery before relinquishing her prey.

"She is yours, Chloe," the vampire said dreamily, letting the body drop to the floor. "Take her now and drain her completely, only then will you be able to walk with me down the Left-Hand Path."

Mary Gannon opened her eyes and looked up to see the Angel of Death crouching over her, her golden eyes shining with hunger and hellfire, coming closer like twin comets in a faraway night sky. She closed her eyes and waited for the angel to deliver her, almost smiling as the sharp teeth punctured the soft flesh of her neck.

Part Two

Nine

Flipping his hair back, Tom Ross considered his reflection peeking over the tops of the liquor bottles in the mirror behind the bar. Hair's getting pretty long, he thought as he drained his glass of Old Style. Almost as long as Mark Farner's, the lead singer of his favorite band, Grand Funk Railroad. Pretty soon he'd have the longest hair in town, seeing as how Greg Tuscher had to get a haircut for that job his old man had lined up for him at the refinery. Funny, but he never thought Greg would buckle under like that, especially when it came to something as important as hair. He dug into the pocket of his shirt and fished out a crumpled pack of Cheyennes. He took a quick count and calculated the pace he'd have to keep if they were to last him the night. Only eight left. That came out to about two an hour if he hung around this shithole till two. He was never going to make it at that rate. Fuck it, he thought, lighting one up. I'll just bum 'em the rest of the night when I run out.

"Mike! Another draft down here when you got a second, buddy?" he called down the bar. Mike O'Connor looked up from his paper, slightly annoyed. Now there's one lazy sonofabitch if he ever saw one, Tom thought. Yeah, sorry you had to get up off your ass there, Mikey boy, don't strain yourself, ya prick. I'd hate to see you have a heart attack and die. He smiled with that last thought. He actually hated Mike O'Connor. The big asshole had been three years ahead of him in high school and beat his ass one day just because he'd been fucking with a friend of Mike's sister. That's okay, payback's a bitch, he thought, watching Mike place a fresh draft in front of him.

"This one's on me, Tom," the bartender said, waving away the crumpled dollar bill Ross pushed toward him.

"Hey, thanks, chief," Tom replied. Maybe he wasn't such a bad guy after all. He took a good long swallow of the icy draft and recounted his money sitting before him on the scarred wood of the bar. A grand total of $6.25. He was in pretty good shape actually, this being Thursday, fifty-cent draft night. Hell, he might even splurge and pour a dollar in the jukebox. Nah, on second thought, why waste money on those golden moldies when he could buy two beers with it. Besides, the songs hadn't been changed on that jukebox since 1972, and if he heard "White Rabbit" one more time, he might have to kill the son of a bitch who played it. He took another swallow of Old Style and looked around the nearly empty bar, resigned to the fact that this was probably as happenin' as the joint was going to get. Dry-balls, even for a Thursday. The only other people in the joint besides him and Mike were Fat Pat and some real old guy whose name he forgot but who always smelled like he pissed himself. Tom figured everyone was on the other side of the river in Cincinnati. It was ladies' night at the River's Edge and they had a band and a two-dollar cover. Two dollars! Just to walk in the door. He was no lawyer, but he was pretty damn sure shit like that had to be illegal.

The opening theme music to *Barney Miller* distracted him from his legal musings, and he looked up to see O'Connor stretched out and fiddling with the reception knob on the ancient television perched high in the opposite corner. Fat Pat bent his ear.

"Best show on TV, don't ya think? Whoa! Hold it, right there, that's as good as it's gonna come in. Did you see it last week? They were all stoned, Deitrich, Harris, even Wojo! Someone brought in brownies and they were laced with hash! Funniest goddamn thing I ever saw in my life. Laughed my ass off." He turned and looked at Tom. "Did you see that one, longhair? I bet you would've liked it. You like all that drug shit, don't you?"

Tom took a deep drag off his Cheyenne and considered the fat man, trying to figure out if he was fucking with him or not. Fat Pat was probably one biscuit under four hundred pounds, but that didn't mean he was going to take any shit from him. I mean, it was all the fat bastard could do to get up from his bar stool to take a leak without breaking a sweat. He decided to shoot one right back at him.

"Nah, I must have missed that one, Pat," Tom replied, feigning politeness. "But you must've really got off on the brownie part of it. You like all that *food* shit, don't you?"

Fat Pat's neck grew redder, the blush spreading up to his tiny ears as he glowered at Tom. "I'll have you know that I have a glandular problem, asshole. I probably eat less than your skinny ass. I even drink light beer—see, it says right here on the can, 'contains one-third less calories then your regular beer.' That means I would have to drink three cans to every one of yours to end up with the same amount of calories."

Tom smiled. The big bastard was backing down, trying to save face in front of Mike. "Do the math, ya dumbfuck, and try to follow along here. It says 'one-third *less* calories,' not one-third *of* the calories. That means you're still getting two thirds of the calories and you're drinking watered-down shit that tastes like—" He stopped as the door to the little corner tavern opened and the girl walked in, bringing an immediate halt to one of the most mathematically complex conversations ever heard inside its humble walls.

Everyone, even the old piss-pot, stared at the small striking blonde as she made her way down the narrow aisle between the bar and the cinder block wall before taking a seat just two stools down from Tom. Tom shifted in his seat and shot her his most effortless smile, unable to believe his good fortune. She was wearing a black leather jacket with fringed sleeves and tight, faded blue jeans that showed every supple curve tucked into little black cowboy boots. A fine mesh gear chain with an oversize Harley-Davidson belt buckle ran through the belt loops, accentuating her tiny waist. She was a looker this one, classy too. Definitely not one of the local scags. Looking slightly self-conscious, she smiled back at him, a quick but dazzling smile, all white teeth and soft pink lips that almost made his heart skip a beat.

"What'll it be, young lady?" Mike asked, setting a new personal standard for efficient and courteous service.

"I haven't quite decided what I have a taste for. Can you give me a moment?" she replied, looking demurely at Tom, as though he had asked the question.

Now his heart did skip a beat. Jesus, it was getting hot in here. He could feel the blood rush into his face, betraying his cool facade and exposing his uneasiness.

"Yeah, sure, take yer time," Mike said, somewhat irked by the snub.

"Another draft for me, Mike," Tom blurted out, thankful and amazed he could speak at all. "And when the lady decides what she wants, take it outta here," he continued, pointing to the crumpled pile of bills in front of him.

The girl raised an eyebrow and pursed her lips ever so slightly, causing the blood to disappear from Tom's face and head to regions south. "A glass of merlot, please. Very dry," she announced, still smiling at Tom.

"Mer-low? We don't have . . . I mean, I think we're

fresh out of mer-low. I have a nice rosé, but last I checked, it was pretty wet." Mike laughed, very pleased with his quick wit.

"That will be fine," the blonde replied, ignoring the pun and pissing Mike off to no end.

Wine! Tom panicked. That was probably going to set him back at least $2.50. Five beers! Almost half his budget for the night.

"On second thought," she said as Mike screwed the twist cap off his finest vintage, "I'll have what the gentleman is having. A draft beer, please."

With that declaration, Tom Ross silently pledged his undying love for her. She giggled, a light, airy titter, as if the two of them were in on their own private little joke. Just one of the many intimate secrets they shared, he thought, as he stared, speechless, into her golden eyes.

"Here you go, draft beer—just like the *gentleman*," Mike said with a mocking grin. He set the beer down in front of her and slid a fresh refill toward Tom without looking at him. Gingerly plucking a dollar bill off the meager pile in front of Tom, he headed back down the bar—no doubt to snicker and whisper with Fat Pat and the old shitbag, like a bunch of old hens at a knitting circle. Thankful for the interruption and a chance to regroup his thoughts, Tom blinked the cobwebs out of his head and decided to move right on in.

"Tom. Tom Ross," he said, extending his hand as gallantly as he could. He almost flinched as her icy fingers wrapped around his callused hand like tiny, frozen sausages. Jeez, it must have really gotten cold outside.

"Chloe, just Chloe," she said. He wasn't even sure if her mouth moved.

"Ah, mystery woman, eh? I take it you're not from around here. I know I would have remembered you if I saw you before."

"No, you've never seen me before," she replied. "And

where I'm from is not important. The past is inconsequential—a burden really—" She stopped abruptly. A puzzled look flashed through her bright eyes, as though she were weighing the validity of her own words. "Only the future matters," she continued with a seductive smile, the sparkle back in her eyes. "And the future starts here and now."

"To the future, then," Mike said, raising his glass.

"To the here and now," she added, tipping her glass. She watched the rhythmic rise and fall of Tom's Adam's apple along his exposed throat as he drained half his beer in a rapid succession of long swallows.

"Not thirsty tonight?" he asked, motioning to her untouched beer. He contentedly licked foam from the corner of his mouth.

"As a matter of fact, I'm extremely thirsty," she replied. "It's just that I prefer my drink a little warmer."

"Well, this place may be a shithole, but they have the coldest beer in town. You may be waiting—"

"You have beautiful hair," she interrupted, reaching out to stroke a shank of the long auburn locks falling over his shoulders. "I wish I could grow mine that long."

"Why don't you?" he asked, beaming. "Just let it grow."

"My hair will never be longer than this," she replied, twirling a finger lazily around her golden tresses. He thought he saw that same puzzled look pass over her face before she brightened and asked, "Any Grand Funk Railroad on this jukebox? They're my favorite."

As they walked out of Sherm's Tap together at midnight, Tom Ross was convinced that this was the girl he had been waiting to meet his entire life. Sure, he had had her figured for a quick lay when she walked in the door and almost sat down on his lap, but it was much more than that. When they talked, it was as if she anticipated his every word, and when he looked into those amazing eyes of hers, he could swear she was looking right into his soul. This was something special, something that was meant to be. He was sure of it. Watching her now sitting in the tattered bucket passenger seat of his '69 Cutlass, he knew that this was the woman he would spend the rest of his life with.

"Yes, however short and insignificant it may be," Chloe said under her breath as they cruised down the narrow backstreets between the squalid row houses that lined the riverfront.

"Huh? What'd you say?" he asked.

"Nothing," she said with a soft smile. "Just talking to myself. Sometimes I get lost in my own thoughts."

"Happens to me all the time, especially after I burn a doobie. Hey, you wouldn't have any smoke at your place would you?" he asked. "If not, I may have a couple of roaches in my ash—"

"You'll want to turn left up here and head toward the top of the hill at Goethe Street," she interrupted, tiring of the game and eager to finish him.

"Jeez, tough neighborhood," he said, just a little uneasily. He was poor white trash and he had lived in Fontana, Kentucky, his entire life, but he had never ventured this far into the seedy riverfront district before, especially at night. I mean, shit, people get killed around here, for Christ's sake.

"You're not scared, are you, Tom?" she asked, feigning surprise.

"Hell, no," he shot back, not wanting to sound like a pussy. "I'm just kind of surprised a girl like you would live around here. I mean—"

"I don't live around here. I don't *live* anywhere," she said, dead serious.

He let that sink in as he eased the Hurst shift lever into first gear and motored the Cutlass up the steep incline, eyeing the shadowy figures lying in the doorways of the run-down dwellings built stubbornly into the side of the bluff. The row houses leaned hard into the hill, like tired old derelicts walking into a cruel wind. The crumbling sidewalk sliced into their foundations at incongruent angles, growing more extreme as they neared the top of the bank, giving one the impression they were pressed haphazardly into the earth like candles sinking into a forgotten birthday cake.

"Up here on the left," she said, lightly grazing his thigh with her fingertips. She indicated a crumbling bungalow sitting at the top of the bluff, overlooking the river.

It looked no more capable of sustaining life than any of the other candidates for demolition on the street, but this one was quite obviously inhabited. An iron security gate was bolted to the front door, adorned with a massive chain looping through its rungs and secured with the biggest padlock he had ever seen.

"A girl's got to protect herself, don't you think?" she asked, flashing that knowing smile again. Christ, it was almost as if she could read his mind.

"Reckon so," he said, nudging the Cutlass over to the curb. He got out of the car and looked around cautiously, somewhat unnerved by the unfamiliar surroundings. "It would take a tank to get through that thing."

"A tank wouldn't make it up that hill." She laughed and grabbed his hand, leading him around to the side of the house. He noticed all the windows, also padlocked shut, were painted over black and recently sheathed in iron. "Come on, I've got some cold beer in the fridge. We can relax and get to know each other a little better," she added, tossing him a look over her shoulder that made his knees weak.

The prospect of cold beer and warm sex dispersed any nagging concerns Tom Ross may have had for his own safety, and he eagerly followed her down the back stairs. He watched as she fished a key out of her leather jacket and popped open the Master lock on the steel basement door.

"Here, take my hand," she said, effortlessly navigating her way through the darkness. He shuffled along behind her, unsure of his footing and disoriented by the complete lack of light.

Darker than a grave digger's ass crack at midnight, he thought to himself.

"Yeah, sorry about that. The light switch is broken," she answered, as though he had spoken aloud. "Careful now, here are the stairs."

They banked left and he followed her ascension toward the sliver of light filtering under the door above them like a slash in a black curtain. He heard the fall of tumblers in a lock and then a click as the door swung open. The light broke from the jamb in a pencil-thin crack, then poured out in a sweeping arc, flowing off the edge of the door and bathing them in the harsh glow of the naked sixty-watt bulb dangling from the hallway ceiling. The smell of decay and human waste hit him like a blindside haymaker. He choked back the gag reflex and pulled his Led Zeppelin T-shirt over his nose, breathing through his mouth as he followed her down the narrow hallway. Christ! Couldn't she smell it? What the fuck was . . .

"You won't have to put up with the smell long, Tom, I promise," she said, a reassuring but apologetic smile breaking out over her delicate face.

With a final look back down the stairs into the black recesses of the basement, he reluctantly followed her down the long corridor, picking up voices and background noise coming from a room just around the bend. He turned the corner and blanched, realizing he had just walked into his own grave.

The scene was so riveting, so unbelievable, he could only stare, unable to move or speak, much like the first wave of Allied troops upon discovering the atrocities of the Nazi death camps. He took it in slowly, from left to right, overwhelmed by the depravity and obscenity of it all.

Thrown into one corner were the battered remains of what may have once been a young woman in her early twenties. The corpse displayed the telltale signs of an animal attack, but a closer look suggested something even more ghastly. The strategic placement of the wounds—concentrated on the breasts, buttocks, and legs—pointed to a premeditated and deliberate assault. Nothing like the random bite pattern an animal might inflict, whether eating or striking out in self-defense.

No, whatever did this, did it with malice and took its time.

Despite the severity of the wounds, there was a marked lack of blood, save for the dark red pentagram that was painted on the floor and dominated the middle of the room. Just outside the circled star, in the opposite corner directly to his right, a striking older woman with long, wavy dark hair sat sumptuously in an old, ratty high-back chair. She was casually watching the late edition of the evening news on a new Sony TV atop a wire milk crate. Her black gown was thrown open, exposing full white breasts topped off with large bright-red nipples, and her legs, long and milky, were thrown over the shoulders of another naked young girl. This one, unfortunately, was still quite alive. The woman in the chair seemed oblivious to their presence, writhing sensuously as she forcefully manipulated the head of the moaning, bloodied girl between her thighs. She raised her head slowly and looked directly at Tom. Her bloody red lips stretched into a leering smile, exposing the long, white canine teeth. It was then that he knew what they were.

Lizabet's laughter rang in his ears as he turned to run. Chloe snatched him and pinned him up against the wall, trapping him like a mouse under the playful paw of a cat. She looked at him, expressionless, her eyes starting to glow with the feverish and infinite blood lust that had defined her kind since the beginning of time.

"Please . . . ," he whispered through his dry throat as he struggled in her firm but gentle grasp, "please let me go . . . I won't tell anyone, I swear . . . we—"

She pressed a finger to his lips as if silencing a precocious child, opening her mouth with a dreamy, almost detached reflex. He stared at the tips of the white fangs pressing lightly into the soft pink of her full lower lip and heard her voice in his head as if from far away.

"Trust me, Tom Ross. It's better this way. Your time here was short, even by mortal standards." In a flash she buried her fangs into the soft nape of his neck, puncturing the jugular with pinpoint accuracy. The words—her thoughts—swam in and out of his head with his fleeting consciousness.

"I am only putting an early end to a fruitless and painful folly. . . ."

She clamped down and tightened her grip as she started the draining process.

". . . meaningless parade of heartbreak and misery. . . ."

He surrendered and went limp in her arms as the blood flowed out of him, the feeling of the fluid leaving his body growing increasingly pleasurable, climbing toward an almost unbearable plateau before the darkness started to overtake him. Yes, she was right . . . now he would be with her, part of her, forever. . . .

Feeling him slipping away, Chloe bore down on him with more intensity, sucking the last vestiges of life from him in deep, desperate gulps until his deafening heartbeat, throbbing through her head, slowed, then fell silent forever. She stepped back from the lifeless body as if it were impure, and let it slide down the wall, hitting the floor with a thud while she basked in the rich sensations of the feeding. Her face was flushed with the afterglow of a contented lover, while she swayed, almost humming, and reveled in the fleeting ecstasy. The Old One's voice rang in her ears, pulling her out of her swoon.

"Chloe! Snap out of it. Listen to this, girl! On the television!"

Blinking back into focus, Chloe turned her attention to the Sony and the blow-dried, solemn-looking anchorman on the evening news.

". . . the fifth young woman to disappear from the greater Cincinnati area in as many weeks. Police refuse to acknowledge any connection between the women's disappearances and the grisly discovery two days ago in a Dumpster behind the Little Slice of Heaven pizzeria on the east side of the city, where the body of one Darlene Donovan, an exotic dancer at the Blue Moon Gentlemen's Club, was found. Details are sketchy, but we have unconfirmed reports that the young woman's throat was torn open and the body drained of blood. News Four has learned exclusively, however, that forensic specialists from the FBI have been brought in to consult, raising speculation of a possible link between this murder and the twenty-six bodies unearthed from a shallow mass grave in Huntington, West Virginia, last year. As you may recall, those victims, all young men and women in their late teens and early twenties, had their throats ripped out, and as autopsies would later show, many had been tortured. This puts a chilling twist on a recent spree of murders that has left Cincinnati holding its breath, waiting for the next—"

Lizabet Bazore simultaneously clicked off the TV with the remote control and casually broke the neck of the hapless girl laboring between her legs. She tossed the body aside and rose up from her makeshift throne in one deceptively simple motion.

"Our time here has run out. Dispose of the bodies at once," she said, looking around the room. "Secure the house against the day when you return. We will sleep in the cellar tonight, and tomorrow at nightfall, we head north, far from here." She brushed past Chloe, then paused, noticing the slightly irritated look on the young vampire's face.

"Don't fret, child," she cooed, reaching out and stroking her cheek. "Lizabet will not let you go hungry. There will be plenty to eat on the road."

Ten

For as long as he could remember, Johnny Coltrane's dreams were void of color, painted in the subdued tones and shadowy grays of film noir. He pondered this as he looked down and touched the pebbled brown leather of the car seat, running his fingertip along the red piping of the upholstery. He turned his attention back to the blighted urban landscape rolling past the dirty windows of the old sedan. He had no idea how he had come to be here, sitting in the backseat of this ancient car driving through the wrong side of town with the two faceless, silent men sitting in front. He said nothing, choosing to wait the situation out, rather than bring unnecessary attention to himself. They seemed to be men of direction and purpose, and he was not about to waste their time with foolish questions.

They slowed to a crawl and came to a halt in a cinder lot sitting between two dilapidated buildings. These were the only two structures for as far as he could see, standing alone in a sea of concrete. Somehow he knew that neither could exist without the other. Their crumbled facades faced each other across the cinder lot like two aged adversaries, wary and spent, saving themselves for one more round. The larger was an old two-story, its brickwork covered with countless layers of peeling whitewash that contrasted with the pitch black pouring from the empty window frames, which had long ago forgotten the feel of glass in their sills.

The other building, which was somewhat smaller and appeared to be made of wood, was also covered with flaky, thick coatings of cheap whitewash and topped by a crooked spire that had not pointed directly skyward for generations. The two men sitting in front of him hefted open the massive car doors with a tortured squeal of metal and walked slowly and purposefully toward the middle of the lot. He watched as men and women—people he recognized from his hometown of Belvidere, Illinois, began to approach as if from nowhere and migrate toward the epicenter between the two buildings. The congregation, maybe fifty strong, slowly dissipated, and a flurry of methodical activity ensued. Things were happening very quickly now. Men were grabbing wooden posts strewn about the lot and pounding in the rotted sides of the old wooden structure, until dirty shafts of sunlight penetrated the interior with each violation. After knocking a sufficient hole in the side of the building, they began a hurried but systematic transfer of small bundles between the two structures. Despite their efficiency, Johnny knew the mob had no idea of what this activity was accomplishing. They were simply going along, following random, isolated instructions in the manner of worker ants or drone honeybees.

Suddenly he noticed four or five people in what appeared to be radiation suits milling about, monitoring the proceedings. He noticed one small figure in a silver radiation suit walking toward him and he hurried out of the car and ran to her, knowing she meant him no harm. They stood in silence for a moment, facing each other. He gently pulled back the hood of the radiation suit and stared into the face of what could only be an angel. Although they had never met, he knew her immediately, and he knew that he loved her. He loved her deeply and more than anything in the world. Her hair was short and spiked, flowing off her head like rays of sunlight. And gold. As gold as her eyes, sparkling so brightly it almost hurt to look into them, although he could not bear to stop. Her features were elfin, almost more girl than woman, but strangely beautiful.

"What is all of this? What's going on here?" he blurted out, painfully aware that the others were still working all around them. Time seemed to be growing very short indeed.

As she opened her mouth to speak, she reached up and gently touched his cheek, nearly causing him to faint.

"Don't you see, Johnny?" she asked tenderly, looking into his very soul. "We have work to do here. Time is short, but you and I will have some time to play, and then we will die."

The finality of her words hit him in the chest, robbing him of his breath.

"No!" he screamed, "no!" The tears welled up hot and furious in his eyes. She pulled him close, gathering him in to her like a mother comforting a distressed child. They kissed and became as one, like lovers who had melted into one another for all time. All he had ever known or believed, ceased to be, replaced by the knowledge of the ages, the very knowledge that had caused his earliest ancestors to be banished from the Garden. At that moment he knew the answer to the eternal question. He knew the reason for man's existence. The meaning of life, the how and the why of the laughter and the heartache, the joy and the sorrow. He had crossed the threshold into the Temple of Man, and that moment of clarity had him drunk with the awful beauty and wonderment of it all. My God! It's all so simple! So . . .

Suddenly he woke up. Springing up from the bed and looking around the room wildly, the tears streaming down his face, searching for . . . for . . .

He forgot! Oh God! To know such a thing and have it taken away! And where was she? Who? . . .

He stumbled to the bathroom sink, trying to see through the stinging tears that would not stop pouring from his eyes. He splashed cold water over and over onto his face, trying to stem the flow of tears. Finally, as the sobbing subsided and he began to regain his composure, he looked into the mirror at his scared face and his burning red eyes. For a moment he knew. *He knew!*

"Jesus Christ," he muttered. Could it have been real? He closed his eyes and tried to remember what she . . . had conveyed to him, but it was no use. With each passing moment it slipped further away from him, leaving him bewildered and uneasy. Still shaken, he walked naked to the bedroom where he sat down on the edge of his bed and lit up a smoke, trying to calm his jangled nerves and gather a little perspective.

"It was just a dream," he said aloud, taking a long drag and pulling the smoke deep into his lungs. He welcomed the refreshing bite that only the first cigarette of the day could provide. At least it was real.

He checked the digital alarm clock next to his bed. Rolling into 5:42. He still had another hour before he had to get up and go to school. For a moment he contemplated crawling back under the covers for a quick forty winks, maybe catching a ride on that same dream. Finding the girl . . . and the answers.

Fuck it, he thought, I'll never get back to sleep. The whole thing will be forgotten by lunchtime. . . .

Johnny bolted into the studio, which made up the remainder of his two-room apartment, and sifted wildly through the clutter sitting atop his drawing table, searching for his notebook. The private one, where he kept his random scribblings. Thoughts, song lyrics, the occasional poem. More of a journal really, not a diary, he would tell people. Only chicks and fags kept diaries. Finding it, he flipped to an empty page and jotted down the entire dream, struggling to capture what was left before it vanished forever. When he had completed it to his satisfaction, he had filled up three pages, and although his hand was sore from writing so fast, he knew he was nowhere near done. Clearing his head, he sharpened a fresh 2B Grumbacher pencil and braced himself for a short period of intense concentration. He opened his hard-bound sketchbook and set about drawing the face of the girl from the dream. The Grumbacher moved cautiously over the page at first, touching down lightly when the feeling was right, finding reference points, building a foundation on which to work. An eye began to take shape. Then, satisfied with the soft outline, he skimmed the pencil lightly across the surface of the smooth bond paper, stopping at just the right spot before starting the other eye. Blocking that in, he traveled down the page, struggling to capture the slightly turned-up nose. He closed his eyes, straining to recollect that mental snapshot as best he could. He nailed the lips, usually a problem for him, perfectly capturing the reluctant purse and full texture he remembered so fondly.

Stepping back from the table, he put some distance between himself and his drawing, literally and figuratively, in order to gain an objective viewpoint. Pleased with what he saw symmetrically, he moved back in, establishing the shadows and highlights with quick cross-hatching strokes, deftly adjusting the pressure on the Grumbacher, letting the soft lead of the pencil find the lights and darks. He stopped suddenly, knowing it wasn't going to get any better than it was right now. He had ruined many a drawing in the past by overworking them, going too far, not knowing when it was done and should be left alone. This one was different, though—he didn't even have to take another step back and consider it. He knew at the end of the last pencil stroke that it was finished. Johnny looked at it for a long time, very pleased with himself. It was rough, sure, but what could you expect? It was from memory, and a somewhat distant one at that. It was by no means dead-on, but he had captured the essence of the angel's face, and that was all that mattered.

He blew the carbon off the tip of the pencil like a gunfighter dispelling the smoke from his six-shooter. Amazing what the right pencil can do for you, he thought. His drawing had improved dramatically after Kenney had urged him to draw with more spontaneity and abandon the wide range of leads he used to cart around.

"Try a 2B, Venus or Grumbacher," Kenney had told him. "That's what I use. You'd be surprised at the range you can get with a nice soft lead—not too soft, though, or you won't be able to go light. Stay away from the fives and sixes. A lot of guys fall in love with the darkness, mistaking it for strength. Only use those for large, complex drawings where you need a variety of leads."

Three years of art school under his belt and the single best piece of advice he received came from another student. Although he was only three years older than Johnny, Kenney Brandt seemed much older—wiser than his chronological age of twenty-five. Maybe it was the hard thought lines around Kenney's eyes, or his slightly cynical take on art and life in general, but Johnny regarded him as one of the few people he had met since arriving at the Chicago Institute for Artistic Study who wasn't full of pretentious bullshit.

Johnny had arrived in Chicago three years ago, fresh out of high school, by way of Belvidere, a cow town about one hundred miles north of the city, near the Wisconsin border, one of the last notches in the great Midwest Bible Belt.

It may as well have been on the other end of the earth.

The bewilderment he had felt walking through the chaotic, bustling streets of the Loop and riding the crowded, noisy subway was nothing compared to the culture shock that had greeted him upon his arrival at art school. He'd felt out of place in his flannel shirt, blue jeans, and Converse All-Stars amidst some of the outlandish, eye-catching garb sported by his classmates. There were plenty of hippies around like himself, but even they seemed pretty extreme to his wide, naive eyes, trudging into class barefoot, looking like they had slept all night in the woods.

He had met Kenney Brandt midway through his freshman year at one of the raucous Institute parties that never failed to materialize on the weekends. Johnny had been hanging out in the kitchen, close to the kegger, when he'd heard the unmistakable, rapid-fire opening riff to "Mama Kin," an Aerosmith tune, being pounded out on an acoustic guitar down the hall. He went to investigate. There was Kenney sitting in a stairwell playing an old Stella Harmony twelve-string with a small crowd gathering around like rodents to the Pied Piper. Maybe it was the beers, the song, or a combination of both that led Johnny to abandon his shy, reserved nature and pull his Marine Band harmonica from the front pocket of his shirt. He joined right in, blowing on that harp and grooving like he was at home, sitting safe and alone in his bedroom instead of standing in a stranger's house in front of a crowd of people he barely knew. They went together like syrup and pancakes, switching rhythm and lead on the fly, and when Kenney nodded to him and yelled "sing it," he did, reaching down and pulling the lyrics from deep in his throat, coating them with a raspy edge that would have made Steven Tyler proud. Without waiting for the applause to die down, they eased into "Howlin' For My Darlin'," with Kenney taking over the vocal chores while Johnny carried the meat of the tune on his harp.

They had gone back to Kenney's place after the party broke up, and the two of them stayed up till dawn talking and listening to Kenney's extensive collection of obscure blues albums. They found that their common interests stretched far beyond music, and riding the "El" back to his dorm that morning, Johnny knew that he had stumbled into one of those rare friendships that would last a lifetime. Their mutual love of the blues led to the formation of a band, and they were actually starting to pick up some bookings, including a regular Friday-night gig at The Drop Zone, a bar not far from Johnny's apartment. As Johnny would soon find out, though, Kenney Brandt's real talent lay not in his music but in his painting. Johnny was a pretty damn good artist, the best his high school had ever produced, and he had won plenty of local awards, but next to Kenney he was a hack.

Kenney was a tireless technician and purist, going so far as to size his large canvases with a carefully prepared mixture of rabbit-skin glue and paste, rather than take a shortcut with store-bought gesso. Landscapes were his passion and he did countless sketches in preparation for a scene on site, returning at different times of the day in order to find just the right light before he even stretched a canvas. Kenney employed a technique borrowed from the old masters of the fifteenth and sixteenth centuries known as glazing, which allowed his paintings to pop with a luminosity of tone and depth that conventional methods could not touch. After thinning his oils with a mixture of damar varnish, stand oil, and pure gum turpentine, he carefully built up transparent glazes, layer upon layer, until the desired effect was achieved. Johnny had no doubt that if the Hudson River School style of painting were ever to make a comeback, Kenney would be a rich man. But this was 1977 not 1877, and not too many people were rushing out to buy photo-realistic landscape paintings to fill the empty spaces on their walls.

The harsh realities of life after art school were not lost on Johnny. Kenney had kicked around for months after graduating last year, trying to land any kind of art-related job before settling for a low-paying paste-up job a few nights a week at a graphics house down the street from where he lived. To make ends meet, Kenney had registered with the local school district and worked as a substitute teacher during the day, squeezing in his painting whenever he could find the time.

It scared Johnny that a guy that gifted couldn't make it on talent alone—scared him enough to change his whole way of thinking about his course selection. He opted to load this semester's schedule with commercial and graphics courses, taking only one studio drawing class.

"Doesn't hurt to be safe," he said to the rendering of the angel looking up at him from his open sketchbook. A profound melancholy and sense of loss began to overtake him as he pondered the drawing, replacing the swell of satisfaction he had felt after producing it.

"No," he said to himself, abruptly flipping the sketchbook shut. "It certainly doesn't hurt to be safe."

Eleven

The seemingly endless flat prairies rolling past the windows of the Ford Econoline van made the long trek up Interstate 65 seem longer than it actually was, even to the vampires' preternatural sense of time and space. Fontana, Kentucky, was more than four hundred miles behind them. The local police were left clueless and the FBI was without a trace of the unseen terror that had plagued the region for nearly a decade. The impregnable fortress on Goethe Street stood no longer, consumed by the strange blue flames that had kept firefighters at bay until the whole structure was reduced to a smoldering pile of rubble. The intense heat liquefied what it did not turn to ash, making it next to impossible to identify the skeletal remains of the damned scattered about the site.

They had stopped only once, at a roadside rest area, where they had fed on two young lovers from Terre Haute who were running away to Florida to get married and start a new life together. After cutting their throats to disguise the wounds and dumping the bodies in the woods, the vampires ransacked the couple's Camaro, discovering a tidy eight thousand in cash. Not a king's ransom by any stretch of the imagination, but it was a nice addition to the small fortune they had accumulated in the last eighteen years together.

"Has it already been eighteen years since I found you, child?" Lizabet asked, turning her head from the dark flat landscape rushing past the window. She looked with pride at the precious jewel of a vampire she had sired.

Chloe sat ramrod straight. Her body, unhindered by road fatigue or muscle cramps, rested in the contoured captain's chair like a crash-test dummy. She moved her limbs only when called upon to control the van, which she had been pushing up the Interstate at a steady eighty-five miles per hour.

"If you say it is, then it must be so, Madam," Chloe answered, never taking her blazing eyes from the road. She banked off the exit ramp and accelerated into the traffic flow on Interstate 95.

Lizabet smiled. The girl really was an amazing pupil. The Master had been wise to send her one such as this. She learned quickly, mastering the subtle nuances of the Dark Craft faster than anyone she had ever seen before. Her thirst for this knowledge sometimes exceeded even Lizabet's expansive wisdom, and they would search for the answers together, delving further down the Left-Hand Path than Lizabet had ever traveled before. Oftentimes Lizabet would find herself regretting she had killed the brother before finding out more about the girl, other than her name.

It was obvious she had come from the upper class, perhaps even some modern-day American version of royalty. She possessed the refinement and quiet inner dignity that could only come from superior breeding—nothing like the simple human cattle that seemed to populate this New World. The hunt was second nature to the child, and on occasion Lizabet would watch her choose her prey, fascinated at the way Chloe would pass over a perfectly desirable feed before moving on to another for no apparent reason. It was rare for Chloe to take more than one in a single night, and she was always careful to mask the true cause of the death or dispose of the body altogether. The child killed quickly, cleanly, and without emotion of any kind. She showed no pity, yet she displayed none of the rapturous jubilation Lizabet herself felt when taking a life and making it her own. It was this same lack of emotion that sometimes worried her. One could not read a closed book, and Chloe had become quite adept at masking her thoughts.

"Time is such a relative thing," Lizabet announced, her mind drifting back to her last years as a mortal, imprisoned in the tower at Castle Cachtice until the Evil One came and claimed her as one of his own.

For three years she had wasted away in that walled-up cell, like an animal, deprived of the aristocratic excesses she so treasured: the travel, the food, the fine clothes, the whores, and the blood.

Especially the blood.

She had marked the passing of each impossibly long day by the progress of the musty shaft of sunlight that poured from the lone aperture notched in the west wall high above her head as it crawled slowly across the dank floor. Not a century had passed since she was reborn to the night that was as long as just one of those day. She had little to do then but wait to die, lamenting the corruption of her beauty and her inability to replenish her fading youth. She had lived fifty-four years as a mortal before crossing over into the arms of the Master, but the years spent swimming in the blood of the whores had paid handsome rewards. Indeed, the cretins who gathered at her interment could scarcely believe that they were looking at the remains of one so old, awed by the youthful beauty of the corpse, whispering among themselves that it was the work of the devil.

"Time is what you make of it," Chloe answered after a short pause. "Lost time is lost opportunity and it can never be taken back." Her brow furrowed. She wondered where that could have come from, not realizing it had been one of her father's favorite expressions.

Lizabet pondered this for a moment, reflecting on the three years lost—no, *stolen* from her last days in the sun. "That may be true, my dear," Lizabet replied. "The time lost is lost forever, but the ambitious and resourceful will find more time, taking it from the feeble and the undeserving."

"Which only follows the natural order of things," Chloe interjected. "The strong and superior feeding off the weak and the insignificant, reaffirming the natural ideal by weeding out the inferior and ensuring the propagation of the Chosen."

Lizabet beamed and reached over, stroking Chloe's cheek like a proud parent.

"I've taught you well, child."

Chloe recoiled ever so slightly from the caress, masking the inherent revulsion she felt whenever Lizabet touched her.

"The lights," Chloe blurted out suddenly, thankful for the distraction and motioning to the sprawling pool of electric glitter twinkling on the horizon. "That is Chicago. I'm sure of it. We will arrive well before sunrise, maybe in time to feed again before we sleep," she offered, hoping Lizabet didn't notice the involuntary shudder that her touch had elicited.

The centuries-old revenant turned and stared, her dark eyes shining as she took in the size of the approaching city. "Five million souls," she said dreamily. "Five million."

Chloe eased off the accelerator, bringing the cargo van in line with the flow of traffic that was beginning to build as they approached the city. Tufts of urban clutter began to accumulate around them, growing denser until the empty pockets of the night sky were packed full with concrete and steel. The downtown skyline loomed up into their field of vision to the left, a picture-postcard panorama dominated by the simple elegance of the Sears Tower and the brawny Hancock building.

"Ah, the things they can accomplish when they are not destroying each other," Lizabet said, showing an uncharacteristic empathy for the species she had held in such contempt. "How far they have come in only three hundred years in terms of science and technology, yet they are no closer to answering the questions of their own mortality than they were two thousand years ago! They mill about as if in a daze, sleepwalking through their dreary day-to-day existence, just waiting to die and be delivered into the glory of some fairy-tale afterlife that they imagine is their birthright!"

Chloe, noticing the hatred beginning to build in her mentor, was actually relieved to see the telltale purple light of dawn seeping into the sky over Lake Michigan. She had seen Lizabet before in such an agitated state kill as many as five or six in one night as if in a frenzy, giving no thought to the consequences or the cleanup involved. Afterward, she would stare down at her bloody hands, puzzled as though she had just awoken from some sort of spell, leaving Chloe to dispose of the carnage while she retired, complaining of exhaustion and light-headedness. Instances like these disturbed Chloe, not because of any pity or compassion for the victims—although she held them in a slightly higher regard then Lizabet, but because such recklessness might one day spell their doom.

"The sun will rise in less than an hour," Chloe offered, casting an eye to the east. "We will have to find accommodations quickly or sleep in the back."

Lizabet checked the sky, then craned her neck, looking over her shoulder at the mound of desecrated soil piled high in the back of the Econoline.

"Get off the first chance you can, Chloe, and get into the heart of the city," Lizabet said firmly. "I would prefer to lie in more secure surroundings if at all possible."

Anticipating a hasty exit, Chloe maneuvered toward the right-hand feeder lanes and weighed the options offered by the forest-green destination signs approaching overhead: 22nd St/Chinatown 1/2 mile, 55 North Stevenson Expressway/Lake Shore Drive 1 mile. The young vampire accelerated and cut the wheel hard to the right, slipping the large cargo van rudely in between a Peterbilt tractor and a '72 Mustang that had been riding its ass. Ignoring the blaring horn and screeching brakes from behind her, she followed the bobtailing Peterbilt around the sweeping exit ramp and cruised leisurely down Cermak Road before gliding to a stop at the red light on Harrison. She was preoccupied, thinking how peculiar the pagodas and mock temples of Chinatown looked nestled between the barren emptiness of the housing projects and the glass and steel grandeur of the office buildings rising from the downtown area. It was, she thought, almost as if the structures had appeared magically overnight, when no one was looking. The squeal of tires behind her and the slamming of a car door shattered her momentary calm. Lizabet, who had been keeping a keen eye on the situation, smiled to herself, anticipating what was about to transpire.

"Breakfast is served," she said, still staring straight ahead.

Chloe looked in her side-view mirror and saw a muscular man in his late twenties emerge from the black Mustang that she had cut off on the expressway. He was walking purposefully toward them, brandishing a tire iron and a very bad attitude. She stole a quick glance into the cab of the tractor idling in front of them at the stoplight. The light had turned green but the driver was in no hurry to get anywhere, his eyes riveted on the show unfolding in his rearview mirror.

The adrenaline pumping through his veins was increasing with every step Tony Ramos took toward the cream-colored van, causing his heart to beat in the crazy, accelerated rhythm that always possessed him before a fight. Tony had never taken shit from anybody the whole twenty-eight years he had spent on this planet and he wasn't about to start tonight. Oh no, once you start eating shit, you begin to like the taste. This sorry son of a bitch had almost run him right into the retaining wall— probably laughing at him like he was some sort of asshole! Sorry, buddy, but it was clobberin' time. Time to pay the fuckin' piper! Time to reap what you have . . .

But suddenly the strangest thought struck him. Maybe this wasn't such a great idea after all. Maybe the guy just plain didn't see me. Shit happens. Wouldn't it be a good idea to just head back to my car and drive home and kiss my wife and daughter—maybe take them to the zoo today, let them know how much I love them? Hell, you don't want to *die* tonight, do you, Tony? Not quite sure where this newfound logic and complacent attitude could have come from, Tony "the Tiger" Ramos relaxed his grip on the tire iron and walked somewhat hurriedly back to his car. The trucker in the Peterbilt chugged away from the stoplight, disappointed he didn't have a story for the boys back at the terminal. Inside the van Lizabet did a slow burn, glowering at her protégée, waiting for an explanation.

"It was for the best, Madam," Chloe offered before the ancient one's anger could build. "There was a witness. A witness with a citizens band radio. I don't know if I could have taken him out in time." As if to underscore her point, a blue-and-white Chicago police cruiser rolled through the intersection. It slowed, taking note of their out-of-state license plates, before turning left out of sight.

Lizabet softened somewhat. It was not the first time the child's calculated reserve had buffered a potentially hazardous situation, but the boldness of the move—interfering with a kill without consulting her first. It just didn't sit well with her.

"I admire your instincts, child," she said after a pause. "But in the future it would serve you well to acknowledge my authority and confer with me first. It is a matter of respect, something I do not take lightly."

"I apologize, Madam," Chloe replied, sounding, she hoped, properly chastened. "No disrespect was intended."

"No need to apologize," Lizabet said, satisfied their roles were firmly reestablished. "We have more pressing matters at hand. Dawn will be breaking soon."

They drove on in silence. Chloe hooked left on to Clark Street and cruised through the Loop, which was deserted except for a few sailors too drunk and stubborn to go home after coming up empty on their Friday-night excursion to Rush Street. The vacant office buildings loomed over them like sleeping giants, settling in for the weekend before reopening their doors to the press of nine-to-fivers that would flood these streets Monday morning. Crossing the State Street Bridge, Lizabet stared solemnly out her window. The Chicago River rolled below them, glassy and black, as though it had sucked the waning vestiges of night from the sky, refusing to yield to the oncoming dawn without a fight.

There were times, Lizabet would admit to herself in moments such as these, that she longed to see the world again bathed in bright sunshine. To see, with her vampire eyes, the deep purity of color denied her by the absence of natural light: the blood, puddling in the freshly fallen snow, so red it seemed to vibrate with a life of its own; the skin of the peasant whores turning blue as the icy water was poured over their naked bodies, freezing them into the winter landscape.

She was untouchable back then—before the discovery; doing what she wanted, whenever she pleased, without fear of reproach or prosecution. Oddly enough, she had yet to reclaim such sovereign power since crossing over. She was frustrated, confounded by her inability to effectively parlay the dark secrets of the Left-Hand Path into a new kingdom on earth. The Old Ones of Europe were too shortsighted and set in their ways to grasp her vision of supremacy, preferring to lurk in the forests and mountains waiting for the slow death that time and the advent of industrialization would bring. She closed her eyes for just a moment, shutting out the pain and anger that the memory of her own slow death had always instilled in her. When she opened them, what she saw lifted her melancholy as quickly as it had descended.

"Turn here," she ordered. "That building there on the corner. Quickly, pull over to the curbside."

Chloe wheeled the Econoline onto Ontario Street and pulled up next to a massive edifice of black stone that seemed to have sprouted full-blown from the cracking sidewalk, claiming nearly half the city block as its own.

Lizabet was out of the van in a flash, slinking along the foundation of the building. She placed her hypersensitive fingertips on the massive flagstones, canvassing the interior of the building for any fluctuation in temperature that might indicate a life-form inside.

"It is unoccupied," she announced, pulling her face away from the cold stone. "Look at it, Chloe. Isn't it magnificent? It reminds me of the castles of the Old Country."

Chloe stepped from the van and walked pensively around the imposing structure, puzzled as to what its original purpose may have been. The whole building was constructed of massive blocks, which upon closer inspection were not black at all but speckled gray, darkened by decades of industrial city air. She looked up at the transept jutting out slightly from the side of the building at a right angle in the fashion of the cross-shaped churches constructed in the latter half of the Dark Ages. A peaked roof crowned the transept over a rounded arch housing an intricate vaulted window, giving one the impression of the facade of a twelfth-century abbey. Making her way around to the front, she paused to read the date, November 12, 1892, chiseled into the cornerstone. She was somewhat surprised such a building was less than one hundred years old.

Chloe turned the corner just in time to see Lizabet crawling like a lizard straight up the rugged face of the dwelling toward a small terrace cut over the entryway. She could not help but admire the nubile grace of her mentor as Lizabet picked her way along the craggy facade, her long dark hair trailing behind her like an extension of the night breeze. Her moves were so fluid and deceptive that any mortal watching from below would have mistaken her for a shadow or a trick of the moonlight fluttering on the wall. It only took a moment for her to touch down silently on the balcony and pry open the boarded-up window just a crack before squeezing herself in through the tiny opening like a cockroach disappearing under a refrigerator.

With Lizabet inside, Chloe stepped back and considered the building as a whole. The overall appearance was that of a medieval fortress—dark, imposing, and impregnable, but not without its own charm. A large metal sign, looking terribly out of place hanging between the two tremendous pillars flanking the open entryway, announced the property's availability in easy-to-read, bright-red box text:

FOR SALE OR LEASE.
CONTACT KNEBLOFF AND ROTTMAN REALTORS
312-436-4120

Just as she was thinking that fate may have indeed brought them here, the big oak doors swung open and

Lizabet stood in the foyer, opening the door as if to a late-arriving dinner guest.

"Our days of wandering from hovel to hovel are over," she said matter-of-factly. "This is our new home."

Twelve

Struggling to remain focused on the thick volume of tax codes open on the table before him, Drew Richards found his hand once again drifting toward his groin. He had been absentmindedly fiddling with himself since he sat down to study, and as he took a moment to review his progress, he realized he had absolutely no idea what he had just spent the last hour and a half studying. Expelling a long sigh, he pushed an oily shank of hair back from his forehead and wondered how he had come to be cursed as the "Horniest Man in the World." How much could one person masturbate? Did anyone keep track of such things? Maybe he could win some sort of prize. Shit, he'd just finished choking the chicken two hours ago, hoping the relief could get him through the municipal codes and real estate revisions without distraction, but to no avail. Feeling more disgusted with himself than usual, he walked to the bathroom and splashed some cold water on his face, taking a good long look at himself in the vanity mirror as he pulled his head up from the lead-stained sink.

"Marvelous. Now you're a wide-awake, horny jag-off. Congratulations," he said mockingly. Drew Richards was not an attractive man, but his physical shortcomings were more self-imposed than genetic. A lack of proper hygiene and low self-esteem contributed to an aura of unpleasantness that at times bordered on repulsive.

Women were more than a mystery to him. They were a myth. Strange, untouchable creatures, much different from him, that he knew only from stroke books and the occasional porn flick. Real women, he was convinced, would have nothing to do with him. He could feel them laughing at him at work, at school, when his back was turned, whispering through their wet, painted lips. . . .

The hell with it, he thought, and grabbed his coat. He wasn't going to get anything accomplished tonight anyway. The rush of anxiety that always preceded a visit to the Saints and Sinners Adult Bookstore and Video Arcade swept over him, accelerating his heartbeat and deepening his respiration. He took the stairs down from his third-floor apartment two at a time, his mounting anticipation adding an uncharacteristic urgency to his normally laconic step. Walking up Clark Street, he felt a chill rise on the back of his neck that he could not attribute to the cool night air. He'd felt it several times over the last week—when sitting in his apartment at night watching TV or studying—the strange feeling that he was being watched. More than once he had gotten up and checked the windows and doors, so certain he was that he was not alone. He glanced around furtively now, unable to shake the sensation, relieved to see the gaudy neon lights of Saints and Sinners just up ahead, glowing like a deceitful beacon to the lost souls cast adrift in the black sea of loneliness.

A cowbell sounded above his head, announcing his arrival as he walked through the painted glass door. Several of the patrons looked up nervously. A dank fluorescent glow illuminated the cramped space, its sickly light shining off the slick covers of the magazines hanging tempestuously in their wire racks. Despite the bright lights and loud colors, a sodden emptiness permeated the place. And empty it would always be, no matter how many men milled about shuffling self-consciously from rack to rack, searching for that certain oddity that opened the door to secrets so dark they dared not even tell themselves. Drew stood in the doorway, in a state of numb bliss, seeing only salvation and gratification.

"Dollar to browse."

Drew turned to see the old troll perched behind the elevated counter glaring at him with wary contempt through his thick glasses. His shirt, which may have been white at some point in the long-forgotten past, was a dingy yellow. The glow of the overhead fluorescents cast spotty reflections off his balding, misshapen head.

"Oh, it's you," the troll said, his scowl melting into a knowing grin. "Catch those Blackhawks last night? They fuckin' suck, I—"

"No, didn't see 'em," Drew said quickly, bristling at the prospect that the disgusting little bastard would take such a familiar tone with him. Christ, you'd think he was in here all the time or something. He fished a dollar out of his front pocket and handed it to the troll, taking great pains not to touch his fingertips during the exchange.

"Refunded with the purchase of a film, magazine, or novelty," the troll said, all business now, sensing Drew's aloof tone. The cash register clanged open and Drew waited for what seemed like an eternity as the machine spit out the receipt, which the troll tore off and handed to Drew. Making his way up the narrow aisles, Drew's eyes skimmed over the racks of standard hard-core, searching for the truly exotic, a new and exciting quirk to really tickle his desensitized libido. He ended up as he always did, standing in front of the bondage-and-discipline section. Catching his heart in his throat, he stared at the powerful, beautiful women splashed across the covers, squeezed into their rubber and latex garb like goddesses from hell. Oh yes, these were dirty women all right, and they knew . . . yes they knew, what made him tick. Barely conscious of the trembling in his hands, he thumbed through nearly every title in the rack, his eyes lingering on the untouchable two-dimensional dominatrixes calling to him through their cruel, painted mouths. Unable to contain the excitement straining against his blue jeans any longer, he shuffled back toward the counter, where the old troll sat reading his paper, glancing up occasionally.

"Five dollars in tokens, please," Drew croaked, his voice tiny and subdued.

The troll took the fin from Drew's hand and quickly dropped a precounted stack of copper tokens into his outstretched palm in the mechanical fashion that only comes with an act repeated over and over again, hundreds of times a day. Heading to the back of the store with his tokens clutched in his sweaty palm, Drew was surprised, and more than a little uncomfortable, to find that he was the only customer left in the empty store. Swallowing whatever dignity he had left, he walked across the sticky floor of the peep show corridor, well aware that the troll would see him enter whatever booth he chose—would know what he was doing in there. . . .

Fuck it, Drew thought. Who the hell is he that I give a shit about what he thinks? Doing his best to appear nonchalant, he entered a booth adorned with a poster of a woman placing nipple clamps on a fat, whimpering biker-type dressed only in a diaper. He closed the door behind him and fumbled around a bit in the dark searching for the coin-drop slot, wincing each time he touched the sticky surfaces in the darkened booth. Fighting off the nearly overpowering odor of dried cum and mildew, he finally hit pay dirt and felt the token drop into the metal slot.

The entire booth vibrated with an automated, resonant hum. The unseen projector sprang to life, casting a tiny elliptical window of dusty amber light on the wall directly in front of Drew's face. Test patterns and target numbers flickered haphazardly on the makeshift screen as the eight-millimeter loop rattled past the lens bulb at twenty-four frames a second. Drew braced himself for the perverse delights about to unfold before him when suddenly the booth went dark and silent as a tomb.

"Shit!" he said aloud, appalled at being short-changed. Licking his dry lips, he immediately fed another token into the cold metal slot only to hear it drop with an empty clink to the bottom of the box. "Son of a bitch!" With his brow knitted in frustration, he administered a solid shot to the side of the coin box with the heel of his palm, hoping to knock some mechanical sense into the stubborn device. He jabbed repeatedly at the coin-return button with his finger before reluctantly dropping another token into the metal bandit. Coming up empty, he unlatched the eye hook on the door and stormed out of the booth with his fly undone, intent on extracting justice for this grievous impropriety.

But when he turned the corner, he could scarcely believe what he saw. It could not possibly be real.

A stunning woman, propped up on one elbow and wearing little more than a leather Merry Widow, lay stretched out sensually across the glass countertop. She smiled wickedly at him while her fingertips caressed the pronounced curve of her garter-belted hip.

He blinked, fully expecting to see the troll glaring at him from behind the counter when he opened his eyes.

She was still there.

She laughed. A husky, sly laugh bordering on a moan.

Drew Richards's legs grew weak, then failed him altogether. He fell to his knees in abject surrender, unable to tear his eyes away from the vision perched on the counter. The long dark hair, which sported just a whisper of auburn, blew lightly around her head, although there was no breeze to speak of in the stuffy room. Her full breasts jiggled ever so slightly, brimming over and out of the black bustier wrapped tightly around her torso.

She swung her long legs off the counter in a fluid arc, the stiletto heels of her knee-high boots touching down on the tiled floor with an audible click. She walked slowly and deliberately along the counter, turning once, giving him a very good look at the high, rounded swell of her ass, the meaty, fishnet-clad thighs, and just a hint of the wonders that lay nestled, forbidden and warm, between them.

"Drew . . . ," she whispered softly through her wet lips, ". . . my darling boy. You have waited so long for me, have you not?"

Drew, overcome with emotion, could only groan. Yes, he had been waiting forever—but he had known—he had always known deep down that she would come. She stood before him now, a shimmering angel encased in black leather to deliver him from this hell on earth. He nodded stupidly, the tears welling up in his eyes.

"You hear their laughter," she said gently. "You feel their scorn. . . ."

"Yes . . . oh yes." He knew she would understand.

"Whores," she said, echoing his own thoughts. "Whores that are unworthy of your affections. Unworthy of your loyalty, your desire to please . . . to serve."

She walked slowly toward him. His eyes took in every carnal stride until he could see only black leather squeezing the gap between her thighs, just inches from his face.

"Is this what you want, Drew Richards?" Lizabet asked, running her gloved fingers through the shock of disheveled hair atop his head. "Is this what the miserable whores have been denying my sweet boy?"

Unable to contain himself any longer, Drew broke down. He lunged forward, crying uncontrollably, and wrapped his arms around the long legs of the ethereal dominatrix in a desperate, clinging hug. Lizabet Bazore brought her open hand down hard across his face, knocking him on his back and leaving him stunned but a bit more coherent.

"You are never to touch me, Drew Richards. Ever. The flesh of the whores you crave will be yours in abundance— more than you could ever ask for, but you are never to touch me without my permission. Do you understand?"

"Forgive me . . . ," he whimpered, although he actually kind of enjoyed it. "I beg of you."

"I have a place for you, sweet one," she cooed, softly stroking his cheek, where she had slapped him only moments before. "I sense you are anxious and worthy to serve, but I must know, is there anything you will not do for me?"

"Nothing . . . nothing!" he shouted through his tears, never more sure of anything in his life.

"Of course, darling," she said, bending low, until her lips, so full and red against her white face, were just inches from his. "But there are so many who wish to serve. You must prove your devotion before you can taste my kisses. There is a test. . . ."

"Anything . . . ," he whimpered, feeling himself rise up off the floor, following the lead of her gloved fingertips underneath his chin.

"That one," she said, pointing to the store clerk, who was trying to crawl out from behind the glass counter. "The troll. That grotesque fiend is intent on destroying our happiness. If he had his way, he would keep us apart forever. There is nothing that would please him more than my destruction. Can you feel it?"

Drew looked at the little man crawling on the floor, barely conscious, searching in vain for the shattered thick glasses that once covered his bloodstained face. A low gurgling sound emerged from his throat as he struggled to his feet, trying to gather his senses. Never in Drew's life, through the horrors of high school or the hell of his job at the assessor's office, feeling the jeers and the scorn of everyone around him, had he felt so much hatred for another creature. He fought to control the rage rushing through his body as he walked over to the counter and hefted the bulky cash register high over his head. The clerk looked up, terrified, as the horrible reality of what was about to happen sunk into his muddled brain.

"Oh no . . . please . . . ," he begged, his wide eyes staring into Drew's, looking for a trace of humanity but seeing only his doom. He had just enough time to close his eyes as Drew brought the cash register down on his skull with a sickening crack, driving him back down into the tile floor like a tent stake. Drew pulled the register up and out of the old man's head and brought it down again, over and over, until only unrecognizable fragments and pulp remained strewn about the floor and walls. When he no longer had the strength to lift it, Drew let the cash register drop from his hands and leaned back against the counter in elated exhaustion, collecting oxygen in deep, raspy breaths.

"This pleases me a great deal," Lizabet said, savoring the smell of the freshly spilled blood. "I knew when I chose you that you would not disappoint me." She walked casually through the gore toward him. Her boots crunched wetly on the human debris, but Drew heard nothing but the beating of his own heart as he watched her approach. She lifted him up off the counter and pulled him close, bringing him in tight against the saucy curves of her body. "I will allow you to lay at my feet for all your days on earth," she whispered softly in his ear, "but if you ever disappoint me, the joy you feel at this moment will pale compared to the pain that will follow you into eternity."

"N-n-never!" he stammered, horrified that she would ever doubt his loyalty. "N-never, I swear, I . . ."

"Shhhh. . . ." She smiled, exposing her long canine

teeth. "Of course not, darling. You have done such a fine job for Lizabet. Would you like a kiss?"

He stared at the hard enamel of the sharp white teeth set in the soft red mouth and moaned, longing for the moment of release. "Yes . . . please . . . God, yes . . ."

His body shook with a violent orgasm as the fangs pierced his throat, and the wet lips champed at the nape of his neck, gently drawing the vital fluid from his body in carefully metered doses. He surrendered completely, letting the rapture wash over him like a wave, until the lights exploded in his head and only a buzzing darkness remained. He felt himself being carried through the black painted door of Saints and Sinners into a new world, a world of endless, starlit skies and long, wet kisses, far from the mocking laughter and the pain.

He had never been so happy.

Thirteen

The morning was dark and overcast when Dragana Navokovich pulled her weary bones from her bed at 5:30 A.M. on the nose, just as she had done every morning without fail for the better part of the last forty years. It was getting harder every morning it seemed, the pillow being so inviting, and the bed so comfortable. But she had never been one to lay about wasting perfectly good daylight while others were sleeping the day away. She was semiretired now at seventy-seven, cooking only for the Vucinic Brothers Catering a few days a week, or for *slavas* down at the Serbian Manor. More out of a need to keep busy than a need for money, really. Money had never been much of a problem since arriving in America more than half a century ago from Yugoslavia with her husband, Nicolai. America was indeed the land of opportunity, and a good living waited for those who were willing to work hard for it. It had been rough at first, but Nic had found work in a matter of weeks at the Schwinn bicycle factory, making forty dollars for a sixty-hour workweek, good money in those days. They had set up house at 22nd and Cullerton, off Taylor Street on the outskirts of Canaryville, a community on Chicago's near-south side populated mostly by first-generation Italians and Irish.

She thought of Nicolai now as she padded to the kitchen to prepare her morning coffee. It had been twenty-one years since God had taken him from her. She had forgiven Him for that. Nicolai was sixty-two when he died and full of the cancer. But Vesna—she would never forgive God for taking her.

Vesna was their only child, but she was all they had needed to make their lives complete. Ten children could not have filled that house with as much love as Vesna, so special in every way. A combination of the very best of her and Nicolai with none of the faults. She did well in school, always at the top of her class—learning English so well that by fourth grade she could speak it better than her parents. She grew into quite a beauty, tall, with long dark hair and high cheekbones, like that Sophia Loren. She could have had her choice of any of the boys in the neighborhood, but she rarely dated, preferring to study or practice her harp. A harp! Of all the instruments she could have played, she had to play the harp.

Pulling her coffee mug out of the cabinet above the sink, she smiled sadly, remembering the day Nic had brought home the thirty-two-string midsize from Chelsey's Music for Vesna's fifteenth birthday. She remembered the joy on Vesna's face when she looked out the window and saw her father and Milan Borgia taking it off the back of Milan's flatbed truck. It was secondhand, of course, they could not afford new, but it was well maintained. It had a beautiful mahogany soundboard decorated in gold leaf, which was almost as beautiful to look at as it was to listen to. Vesna had mastered the subtle nuances of the obscure instrument by the time she was twenty, prompting an invitation to play at the Arts Festival in Bridgeport, a big, fancy to-do that the mayor himself attended. It was there that she had caught the eye of Luigi Rosario, an Italian stone carver of some renown. He had heard about the raven-haired beauty who could play the harp so beautifully, you'd swear you were in heaven with the angels.

Luigi was a handsome bull of a man with black curly hair and thick arms, lined with muscle from hammering marble all day. He was already a success at twenty-three, having opened his own monument company, an exclusive little shop that dealt in elaborate statuary and grave markings. A Rosario monument on a loved one's grave was something of an honor in the neighborhood. People from all across the city would come to the little studio on 35th Street to admire the beautiful handiwork of the young sculptor.

Being a proper young gentleman, Luigi appeared at their doorstep one day and asked permission from Nicolai to speak to his daughter. Although she had suspected Luigi was already quite familiar with her daughter, Dragana was charmed by the smooth-talking sculptor and told Nicolai to invite the young man in for lemonade. The two of them were married sixteen months later in a beautiful ceremony at All Saints Church, which nearly the whole neighborhood had turned out to see. She knew full well that some of the Serbs, being the clannish bunch that they were, looked down on her and Nicolai for letting their daughter marry "that Italian," but she didn't care. Luigi Rosario was a fine man and a good husband. In 1954, he and Vesna blessed them with a grandson, Vincenczo Rosario, the most beautiful thing in her life to this very day.

Nicolai was only a grandfather for two years before the cancer ate him up and took him in the fall of '56. Then, almost one year to the day Nicolai died, Dragana received the phone call telling her that Vesna and Luigi had been killed in a head-on collision coming home from a late dinner and show downtown. A drunk driver had crossed the center lane and plowed into them before walking from his own wreck and falling asleep on the side of the road. The worst part was telling little Vincenczo, who was sleeping at her house that night, that his mommy and daddy were in heaven now and that he would never see them again. She never stepped foot in a church from that day on, not wanting anything to do with a god that would make her tell such a thing to a three-year-old boy.

The percolator let loose with an exasperated wheeze, and she looked up and saw the sun burning a hole through the thick blanket of clouds that refused to let the day break over the city.

Might be a nice day after all, she thought as she opened the refrigerator door and searched for the cream behind Vincenczo's bottles of beer. The familiar jingling of metal dog tags that always followed the sound of the fridge opening brought a knowing smile to her face. She turned around and saw Thor, their yellow Labrador retriever, trotting into the kitchen, blinking the sleep out of his eyes.

"Finally wake up, you sleepy old pup?" she asked. "I hope you would be that quick to come running if you heard a burglar coming through the back door." With his tail wagging, Thor opened his mouth and yawned loudly, brushing himself against her legs in a pure and shameless display of love. The old woman laughed and returned the favor with a pat on his broad head and a good-hearted tug on his floppy ear.

"Come sit with mama while she has her coffee and then we'll cook breakfast for Vincenczo, huh?" she said. The animal's eyes lit up at the mention of both Vincenczo and breakfast in the same breath. Thor followed her to the little kitchen table and laid his chin on her lap, his doughy jowls, bred for generations to carry game fowl without crushing the delicate bones, splayed out across her thighs.

"Save that sad face for your begging," she scolded him with a smile. "There is no food on this table." Looking into his face, she noticed the telltale white creeping into the yellow fur around his bright eyes and wondered, not for the first time, who would be the first to go, him or her. He was eleven years old now, as old as she was in dog years, if what they say is true. Goodness, where did the time go? It seemed like only yesterday when they had brought him home from the animal shelter on the bus, just nine weeks old, his tiny face peeking out from inside Vincenczo's jacket.

There was little she would deny the child back then if it were within her means, and a dog seemed like such a natural thing for a boy to have. She never dreamed the animal would become so important to her, such an integral part of their lives. As the years passed and Vincenczo grew older and more independent—as teenage boys are apt to do—the dog grew closer to the old woman, perhaps sensing that his best days with the boy were in the past. As if to accentuate this, Thor placed his big paw squarely on her knee and sighed, apparently dissatisfied with her delay in starting breakfast.

"Well, someone is awful bossy this morning," she said, bending down and nuzzling his noble face, taking in the softness of his fur and the hammy smell of his ears. "Oh all right, then, let's get started," she sighed, pushing herself away from the table and topping off her cup with another splash of her strong black coffee.

She moved methodically around the kitchen, each action following the previous one in a sequential and necessary order that was second nature. Within minutes, the smells of breakfast were wafting through the kitchen. Thor stood by dutifully, his leathery brown nose twitching as he caught the scent of the bacon frying up in the iron skillet, ready at a moment's notice to scoop up any wayward food that might find itself on the floor. Grabbing the most businesslike blade from the selection of knives in the butcher block, Dragana sliced four two-inch segments from the roll of French bread she had bought the night before and carved a circular niche out of their centers with a shot glass. She checked the bacon's progress and placed the four cuts of bread into the thin layer of butter already melted to perfection in the Teflon frying pan occupying the low flame on the opposite burner. After letting the bread sear for just a few seconds, she cracked an egg over the rim of each slice. The contents spilled cleanly into the empty cores left by the shot glass, the yokes sitting dead center while the whites clung to the soft, spongy bread surrounding them.

The sudden and rapid thumping of Thor's broad tail on the floor alerted her to her grandson's presence before he could sneak up behind her and plant an affectionate kiss on her wrinkled cheek.

"Mmmm . . . something smells good," he said, peering over her narrow shoulder in mock curiosity. "Oh what a surprise! My favorite! Egg *sang-wiches!*" he teased, borrowing the odd inflection from his uncle Tony, an old mustache Pete–type from Canaryville who was supposedly mob-connected, if you could believe the hints he liked to drop.

"Good morning to you, too, Mr. Funnyman," Dragana replied, trying to suppress her laughter. "Make yourself useful and get the milk out of the fridge for me. And don't drink out of the bottle."

"Slave driver," he teased, bending over and giving her another peck on the cheek for good measure. "Hey, how's my boy, huh?" he asked, ruffling Thor's ears and cuffing him gently on the side of his face. "The mighty Thor! Are you standing guard over Nana's breakfast? Make sure she doesn't burn it!" Thor responded with a muted bark, as if he were joining in on the good-natured teasing, his tail rolling around in a blurry hoop.

"Very funny. Maybe you would like it better if I did burn it, hmmm?" She shook the spatula at him and then looked at Thor. "You too, Benedict Arnold."

Vinnie laughed and poured himself a cup of coffee. He scratched the morning growth of beard that had collected on his handsome face overnight as he rummaged through the overhead cabinets for the table settings.

"You put a shirt on before you sit down for breakfast

at this table, young man," Dragana said, watching her grandson slide his long frame into one of the two rail-back chairs at the little dinette set. "And be quick about it, it's almost ready."

"Aww, Nan," he moaned, but he knew it was no use. He trotted upstairs with Thor galloping behind him and returned moments later with his bathrobe cinched around his narrow hips. "S'all right?" he asked, pulling the orange juice out of the refrigerator.

"S'all right," she answered with an approving nod as she crumbled bacon over the top of his eggs.

They sat and talked while Vinnie wolfed down two of the sandwiches before easing into the third. He has his father's appetite, that was for sure, she thought, watching him in the morning light of the breakfast nook. He was blessed with his parents' good looks, taking from his mother the classical cheekbones and the big dark bedroom eyes sitting under ultra-long lashes that most women would kill for. His father's contributions were evident in the angular blade of a nose and the strong jawline, but he favored his mother, right down to the wavy black hair that fell down to his shoulders the way the young people wore it nowadays. He keeps my Vesna alive in that angelic face of his, she would tell her friends at Bingo, proudly pulling the pictures out of her purse and passing them around the table. She did not mind the long hair on the boys, unlike some of those old hens. He could grow it down to the floor, for all she cared. It was so beautiful it would be a sin to cut it.

If the constant phone calls from the young women were any indication, she was not the only one who thought he was pleasant to look at. Her Vincenczo was a popular boy, and although he never took school very seriously, which disappointed her, he did have his mother's passion for music, his instrument of choice being the guitar. He started his formal training at the age of eight, after she found him in the basement harvesting an impromptu melody from the strings of his mother's harp. His natural ability was apparent even in the random plucking and strumming born out of a child's curiosity. His instructor, Mr. Caravelli, considered the boy nothing short of a prodigy, and at his urging, Vincenczo was schooled right from the start in the disciplined, classical style of playing. Mr. Caravelli pushed the boy hard, demanding more from him than his other pupils. Vincenczo responded in kind, practicing whenever time would allow, as he considered it a pleasure rather than a chore like his schoolwork. After nine years, Mr. Caravelli took his favorite student aside and told him, in his broken English, that he had nothing left to teach him, but he would consider it an honor if Vincenczo would stop by once in a while and "jam" with him. They became close friends, the former student and teacher. Vincenczo would still occasionally drive down to Bridgeport and see the old gentleman, even though his best playing days were behind him, his hands crippled by arthritis.

Looking at him now, feeding the last half of his third egg sandwich to Thor, she felt just the slightest twinge of sadness. She had always dreamed of great things for her Vincenczo, given the incredible talent he had been blessed with. Yet here he sat, twenty-three years old, working as a custodian—a janitor—at the hospital, unable to parlay his talent into a career. He had turned down Mr. Caravelli's numerous offers to take over his vacant teaching slot and lengthy student list, insisting he didn't want to teach, preferring to write his own music and "wait for the right gig."

Oh well, she thought, maybe this new band he joined would bear some fruit. They seemed like a nice enough bunch of young fellows, and Vincenczo seemed to be very excited about their prospects. Listening to them practice in her garage, she could tell that they were very good, even though she didn't care too much for the loud rock and roll music that they played. The singer—a nice, quiet young boy—had a lovely voice and they had even gotten themselves a paying job, playing at some tavern on the north side on Friday nights. Not quite what she had hoped for at this stage in Vincenczo's life, you understand, but it was a start, and the boy was happy and healthy. What more could you ask for, she thought as she cleared the table and began loading the dishes into the sink.

"Sit down, Nan," Vinnie offered. "It looks like it's clearing up outside, I think I'll take the bike to work today."

"Oh, I don't know Vincenczo," she replied, feeling the dread creeping up in her stomach. "The weatherman is calling for more rain, maybe you better take the car."

Vinnie smiled, knowing how she hated his motorcycle, always looking for some excuse to keep him off it. "Nice try, Nan," he said, looking out the window at the clearing skies. "Don't worry, I'll be careful."

She frowned, knowing she had lost this round. "Go on now, get dressed," she said, shooing him away from the sink. "And be careful. No speeding."

"I'm always careful. Especially when I'm getting dressed," he teased.

"You know what I mean, smart guy," she said, whacking him on his narrow behind with the dish towel as he made his way past her toward the stairs.

She had finished up the dishes and was rummaging through the pantry, looking for a side dish to go along with the *sarma* she was preparing for the evening meal, when she heard the clippity-clop of Vincenczo's cowboy boots drumming down the wooden stairwell.

"Worrying about dinner already?" he asked, looking at the package of ground beef and the head of cabbage sitting on the counter. "You're spoiling me, Nan."

"So what else is new?" she asked, only partly kidding.

"Be home around five," he said as he slipped his long

arms through the sleeves of his leather jacket and pecked her on her cheek. "Hey, you be a good boy and keep an eye on the *sarma,*" he said to Thor, patting him on the head. "And maybe when I come home, I'll take you to the p-a-r-k and throw you the F-r-i-s-b-e-e." He spelled the words out, not wanting to rile the animal up, but to no avail. The Lab's eyes and ears perked up and his tail thumped madly on the floor, recognizing the now-familiar syllables as a prelude to a rollicking good time with his master.

"The dog can spell," Dragana said simply.

"I know," Vinnie said, shaking his head. "He's crazy."

Tossing his long hair over the collar of his jacket, he kissed his grandmother good-bye and gave Thor a reassuring nudge on the top of his golden head. "Tonight. Okay, boy? I promise. Bye Nan," he said. "I'll call if I'm gonna be late."

"Be careful," she called out as the door clicked shut behind him. She stood at the window and watched him saunter across the backyard with that odd bobbing gait of his and disappear into the garage.

Vinnie let himself into the garage and stood for a moment in the doorway as he always did, appreciating the clean lines and sleek profile of his Honda 750 SuperSport, sitting patiently like a hooded falcon waiting for flight. He walked around it once, bending low, observing it from all angles, like a museum patron taking in a piece of sculpture. He climbed aboard and settled in at the controls. Twisting the key between the speedometer and the tach, he released the steering lock on the front forks and switched on the ignition. The instrument panel lit up, illuminating the garage with the piercing high beam of the headlight and the soft amber glow of the rear running lights. Vinnie reached down under the gleaming fuel tank and pulled out the choke, flooding the float bowls in the synchronized bank of carburetors with premium unleaded. Applying just a slight twist to the throttle, he thumbed the starter switch and the Honda's engine instantly came to life, filling the garage with the throaty music of a high performance in-line four. Backing off the choke, he let the engine settle into a smooth idle, and gave the throttle a blip, relishing the muted growl from the four-into-two chromed exhaust pipes. Goddamn, he thought, how could any guy with any serious hair on his nuts not love something like this? He pressed the remote control clip tucked into his inside pocket and watched from his perch atop the Honda as the overhead door rattled open with the creaky machination of a medieval drawbridge. Fishing his mirrored sunglasses out of his pocket, he leaned the bike slightly to the right and nudged the sidestand up with his heel, catching a look at himself in the rearview mirror.

"Looking good," he said with no trace of conceit, just the self-assured righteousness of a man confirming the undeniable. He reeled in the clutch and toed the shift lever into first gear, easing the bike into the alley. He paused and waved to his grandmother, knowing even before he looked up that she would be there at the kitchen window, watching him leave.

In her kitchen Dragana waved thoughtfully, watching her grandson motor down the alley, the back tire kicking up a small rooster tail of gravel and dirt. The sun had burned away the last of the lingering clouds, leaving the sky a freshly scrubbed Windex-blue. It was going to be a beautiful day.

So why did she suddenly feel as though a goose had just walked over her grave?

Fourteen

Oblivious to the sweat that was rolling into his eyes, Drew Richards gingerly adjusted the dial on the Coleman lantern, filling the cellar with a soft, steady hiss of white light. It was unseasonably hot for mid-May in Chicago. The temperature had climbed into the nineties by noon, and the sweltering heat inside the old building may have proved a distraction for a lesser man, a man without the sense of purpose and direction that had driven him all week. With strokes bordering on the robotic, he finished painting the last window along the south wall, effectively shutting out the last rays of the sun. He capped the gallon of black enamel and stored his supplies in the corner, pausing for just a moment to admire his progress. All the windows in the basement had been coated in thick black paint and nailed shut. A deterrent but by no means a stopgap to any prying eyes or curiosity-seekers foolish enough to disturb the sleep of the mistress.

He had been working all week to locate and secure the deed to this property. His access to public records and real-estate holdings through his job at the County Building enabled him to cut through much of the red tape and trivial legalities in a relatively short matter of time. The building, he had learned, was originally built in 1892 to house the Chicago Historical Society and had served that purpose until 1936, changing ownership and incarnations several times over the next few years. It had been vacant for the last decade, repossessed by the city for back taxes after an ambitious but failed attempt by a young restaurateur to turn the sprawling behemoth into a nightclub. It was an unprofitable burden to the city, a white elephant on the outskirts of the Loop. As far as he could tell, it could be had for next to nothing once the back taxes had been paid and the proper repairs made. After pulling the file, it was simply a matter of walking it through the proper channels. He would check outstanding liens and clear the path for a clean purchase and closing, which he was sure he would be able to handle himself if all went according to plan.

That bitch on the third floor, Rita Kramer, had tried to give him a hard time. He glared at her, the look in his eyes silencing any smart-ass remark she may have had waiting on the tip of her whorish tongue. He knew she had taken great pleasure in antagonizing him in the past, before the mistress chose him to serve. She would go out of her way at times, it seemed, to give him grief. Laughing openly at him with her little clutch of slutty friends, while he sat alone in the cafeteria, pushing his lunch around on his plate, burying his head in the newspaper and pretending not to notice. She wasn't laughing at him or rolling her eyes when he walked away from her counter with the plat of survey and zoning restrictions tucked into the neat little folder he had been compiling on the property. No, not this time. Perhaps she knew, as he stood there watching her, grinning and staring boldly at her breasts, that it was only a matter of time before she would be at his feet, existing for the sole purpose of giving him pleasure. Oh yes, he would ask for her when the time was right, and the mistress would hand her over to him just as she had promised. Was her hand trembling ever so slightly when she pushed the completed paperwork across the counter to him? Yes, as a matter of fact, it was. Fear had a funny way of commanding respect, he thought. He smiled as he glanced at the heavy wooden doors of the sleep chamber nestled in the far corner of the basement, where his mistress and the other lay during the daylight hours.

When she awoke tonight, she would be so pleased with him. He could hardly wait to tell her of all the things he had done for her today. There was now a corporate bank account with the tidy sum of $150,000 under the name Cachtice Imports at the First National Bank of Chicago, with Lizabet Bazore listed as the president and owner of the company. The tidy, little blue-haired woman in customer service had made no attempt to conceal her distaste when he appeared at her desk, grimy and unshaven. She was quick to change her tune, though, when he opened the briefcase and counted out the cash, all stacked and wrapped in bundles according to denomination.

Can I get you a cup of coffee Mr. Richards? How about a Danish? Allow me to show you some of our new passbook options while we're waiting for this to process. Cachtice Imports, how interesting. Eastern European furniture, did you say? My husband, Norman, he doesn't know a thing about decorating, but I just redid our living room in a country motif and blah, blah, blah.

Jesus Christ, bitch, he thought to himself, why don't you just shut up? Do you really think I give a fiddily-*fuck* about you or your husband? Sitting there, listening to her ramble on, Drew had felt an almost overwhelming urge to snatch the shiny brass letter-opener from her desk and plunge it into her throat. Wouldn't that be a surprise? He played the scene out in his mind over and over again, the thought of all that blood spilling from the wound and soaking her powder-blue suit, turning it a deep purple as she kicked and struggled underneath him. He actually did pick the letter-opener up off her desk. He had cleaned his fingernails with it, digging the impacted soil from the mistress's sleep chamber out from underneath his cuti-

cles, letting it fall in sordid clumps onto her crisp person-
alized stationery. She hurried it up after that, rushing the
application through in an effort to get him away from her
desk and out the door as soon as humanly possible.

Drew's personal hygiene, never high on his list of pri-
orities, had deteriorated to the point where he had
crossed the line from unpleasant into downright foul.
Trivial pursuits such as showering or brushing his teeth
were of little importance when there was the more pressing matter of serving the mistress at hand. Food was nothing more than an afterthought. He ate only to quell the
growling in his empty stomach and suppress the bouts of
nausea that seemed to creep up on him after any extended exposure to the sun. His diet consisted mostly of
hamburger and calves' liver, which he would eat raw. He
washed it down with the bloody juices pooling on the bottom of the butcher's paper, being very careful not to spill
even one drop. He didn't miss food, or his family, or any
of the day-to-day nonsense that occupied so much of his
time before the kiss. He had wasted his life pursuing the
petty dreams of success and happiness so cherished by the
pathetic fools all around him, the cretins and the whores
walking blindly through their short and hollow lives. Real
happiness, real gratification, he realized now, looking
around at his handiwork, could only be attained by re-
nouncing your own petty ambitions and devoting yourself
to a higher cause.

Lantern in hand, he made a final sweep through the
cavernous basement, checking each window before ascending the staircase to the ground floor. Reaching the
top, he inspected the four-by-four he had bolted across
the doorway, denying anyone without a battering ram access to the basement from above. That would be coming
off soon enough, he thought as he made his way back
down the steps. Once the title was secure and the mistress
owned the building legally, he could start work on the

remaining floors and turn the dwelling into a castle more suitable for his queen. Drew Richards hunkered down in the corner and stared longingly at the doors of the sleep chamber, knowing the sun would be setting in a few hours and the mistress would awaken. Dialing down the gas on the Coleman lantern until the light dimmed and then vanished altogether, he sat in the dark and waited for the mistress to rise with the moon.

Fifteen

Kenney Brandt had to smile to himself as he watched Vinnie "the Razor" Rosario swagger through the double doors of The Drop Zone and make his way down the bar. Vinnie spread himself around, bullshitting and laughing like a diplomat greeting heads of state in a receiving line at a black-tie dinner. Everyone wanted a moment with him and he was happy to grant it. He paused to shake a hand or slap a back, before moving on, working the crowd with the effortless, cocksure attitude of the truly confident and totally cool. His manner was so easygoing, so breezy, it was almost infectious. The promise of a good time hung over his shoulders as surely as his mane of thick black hair, and women and men alike gravitated toward him, seeming to feed off the energy that lingered in the air around him like a familiar aftershave.

Taking a pull off the long-neck Budweiser sitting on the coaster in front of him, Kenney recalled the first time he had ever seen Vinnie the Razor walk through those cheesy red upholstered doors four months ago.

GloryDaze, the band he had formed with Johnny Coltrane, had been holding open auditions for a guitar player. Pete Sullivan, their slated lead guitar and a pretty good backup singer, decided not to return to art school after Christmas break, opting for the security of a union job, working construction back home in Minnesota. Sully's unexpected flash of good sense had left them short

one lead guitar with their first scheduled gig at The Drop
Zone just one week away. They placed an ad for a guitar
player in that Thursday's edition of *The Reader,* and to
their surprise, no less than five candidates showed up at
The Drop Zone at 9 A.M. on a chilly Saturday. They were
setting up on the small stage when Vinnie walked in, shaking the snow off his leather jacket, his eyes hidden behind
mirrored shades, looking very rock and roll. Vinnie sat
expressionless as the first two arrivals finished showing off
their stuff. When it was his turn, Vinnie peeled off his
leather jacket, pulled his custom-made Stratocaster from
its case, and slipped it over his shoulder. He reached back
into the guitar case and produced three sixteen-ounce
cans of Budweiser, which he laid out ceremoniously in
front of him. Without saying a word, he opened each can
and then chugalugged the tall-boys, one-two-three, in
rapid succession. He belched softly as he laid the last
empty can down and plugged into the big Marshall amplifier.

"Pardon me," he said as he casually pulled the pick
from between the strings of the Fender's neck and
launched into a hellacious set of electric firepower that
left everyone just a bit starstruck. In a wild and hairy five-
minute span, he strung together a medley of superlative
Hendrix, Zeppelin, and Sabbath riffs, note for note. Unable to contain himself, Dave Hannon, their drummer,
jumped behind his Pearl drum kit and joined in as the
Razor wrapped it up with a bluesy improvisation. When
he finished, the remaining candidates didn't even bother
going on. They just packed up their axes and slinked off,
realizing the audition was, for all intents and purposes,
over. Vinnie hung around and they all jammed for two
more hours before Tommy Corbett, the owner of The
Drop Zone, and a boyhood friend of Kenney's, had to
kick them out and open the bar for the afternoon crowd
filtering in to watch the Notre Dame game. Those first

two hours had been magical, however, and everyone in the room sensed it.

Covering old blues and R&B standbys like the Yardbirds' "Smokestack Lightning," and "Shake" from Sam Cooke and Otis Redding, they had fallen into a cozy synchronicity, feeding off Johnny's wailing vocals and Vinnie's heavy power chords and hot leads. Kenney was content to lay in the background and supply a steady and unobtrusive bassline to the two front men and the stomping thunder of Dave's relentless drumming. In between songs they talked excitedly, grinning and laughing with each other, bouncing old stories around and feeding off the realization that this might be something special. It was apparent that Vinnie was the star, but it was the interplay between his guitar and Johnny's voice that created the chemistry that made them a band as opposed to four musicians who just happened to be playing together. It was during that first session that Johnny began to realize the untapped potential of his own voice, the sexy, supercharged quality that began to emerge only after he loosened up and got deeper into the set.

After they finished packing up and hauling out their gear, the four of them sat at the bar and shared a quick beer, making arrangements for the next rehearsal. Still giddy from the adrenaline rush produced by the jam session, Kenney turned to their new guitar player and officially welcomed him aboard.

"Congratulations, Mr. Rosario," he said, smiling. "You passed the audition."

Vinnie looked him straight in the eye, serious as a heart attack, and replied, "So did you guys."

With that, he shot Johnny a wink, drained his beer, and headed to the door, carrying his precious Stratocaster out into the cold Chicago winter.

All kidding aside, Kenney knew that a musician of Vinnie's caliber could hook up with just about any group he wanted to. Why he chose a rag-tag garage band like GloryDaze was anyone's guess, but if he had to lay money down, he would bet it was because of something in Johnny's voice. Though he was relatively untrained, with no proper schooling aside from singing in the church choir back in Belvidere, Johnny had great natural instincts and a gritty edge to his voice. They made for an interesting set of front men, the lanky, dark guitar god and the willowy vocalist with the cherubic face, framed with ringlets of curly brown hair.

Even now, as Vinnie pulled up a rickety bar stool and sidled in beside him, Kenney could see the women in the bar casting furtive glances over their drinks and around their boyfriends at the tall, handsome guitarist. Kenney knew damn well that they weren't looking at him.

"How goes it, teacher?" Vinnie asked, slapping him on the back as he sat down next to him. "Rough day at the office?"

"Second-graders," Kenney said, holding up two fingers as he signaled to Tommy for a refill. "Runny noses and pissed-up pants, but I'll be damned if they don't try to scam you just like the older kids do. 'Lets all bullshit the substitute.' Jeez, they must all think we're morons."

"You got a short memory, my friend," Vinnie laughed. "What did you think of substitute teachers when you were a kid?"

Kenney smiled in spite of himself. "That they were all morons," he laughed. "Point well taken, Mr. Rosario."

"Hey, fuck it," Vinnie replied, sliding a fin toward Tommy as he set two beers down in front of them. "I got this one, Tommy. You do what you gotta do. We're gonna be rich and famous rock and roll stars pretty soon anyway, with all the poontang we can handle—well, all the poontang *you* can handle," he said, throwing a shot at Kenney in the well-intentioned manner of two close friends. "Me,

I never get enough. And then you can tell 'em all to kiss your ass."

Kenney thought back to earlier in the day when he had been eating lunch in the teachers' lounge. He could tell by their polite nods and abbreviated manner that the regular faculty disapproved of his hairstyle, not long by modern standards, just touching his shoulders actually, but longer than your average teacher's.

"I can't wait," he said, relishing the thought. "I might even paint a bull's-eye on my cheeks so they all know exactly where they can plant their lips."

"That's my boy," Vinnie laughed out loud, visualizing the scene. "You talk to Johnny today?"

"No," Kenney said. "Saw him in school last night. He stopped by during his break and dropped in on this life-drawing class I was teaching. We had a pretty good-looking model, for a change, and I think word got around. He missed out, though, she was in her robe taking a break when he came by. Too bad for him. You should have seen the ass on her. World-class. I think he was pissed."

"I thought you said drawing all those naked chicks was 'just like drawing a vase of flowers,' " Vinnie reminded him, a slight mocking tone in his voice.

"It is. Only this was a vase of flowers with a great ass," Kenney laughed.

They sat in comfortable silence for a moment, then Vinnie said, "Speaking of great asses, Monique and I are through. For good this time, I think. She found out about that little blonde last Friday night."

Kenney felt a slight sting at the mention of Monique's name. He had carried a torch for the beautiful sculptress ever since he had met her in a figure-modeling class two years ago. They had gone out a few times, had even slept together, but the relationship was pretty much a one-sided deal. She was just out for a good time. A young, beautiful girl, away from home for the first time—nowhere near ready for any kind of commitment. When she'd felt Kenney getting serious after a few weeks, she laid the old "Can't we just be friends?" line on him and dropped him like a bad habit. He should have seen it coming. Kenney was the quintessential nice guy, and Monique was one of those women who liked her men with a little edge, the dangerous type—the kind of guys who would bring her nothing but heartache and grief.

A guy like Vinnie.

She had met Vinnie at an Institute party shortly after he had joined the band, and Kenney knew as he watched the sparks fly from a distance that she wouldn't be sleeping alone that night.

"It isn't the first time she caught you fucking around on her. You guys will work it out," Kenney said, trying to sound casual. Then he added with just a touch of bitterness, "She always comes back for more."

"Naw," Vinnie said, missing the dig. "This is it. She's really pissed. Hey, fuck it, she's too possessive anyway. What does she think? We're married or somethin'? Maybe you should try to catch her on the rebound, Kenney."

"I told you that's ancient history, Vincenczo," Kenney lied. He kept his true feelings about Monique buried. Only Johnny, his best friend, suspected how he really felt. "I don't need to be digging up old bones. There's too much fresh meat out there to keep going back for leftovers."

"You got that right, brother," Vinnie laughed, raising his glass in salute. "And it's all out there waiting for us. Hey, look who decided to show up."

Kenney turned to see Johnny Coltrane and Dave Hannon walk in together. The big drummer towered over the slightly built singer like a wary bodyguard. They elbowed their way through the growing crowd and squeezed into a couple of empty bar stools next to their bandmates.

"How you ladies doin' tonight?" Dave asked, laughing. "Trollin' for blowfish as usual, I see."

"Yeah, if you see any *real* men walk in, let us know," Kenney said in retaliation, needling the carpenter from Wrigleyville.

He'd met Dave a few years back at Play It Again, Sam's, a secondhand record store near Greektown, known for its eclectic selection of hard-to-find imports and bootleg blues albums from the early days of the British invasion. Kenney had been flipping through a stack of scratchy old 45s when he noticed the imposing figure standing next to him with the Moby Grape and Cream albums tucked securely under his beefy arm. They struck up a conversation and Dave discovered that an elusive cut he had been searching for in vain—"Toad," a classic drum solo by Ginger Baker—was a staple of Kenney's personal collection. Kenney copied it onto cassette tape for him and the two of them became fast friends. They had kept in touch over the years, getting together for a few beers at Kingston Mines occasionally, each promising to call the other if they ever decided to form a band.

Jeez, I'd hate to get into a fight with that guy, Kenney thought, watching the tensor and flexor muscles twitch on Dave's tattooed forearm as the carpenter drained his first beer in one long gulp. Dave's childhood buddies had called him "Popeye" in reference to his somewhat out-of-proportion forearms, built up over the years from lifting weights and generally pounding the shit out of things. He had been a football player of some renown in high school, an all-state middle linebacker and fullback. He had earned a scholarship to tiny Millikin College, where he had terrorized opponents for two seasons until he tired of the academic workload after three semesters and hung up his cleats. His uncle, a precinct captain in the thirteenth ward, got him into Washburne Trade School on Chicago's south side and a cushy union job as a carpenter at McCormick Place right after he graduated. Dave made a pretty good buck, not like the rest of them, struggling to pay off student loans like Kenney and Johnny, or stuck in a shitty job like Vinnie. He'd recently purchased two sound monitors so they could actually hear what they were playing, waving off his bandmates' offers to pitch in. His generous nature made him a good man to have around in a tavern, if cash was tight, as it always seemed to be.

"Another round down here, Tommy!" Dave yelled down the bar as he slapped down a pair of crisp twenties. "And keep 'em coming."

"My hero," Johnny said, looking at his empty glass. "So, whadda you guys think? Are we gonna be able to squeeze in an extra rehearsal before Saturday night?"

In addition to their regular Friday night gig at the Zone, Kenney had managed, with some fast-talking and their best demo tape, to get them booked for the upcoming Battle of the Bands at the WhereHouse, a huge converted factory near Lincoln Park. They had secured the spot only two weeks ago after Vinnie had heard through an old girlfriend that TimeBandits, an oldies group from the west side, had dropped out, creating a vacancy on the bill. In addition to the thousand-dollar grand prize, it was an opportunity to play to a big auditorium-type crowd and see how they matched up against some of the city's best bands.

"Let's see," Kenney said thoughtfully, "what's tonight, Wednesday already? We've got tomorrow night open and our regular gig here Friday night. You guys think that's enough?"

"I don't know, boss," Dave said. "I'd like to walk in there Saturday tighter than a virgin's quim on prom night, if you know what I mean. We're gonna have to be kickin' some major ass to walk away with that dough. There aren't any lightweights on that card."

"There isn't anybody on that bill better than us," Vinnie said matter-of-factly. "They can cut us that check right now and save themselves the time as far as I'm concerned. All we have to do is show up and play. Shit," he added, pinching Johnny's cheek, "when they hear pretty boy sing, they'll be throwin' the money at us."

Johnny actually blushed. The shy kid from Smalltown, U.S.A., had no idea how good he really was and was honored that Vinnie the Razor, guitarist extraordinaire, spoke so highly of him.

"I don't know, Vinnie," Johnny said, brushing off the compliment. "I'm with Dave. Maybe we should try to squeeze in one more rehearsal."

"Hey, no problem. I'm all for it," Vinnie replied. "But when?"

"How about Friday afternoon?" Kenney asked. "Me and Johnny are free. Can you guys take a day off work?"

"No problem," Dave said.

"I don't know," Vinnie said, scratching his chin. "Nana's gonna wonder why I'm out in the garage playing rock and roll with you assholes and not cleaning up shit at the hospital. I don't want to get her pissed. How about Saturday afternoon, around one? We'll do a quick run-through, have time for a nap, and be fresh for kickoff at ten o'clock."

"Sounds good to me," Kenney said. "How about you guys?"

"Sure, why not?" Dave agreed, polishing off another beer. "You guys could use the practice."

"So . . . ," Johnny asked, a trace of anxiety in his voice, "just how big is this joint?"

"Capacity's thirty-five hundred," Kenney replied. "And if it's anything like the last one, it'll be packed."

They contemplated that for a moment, taking slow, thoughtful sips of their beers, letting it sink in. Giving voice to their thoughts, Vinnie raised his bottle of Budweiser and looked them each in the eye as he spoke.

"This is gonna be a breakthrough night for us, guys. I can feel it. After Saturday night, our lives will never be the same."

Sixteen

As Vinnie the Razor was prophetically toasting the future and unwinding with his bandmates after a long day, Maureen Reilly was stepping off a bus some five miles north of The Drop Zone and beginning her night. A cold breeze blew in from the lake, mingling with the warm air that had lingered in the wake of the storm the night before, bringing with it a wispy layer of fog that unfolded over the streets. Maureen regarded the fog with the simple amusement of a child, watching the smoky tendrils part around her ankles as her stiletto heels click-clacked across the sidewalk toward her familiar corner on Halsted and Diversey. She looked around pensively, noting the marked absence of the other girls who regularly worked the area, and checked her watch. Nearly midnight. Where the hell was everybody? Come to think of it, she hadn't seen Charlene for days, and those two skanks that worked for that mutt Estoban seemed to have disappeared without a trace. Not that she missed them. She hoped they hauled their big asses up north to Rogers Park, like they were always bragging they would. But Charlene . . . it wasn't like her to miss work. She dug into her purse, past the long-handled razor she kept for dealing with sickos and rip-off artists, and fished out a pack of cigarettes and the Zippo that Charlene had given her for Christmas. Maureen lit up, pulling the smoke deep into her lungs, and took up position at the mouth of the alley next to Burman's

Pharmacy. She looked around, sizing up her prospects for the night.

Foot traffic was minimal. A few rubes from the suburbs slumming and the usual punks from the neighborhood, but it was still early. Business didn't start to pick up until the bars closed down at two o'clock. The johns would drive by, looking for a quick blow job after striking out with the bimbos in the nightclubs. Maureen unzipped her pink PVC jacket and pulled it back away from her skimpy tube top, giving the drive-by traffic some food for thought, just in case the hot pants and seamed fishnets didn't get the point across. Well, at least she had the place to herself tonight, she thought, taking another drag off the Cheyenne. Still, it was kind of creepy being out here all by herself, what with the fog and all. An icy chill raced up the back of her neck with the sudden realization that she was not alone in the alley. She wheeled around, eyes wide. The straight razor was already in her hand, ready to carve someone a new asshole.

"Who's there?" she asked, trying to inject a note of bravado into her squeaky voice. "This shit ain't funny, motherfucker . . . I ain't kiddin'! You mess with me and I *will* fuck you up!" She backed slowly out of the cavernous alley, squinting into the shadows. Vanity prevented her from wearing the glasses she needed, but she could see well enough to realize that there was nothing lurking behind the Dumpsters and trash bins besides the huge rats and the tomcats that tried to stay out of their way.

"Settle down, Mo," she said aloud, ashamed that a little fog on a quiet night could spook her like that. Still, she could have sworn someone had been standing right behind her a moment ago, and her instincts, unlike her mind, were pretty sharp. Dropping the straight razor back into her purse, she leaned back against the cool brick wall of Burman's and actually thought about calling it a night, when she looked across the street into the narrow brick corridor of the opposite alley.

There was a shadow stirring in the fog.

At first she thought it was a trick of the light, but as she narrowed her eyes, the shadow took the shape of a woman, coalescing—gathering substance as it glided out of the tranquil blanket of mist. The young streetwalker stood mesmerized, unable to take her eyes off the dreamy specter as she approached, her footsteps making no sound on the scarred concrete. A long black duster, pulled open in the front to reveal the fluid, almost hypnotic, roll of her hips, trailed behind the woman like a cape, fluttering on the isolated breeze that blew the long dark hair away from her exquisite white face.

The woman was smiling at her. The smile was more apparent in her smoldering green eyes than the hint of a grin that danced on her red lips. She walked coyly around the teenage hooker, sizing her up.

"You're quite the little package, aren't you, sweet one?" the woman asked brazenly. She stared at the teenager's considerable assets, slowly circling her. "How old are you, child?" she asked, reaching out and stroking the soft skin of the girl's exposed midriff, finding it supple with just a trace of baby fat. "Seventeen? Certainly no older than twenty. Yes, exactly what I was looking for . . ."

"Old enough to know a good time when I see one, mama," Maureen replied, no longer afraid. In fact, she was actually a little turned on. The woman was older than she was used to, in her late thirties maybe, but she was a knockout. Little Mo had turned quite a number of dyke tricks during her three-year stint on the street—usually rich society bitches from the Gold Coast, pulling up in their Mercedes-Benzes and Lincolns, looking for a little kink. She didn't mind. They were easier than the men. No mess, no fuss, no worry. Maybe this wouldn't be such a boring night after all.

"Oh, I assure you, Maureen," the woman said, pulling a roll of hundreds from the pocket of her duster and tucking a single crisp bill into the girl's exposed cleavage, "it will be anything but boring." She cupped the teenager's large breast, giving it a firm squeeze. A giggle, almost musical, escaped from her throat. "Oh my . . . ," she cooed with mock surprise, "such large breasts for such a sweet little girl."

"Mmmmm . . . yeah . . . ," the nubile youngster moaned, cocking her shoulders and arching her back. "You like that sweater meat, don't you, mama?" How did she know my name, Maureen wondered, plucking the bill from between her breasts and tucking it in her purse with the speed of a sleight-of-hand magician. Who cares, she thought, inching closer to the vampire, pressing her firm breasts underneath the taller woman's own ample bosom and into her rib cage. Her nipples grew hard, nearly bursting through the taut fabric of her tube top, as the weight of the other's breasts pressed down on her own, adding to the friction.

"Sweater meat!" Lizabet Bazore laughed out loud. "What a delightful term. How appropriate! From the mouths of babes . . . ," she giggled. "Yes, my little darling. I like it. I like it very much. I like sweet young meat best of all. Here let me show you. . . ." She pulled her in close, gathering her up like a spider wrapping up a fly in a tangle of legs, arms, and sweet smelling hair. The vampire's lips brushed against the girl's face, lighting softly for a moment on her cheek before making their way down her neck where the wet enamel of the long teeth brushed against the sensitive skin of the girl's neck. The little streetwalker relaxed, melting into the gentle, whispered kisses. The moisture and warmth began to flow between Maureen Reilly's legs as Lizabet's lips moved slowly back up to her cheek and lingered there, savoring the springy juvenile flesh.

Then with a muted growl, the vampire struck. In a flash of white teeth and a splash of crimson, she tore a ragged mouthful of tissue from Maureen's face just beneath her eye. The scream stopped in the terrified hooker's throat, emerging in spastic, convoluted gasps and half-syllables. The monster released her and the girl reeled backward, disoriented and confused. Her fingers explored with numb disbelief the puddling, elliptical hole in her face, where her cheek used to be. She pulled her hand away from her ruined face, staring at the oily blood pooling on her fingertips. The sounds of laughter, loud and scornful, rang in her ears, snapping her back into the moment. The beast stood before her with the shredded remains of her face locked between her clenched teeth in an awful, mocking grin. So unexpected and violent was the attack, that anger and retaliation were never an option. The surreal nature of the incident left the street-tough runaway gasping incoherently through her welling tears.

"How . . . how could you do this to me?" she stammered, still fingering the hollow void beneath her eye. "How . . . look what you've done! Look at my *face!*"

"Shush, child! Where are your manners!" the vampire scolded, barely able to stifle her laughter. "Can't you see I'm trying to eat!" With that, she jerked her head back and champed the quivering crescent of tissue down her throat. She swallowed obscenely, and the smile disappeared from her face, leaving behind a mask of abomination, her eyes shining with menace.

Now Maureen Reilly did scream. She turned and ran headlong into the alley, the blood from the awful wound nearly blinding her. She careened off a Dumpster and spun into a row of garbage drums. The heel on one of her pumps snapped off as she tried to right herself. She fell hard, landing with a dirty splash in a puddle of tepid rainwater. She winced at the pain racing up her leg as she scrambled to her feet. The laughter of the demon rever-

berated down the alleyway and through her head. She
shot a brief, desperate glance over her shoulder as she
hobbled down the alley on her broken ankle. The thing
was right behind her, walking slowly, casually, its eyes burning like twin pinpoints of hellfire.

"Where are you going, Maureen?" the phantasm asked,
the voice seeming to come from all around her. "I do so
want to give you another kiss."

Maureen screamed again, a wail of anguish and despair
welling up from the realization that she would not leave
this alley alive. Just as she was about to surrender to the
pain in her ankle and the loss of her will, a Ford Econoline
van pulled up and rolled to a halt some twenty feet in
front of her at the mouth of the alley.

"Stop! Please help me!" she screamed, almost running
now, ignoring the crippling pain that shot through her
ankle with every step. "Please, please stop!"

Unbelievably, the cargo door slid open, and she pitched
herself headlong into the van. She turned in time to see
the vampire still walking toward her with that same maddening, methodical step.

"Drive! Go! Now! There's a monster out there!"
Maureen yelled, slamming the side door shut on the sight
of the grinning nightmare now only ten feet away. Without
a word, her savior, sitting unseen in the driver's seat,
dropped the transmission into drive and pulled away from
the curb with the careful, exaggerated patience of a
driver's-ed student.

"Hurry up, motherfucker! She'll kill us both!" she
screamed in frustration. "She ain't human, she's some
kind of fuckin' monster, she—"

"Are you working tonight, cupcake?" the man asked
from behind the high-backed captain's chair. He motored
slowly down Diversey like a meandering sightseer with no
agenda and not a care in the world.

"Huh?"

Drew Richards craned his head around and looked at the hysterical young woman with the gaping wound in her face and repeated the question. "Are you working tonight? You know—selling your body for money. That is what you do, isn't it? I imagine your mother and father must be very proud of you."

The sharp words had little sting, unable to penetrate the wall of trauma that surrounded her, eliciting only more bewilderment and panic.

"Please, mister, you gotta get me to a hospital. I'm hurt bad. She bit me, she bit my . . ." She paused and brought her hand cautiously up to the recessed gore underneath her eye. "She bit my face! Look at what she did to my face!"

Drew turned around again and carefully considered the ragged hole in her cheek. He made no effort to hide his revulsion as he squinted at her in the green glow from the dashboard lights. "Eeeew, yuck! You're gonna have to find another line of work, honey. Maybe you can be a doctor or an astronaut. No one is gonna pay good money to have an ugly kisser like that bobbing up and down on their lap."

The tears came, racking her body in great sobs. She collapsed on the grooved metal floor of the cargo van, her senses numb, reduced to a pool of blood, tears, and ruined flesh. "A monster," she mumbled. "My God, she was a fucking monster!"

"There, there, cupcake," the greasy little man said from behind the wheel. "I realize you're upset right now, but there's no need to resort to name-calling." He pulled the van to a stop and turned to look at her as he spoke. "You know, I really think you should apologize."

"What?" she asked, lifting her head from between her hands. "What are you talk—"

The cargo door slid open with a shimmy of rolling metal and the beast stood there, backlit by the stark gleam of the streetlight. Blood—*her* blood—smeared its lips and stained the sharp teeth. Lizabet Bazore leaned in close, her eyebrow arched in feigned curiosity.

"Now then, child, what's all this talk about monsters?"

Maureen didn't even have time to scream.

Seventeen

From her vantage point on the fire escape, Chloe Covington searched the heavens in vain for the billions of stars muted by the electrical luminescence of the city lights. It was her least favorite aspect of habitation in the big city—the corruption of the night sky, one of the few things she felt a link to in her wandering, nocturnal existence. For as far back as she could remember (which happened to be the night she was conceived by the mistress), she had loved to walk the night under the blanket of celestial glitter, feeling plugged into, yet humbled by, its infinite majesty.

It was a little better tonight. The sky was clear and cloudless—a marked yet lovely contrast to the fog that dusted the streets below her. The reemergence of a few familiar stars warmed her heart. Peering out over the opposite rooftop, she could see the increased activity along Division Street as the bartenders signaled last call and the desperate lost souls scurried about, searching for a quick and easy cure for their loneliness.

The city was not without its upsides. The food supply was seemingly endless, offering a wide variety of the defeated and the forsaken. Most were more than willing to forfeit their souls in exchange for a quick end to the pointless redundancy of their day-to-day existence. Looking into their thoughts as she walked among them, she would pick and choose, sorting through the vacuous and the superficial, searching for a particular quirk or poignancy that would strike her fancy. There was a certain intimacy to the kill. The limp, almost grateful surrender of the victim, the robust and dizzying surge of the blood, the fleeting covenant that passed between them as the intended's life force slipped away and became her own. She took no pleasure in watching them suffer as Lizabet did, nor did she believe that their suffering in any way enhanced the purity of the transfer as the mistress had suggested.

Lizabet's eccentricities had landed them in precarious situations on more than one occasion. Although there was probably not another creature walking the earth as skilled in the Dark Craft, Chloe wondered at times how Lizabet had managed to survive so many centuries in such a reckless manner. Like most hedonists, Lizabet lived for the moment and gave little thought to the future or the consequences of her actions, unlike Chloe, whose calculated, systematic approach was apparent even in her killing.

She glided away from the railing and pressed herself against the side of the building before the couple had even turned the corner off Clark Street and made their way toward her from the far end of the alley. Their footsteps were heavy, suggesting two large males, although the rhythm of one set was unnatural and stilted, carrying the trademark click-clack of high heels. Thinking her ears may have deceived her, she focused on their scents, discovering one buried beneath a thick layer of feminine perfume, although both subjects were testosterone dominant. They came into view just as she was able to isolate their thought patterns from the cacophony of alpha waves emanating from the nightclub behind her. What she saw brought a wry smile to her wet red mouth.

One mortal, a disheveled male in his late twenties, apparently quite drunk, was being led down the alley by a tall, rather unconvincing transvestite, also walking the night in search of prey. They stopped directly beneath her.

Chloe watched, fascinated, as the big male in the tight, body-hugging dress worked the drunken john into the recesses of a doorway and cooed into his ear. He spoke huskily of the magic he would work with his lipsticked mouth, distracting the mark while he dug through his designer handbag, searching for the heavy leather blackjack that lay at the bottom. Chloe settled back, contemplating which one she would kill first, when the thoughts of the john drifted into her head and made her reevaluate the situation unfolding below. Oh no, she thought, combing past the clouded, debauched confusion, deep into his subconscious, this one could not die. Not tonight. Not yet. He was far too valuable. She intervened just as the transvestite drew the weapon and prepared to bring it down upon the besotted lawyer's head.

"Not so fast, deary," Chloe said, causing both of the mortals to look up, surprised that their clandestine rendezvous had not gone undetected.

Chloe Covington altered her molecular structure, made it less dense, and stepped off the iron grating three stories above them into the nothingness of the night sky. Catching the air currents coming in off the lake, she drifted, featherlike, and descended like a seasoned sky diver directly between the two humans.

"Who, the fuck . . . ," the transvestite complained, dropping the feminine pitch from his voice.

Chloe turned and considered the leggy cross-dresser, surprised to see that in the muted light of the alley, he was actually kind of pretty, in a trashy, overdone way. "Party's over, Keith," she declared, calling him by his given masculine name. "Time to call it a night."

Enraged by the slight to his femininity, rage replaced the shock on Keith's face. He waved the blackjack ominously and squared off, taking on a combat stance, drawing the vampire into the center of the alley. "Bitch, you are so done and you don't even know it! I am gonna fuck up that pretty little face of yours so bad your own mother won't recognize . . . ."

For reasons she could not remember or understand, the mention of her mother touched a raw nerve in the vampire's brain. Her angelic face, a child's face really, contorted, twisted for one mad moment into the mask worn by the demon within her.

". . . it." Keith continued, the last word, dangling stupidly from his mouth as he backpedaled, unable to believe what he thought he saw.

With her back to the barely cognizant john, she advanced calmly, casually, toward the man in the dress.

"It's over, Keith," she said, her words ringing with somber finality. "The confusion, the pain. The anger and the resentment you feel for your God when you cry yourself to sleep. The disgust you feel for yourself when you bring the shaving razor to your hairy face every evening. It all ends tonight."

A shriek welled up from deep within the transvestite's tortured soul, a mad, howling wail of pain and fury that reverberated through the alley. He charged at the diminutive blonde, intent on breaking her to pieces.

With the fluid grace of a prima ballerina, Chloe took the charge. She stepped deftly away at the last possible moment and caught the enraged mortal by the throat, cutting off the war cry as her tiny hand closed like a vise around his bulging Adam's apple.

"Trust me," she said, a note of condolence in her voice as she forced the gasping man to his nyloned knees in the squalid alley. "It's better this way. You didn't have long to go, anyway." With that, Chloe reached into the mass of dark cascading hair and yanked the wig from his balding head. She twisted hard, breaking his neck clean and severing his spinal cord.

"Good night, Karla," Chloe said, invoking his feminine name one last time as he crumpled lifelessly to the ground. The dazed man in the wrinkled six-hundred-dollar suit stood nestled in the doorway, staring numbly at the wig lying in the alley like some alien roadkill.

"God . . . ," he moaned, more affected by the unveiling of the transparent masquerade than by the execution he had just witnessed. "It was a guy! I kissed a fucking guy!" He looked at his savior with wide, innocent eyes. "I didn't know. I swear, I thought it was a chick. I'm not gay or anything, really, I—"

"No, Arthur Melbourne," Chloe said, confirming his embarrassed and clumsy denials as she approached him. "You aren't gay. But you did know that that was a man, didn't you?"

The fact that she knew his name did not surprise him in the least. Of course she would, it was only natural. "Yes," he admitted shamefully, not only to her but to himself. He found it impossible to lie, staring into the glittering gold eyes of the beautiful creature that stood before him. It would be fruitless anyway. She knew everything about him, all his secrets, all his desires. And she understood and accepted without judging.

"And you knew," Chloe continued, gently stroking his cheek, "that walking into this dark alley with him was a dangerous and reckless thing to do, didn't you?"

"Yes," he said, his lip trembling.

"But you didn't care. You came anyway," she said. "You followed him into this alley, knowing full well that nothing good could possibly walk out of here with you." She smiled a secret smile to herself, fascinated by the complexity of the human psyche.

"No, I didn't care," he said, admitting his true nature aloud for the first time in his life. "I liked the risk, the danger. It was exciting."

"Yes," Chloe replied, her voice so understanding, so

supportive. "You like to take risks, Arthur. That is why I chose you. I need you to do something for me that may involve some risk, some danger. You know," she continued, her lips close to his face, "if I hadn't come along, you may very well have been killed."

The vision of the specter descending like an archangel from the fire escape flashed into his head. The sudden realization that she was not of this earth exploded like an epiphany through his alcohol-muddled brain. Arthur Melbourne's head reeled with an overwhelming rush of emotions, convinced now that he stood face-to-face with a messenger from the afterlife, a shimmering, heavenly spirit from the great beyond. "You saved me," he whispered, humbled by the divine intervention. "You saved me from that . . . that *thing!*"

"Yes," Chloe said, taking his head gently between her hands as her lips curled back to reveal the sharp teeth that would spell his doom, "but I cannot save you from yourself."

Eighteen

Kenney Brandt was more than a little puzzled as he followed the well-oiled gait of the pretty teacher's aide down the glossy brown and yellow tiled corridor of Saint Nicholas Elementary School. They turned the corner past the sun-splashed nook with the life-size statue of the Virgin Mary, so bizarre with her garish, painted Sacred Heart sitting exposed, blood-red between the suggestion of breasts on her white flowing gown. He hoped it didn't reflect badly on him—receiving a phone call just one hour into his day. It was highly unusual to be pulled from class like this and he couldn't for the life of him think of who could be calling him at work. For that matter, who even knew what school he would be working at today? This was, like most of his appointments, an unscheduled assignment. Although on occasion he would be called in advance to take over a class, the majority of his work was of the same-day variety, a one-shot deal to cover a teacher who couldn't make it in. Good substitute teachers were in great demand and he could usually count on three or four calls every morning from the various school districts he was registered with in the southwest suburbs. He would usually take the first call, and he rarely refused a request to fill in unless it was from one of the more notorious high schools, bordering on the city limits. He preferred to take his chances and wait for a gig where he wouldn't have to worry about a knife in his back for the lousy thirty-five bucks they paid him.

He had been relieved this morning when the phone rang and he heard the pleasant voice of Mrs. Anderson from St. Nick's on the other end. The Catholic school jobs were a breeze, especially the elementary schools. The kids were generally from good families and well behaved, allowing him some quiet time to sit at his desk and read or draw in his sketchbook after assigning the lesson. If he was required to actually teach, well hell, that was okay, too. He took more enjoyment from teaching than he would care to admit and he was damn good at it. He had a genuine rapport with the students, who generally thought it was pretty cool having such a hip young sub. His ability to make a quick connection with a class made him a popular choice of the school administrators willing to look past his shoulder-length hair and John Lennon–inspired reading glasses.

"Right this way, Mr. Brandt," the tiny brunette in the tight skirt said with a sly smile as she led him through the administration office to an unoccupied desk. Shit, did she catch him looking at her ass? "You can take your call on this phone."

"Uh, thank you," he said, slightly embarrassed. Jeez, he'd have to be more careful. He stared at the black phone with the sterile row of white call buttons protruding from the base like miniature tombstones. He picked up the receiver and punched the lone red button, halting its angry, incessant flashing. "Hello?" he said. More of a question than a salutation.

"Hey, dipshit, how've you been?"

The blood drained from his face as the voice, *his* voice, mocked him through the plastic earpiece.

This was impossible.

Kenney's knees turned to gravy. He leaned against the

desk to steady himself, defying all logic and rational order as he spoke his dead brother's name. "Ronny?"

"Bingo!" Ronny replied. "Give the teacher a cigar, or maybe an apple would be more appropriate?"

Kenney swallowed hard. Ronny, two years his senior, had died a year and a half ago from a rare form of cancer. It had started as a lump in his scrotum and six months later had spread through his body like wildfire. The doctors couldn't remove the diseased organs from his body fast enough, and when he had finally surrendered, there was little left of Kenney's big brother but a withered shell. Ronny died at the family home, emaciated and spent, in his old bedroom while Kenney read aloud to him from his favorite book, *Breakfast Of Champions*. Ronny had reached out, given Kenney's hand a weak squeeze, and he was gone, just like that. Forever.

"What's the matter, buddy?" Ronny asked, sounding vital and slightly amused. "Cat got your tongue?"

The tears came and he could not stop them. Tears of exultation and rapture poured down Kenney Brandt's face as he spoke, impossibly, to his brother. "Ronny, I t-t-thought you were . . . you were—were dead," he stammered through the tears, oblivious to the wide-eyed stares of Mrs. Anderson and the office staff. "I saw you, you—"

"Oh, I'm dead, Kenney. Dead as the proverbial door-nail," Ronny interrupted. "Let's not lose our perspective here, okay?"

"But . . . how . . ."

"How is not the issue here, Kenney. A lot of metaphysical mumbo jumbo we don't have time to get into," Ronny replied. "Let's just say this was the only way I could get in touch with you. Direct contact with the other side is a no-no, but there are ways to circumvent the rules. It's been going on since the beginning of time."

"Oh God, Ronny, I've missed you so much," Kenney

said, biting back the flow of tears. "I love you. I never thought I'd hear your voice again."

"Get a hold of yourself, little brother," Ronny said seriously. "We don't have much time. Now listen up. An evil wind is blowing your way. An evil so powerful it has survived for centuries, refusing to die. It walks the earth in human form, yet it is so wretched it cannot tolerate the light of day. It comes at night when its true essence is masked by the stars, tempting and seductive, corrupting all that it comes in contact with. Recognize it for what it truly is and don't be blinded by your own vanity and the delusions of grandeur fostered from human arrogance. Open your mind to the impossible and see the world through the eyes of a child. Everything happens for a reason, Kenney. Don't ask how or why. Think of it as a test. In your darkest hour you will be standing alone, facing the beast with only—"

Another phone line rang through, shrill and piercing, cutting his brother off in midsentence. Startled, Kenney looked down to see that another call-light was indeed flashing on the black office phone. He looked around the office helplessly, hoping someone would pick it up.

"You better get that call, bro," Ronny said, barely audible over the persistent ringing. "It's for you."

The ringing grew louder in his ears until it was the only sound in his universe. Agitated and disoriented, he punched the flashing button and fumbled with the receiver. Kenney pulled the covers back from his body as he gurgled a confused and muddled greeting, making no attempt to hide his aggravation at being interrupted in the middle of such an important call.

"Hello?"

"Hello, Mr. Brandt. I hope I didn't wake you," Mrs. Anderson said in her sweet, professional voice.

Kenney looked around his bedroom, dazed from the

intensity of the dream, trying to pull himself back into the moment.

"I was hoping," Mrs. Anderson continued, "we were lucky enough to get to you first. Miss King is out today with the flu. Are you available today?"

"Uh, yeah, yes—sure . . . ," Kenney said, unsure of his surroundings. The dream was still in his head and he was in a hurry to get back on the other line and talk to his brother.

"Fine, then," Mrs. Anderson replied. "We'll see you at seven-thirty?"

"Seven-thirty . . . fine, then," he repeated stupidly. "Yes, I'll be there. Thank you. Good-bye." He terminated the connection before she could reply and pressed the receiver to his ear. The faraway sonic hum of the dial tone pierced through the fog of his waking consciousness.

Ronny was not on the other line. It was just a dream. Limp and numb with disappointment, he cradled the phone and settled back into his pillow. He fought back the lump rising in his throat as the sound of his brother's voice, so clear, so real, played over in his head. "Christ, Ronny, was it really you?" he asked aloud. He closed his eyes, struggling to recover the conversation that was already dissipating, drifting away from him with each passing moment. Fumbling for the notebook next to the phone, he jotted down bits and pieces from the cryptic warning Ronny had voiced. The actual act of putting them to paper lent a stark credence to the words: *An evil wind is blowing your way.*

He grabbed the pack of Cheyennes sitting on his night-stand and lit one up, watching the smoke rise slowly toward the ceiling. It wasn't unusual for Ronny to talk that way. He had a colorful way of turning a phrase and was known at times to be a little over the top, but that was downright grim. Lying in his bed with the full light of the

morning sun filtering in through his window, Kenney
Brandt felt a shiver race up his spine.

Looking back over his notes, at the random fragments
he had jotted down, Kenney could hear his brother's voice
as he read along. The recollection of its sound infused a
reassuring warmth into the chilling words he had scrib-
bled across the page. Although he had abandoned his
Catholic faith long ago, there was a small part of him, a
desperate need to believe, that clung stubbornly to the
comforting possibility of an afterlife. Perhaps the horrify-
ing alternative, the prospect of eternal nothingness, the
total and immediate cessation of consciousness—of being—was simply too depressing. The electric scream of
the alarm clock startled him out of his musings, and he
silenced it with an irate swat. Swinging his legs abruptly
out of bed, he felt the twinge of a headache lying in wait
at the base of his neck. A warning from his body that he
had stayed out just a little too late with the boys at The
Drop Zone last night. He mashed the cigarette out and
sat naked on the edge of the bed. He considered his be-
draggled reflection in the dresser mirror, taking note of
the bloodshot eyes staring back at him through the puffy
lids. Six-fifteen arrives far too early when you drag your
sorry ass in at two. He shuffled to the bathroom, silently
cursing his delinquency.

Kenney Brandt emerged from the shower, alert and refreshed, having stood every nerve in his body on end with
an arctic blast of cold water after his usual fifteen-minute
scalding. He wiped the condensation from the mirror, and
after shaving and brushing his teeth (twice, just to be
safe), he looked at the face that would be greeting the
students of St. Nicholas Elementary School in less than
an hour.

"Can't fool a seventh-grader with eyes like that," he
said to the reflection staring back at him. Feeling just a
bit guilty, he pulled a bottle of Visine and a tube of Prepa-

ration H from the medicine cabinet. Trying not to think of the product's intended purpose, he squeezed a tiny dollop of the hemorrhoid cream onto his fingertip. He carefully worked the ointment into his swollen eyelids and topped off his routine with an expertly placed drop of Visine.

Blinking the sting from his eyes, he picked his way down the hall into his modest but neat kitchen and prepared a cup of instant coffee, doubling the measure as he usually did when he felt in need of an extra caffeine blast. While the water boiled he rummaged through his closet, searching for a clean dress shirt and slacks amidst the blue jeans and flannel shirts wedged into the cramped cubicle. He pulled out a button-down shirt, still crisp and wrapped in plastic from the dry cleaners. He felt the same awkwardness he had always felt whenever he dressed in Ronny's clothes. His wardrobe had taken a quantum leap in both quality and volume after Ronny had died. One of the little perks you get when your brother, the snappy dresser, is struck down in the prime of his life. He dressed quickly, stringing the whole ensemble together with a skinny leather tie and a sport coat, taking a moment to consider the results in the full-length mirror on his bedroom door.

"Fresh as a flower," he said, looking at the handsome, professorial gentleman staring back at him. Strolling back down the hallway to the kitchen, he paused and stuck his head into the spare bedroom that he had converted into a studio. The smell of turpentine and linseed oil lured him deeper into the room and he stared, transfixed at the expansive canvas cradled securely in the industrial-strength easel. It was the second panel of a triptych he had been working on, a huge stylized landscape, that would be hanging in the lobby of the new Beverly Library under construction on Western Avenue. Although winning the commission was a major personal coup, he couldn't help but feel slighted when he considered all

the work it would take to complete the project. He had
low-balled his bid when he submitted his proposal, trying
to gain any edge that he could. After listening to the
project coordinator blather on endlessly about limited
funding and budget constraints, he had ended up ac-
cepting seven hundred dollars for the piece and the
promise of more work in the future. Midway through
the second panel he had already put more than one hundred hours into the project and as he stood there, tal-
lying his time, he realized he was working for about $3.50
an hour. Frustration replaced the pride he felt whenever
he viewed his work. He walked dejectedly out of the studio with the words his brother had spoken in the dream
echoing in his head: . . . *don't be blinded by your own vanity
and the delusions of grandeur fostered from human arrogance.
Everything happens for a reason, Kenney.*

"Thanks, Ronny," he said aloud, "but you didn't have
to scare the shit out of me just to keep things in perspective."

Okay, so the money sucks, but it's a city commission
and they like your work, he reasoned. Do a good job on
this one and you'll get more. He took a long pull off the
cup of double-dose instant and grabbed a Pop-Tart on his
way out the door, wondering if he was ever going to catch
a break.

Driving to work in his piece-of-shit blue Maverick did
little to lift his spirits. The brakes were going and the wrinkled driver's-side door was held shut with a rubber bungee
cord, the result of a hit-and-run outside The Drop Zone
a few months ago. He cruised down the sun-dappled
sidestreets toward St. Nicholas School and cursed the non-
stop chatter of the morning-drive disc jockeys as he
searched the dial in vain for some serious rock and roll.
Fishing through the jumble of cassettes in the glove box
that never really closed properly, he popped the latest
GloryDaze demo tape into the mouth of the Kenwood cut

into his dash. The sound of Johnny's voice poured out of the speakers.

"Goddamn, that's good," he said, wolfing down the remainder of the strawberry Pop-Tart in three quick bites. Maybe Vinnie's right, he thought as he wheeled the Maverick over the curb into the school parking lot. We just might be good enough to win Saturday night after all. Pulling down the visor flap, he checked his appearance in the vanity mirror and noticed the driblet of strawberry filling that had found its way onto his freshly cleaned shirt. "Shit!" he cursed in frustration, carefully lifting the globule off his chest with the edge of a business card. A bright-red stain remained, soaked into the fiber of his shirt.

It looked just like blood.

Nineteen

The confined space did little to mask the discomfort of the other passengers sharing the compartment with Arthur Melbourne as the elevator labored steadily toward the seventeenth floor. They pressed themselves tight against the dark wood and brass rails, trying to get as much air space as they could between themselves and the loathsome, unshaven madman in the rumpled suit. He stood oblivious to those around him, staring through dark, sunken eyes at the polished mahogany doors. His mouth twisted into a tight grin, hinting at insanity. You could almost hear the collective rolling of eyeballs in their sockets over the whispered, nervous chatter and sighs of relief as he stepped off the elevator and lurched down the hallway.

Arthur Melbourne glanced at his name painted majestically in gold leaf across the massive double doors rising like twin redwoods from the thick carpet at the end of the corridor.

Levy, Melbourne, and Elovitz
Attorneys at Law

The smug pride he usually felt was replaced by a deep-seated contempt.

"Assholes . . . ," he mumbled to himself as he flung the door open, splitting his name between the "o" and the "u." "Melbourne, Levy, and Elovitz. Or," he added in a flash of muddled inspiration, "Melbourne, Elovitz, *then* Levy! Melbourne! It just sounds better!"

"Er . . . good morning, Mr. Melbourne," the young receptionist said nervously from behind her rounded desk in the foyer. "I have some messages for you. Quite a few, as a matter of fact." She held the short stack of "while you were out" chits at arm's length, as though she feared he might actually bite her.

"Messages?" he asked, leaning in close, just inches from her face. He could feel her heat. Her perfume, sweet and heady, filled his nostrils, overwhelming his frazzled senses. "I think I'm getting *your* message loud and clear Miss Montgomery," he said with exaggerated cleverness as he leered unabashedly down her white blouse. "Did anyone ever tell you that you have great tits? Magnificent, I would go so far to say."

"I'm sorry?" she asked, recoiling in disgust. His breath smelled, and for one awful moment she thought she was going to be sick.

"Don't be sorry," he said, bolting upright and striking a theatrical pose. He launched into song like a lead in an old Busby Berkeley musical. "Be proud, Miss Montgomery! Sing it clear! Sing it LOUUUUDDDDD!"

"Do you feel okay, Mr. Melbourne?" she asked, her uneasiness escalating into genuine fear. "Would you like me to . . . call someone?"

He stopped singing, agitated that she would dare to interrupt him in the middle of his number and collected himself as though he had suddenly grown self-conscious. Insulted, he screwed his face into a mask of contempt, glowering at the young woman cringing behind her elevated desk.

"Fuck you," he sneered. He picked up his briefcase, snatched the messages from her hand, and shuffled down the hallway to his office.

The bluntness of the obscenity shocked her more than the remark about her tits, leaving her confounded and frightened. She waited for his door to slam before picking up the phone. Pausing for a moment, she checked her watch and recradled the receiver. Who was she going to call? The "Colonel," as old Mr. Levy liked to be called, had left last night for his battalion reunion in Cleveland and wouldn't be back until Monday. Marty Elovitz was vacationing in San Francisco and it was only five-thirty on the Coast. Did she really want to wake him up and tell him that Arthur Melbourne was drunk and singing show tunes in the foyer? She didn't want to risk losing this job. There were too many good-looking, rich young lawyers in and out of this place all day and she intended to land one of them before she got too old.

Leaning over her desk, she peered cautiously down the hallway at Artie's locked door. She wasn't thrilled about being alone with him in his present condition, but it was almost eight o'clock and the rest of the office staff would be drifting in soon. Janine, Marty's secretary, would know what to do.

Art Melbourne was a boozehound and could be a little rude at times, but this, this was . . . different, like he was having some sort of nervous breakdown. He had blown in yesterday around eleven, wearing the same suit he had worn the day before (he *still* hadn't changed since they had all gone out for drinks on Wednesday night), and locked himself in his office for a few hours before leaving without a word at one-thirty. Spooky, that's what it was.

The phone rang, scaring the shit out of her.

"Levy, Melbourne, and Elovitz," she answered in her sweet, practiced fashion.

"Good morning, Mary Anne. How's everything at the fort?"

It was the Colonel. She had never been so happy to hear the sweet old gentleman's voice.

"Good morning, Colonel," she said with genuine affection. She really liked the foxy grandpa. "I'm so glad you called."

"Miss me already, eh?" he laughed. "Is everything all right? I got the strangest phone call from Paul Brown at the Northern Trust last night. Is Artie in yet?"

"Yes, sir, he is," she said with relief. "Would you like me to put you through to him?"

"If it's not too much trouble, dear. And drop the 'sir.' I heard enough of that in the Army."

"Yes, sir . . . er, Colonel. One moment please." She placed him on hold and punched up Artie's extension. Artie picked it up immediately but did not answer. "Mr. Melbourne?" she asked nervously, hearing his muted breathing on the other end of the line.

"Yes, angel tits?" he finally replied, mocking her tone.

"I have Mr. Levy on line one. He'd like to speak to you," she said, a note of smug satisfaction in her voice.

"Shit!" he said, sounding a little surprised. "Put the old cock-knocker on."

Arthur Melbourne stared at the flashing red button on his elaborate telephone network with trepidation and took a deep breath. This was a critical move. He would have to be very careful. "Good morning, Colonel," he said jovially, trying to interject just the right blend of servitude and professionalism into his voice. "How's everything in Cleveland?"

"Arthur, my boy," the Colonel said, cutting right to the chase. "What the hell is going on with the Rothenburg estate?"

"The Rothenburg estate?"

"Yes, Arthur," the Colonel replied, obviously annoyed. "The goddamn Rothenburg estate. Paul Brown called me last night and told me you had walked in and cashed out the entire ledger. The savings account, checking, bonds even the Christmas Club! Arthur, have you lost your fucking mind?"

"Whoa, now, Colonel, hold on just a second," Arthur replied, trying his best to sound indignant. "I liquidated that account under the written request of Joyce Rothenburg herself. She called me yesterday morning at home before I even got to the office and insisted that I drive out to her place in Lake Forest. When I got there, she told me she was sick and tired of her children fighting like a pair of buzzards over who was going to get *what* when she died. She told me she wanted everything, *everything,* cashed out and in her hands by that afternoon. I tried to—"

"Goddamn it, Arthur!" the Colonel screamed in disbelief. "Joyce Rothenburg is in no fucking condition to make decisions like that! That's why we're angling for power of attorney—to prevent just this sort of thing from happening. She—"

"I know, Henry, I know, but she insisted. I couldn't refuse a written request. It is, after all, her money. She—"

"You could have stalled her Arthur!" the Colonel cried. "You could have bullshitted her, told her it would take a while. My God, Arthur, where's your tact? Your savvy? Your goddamn common sense!"

"Now hold on, Henry," Arthur interjected. "I told you I really didn't have much choice in the matter. Besides, there was a lot of money that I, eh . . . *she* couldn't get to. Some long-term bonds. The trust funds and the property holdings are all still intact."

"Well, thank Christ!" the Colonel said, sounding just a bit relieved. "So, exactly how much did she end up cashing out, Arthur?"

"Ohhh . . . let's see," Arthur said with a goofy grin as he fondled the alligator textured lid of the briefcase sitting on top of his desk. "She really took a beating with the early withdrawal penalties, and you know it was an off day down at the Merc yesterday when she liquidated her futures." He paused as though going through the figures again as he popped the latches on the briefcase and stared at the fortune bundled neatly inside. "Exactly nine hundred seventy-eight thousand, five hundred and twenty-six dollars."

The line was silent for a moment as the Colonel, sitting on the edge of his hotel bed in Cleveland, let the number sink in. Joyce Rothenburg was worth over seven million dollars the last time he had checked.

"Almost an even million," the Colonel said finally. "Well, I guess it could be worse. Where exactly is the money, Arthur? She didn't give it away to the Little Sisters of the Fucking Poor or anything like that, did she? Please tell me she didn't give it away."

"It's right here, Henry," Arthur said, running his fingertips over the neat stacks of crisp currency. "In the safe in the office. I was afraid she might do something stupid with it, so I told her I wouldn't be able to get the actual cash until this afternoon. I stalled her," he chided contemptuously. "I used my savvy, my tact, my goddamn common sense."

"Well, thank Christ," the Colonel replied, ignoring the jab. "This isn't quite a full-blown disaster, but it's awful goddamn close, Arthur. Don't do a thing with that money until I get back on Monday, and if Joyce calls, you're not in. Don't even take the fucking call. Shit! I hope we don't have to get her declared unfit. Under no circumstances is she to get her hands on that money, Arthur. Under no circumstances."

"Oh, you can count on that, Colonel," Arthur replied, stifling a childish giggle. "She'll never even see it."

"Are you feeling all right, Arthur?" the Colonel asked apprehensively. "I can't help but feel that this could have been handled differently."

"I assure you, Colonel, this was the only way. And I've never felt better."

"I'll see you Monday morning, Arthur, first thing," the Colonel said sternly before hanging up.

"I'll see you in hell first, you crotchety old piece of shit!" Arthur hissed into the empty phone, his indignation rising as the anxiety of the confrontation dissipated. He slumped back in his chair and tried to sort through the conversation in his polluted mind. Did the old cock-knocker buy it? Probably not, but that didn't matter now. There was little he could do about it. It would all be over soon anyway.

Joyce Rothenburg was either dead right now or still sleeping in the arms of Morpheus. What a delightful old gal she was! She had been so happy to see him yesterday when he had driven onto her grounds in his new BMW convertible. They had gone for a drive with the top down along the lakefront, and she had been as happy as a schoolgirl. Her crown of matronly white hair fluttered in the slipstream as she talked of her long life, her children, and all manner of other things he couldn't really give a shit about. Afterward, they had sat in the shade (and not a moment too soon, all that time in the sun had made him nauseous) overlooking her meticulously landscaped grounds. He had pretended to listen as she prattled on endlessly and signed all that legal mumbo jumbo he had put in front of her.

Nothing for you to be concerned about, Joyce, just some technical legalese, you know how those damn lawyers are, ha-ha. Oh, don't forget to initial that, right there. Yes, thank you. She was starting to get groggy just as he left and he had walked her into the sitting room so she could lie down a bit. Such a busy afternoon. She wasn't used to so much activity, you know. Yes, and those two quaaludes I ground up and dropped in your lemonade probably didn't help, either, he had thought as he helped her to the sofa. You lie down and take a nap, old girl, and don't bother to answer the phone if it rings. Get your beauty sleep—not that you need it of course, ha-ha. You're a devil, you know that, Mr. Melbourne, she had told him with that goofy grin on her leathery old face. Within minutes she had closed her eyes and drifted into the one realm of true, uncomplicated happiness available to the human animal.

She really had quite a constitution for such a skinny old bitch, he thought as he spun around and stared out the window at the throng of human cattle bustling through the streets of the Loop. I wonder if she ever woke up? Well, who really gives a shit. He checked his watch and shuffled over to the bar in the corner of his office. Bending down, he opened the mock door of the tiny refrigerator and dialed open the safe it concealed, pulling out the small fortune he had stashed there last night. He opened an empty briefcase and counted the bundles as he stacked them carefully, one on top of the other, lining them up just right. He wanted everything to be perfect for his savior. His entire life's savings was there, as well as most of the firm's liquid assets. A lost, pathetic smile etched its way across his unshaven, sweaty face as he placed the heavy briefcase carefully on his desk next to the other stash of ill-gotten booty. This was his ticket to paradise. All the unspoken promises, everything he had seen in her eyes, all the wonder and the glory of the ages, awaited him if she deemed this offering worthy. He sat expressionless and numb, his head filled with liquid dreams of soft, wet kisses and sharp teeth. He drifted further from reality with each passing minute, waiting for the rapture to come and sweep him away from all the pain and heartache forever.

A distant ringing in the back of his head broke the spell. The ringing grew louder, jolting him out of his trance. He found himself back in his office surrounded by endless rows of law books and the trappings of his pointless profession. He stared stupidly at the button on his phone, again flashing that angry bloodlike red. Startled, he jabbed at it, repeatedly, violently, knocking the handset off the receiver onto the floor.

Miss Montgomery's voice, circumspect and wary, sputtered out of the plastic speaker with a hollow electric titter.

"Mr. Melbourne?" she asked, from the floor near his feet. "There's a . . . gentleman here to see you."

Mary Anne Montgomery's disembodied voice calling to him blindly from the handset on the carpet struck him as comically absurd and he tried his best to answer her in a businesslike manner.

"Is he wearing a red carnation?" Arthur asked, clasping his hand over his mouth in a childlike attempt to stifle the oncoming giggles.

"Uh, no, sir, he—"

"Well, that's good," he replied with a snicker. "Flowers make me sneeze. Tell him to fuck off please. I'm very busy!"

"He says he's here to take you home, sir," Miss Montgomery said, her voice wavering. "He said—"

Another voice, a man's somber voice, poured out from the speaker, as if from a great distance, strangely soothing and compassionate. "I'm here to guide you down the Left-Hand Path, Arthur. *She* sent me."

Arthur Melbourne bolted upright in his chair and looked around wildly. "Send him in! Send him right in, Miss Montgomery!" In a comical and pathetic attempt to appear presentable, he patted down his dirty, tousled hair and straightened his tie—all business now—preparing himself for the celestial herald that would take him to the other side. To *her*. His *savior*. His *queen*. He could hear the footsteps of the dark archangel echoing down the corridor. As the tumbler in his doorknob turned, he instinctively squinted, bracing himself for the blinding white light of divinity that would surely be glinting off the angel's sword of fire.

The door opened and Drew Richards shuffled in, his scrawny frame swimming in an old army jacket, his face expressionless underneath a floppy hat and an oversize pair of wraparound sunglasses. Sliding along the wall to avoid the slivers of direct sunlight shooting in from the window, the scruffy vagabond wordlessly adjusted the venetian blinds behind the dumbfounded attorney. He sighed audibly as the last poisonous rays of daylight dissolved into harmless microsplinters, barely visible beneath the plastic slats.

"Yesss . . . ," he said thickly. "That's so much better, don't you think, Arthur?"

Arthur Melbourne, Esq., nodded, grateful for the relief. Now why hadn't he thought of that?

Drew Richards removed his sunglasses and peered at the briefcases on the desk before him, overflowing with stacks of cold, untraceable cash. "This is all of it, Arthur?" he asked, like a mob bagman shaking down a timid shopkeeper. "You know," he continued in a softer, comforting tone, "she demands a total and complete sacrifice. You must abandon all your mortal possessions before you can pass through the portals into her kingdom. She will know, Arthur. She—"

"This is all of it!" he cried, a lost desperation choking his vocal cords. "Everything I have and more!" He jumped to his feet and ripped the ribbon of white paper from the mouth of the adding machine, his eyes shining as he read off the total. "Exactly one million, four hundred seventy-six thousand, nine hundred and forty dollars!"

"Oh, that is excellent, Arthur," Drew replied, snapping the cases shut and propping them up on the desk. "She will be pleased. You've done well. Now there is only one more bridge you have to cross. I can't take you there,

Arthur. You must pass through alone and of your own free will."

Arthur Melbourne stared at the divine courier as the revelation swept over him, blowing the fog and clutter from his mind like a cleansing storm. It was all so clear now.

"Waste no time, Arthur," Drew said over his shoulder as he pulled the briefcases off the desk and headed out the door. "She's waiting for you. Kisses like you've never tasted before, until the very end of time."

Arthur Melbourne was already rifling through his desk drawers as the door clicked shut, searching for the key that would unlock the gates to paradise. Blinking through the salty tears pouring from his eyes, he groped blindly through the deep well of the bottom compartment, his hand finally coming in contact with the cold reassuring steel. He pulled the semiautomatic from its hiding place and held it in front of his face, staring triumphantly at his elongated reflection in the shiny blue barrel.

Yes, he thought as he stepped back and stripped the filthy clothing from his body, it won't be long now. Pulling off his shoes, he stepped out of the crumpled pants wadded around his feet and stood naked and unashamed at the window. He winced at the sting from the bright morning sunlight as he rolled the blinds away and hoisted the wooden jamb high over his head.

"Pure . . . ," he whispered as he stepped out onto the ledge, oblivious to the early rush-hour bustle on LaSalle Street seven stories below. "Pure and untainted by the shame of man and his pretensions . . . that is how she will receive me. . . ." Holding the Glock in his folded hands like an offering of prayer, he pressed the oily muzzle to the side of his head, his finger tightening on the trigger as it found the natural groove of his temple.

"I'm coming, darling . . . ," he whispered.

Drew Richards did not look up when he heard the shot

ring out, a fleeting pop that may have gone undetected by the engrossed masses flowing over LaSalle Street if not for the sickening thud of the lawyer's naked body as it met the sidewalk moments later. A single hysterical scream some twenty feet behind Drew touched off a chaotic uproar among the nine-to-fivers as they scurried about, excited and repulsed by the bizarre interruption of their morning routine. He continued walking north, toward the river. He smiled contentedly as they ran past him, their eyes wide and full of anticipation, eager to get a look at the dead man.

"No need to rush," Drew said to no one in particular as he walked unnoticed across Wacker Drive to the bridge. "Plenty more where that came from."

Twenty

She was there waiting for him as he rounded the corner, bathed in the glow of the streetlight, her face strangely familiar under the flowing mane of fiery red hair. It seemed she had existed forever, elusive and out of reach, lingering like a dark, whispered secret in the recesses of his earliest boyhood fantasies, an unrealized vision of sexual indulgence. She stood before him now, finally, the embodiment of his most wanton cravings, the culmination of his deepest desires brought to the flesh.

"Vincenczo . . . ," she cooed, adjusting the full-length white fur coat, exposing her bare shoulders and a hint of the milky naked perfection of regions farther south. "At last. I have been waiting so long to give you a kiss. Come to me, my darling"

He floated across the street, his feet barely touching the pebbled texture of the asphalt until he stood just inches from her, so close he could feel her breath on his lips, warm like a summer breeze and smelling of lilac. A low moan came from somewhere deep within him as he looked into her eyes, wet and neon-green beneath the long lashes, sparkling with flashes of starbright stolen from the night sky. She opened her coat and stood there boldly, letting his eyes roam over the succulent prize beneath the fur wrapping. He stared unashamed at the supple breasts crowned by rosy nipples, puckering and stiffening in the cool night air.

His hands slipped around her waist and she pulled him to the ground, entangling him in the luxuriant fur. Her fingers found the belt loops of his Levi's and she pulled them down rudely, covering his face with tender kisses. Beneath him, her legs spread open like the petals of a rose, her hips rising and falling in a throbbing, undulating rhythm against his loins. He grimaced, trying to contain his excitement as his manhood slapped rudely against his flat stomach. Long red fingernails reached up underneath him, stroking the length of it as it grew harder still, turgid and bobbing like a separate entity with a life of its own. It brushed blindly against the flesh of her inner thighs, the delicious friction almost unbearable, before finding the sticky warmth of her damp portal. He lingered there a moment, gritting his teeth, savoring the tight, wet heat as she slowly took him in. The sensations were overwhelming, nearly causing him to swoon as he buried it to the hilt and she met his thrust, their pubic mounds grinding together in a scratchy embrace. Panic crept up on him as he felt the deep rumbling in his balls, and he fought to regain some semblance of self-control, pulling back slowly in an attempt to buy more time, but to no avail. He surrendered to the inevitable—the release almost crippling in its intensity, his body convulsing as wave after wave rolled through him, freezing him in time and space.

A sudden bolt of pain tore through the curtain of bliss as her nails dug deep into his buttocks, scooping out ribbons of flesh in a frenzy far beyond the boundaries of passion. His initial yelp of surprise ended in a shriek of pain and a flash of silver fur as her jaws clamped down on his shoulder, just below his neck. He could hear his own screams, as if from a great distance above the growling and snarling as he fought to tear himself away from the thing transforming beneath him. The beast wrapped its hairy canine legs around him, pulling him farther inside the foul cavity, cold as a tomb now, and gripping his spent penis in an icy stranglehold. With a grisly wet crunch of bone and tissue, the werewolf bit cleanly through his trapezius, freeing his upper torso. He pinwheeled backward, striking his head on the hardwood slats of his bedroom floor.

The rapid knocking was followed by his grandmother's voice, shaky and frightened.

"Vincenczo! Open the door! Are you okay?"

"Uh . . . yeah, fine Nan," he said out of pure reflex. He looked around in a daze, surprised and relieved to find himself in the safety of his bedroom.

"I thought I heard a scream. What's going on in there? What's all that racket?" she asked, agitation replacing the worry in her voice.

"Nothing!" he replied a little too quickly. "It was a dream," he added, finding the statement very comforting. "I had a dream and fell out of bed."

"Fell out of bed? What kind of dream was that?" she asked, the worry back in her voice.

Collecting himself off the floor, Vinnie the Razor stood up and inspected the sticky discharge matted in his pubic hair and dripping down his stomach.

"A wet one," he said under his breath, taking note of the generous emission with more than a little pride. A *real* wet one. Because he couldn't keep talking to his grandmother through the bedroom door, he grabbed a handful of tissues from the box on his nightstand and wiped himself off before slipping into his bathrobe and belting it loosely around his waist.

"A weird dream, Nan," he said, opening the door and showing himself, letting her see for herself that he was okay, "with scary monsters."

"I'll give you scary monsters, smart guy," she scolded. "Have you been sleeping with your bare ass in that bed again?" she asked, noticing his lack of clothing underneath the robe. "What have I told you about that? I didn't raise you to be a savage."

"C'mon, Nan," he chided. "Its only natural. That's the way people should sleep. That's why it's called au naturel."

"You can sleep *aw nach-er-awl* when you're washing your own bedsheets, Mr. Big Shot. Until then, you'll wear the pajamas I bought you," she said, putting an end to the discussion.

"If I wear the pajamas, can I stay with you forever?" he teased, turning on the charm and breaking down her defenses.

She softened a little. It pained her to think about the day her Vincenczo would move out on his own. Maybe she would die first. She hoped so. "We'll see," she said, then as if she suddenly remembered, "I was coming upstairs to wake you up anyway. Did you plan on sleeping all evening? Don't you have to get ready for your big jig tonight?"

Vinnie smiled and shook his head, a heartfelt smile born of pure love and genuine affection. *"Gig,"* he corrected her, still smiling, "We got a big gig tonight, Nan. It could be a big break for us."

"I'm sure you'll do fine," she said, heading back down the stairs. "Oh, I washed those old blue jeans you like to wear," she added knowingly, "the ones that are far too tight for you."

"Thanks, Nan," he called down after her, "you're the best." Closing the door behind her, he looked down, puzzled and slightly disgusted at the sticky discharge drying on his stomach. When was the last time he'd had a goddamn wet dream? Ten years ago, at least. And what a dream! He could still see the pink areolas surrounding the eraserlike nipples protruding from those perfect tits as she opened her coat for him. A twinge of déjà vu passed through him, fleeting and ill-defined, bringing with it an empty melancholy. He touched his shoulder, absently fingering the spot where she had bit him, shivering slightly at the recollection of the wolf's jaws tearing the flesh from his body while he lay locked in that unspeakable embrace.

"Too much acid in high school," he mumbled. He grabbed a big fluffy towel from the hall closet and padded down the stairs to the bathroom.

He stayed in the shower even longer than usual, letting the water, hot as he could stand it, pound into his body, washing the soiled remnants of the dream from his consciousness. He toweled off quickly, lightly patting down his sumptuous mane of black hair and giving it a good shake, letting it dry into the relaxed curls that fell so naturally over his shoulders. After a careful shave and a little preening, he slipped directly into the freshly washed jeans his grandmother had laid out for him, ignoring the Fruit of the Loom briefs she insisted he wear (unless, of course, he wanted to become sterile and ruin any chance of her becoming a great-grandmother). With a few well-placed tugs on the crotch of the faded Levi's to settle himself in properly, he strolled through the living room. Nana was nestled into her high-back comfy chair with a cup of tea and the five o'clock news.

"Terrible thing about that poor man jumping out that window like that," she noted. "Naked as a jaybird, he was. Left behind a wife and two children, they said."

"Yeah, I saw that. Big-shot lawyer," Vinnie said, turning his attention to the television for a moment as the story was wrapping up. "Left behind a big stain on the sidewalk, too."

"Vincenczo!" she said with mock horror. "That's terrible."

"It's terrible, all right," he said, stooping to pet Thor. "Taking the coward's way out after stealin' all that dough. I heard the cops are still lookin' for it. In the end I guess he just didn't have the guts to carry it out. Of course," he added, setting her up, "the guy who had to clean the sidewalk might argue that last point."

She laughed in spite of herself. "You're impossible. There's a meatball sandwich in the fridge or leftover *chufte* from Wednesday. Just make sure you clean up after yourself. I'm taking the day off."

"Slave driver!" Vinnie laughed, ruffling the dog's ears. "Whadda ya got a taste for Thor? Meatball *sang-wich*?"

Thor's tail thumped on the floor, indicating his approval, and he followed Vinnie into the kitchen. Thor watched with the keen eye and rapt attention of a seasoned hunter as his master flushed their prey from the refrigerator and laid it out on the counter. He peeled the plastic wrap away from the half-loaf of French bread, and sprinkled crumbled Romano cheese generously across the top of the giant meatballs before sticking it in the oven. The smell of homemade red sauce wafted through the kitchen as he pulled out the steaming sandwich and set it down on the table next to a jar of his grandmother's hot peppers and two ice-cold cans of Coke. With Thor's heavy head resting on his knee, he set one meatball aside before spooning the hot peppers liberally over the top of the sandwich, the final brush stroke of the culinary masterpiece.

"That one's for you if you promise not to drool on me," he said, before biting into the sloppy creation. Not wanting to blow his chances, Thor apologetically pulled his head off his master's knee and lay patiently at his feet. As he ate in the calm quiet of the little kitchen, Vinnie the Razor reflected on the afternoon rehearsal and the general lack of firepower that seemed to permeate the two hours they spent fine-tuning their playlist. They were tight but uninspired, and this had him a little concerned after the somewhat lackluster set they had put on at The Drop Zone last night. Kenney was his usual steady, professional self, and Dave—well, he never had to worry about Dave. Just keep him well oiled with Budweiser and he could pound the shit out of that Pearl kit all night without missing a beat. Johnny had him a little worried. The kid had an incredible set of pipes, but he could tell the farm boy from Belvidere, Illinois, was still a little nervous about singing in front of a packed venue the size of the WhereHouse. Nervous? Shit, you couldn't pull a pin out of the kid's ass with a tractor.

"Whadda ya think, boy?" he asked Thor, lifting the promised meatball from his plate and holding it over the Labrador's nose. "Johnny 'Golden Pipes' gonna be okay tonight?"

The animal responded with a loud affirmative bark. Vinnie lobbed the meatball and Thor snatched it out of the air.

"What did I say about making a mess?" Nana asked as she entered the kitchen, shaking her head. "Look at what you did to my clean floor!"

"Oops," Vinnie said sheepishly. "Caught me again. Don't worry, Nan, I'll clean up."

"Thor's got it," she said. "You go on, get ready for your gig. I'll finish up in here."

"Thanks, Nan," he chirped, rising from the table and planting a kiss on her cheek. "You're the best."

"I know," she said, watching him clop up the stairs to his room. "And don't you forget it."

In the far corner of the bedroom, apart from the clutter and disarray that typified the rest of the converted attic, Vinnie the Razor pulled his custom Fender Stratocaster from its case and carefully restrung the worn E string with .012 gauge wire. After double-checking the feel, he plugged into the Vox AC 30 amplifier for a retune, coming down one half step for the spiky, bladelike sound that had earned him his nickname. Satisfied with the tone, he played a couple of quick riffs out of habit and love before laying the guitar, which he had dubbed "Thor's Hammer," back into its case.

The Hammer was one of a kind, distinctive in both its looks and sound, owing to a variety of modifications made over the years since rescuing it from a Bridgeport pawnshop when he was nineteen. It had caught his attention purely by chance one summer day as he stepped off an Archer Avenue bus and strolled past the window of Another Man's Treasures on his way to see a buddy from the old neighborhood. A keen eye and a soft spot in his heart for classic Stratocasters convinced him it was worth a good long look, and he was back the next day with all the money he had to his name, ready to strike a deal. He had walked nonchalantly into the cluttered shop, pretending to eyeball the cameras on the shelves and the watches in their glass cases before going in for the hook.

"How much you want for that old beat-up guitar in the window there?" he asked the counterman, a heavyset, faded fellow with a dirty toothpick tucked securely in the corner of his mouth, deeply immersed in an issue of *True Detective* magazine.

"Three hundred dollars," the big man replied without looking up.

"Three hundred bucks?" Vinnie shot back. "You gotta be kiddin'. For that old thing?"

With an exaggerated wheeze of exasperation, the old guy closed his magazine and tucked it carefully under the counter. As if noticing him for the first time, he squinted hard at the cocky longhair and sized him up for a sale. "That there is a gen-u-ine Fender Strat-o-caster, son," he said, lumbering out from behind the counter toward the display window. "A real guitar player's guitar," he explained, as if talking to a child. "That ain't no toy." The toothpick moved back and forth across the expanse of his ruddy lips while he talked.

"The neck's cracked," Vinnie replied, dropping the naive bumpkin act. "Right here, at the mortise and tenon joint where the neck joins the body. See?" he said, pointing the flaw out to the old huckster who stared at it with mock surprise. "No *real* guitar player will give you three hundred bucks for that. The vibration transfer between the neck and the body is corrupted. The pitch is shot. I bet it sounds like shit."

The toothpick stopped dead on its invisible track, and the fat man's eyes narrowed as he glared at the young punk with newfound respect. "Well, then, why do *you* want it?"

"My uncle bought a joint just south of the Loop. He wants to turn it into a blues club," Vinnie said, trying not to sound too lame. "He needs some shit to hang on the walls. I thought this might look good behind the bar."

The man's thick lips curled up into something that was supposed to be a smile as he wiped a wayward wisp of thin white hair away from his forehead. "Okay," he said grudgingly. "I'll let you have it for two-fifty."

"The fingerboard is warped, too," Vinnie said, peering down the length of the neck as he held the guitar body out at arm's length. "It isn't worth fifty bucks. Sorry to waste your time." He placed the Fender back on its stand and turned toward the door.

"You're killing me here, kid," the old man called out, watching his sale disappear. "Two hundred. That's as low as I go."

Vinnie turned and pulled two bank-crisp fifties from the pocket of his Levi's. "I got a hundred cash. That's it, and only because I love my uncle so much."

They haggled and tossed bullshit back and forth for another fifteen minutes before Vinnie walked out of the musty den of cast-off memories with a vintage Stratocaster, leaving the counterman grinning like a thief with three fresh fifties burning a hole in his pocket.

With the help of Mr. Caravelli and a lot of phone calls,

Vinnie had been able to locate an authentic Fender "D" neck from 1961, the longest neck Fender had ever made. He'd had the neck's fret board, which was a rosewood "slab" type, removed and replaced with a curved veneer board refitted with Gibson Jumbo bass frets to better handle his aggressive playing style. A peek inside the body cavity when the old neck was removed showed the date 1963 handwritten, as was common in those days, confirming his suspicions about the Strat's pedigree. The body, which was solid alder, had at some point in time been painted fire-engine red. As the years passed, the original sunburst paint that the factory had applied began to wear through around the edges and above the pick guard where his hand oils had rubbed into it. He would later add hand-wound Humbucker pickups with high-output coils and a five-way toggle switch. The latest modification was a gold-plated tremolo arm, a gift from Mr. Caravelli to his most accomplished student.

He looked at it now, lying snugly in the cushioned recess of the guitar case, the way an adoring parent may gaze at a sleeping child. Love might be too strong a word, but aside from his grandmother and his dog, he could think of nothing in his immediate life that was more important to him. It was virtually irreplaceable, and when he played a gig, he never let it out of his sight, sometimes simply unplugging and leaving it around his neck when he bellied up to the bar between sets rather than leave it unattended.

"When we hit the big time, I'll hire a full-time roadie just to watch over you," he promised as he wiped the body with a hank of treated cheesecloth. A quick look at the clock on his wall showed six-fifty. He cursed his procrastinating. "Shit, Kenney's gonna be here in ten minutes and that fucker's never late."

Vinnie finished dressing quickly, pulling on his good snakeskin cowboy boots and a black leather vest that he slipped directly over his naked torso. Looping two freshly ironed red bandannas together, he laced them through the belt loops of his Levi's and tied them tight around his waist just as the doorbell chimed, signaling the arrival of his bass player. Vinnie tossed his dark wavy hair over his tanned shoulders and checked out the striking figure staring back at him from his dresser mirror, satisfied that the look was just right.

"Enough with the bullshit already," he said aloud, screwing his game-face on. "It's time to rock and roll."

Part Three

Part Three

Twenty-one

The two vampires filtered through the crowd like wisps of smoke, sorting through the mad cacophony of bio-rhythms generated by the sweaty throng. The building was filled to well past capacity and the crowd mentality, fueled by alcohol and all manner of recreational drugs, was bordering on riotous. Chloe generally disliked scenes like this. Lizabet, on the other hand, was in her glory, feeding off the excitement. It had been her idea for the two of them to hunt together tonight. Having grown somewhat bored with the usual feedings on streetwalkers and runaways, Lizabet had suggested that a girls' night out might provide a needed break in the routine. Her hunch had paid off when they zeroed in on the energy emanating from the industrial district off Canal Street and happened upon the long line of souls filing into the WhereHouse.

"Can you smell the vitality, the potency of the life force?" Lizabet asked her with a delighted grin as they walked somehow unfettered through the outer concourse's crowded beer stands and bathroom lines. They were a striking couple, the centuries-old queen of hell and her young disciple, what with their pale skin and black clothing. Heads turned as they moved past, drawing appreciative looks from the men and whispered innuendo from the women. All around them, young men, shirtless and full of bravado, mingled with the ripe assortment of nubile women in crop tops and hip-huggers. The air was thick with the smell of beer and the pungent aroma of marijuana and cigarette smoke. Despite her uneasiness, Chloe found herself slightly exhilarated by the sheer body heat and enticed by the comely array of flesh on display everywhere she turned.

"I must admit, it is quite appetizing," Chloe answered. Perhaps a bit too appetizing, she thought, casting a worried eye at her maker. Lizabet had a wild look in her eye and this was no place for a bloodbath. "There's plenty of time to feed," she continued, trying to buy herself some time. "We must be discreet—discerning, take our pick. There's no need to rush with a selection like this."

"Mmm . . . perhaps you're right, young one," Lizabet replied, staring boldly at a winding line of young women waiting to use the rest room. "But I'm so hungry now. A quick bite wouldn't hurt, do you think? Look at them. It's like they're waiting for me. That one there," she continued, motioning toward a willowy little brunette with a black lace top and cutoff blue jeans, angrily smoking a cigarette. "She just had a fight with her boyfriend. In fact," she said, "she's even thinking about leaving him here and going home with another man! Could you imagine? The little tart. She's perfect. Yes, I think I'll start with her."

The houselights dimmed twice, indicating the next band was due up in five minutes. The crowd in the outer concourse began to disperse, gradually breaking away from the beer stands and T-shirt booths to reclaim their ground in the concert hall. Taking advantage of the flurry of activity, Lizabet approached the comely brunette as she stood anxiously shuffling her feet in the shrinking line.

"Men," Lizabet said offhandedly as she sidled up to the teenager, "who needs 'em?"

"Huh?" the brunette replied, looking up blankly.

"I hate them," Lizabet continued, telling the girl exactly what she wanted to hear at the moment. "They're only good for one thing and half the time they can't even do that right."

"Goddamn straight!" the little stoner replied, looking into the older woman's beautiful dark eyes. What a funky-looking chick, she thought. Older, but real sharp-looking. I bet she's in the business. I wonder if she's got any . . .

"Coke?" Lizabet said, finishing the girl's thought. "I wouldn't be caught dead without it, my dear. Would you like some?" She reached up and gently pinched the soft skin of the girl's cheek like a doting grandmother.

"Oh, that would be too fuckin' cool," the girl replied, nonplused by the squeeze. "You mean it? This is great. Hey," she said, rummaging through her purse, "I even got a mirror and a fresh blade."

Lizabet plucked the razor blade from the unsuspecting girl's lacquered nails and considered it for a moment. She smiled, truly delighted. "Yes, I think we can use this."

Chloe watched Lizabet and her victim disappear into the bathroom, apprehensively scanning the surrounding area for the girl's wayward boyfriend or anyone else who may have taken notice of the two of them together. The houselights dimmed again. A thunderous roar erupted from behind the doors of the main hall as the feedback whine of an amplifier being switched on pierced the din. Lizabet emerged from the rest room, bleary-eyed and flushed from the feed, casually wiping her crimson-stained teeth with the back of her hand.

"We should leave," Chloe said as Lizabet glided toward her, light-headed and giddy, "before someone finds her. There's no telling who saw the two of you together."

"Oh, now . . . ," Lizabet giggled, pressing her finger, wet with the girl's blood, to Chloe's moist lips. "Relax, darling. We're going to have fun tonight, remember? It seems like ages since I've watched you feed."

The blood, warm and slick under her nose, silenced

Chloe's objections. Unable to stop herself, she succumbed to the coppery temptation and licked the blood from her mistress's fingertips.

"There we go . . . ," Lizabet whispered, knowing full well she could not resist the hunger. "Now don't worry about our little friend. I stuffed her up underneath the ceiling tile. No one will find her until she starts to stink."

Chloe pulled back, her lips sliding off the oily fingertip with a wet pop. "And the blood?" she asked, suddenly very hungry.

"A few puddles on the floor. Nothing unusual in a woman's bathroom stall, my dear." She laughed, producing the stained razor blade. "It was a clean feed. Now," Lizabet said over the booming power chords emanating from the concert hall, "let's go and see what all the fuss is about."

Twenty-two

Johnny Coltrane was contemplating the pebbled surface of the Jack Daniel's bottle he was nursing when the knock came at the door, giving him such a start that he almost dropped the bottle to the floor.

The man known only as Steve the Soundman stuck his lionlike head into the tiny dressing room and flashed his trademark thumbs-up.

"Five minutes, guys," he urged, his lips moving unseen beneath the profuse mustache that flowed seamlessly into the long beard.

"Thanks, Stever," Vinnie called out from the ratty old sofa, where he sat calmly rolling a joint.

"Goofy-lookin' son of a bitch," Dave Hannon mumbled as he nervously pounded out a steady beat on the coffee table with his huge drumsticks. "Fuckin' guy looks like Cousin It from the goddamn Addams family."

"Don't worry about how he looks," Vinnie replied as he lit up the joint and handed it to Johnny. "He's one of the best boardmen in the city. We're lucky we got him."

"You work with him before, Vinnie?" Kenney asked, strapping on his bass.

"Few years back. I was in a band called Majik and we were on a bill with about five other bands at some fest out in the north burbs. Not a bad group, but we didn't have anyone who could sing like Golden Pipes here," Vinnie said, slapping Johnny on the back.

A violent burst of racking coughs exploded from Johnny's throat as he fought in vain to hold the acrid smoke in his lungs. "What is this shit?" he asked Vinnie, still hacking as he wiped the moisture from his tearing eyes.

"Thai-stick. I told you to take it easy, didn't I?" Vinnie asked. He shot a worried glance at Kenney, who could only raise his eyebrows and shrug.

"Gimme a hit offa that, puppy lungs," Dave Hannon said, needling Johnny lightheartedly as he pulled the doobie from his hand and took a deep drag.

"This is it, boys," Vinnie said, adjusting his guitar strap around his neck and popping open a fresh Budweiser. "Just let it hang out and kick some ass. You ready, Johnny?"

"Don't worry about me," Johnny said, raising his head up from the sink, where he had splashed the red from his face and eyes with cold water. He toweled off and considered his handsome reflection for a long moment in the mirror. The ugly gremlin of self-doubt and apprehension that had jumped on his back when he had boarded that first Greyhound bus to Chicago three years ago crept into the deepest recesses of his gut. C'mon Johnny, he said to himself in an attempt to calm his jangled nerves, this ain't no different than singing at home in your bedroom.

Except, of course, you got a few thousand people watching you!

The vomit rose up from the pit of his stomach without warning, violently spraying the sink with Jack Daniel's, Budweiser, and most of his dinner. The dizziness and fear he had been feeling for the better part of the evening lay there with it, bubbling in the aftermath. Suddenly he felt remarkably clearheaded and in control. He adjusted his light flannel shirt, tying it in a knot at his waist and flipped his hair back over the collar.

"I'm fine," he said, looking at his startled bandmates. "Now, let's blow 'em into the weeds."

The muted rumbling of the crowd grew louder as they walked, single file, between the tall sheets of pressboard that made up the narrow makeshift corridor and made their way toward the darkened stage. Johnny led the way and stepped confidently toward the microphone, where Bobby Stagg, a disc jockey from WDAI, Chicago's best rock station and the Battle of the Bands' main sponsor, was trying to work the raucous crowd.

"How y'all doin' tonight?" Bobby Stagg asked the mob in his best DJ voice as Vinnie the Razor and Kenney Brandt discreetly plugged into the towering stacks of amplifiers and Dave settled in behind his drum kit. "You ready for some more rock and roll?"

"You suck, Bob!" someone yelled above the ensuing roar, prompting laughter and cheers from the rowdy mob.

"All right!" Bobby continued, ignoring the insult. "I want you all to put your hands together and give a big WhereHouse welcome to some real up-and-comers, making their first appearance at the WDAI Battle of the Bands. Ladies and gentlemen . . . let's give it up for GloryDaze!"

The lights faded to black. Vinnie spotted Steve the Soundman standing at the controls of the soundboard on his elevated platform. The thumb popped up from behind the console and the Razor's long fingers latched onto the Stratocaster's low E and A strings. He squeezed out the opening riff to "Thrush," a song he had written as a teenager. With the dark and gloomy power chord still resonating through the amplifiers, he tore off a series of hot licks that threatened to peel the paint from the walls. He paused, basking in the lush reverb, as he toed the effects pedal at his feet. In the minuscule window of silence that followed, Dave Hannon brought the thunder down from the heavens, pounding out a killer backbeat as the stage lights flashed on, giving the audience its first look at the band. Kenney jumped in, laying a solid foundation for the Razor's showcase leads. Johnny Coltrane took his cue and stepped up to the microphone, his voice a tortured wail fusing with Vinnie's lead, then rising up and over the accompaniment like a wave breaking on the rocks in a tempest.

A blue floodlight bathed him in an ethereal glow and he paused dramatically, flipping his hair back away from his face, letting Vinnie's guitar fill the air before joining the rest of the band chanting the one-word chorus, hypnotically weaving in and out of the leads.

Pulling the mike from its stand, he reared his head back and flexed his vocal muscles, letting his voice climb over the wall of sound rising up behind him.

The chorus picked up tempo, chasing the runaway train that was Vinnie's guitar as it blasted clear from the rhythmic violence of Dave's explosive drumming and cut like a knife through the smoke and sweat of the packed arena. A well-placed laser beam bounced off the Stratocaster's pick-guard and accentuated the blur of the Razor's hand as it flailed across the strings like a crazed spider. Stepping into the multicolored spotlights at center stage, he sawed away unmercifully at the guitar slung low on his bouncing hip. He finished off the brief burst with an open G-string note ringing eerily through the arena before settling back into the chorus riff.

With a grin and a nod to his cofrontman, Johnny shimmied back up to the mike, singing the closing verse with a haunting, solemn edge to his voice.

He stretched out the last note and Dave Hannon brought it home, slowing down the backbeat with a cryptic rattling of the cymbals and a final flurry topped by a closing "chunk" from Vinnie and Kenney Brandt. Pausing for just a moment to take in the deafening applause, they segued into an electrified cover of "Howlin' For My Darling," giving the house a taste of Johnny's vocal range and Vinnie's exquisite blues technique. Midway through "Howlin'," Johnny pulled out his Marine Band harmonica and set the table for "Ice Cream Headache." This was Vinnie's showcase guitar solo, incorporating the best he had to offer in an eclectic blend of rock, blues, and jazz fusion, plus some classical tables thrown in for good measure.

Wolf whistles and cheers rose up as the number wore down, and Vinnie raised Thor's Hammer high over his head, acknowledging the audience with a modest wave of his guitar pick.

"Mr. Vincent Rosario on guitar!" Johnny bellowed into the mike, grinning from ear to ear. "We're going to switch gears a bit here, people," he continued, working the crowd like a seasoned pro, "and play something a little funky, a little cool, just because it's so damn hot in here!" Turning around, he nodded to Kenney and Dave and mouthed the word "Fever" to his puzzled rhythm section. "Fever" was not on the playlist, and although they had been tossing it around in rehearsal, it was far from polished and they had never shared it with an audience. Kenney shrugged and began plucking the loping beat of the old classic from the meaty strings of his bass, watching Vinnie closely, trying to gauge the guitarist's reaction to this break in routine.

Dave joined in with a remarkably subdued and steady cadence on his bass drum, embellished by the slinky rattle of the cymbals. With the earthy bass line pounding out behind him, Johnny stood confidently at the mike, snapping his fingers in time to the addictive beat. Vinnie casually sidled up next to him, waiting for his cue to join in.

"You think this is a good move?" he asked under his breath.

"Trust me," Johnny said discreetly. "They'll eat it up."

Vinnie nodded and backed away, leaving the singer alone under the rainbow of multicolored spotlights. Laying off to the side of the stage, he added his own signature sparkle to the song, squeezing out one perfectly timed

note after another. Johnny handled the old lounge standard like a classic crooner. It went off much crisper than
Vinnie would have imagined, the spontaneity and
Johnny's showmanship making up for any lack of polish.
If anything, it was one of their better efforts of late, and
the crowd broke into early applause as they sensed the
song winding down.

Kenney closed the number out with a long fade amidst
the cheering, laughing with relief. Dave, pumped from
the crowd reaction and countless Budweisers, stood up
behind his drum kit and howled triumphantly, waving his
meaty fists in the air, sparking the crowd into a standing
ovation. Vinnie, surprised and delighted by the response
to the quirky tune, waved off in deference to Johnny, who
stood silently at the mike, seemingly oblivious to the enthusiastic pandemonium breaking around him.

With the applause winding down, Vinnie shuffled over
to his glassy-eyed lead singer. "All right, ace, let's wrap it
up," he said a bit impatiently, concerned that Johnny
might be milking the ovation a bit too long.

Johnny Coltrane continued to stare straight ahead, as
though struck dumb by rapture, gripping the mike with
both hands in a gesture that was strangely prayerlike.
Then, as though suddenly released from a parlor magician's trance, he blinked and found himself looking directly into the distressed face of the lanky guitar player.

"C'mon, Johnny, snap out of it," Vinnie said, a little
uneasy. "Jeez, you look like you seen a ghost."

Twenty-three

It was the voice more than anything else, hard edged yet melodic and soulful, which sparked her initial interest. Watching him from amidst the bustle and heat generated by the mortals, she felt an unfamiliar temptation, an exotic enticement that had nothing at all to do with hunger or blood lust. A fuzzy halo, cast from the spotlight, shimmered around the mane of sandy brown hair that fell in soft damp ringlets around his neck, framing the exquisite throat from which the songs poured out like water from a faucet. An intrinsic charm surrounded his aura as he performed, born out of the pure elation that comes from doing what one loves and doing it better than most everyone else. The mob of mortals felt it also, to a lesser extent of course, but it was that charisma as much as the seductive appeal of his voice and the delicious energy of the music that held them in such thrall.

Chloe was rifling through the electronic thicket of sound waves and alpha rhythms reverberating through the hall. She had finally managed to isolate his thought patterns from the chaotic tangle when Johnny Coltrane happened to look past the faceless thousands packed into the arena, directly at her. Their eyes locked across the crowded auditorium and she knew, staring back at him, that she had somehow been discovered trespassing in the private recesses of his psyche. She stood motionless, cautiously waiting for his next move. A glimmer of recognition flashed across his face, before melting into a forlorn mask of longing. In the fleeting moments that followed, a smoldering ember of her lost soul rose up briefly from the flames that had consumed it for nearly two decades.

"He's beautiful, isn't he?" Lizabet asked suddenly.

The words jolted her free from the telepathic union and she looked up, startled. The mistress was staring intently at the stage, a wicked smile dancing in her eyes. Had she seen what transpired between the two? Embarrassed and somewhat flustered, Chloe moved to one side, blending deeper into the crowd and taking herself out of the singer's field of vision.

"Yes," Chloe answered nervously, trying to gauge her maker's level of interest while undermining her own. "I suppose he is. And he can sing, too. Quite a lovely voice for a mortal."

"Not him!" Lizabet scoffed. "He's just a child. I'm speaking of the one with the raven hair and the olive skin. The guitar player. Have you ever seen a man with such flawless skin? Come, I simply must have him!"

A wave of relief washed over the shell that was Chloe's body as the Ancient One took her hand and led her from their vantage point on the outskirts of the arena. They slithered through the sweaty mob, virtually unseen, until they found themselves on the far end of the stage concealed discreetly behind a towering stack of amplifiers.

Lizabet Bazore gazed at the flaming guitarist as the band rolled into their next number. Chloe had never seen her quite like this, almost like she was smitten. It was highly unusual for her to be even remotely interested in a male of the species. Lizabet preferred the pliant suppleness and sweet smells of the female. She would obsess over their soft skin, playing with it, poking it, puncturing it, sometimes for hours on end as they lay screaming or begging for mercy. Lizabet stood perfectly motionless, peering out silently from between the booming amplifiers, her dark eyes offering no clue to the secrets lurking behind them. She found her mind drifting back to the old days, before she had crossed over—before the discovery. She thought longingly of her clandestine afternoon dalliances in the Vienna woods with Ladislas while her husband, Ferenc, was leading a campaign against the Turks. The wife of a warrior had a lonely existence, and she found many diverse ways to amuse herself while the Black Knight led his long and bloody forays through the Pyrenees Mountains. Barely in her twenties at the time, she had already had more than her fair share of both men and women, but no man thrilled her like the handsome young nobleman from the imperial court. The young musician's resemblance to Ladislas was nothing short of remarkable, but this one was even more beautiful. Streamlined and smooth, he moved across the stage with the grace and rhythm of a natural athlete, animated, it seemed, by the sheer power of the music he played. An undeniable sexual energy flowed from him like the notes from the guitar slung so low over his crotch, bouncing suggestively off his hip.

Her nostrils flared slightly as she picked up his scent, musky and sweet, as she knew it would be. Beads of sweat, sparkling like tiny diamonds, dotted his chest, dripping down in rivulets over the firm, chiseled muscles of his stomach, disappearing into the waistline of his tight blue jeans. She imagined her hands sliding underneath that coarse fabric, over the silky hair on the small of his back, her fingertips lingering over the curve of his ass before squeezing the twin hemispheres of muscle in huge, greedy handfuls. Her mouth watered at the thought of that perfect skin wet with her kisses, savoring the taut flesh, hard with muscle as her teeth danced over the surface. The taste, the texture, as she finally bit . . .

Twenty-four

"Fuckin' ay!" Dave Hannon bellowed delightedly as he brought his big hand down on Johnny Coltrane's back. "Hey, Vinnie, didn't I tell you this kid was a fuckin' musical genius?"

Johnny grinned sheepishly, still staring at the poster-size check in his hands. The hefty drummer threw a muscled arm around him and planted a wet, sloppy kiss on his cheek.

"You trying to make the kid throw up again, you big ugly bastard? Knock that shit off before you break him. We may have to use him again." Vinnie laughed as he tucked his Stratocaster carefully into his guitar case. "A thousand bucks! Hey, professor," he called out to Kenney Brandt, who was packing up his own gear, "you're the brains of this operation. What are we gonna do with all this dough?"

Kenney paused, stroking his chin thoughtfully. "Well, you know, I've been thinking. The Maverick could use a little work . . . no, seriously, why don't we take two hundred right off the top just for the hell of it and have some fun. The remaining eight hundred can go right back into the band. We could use some new equipment. Maybe a soundboard or—"

A knock sounded on the door of the dressing room, and Bobby Stagg, late-night jock and B-list local celebrity, walked in. A short slight man decked out in polyester pants and white shoes with tassels followed him, grinning and nodding as if he were having a minor convulsion.

"Hey, boys," Bobby said, dropping the trademark on-air inflection common to all FM disc jockeys. "Great job out there tonight. No shit, I really mean it. Congratulations. Oh," he paused, fishing into the inside pocket of his jacket, "here's your check. The real one. That one I gave you onstage," he continued, indicating the bogus check in Johnny's hand, "is just for show. If you try to cash that," he laughed, handing the real check to Johnny, "you'll get arrested. By the way, this gentleman is Barry Ruder. Barry manages all the talent for the Sphinx over on Superior. You boys familiar with the Sphinx?"

"Sure," Kenney said, nodding, looking around the room at his stunned bandmates. The Sphinx was one of the best clubs in the city. A real prestige joint that was known for showcasing the best local talent along with big-name acts from across the country. "Nice club. I really like your cheese fries," he added, trying to sound casual but coming up lame. Jeez, what a stupid thing to say.

"Thank you!" the little man exclaimed, pleased by the offhand compliment. Still nodding, he extended his hand to Kenney. "Barry Ruder," he announced. He pronounced it "Rudah." "Nice to meet cha."

"Kenney Brandt," Kenney replied, pumping the little man's hand, hoping he didn't sound too much like an asshole. "And this," he continued, making the introductions, "is Johnny Coltrane, Dave Hannon over there on drums, and—"

"Vinnie 'the Razor' Rosario!" Ruder interrupted. "Seen you play before, young man. Old Town Art Fair, maybe two years ago. Good stuff! Good stuff!"

Vinnie shook his hand, surprised and delighted that the man would recall such an obscure show from so long ago. He could hardly remember it himself.

"We're having a little party in the hospitality suite upstairs," Bobby Stagg said, pulling out a small vial of cocaine and casually unscrewing the cap. "Can you boys hang out for a while?"

"Have a few drinks," Ruder added. "Talk a little business? I might have something you fellas might be interested in."

Vinnie and Kenney exchanged glances across the room and nodded.

"Yeah, I think we can hang out for a little while," Vinnie said, a sly smile working its way across his face. "Whadda ya think, guys? Stick around here for a little while?"

"Talked me into it," Dave Hannon said with a snort as he sucked back the heaping spoonful of coke Bobby Stagg had placed under his nose. "Lead the way, gentlemen."

The conversation was loose and casual as they piled into the freight elevator behind the stage, peppered with nervous laughter and genial small talk, but Johnny Coltrane was so excited he thought he might jump right out of his skin. Bobby Stagg had been a staple in this town for years. Many was the night he would be working in his studio, listening to Stagg's program on WDAI while he labored over his artwork into the early morning hours. Now here he was telling Johnny how much he liked his sound, comparing him to Robert Plant and early Rod Stewart, "before he turned into a pussy and started making music for fourteen-year-old girls." This Ruder guy smelled of big money, and despite the goofy outfit and the gold jewelry, he had an infectious enthusiasm and an impressive résumé when it came to cultivating talent.

After bobbing to an abrupt halt, the doors of the creaking elevator rolled back and they spilled out into the thick carpet of the second-floor suite, which overlooked the main floor and concert hall below. The room, much bigger than it looked from the stage, was already filling up with an eclectic assortment of late-night revelers. Hard-core metal-heads mingled freely with the pinkie ring and cigarette holder–crowd, and women, dressed in everything from stylish designer miniskirts to skimpy gym shorts and leotards, were everywhere, nearly outnumbering the men in the room two to one.

"No riffraff up here, boys. Invitation only," Ruder shouted to them over the blare of the music coming from the speaker mounted directly over their heads. "Come on, I've got a booth reserved for us in the corner, we can talk."

"Man," Dave said, sliding into the sumptuous booth next to Kenney, "would you look at all these chicks! I think I died and went to heaven!"

"Yeah, it's great, ain't it?" Stagg said. "We have a small crew that works the crowd during the show. They hand out passes to all the prime trim." He motioned to the door at the far end of the room, where two huge bouncers were monitoring admission. "No one gets in without one."

"Stroke of genius," Kenney marveled, watching the steady stream of beautiful young women trickle through the tiny door.

"An oldie, but a goody," Stagg agreed, signaling a waitress over to the booth. He chopped several lines of cocaine out on the round mirror that had been sitting on the table.

"A round of beers and a bottle of champagne, Georgia," Barry Ruder said to the waitress as she bent low to hear his order over the blare of the music.

"Coming right up, Mr. Ruder." She flashed Kenney Brandt a dazzling smile, which made his heart ache, before gliding away.

"I'll get right down to it," Ruder said. "We need a house band for the Pharaoh Room at the Sphinx. We had to drop the current band on account of some, eh, personal problems their lead singer was experiencing, and they're on a prolonged hiatus, so to speak."

Vinnie nodded. He'd heard all about Raydio's Tom Condron and the "personal problems" he was having. He had gotten into a fight with his girlfriend and busted her face up pretty good. When the cops finally caught up with him in some dive on the west side he was carrying a .22 and an eight ball of smack. He was going to be on hiatus for quite a while.

"What we're looking for," Ruder continued, "is a group that can step right in and give us three solid sets, eight to two A.M., Friday and Saturday nights. We're talking about a mixed set. Maybe seventy percent cover songs, thirty percent your own stuff. I figure maybe . . ."

Dave Hannon was listening intently, waiting for the mirror to make its way around the table, when he felt a tap on his shoulder. He turned around and found himself looking at a pair of fishnet-clad legs sprouting from beneath a tiny leopard skin-print minidress.

"Excuse me," the blonde said, pressing her hips closer to his face. "I was wondering if you'd like to dance."

"Well, that's awful nice of you to ask, darlin'," Dave said, letting his eyes crawl over the clingy dress. "But I don't really dance."

"Neither do I," she replied matter-of-factly. "I just want to get you out there and dry-hump your thigh until I come."

"Oh, well in that case," Dave said, looking around the table, "if you gentlemen would excuse me. The little lady wants to dance."

"By all means," Barry Ruder said as the big drummer slid out of the booth and headed to the dance floor, his hand disappearing up the blonde's meager skirt. "Now where were we? Oh yes, Friday and Saturday nights, seventy-thirty mix. Maybe sixty-forty down the road. We'll have to see how the crowd takes to your material. Thank you, dear. . . ."

He paused for a moment while the waitress set the silver champagne bucket in the center of the table and laid the drinks out. Her fingertips lingered for just a moment over Kenney's hand as she pulled the tray away, her lacquered nails leaving a tingling sensation across the surface of his skin.

"Here you go, doll," Ruder said, handing a crisp folded twenty to Georgia. "Put it on my account and keep 'em coming."

"Yes, sir. Thank you, Mr. Ruder." That smile again.

"It's a great room," Ruder continued, watching the waitress slink away. "Good acoustics and you'll get plenty of exposure. Our ads run in all the weeklies, including the *Illinois Entertainer.*"

"Plus, they advertise heavily on WDAI," Bobby Stagg said, coming up for air as he lifted his head from the mirror. "The place is happening, believe me. Great crowd for your type of music. Young but sophisticated."

"No question, no question," Ruder agreed. "Whadda ya think? You fellas interested? I gotta know right away. I have to get that slot filled quick, and I think GloryDaze would be a perfect fit."

Johnny looked like a little kid listening to his parents discuss an upcoming trip to Disneyland. Kenney looked at Vinnie and nodded. They both knew they had a handshake agreement with Tommy Corbett to play The Drop Zone on Friday nights, but all parties concerned seemed to know that was a temporary gig.

"How much money are we talking about?" Vinnie asked, getting right to the point.

"Five hundred a week. Two-fifty a night," Ruder said, doing the math for them as he pulled a multipage contract from his polyester sport coat and slid it across the table.

Kenney took a long pull of his beer and looked at Vinnie. That was pretty good cake. Tommy was only paying them a hundred a night at The Drop Zone.

"As I said earlier, I need to fill that slot. I'll be honest with you," Ruder said, suddenly looking very contrite. "The guys down at corporate will have my ass if I don't get a band that can draw in that room by the weekend. We don't make any money if it's empty."

Johnny sat wide-eyed watching his two bandmates. It seemed like forever before they nodded.

"I think we got a deal, Barry," Vinnie said finally.

"Fantastic. Fantastic," Ruder said, pulling a Cross pen from his pocket.

"Of course, we'll have to check with twinkle toes out there first," Kenney laughed, cocking his head toward the crowded dance floor, where Dave Hannon was undressing the diminutive blonde. "And we'd like to read that contract before we sign it."

"Why, certainly, certainly!" Ruder said, standing up and ceremoniously uncorking the champagne. "Plenty of time to read that. This calls for a celebration! Let's have some fun, heh?"

Dave walked up and slid back into the booth with the sweaty, exhausted blonde draped across his sturdy torso. "I hope you ladies weren't talkin' shit about me while I was gone," he said, laughing. "What did I miss?"

"You're playing the Pharaoh Room at the Sphinx," Bobby Stagg said, taking a blast off the mirror and handing it to Dave. "You guys are gonna be rich and famous."

"Well, no shit!" the big man said, bending and snorting a thick line of the flaky white powder up his nose. "Ain't life grand."

Twenty-five

The heavy door shut behind him with a metallic snicker, muffling the relentless throb of the music and mayhem from within. Johnny Coltrane leaned back against the cold steel, sucking in the cool night air like a winded prize-fighter between rounds of a lost cause. His heart was beating like a trip-hammer, racing against the deafening high-voltage hum buzzing in his head, so loud he had to struggle to hear himself think. He stepped gingerly off the concrete stoop, testing the integrity of the footing before allowing his full weight to fall onto the iron grating of the fire escape. Johnny shuffled to the rail, satisfied the whole structure was not going to collapse beneath him and send him plummeting down to the alley below in a twisted heap of flesh and hard black iron. He grasped it with both hands in an effort to steady himself against the wave of vertigo rolling up his legs as a stiff breeze came in off the lake lifting the matted hair from his sweaty face. He stood there, savoring the chilly kiss of the wind, and waited for the world to stop spinning.

He had no idea how long he had been standing there when the realization struck him with deadly certainty.

Someone was standing at the far end of the grated landing. Watching him.

"Don't be alarmed," she said. The voice was soft and silvery, riding the night air like a butterfly with glass wings.

And he wasn't alarmed. Not at all. In fact, hearing that voice, he felt just fine.

It was the girl he had seen in the crowd. He knew that before he lifted his head and turned to look. The moon cast a luminescent glow on her pale skin, making the contrast with her black outfit, a knit tank top and tights, all the more striking. High leather boots rose to just below her kneecaps before folding over on themselves with a swash-buckling flair. A silver band in the form of a snake wrapped itself around her left bicep, the splash of red that was its eye pulled his attention back to her wet mouth, parted in a whisper below her dazzling golden eyes. She stood perfectly straight, the rigid stance lending an imposing peculiarity to her petite frame. The wind played with her glossy blond hair, tossing it across her face before she reached up and pulled it away, her whole body seeming to relax with the simple gesture. It gave him the impression of a statue imbued with the sudden and wonderful gift of life, instantly graceful, moving with the preternatural fluidity of liquid smoke. She was standing next to him suddenly, and although he was sure that she had walked the short distance to where he stood, he could not recall the action taking place.

"You're not well," she said, placing her soft hand against the side of his clammy face. She cupped his cheek in the manner of a concerned mother checking on a bed-ridden child. Her hand was soft but cold, drawing the heat from his fevered skin like a splash of cool water.

"Too much coke," he said, his skin tingling from the caress as she withdrew her hand. "It's really not my drug, I guess. Makes my heart race. Way too much coke. I never did that much before. I don't know how people could do that shit all the time. You wanna go back inside? I could use another blast—" He stopped, vaguely aware that he was starting to babble. She slid her left hand inside the soft cotton of his shirt, her fingers running through the sparse hair of his silky chest before lighting atop his rapidly beating heart. He swallowed hard, somewhat surprised by her boldness, a loud click coming from inside his dry throat.

"I saw you inside," he continued, looking at her amazing eyes. "In the crowd. I don't know how to explain it. We made a . . . connection, you and I."

"Yes, I suppose we did," she said with a sad, beautiful smile. She pressed her palm against his chest with the clinical regard of a doctor. "Shhh . . . quiet now. Listen."

Johnny Coltrane closed his eyes and let the muffled din shaking the walls of the WhereHouse fade into the calm of the spring night. A different sound replaced it, growing louder as though speeding toward him from a great distance. Twin drumbeats wildly out of sync with each other welled up from deep within him, and he realized he was hearing the pounding of their two hearts. The pulse emanating from the base of her thumb accelerated, gaining speed until it matched his own heartbeat, overtook it, and held it in check.

He opened his eyes, refreshed and giddy. The drums, beating in perfect harmony, faded into the night air.

"Wow . . . what a rush!" he said, delighted that his heart wasn't going to explode, after all. "How did you do that? *What* did you do?" he asked, placing his hands over hers, gently stroking.

"I did nothing," she said, lowering her eyes. "You did it yourself. I merely helped you." Somewhat flustered by the display of affection, she pulled her hand from his and ceremoniously buttoned his shirt one notch, patting his chest in a sweet gesture of finalization. "You sing beautifully," she said, looking at him with that haunting, sad smile. "It would be a shame if you were to deprive the world of your voice through avarice and overindulgence."

"Huh?" he said.

"Take it easy on the partying," she scolded with a laugh. "The circulation of blood through your body is robust, but your heart, though young and strong, has a slightly irregular beat."

"Who are you?" he asked, his tongue thick and fuzzy from the alcohol. "How do you know these things? You sure don't look like any doctor I've ever seen." He looked her up and down. "What are you? A premed student or something like that?"

"Something like that," she said. "I'm a student of all things under the stars."

"Johnny Coltrane," he offered, extending his hand. "Student of all things relating to art, and fledgling rock and roll singer."

"Chloe." She smiled and shook his hand. "Just Chloe."

"Oh," he laughed, trying not to stare at the sweet, pliant lips sliding over her white teeth into that inviting smile. "Like 'Cher.' "

"Like share?" she asked, puzzled.

"Yeah," he laughed. "You know, like 'Elvis.' Hey, can I buy you a drink? It's the least I can do after you saved my life."

"You weren't going to die, Johnny Coltrane," she said matter-of-factly. "Not tonight."

"Sure felt like it," he said, tugging on the door. "Shit! We're locked out."

"Allow me," she said, stepping in front of him. With a subtle pass of her left hand, the dead bolt barring their entrance slid back into its hasp and she pulled the door open. The raucous sounds of the backstage party spilled into the uneasy calm of the Chicago night.

"You're amazing, you know that?" he said over the blare of the music. "I don't believe I've ever met anyone quite like you."

"Trust me," she said, turning to him with a sly smile. "If you ever had, you never would."

* * *

"They flock to you, don't they?"

"Huh?" he said, turning from the urinal.

Vinnie the Razor was so startled he had almost caught himself in the zipper of his blue jeans. The woman leaning against the stall had not been there a moment ago. He would have sworn to it.

"The little girls, Vincenczo. The *groupies,*" Lizabet said with a smirk, walking slowly and deliberately toward him. "Throwing themselves into your arms like lemmings racing for the cliff's edge, with little or no regard for the fall they must know they're sure to take when you're done with them. That must make you feel wonderful."

It struck him for the first time that he did rather enjoy that. It was something he preferred not to think about, the blasé manner in which he regarded his sexual conquests. He gave little thought to the lack of emotion or the consequences of his dalliances. But yes, now that he had this moment to reflect on it, it did make him feel wonderful.

"Beats a poke in the eye with a sharp stick," he said, putting on his best front as he gave his zipper a hearty tug. "They know what they're getting into. I don't make any promises."

"My, but you are bold," she said, stepping right up to him. Her breasts, creamy and white as twin scoops of vanilla ice cream, spilled out over the tight confines of the black leather Merry Widow, only inches from his chest. Her breath, behind the thick, full lips and the white teeth, was heady and sweet, smelling of lilac (and something else hidden beneath it?). She was older than he was, older than most of the women he'd had, but her beauty transcended age, and the want rose up in his loins like a firestorm making his cock hard and his knees weak. The defining edge that middle age brings to one's face was on hers, distinctive to the point where it would be hard to imagine her ever being more beautiful at any time in her life. Her auburn hair, long and luxurious, sparkled with the sheen of a teenager's, and her skin, flush and revitalized from the recent feed, had the fleshy tender resilience of a woman half her age.

"Tell me, Vincenczo," she said, well aware of his eyes crawling over her body, "how long has it been since you've had a *real* woman?" With the leisurely and calculated finesse of a seasoned showgirl, Lizabet Bazore pulled the drawstring from the tight Merry Widow, unleashing the full white breasts with a springy jiggle. She stared for a moment admiring her own nakedness before reaching up and pinching the big rosy nipples, rolling them slowly between her thumbs and forefingers. She paused to watch their gradual erection like an artist stepping back to contemplate a brush stroke. She met his gaze with a sly smile, pleased with the wanton desire she saw in his eyes. "Or would this be a first time for you?"

He had no snappy comeback, no quick rejoinder, only a weak moan that croaked up from deep inside his dry throat. Unable to contain himself any longer, he made a move, lurching toward her with the clumsy passion of an ungainly schoolboy on a first date. A delighted laugh escaped her as she deftly stopped his advance and pressed a single fingertip to his lips.

"No, Vincenczo," she said, running her finger along the edge of his mouth. "Don't you see, beautiful one, that you are the prize? I shall be the one to taste the fruit of the flesh. I will partake of your charms and drink deeply from the wellspring of your youth and vitality at my leisure. Only if I deem it so, will you be allowed to sample the glory of my flesh, the splendor of my womanhood, the essence of all your dreams and desires." Pulling her finger from his trembling mouth, she slipped her hands under his leather vest and let her fingertips roam over the broad expanse of his chest. Savoring the taut resilience of his pectoral muscles, she squeezed hard, pinching the flesh until a small droplet of crimson welled up beneath her thumbnail. Now it was her turn to moan.

Vinnie the Razor winced as the sharp pain pierced the dense fog in his clouded head. Too drunk with desire to offer any resistance to the spell of the centuries-old sorceress, he gave himself up willingly, almost gladly. The revenant's warm mouth closed on the wound, champing and sucking the lifeblood from his chest in time with the beating of his heart. Reduced to a near swoon by the gentle rhythmic suckling, he pulled her close and she responded in kind, gathering in greedy handfuls of his ass, nearly picking him up off the floor as she locked in tight. Her head swam with the sweet taste of his blood and the musky scent of his olive skin.

The incessant pounding on the door broke through the veil of intimacy and for one mad moment she found herself back at Cachtice, moments before the marauders stormed into the castle and discovered the evidence of her atrocities. She could hear their heavy footfalls echoing off the walls, growing closer. . . .

She pulled her head back, relieved to find herself surrounded by the antiseptic green tiles of the small modern-day bathroom, centuries removed from the discovery.

"C'mon! Open the fuckin' door already!" the voice yelled from behind the locked door. "I gotta take a piss!"

Wiping the blood from her mouth, she released the guitar player from the unholy coupling. They leaned back against the sink, unfolding from each other's arms, their eyes glazed and heavy like a couple basking in the afterglow of a particularly intense session of lovemaking.

"That was sweet, my darling," she whispered to him as he feebly tried to coerce her mouth back to the tiny crescent-shaped wound on his chest. "But that's quite enough for now. We will have all eternity to enjoy each other." She helped him to his feet, and they stumbled to the door. Mindful of the steady pounding and string of obscenities coming from behind it, they allowed themselves a few moments to clear their heads.

"Hey, I ain't fuckin' around out here! I mean it, I'm gonna—" Dave Hannon stopped in midrant as the door opened beneath his raised fist and he found himself looking directly into the spent, bewildered face of his guitar player. The Razor's arm was draped around a *very* wild-looking chick, and from the look on her face, she was none too pleased that he had interrupted them.

"Oh," Dave said with a sly, drunken grin. "Excu-uuuse me! Hey, where you been, man? We've been lookin' all over for you. We're moving the party down the street to the LakeView." He paused, amused by the blank look on Vinnie's face. Must have been one hell of a blow job, he thought. "Hey, don't worry," he said, still laughing, "you can bring your new friend."

Twenty-six

Kenney Brandt lifted himself from the motel bed in the waning hours of dawn and stumbled to the bathroom. Each step brought a jackhammer pounding in his skull, a harbinger of the violent hangover brewing in his brain. He squinted in the harsh light of the bathroom mirror and let loose with a thick stream, marveling all the while at the capacity of the human bladder. Shaking himself clean, Kenney flushed the toilet with a loud, wet roar and shuffled out of the bathroom trying to piece together the past few hours of his life. The towels, embroidered with the words "LakeView Motel," and the tiny bars of soap wrapped like fancy white chocolates were the only clues he had to his surroundings. In the warm glow of the coming dawn filtering through the vertical blinds, he saw the unmistakable hourglass silhouette of a woman under the covers of the bed he had crawled from only minutes before. With a mixture of hope and trepidation he tiptoed naked across the worn carpet to the far side of the bed and found his silent prayers answered. He stared with blessed relief at the face of the waitress, Georgia, her lips wrapped in a secret smile, sleeping contentedly in the motel bed. His bed.

Never one to question a stroke of good fortune, Kenney slid under the covers and sidled in next to her, carefully slipping his arm around her waist, his fingertips moving gently over the soft, perfumed skin of her body. He traced the marvelous outline of her hip, caressing the flesh of her inner thigh before delicately moving up along the exquisite swell of her tummy and cupping the full breast in his eager hand. She sighed, a warm cozy sigh, and snuggled back against him, melding into him like a formfitting glove. His cock grew hard and strong as her ass ground against it, slapping rudely up against her backside before settling in between the bountiful round cheeks. He lay there for a few minutes, his cock aching and his head pounding, smelling the wonderful fragrance of her hair before sleep came and overtook him once again.

Consciousness returned a few hours later and with it the hellish pounding in his head, augmented by a loud, incessant knocking penetrating the fitful curtain of sleep that had enveloped him.

"Hey, don't you worry about haulin' your ass outta the rack to answer the door, old buddy. I'll get it. You just lay there and get your beauty sleep! Lord knows you need it."

He opened one eye, amazed by the amount of pain brought on by the simple action. Dave Hannon was shuffling past his bed, naked except for a LakeView Motel bath towel wrapped around the expanding paunch of his ex-athlete's waist. Dumbfounded by the sight of the bearish drummer parading through his room, he rose up in the bed, ignoring the series of sonic booms in his head. He instinctively reached out for Georgia, alarmed that the big man would wake her. He came up empty, groping stupidly at the spot where she had lain, staring in disbelief at the rumpled sheets.

She was gone.

The door swung open, letting in a great white blast of morning sunlight, eliciting hearty laughter from Dave. "Well, look who's here! The fucking Prodigal Son returns! Welcome, my son!"

Johnny Coltrane shuffled in, looking only slightly better than Kenney felt at the moment.

"Hey, Johnny," Dave laughed, tearing a can of Budweiser from the six-pack ring at his feet. "Me and Kenney were just about to have a beer. Care to join us?"

Johnny blanched at the sight of the alcohol and collapsed into the boxy motel chair next to the TV set, which was bolted to the table against the wall.

"You look like you been rode hard and put up wet." Dave laughed, taking a long swig from the warm beer. Kenney thought he was going to be sick. "Where'd you and blondie disappear to last night? I thought maybe the two of you ran off and got married."

Johnny moaned and shook his head. "Maybe we did, for all I know. The last thing I remember is walking over here from the WhereHouse and filling the bathtub up with beer and ice. After that, everything is pretty much a blank. The next thing I know, it's six in the morning and I'm walking down Sheridan Road all by myself. I'm tellin' ya, it's like I woke up from a dream. Like I was sleepwalking or something."

While Dave laughed and needled Johnny, Kenney sat up and swung his legs over the side of the bed, his eyes lingering on the subtle emptiness of the shallow indentation next to him. Wrapping a sheet around his waist, he lumbered toward the bathroom, wondering where Georgia had gone and where the hell Dave had come from. Another surprise awaited him behind the bathroom door in the shapely form of a young woman, naked except for a pair of red lace panties. She was bent over the vanity, expertly applying a layer of lip liner to her pursed mouth. She looked up, genuinely pleased to see him.

"Hi, Kenney," she said, as if bumping into an old friend on a street corner. "You're the bass player, right? God, you guys fucking *rock!*"

He nodded blankly, averting his eyes from the large

brown nipples on her jiggling breasts. Over her shoulder he saw the open door to the adjoining suite, framing a rectangular still life of rock and roll decadence. Articles of clothing lay strewn about the floor amidst the beer cans and liquor bottles; a bra, a leopard-print miniskirt and Dave's Harley-Davidson T-shirt were hanging helter-skelter from the blades of the ceiling fan. A pair of pantyhose draped over the lampshade on the nightstand led his eyes to a pair of long, supple legs dangling off the side of the bed. He followed them, from the tips of the red painted toenails dangling inches above the worn carpet to the supple calves and taut thighs before they disappeared into the doorjamb, robbing him of the rest of the view.

"That's Kristen," the girl said suddenly, making him painfully aware that he had been staring. "She never could hold her liquor. Come to think of it," she said, noticing the pallor of his face, "you don't look so good yourself."

Clutching the sheet around his waist, Kenney could only nod. "Could you excuse me, please?" he asked humbly. "I think I'm going to be sick."

"Sure, hon," she said with that sympathetic, mothering tone exclusive to the female of the species. "Could you tell Daveykins to get his ass back in here when you're done?" she asked, gathering up her things. "He said he'd give me a ride home."

As the door clicked shut behind him, he dropped to one knee and bent low to the bowl, feeling the cold rush of the toilet water inches from his clammy face. He hung there until the nausea passed, knowing the relief was temporary at best. Kenney forced himself up off the floor, repelled by the ashen face staring back at him from the mirror.

"You are one sick puppy," he mumbled, barely able to look at his own reflection. He lowered the sheet around his waist and voided his bladder, trying to wrestle the lost fragments of the night from his failed memory. It wasn't like him to black out like that, and losing the time he and Georgia may have had together made him feel as though he had been robbed.

She had come to the motel after finishing up her shift at the WhereHouse, arriving a good half hour into the party, a vision of class and elegance amidst the stoned groupies and hangers-on milling about the crowded rooms. He allowed himself a sappy smile at the thought of her standing in the doorway, casually scanning the room, and didn't her eyes light up when she saw him in the corner talking to Barry Ruder . . . Ruder! Shit! He had been talking to Ruder about finalizing the contract to gig at the Sphinx. Did they agree to terms? Did he sign the goddamn thing in the condition he was in?

Swearing he would never drink again, he flushed the toilet and ambled back into the room where Dave was coercing Johnny into having "one more beer" with him.

"Hey, loverboy," Dave laughed, reaching into a bucket and tossing him a wet can of Budweiser. "Have some breakfast."

"You're fucking nuts, you know that, Dave?" Kenney said, amazed at his friend's constitution. "Didn't you have enough last night?"

"Last night is still going on for me, pal," Dave replied. "The trick is not to stop. I haven't been to sleep yet!"

Kenney looked at Dave's dilated pupils. He was still cresting on the cocaine. "How could you sleep, you greedy bastard? By the way, *Daveykins,*" he laughed, cocking a thumb over his shoulder, "I ran into a friend of yours in the john. She says you're giving her a ride home. How many women you got in there anyway?"

Dave leered and held up two fingers. "Just two, babe. Davey the wonder horse was tired after that wicked gig we played last night. I hope I didn't wear them out."

Johnny managed to raise his head off his chest high

enough to look at the big drummer with a mixture of disbelief and jealousy. "Two? You gotta be shittin' me. You made it with two chicks last night?"

"Like I said, my boy, I was tired." Dave smiled broadly, as if reliving the moment over in his mind, then dropped the bravado. "Can you believe it? I can get used to this rock-star shit real quick. We never got this kind of action playing The Drop Zone. Hey," he continued, looking at Johnny, "there had to be a dozen chicks in here last night and you could have had your pick of the litter, but you were all wrapped up with that little blonde. We could hardly tear you away from her to get you to sign the contract with Barry. You and Vinnie both. Did you see that wild broad he was with all night? I hope you at least got—"

"The contract!" Kenney interrupted. "Where is it, Dave?"

"Whoa, settle your nuts down, professor," Dave said, surprised by Kenney's anxiety. "I think you put it in the nightstand drawer over there for safekeeping. Why? Is there a problem?"

"Uh, n-no . . . ," Kenney stammered, not wanting to let on that he had no idea what he had signed. He was more or less looked at as the unofficial manager of the band, and the rest of the guys trusted him with the business dealings. "I just wanted to make sure I didn't lose it." He opened the nightstand drawer. There it was, folded crisply between the pages of the Gideon Bible. He pulled it out and looked it over quickly, noting their four signatures on the last page before casually slipping it into the pocket of his jeans hanging over the side of the bed. It looked pretty standard. He would give it a good read when he got home. Hopefully, they didn't do anything stupid. He paused for a moment as he fished around, surprised to find a sheet of LakeView Motel stationery buried deep in the front pocket of his Levi's.

"Everything okay, Kenney?" Johnny asked, still slumped in the chair.

"Everything's fine, pretty boy," Kenney said as he unfolded the stationery and quickly read the three words scripted in the flowing feminine handwriting: Call me! Georgia.

Her phone number was there underneath a little smiley face she had drawn. Suddenly he felt much better.

"A little love note from your sweetie pie, Romeo?" Dave asked, noticing the stupid, slack-jawed smile on his friend's face.

"Hey, what can I say?" Kenney said, reading the note once more before refolding it and stuffing it back into his front pocket. "So . . . ," he continued, casually trying to extract as much information out of Dave as he could, without letting on that he had blacked out, "what time did Vinnie leave last night?"

"Shit, he didn't stay long at all," Dave said. "An hour at the most. He left with that smokin' brunette without saying a word. I never saw him pussy-whipped like that. It was kinda scary. Did you get a load of her? Talk about a wild-looking piece of ass."

Kenney remembered her. She was not the type one would forget easily, even after a night of excessive drinking. Older, midthirties maybe, but really good-looking.

"Yeah," Kenney answered, recalling the offhand way she had regarded him. "She was kind of spooky."

"You can say that again," Dave said, shaking his head. "I offered her a beer and she looked at me like I was a booger stuck on the end of her finger."

The phone rang, scaring the shit out of Johnny. He reached over and snatched up the receiver, silencing the annoying jingle in midring. "Hello?" he said, listening intently for a moment, a quizzical expression on his face. "Yeah, thanks," he mumbled, hanging up the phone.

"That was the front desk. They want Mr. Ruder to know that it's eleven o'clock and checkout is in a half hour."

"Well," Kenney said, walking around the room and gathering up his clothes amidst the jumble of trash on the floor. "It's eleven-fifteen by my watch. Let's haul our asses out of here before they see what we did to these rooms."

"Fuck 'em if they can't take a joke," Dave said, laughing as he rose up out of his chair and lumbered toward the adjacent bedroom. "I'm gonna see if the ladies are up for one more Hannon sandwich before I take 'em home."

Kenney's blue Maverick was parked right outside the room. He and Johnny piled in just as the maid was wheeling her utility cart up to the door.

"Whoa," Johnny laughed, shaking his head. "The proverbial nick of time."

Kenney snorted and pulled the door shut, securing it with the black bungee cord he had to use in lieu of a lock. He felt a pang of sympathy for the maid, pushing that heavy cart around and making her living cleaning up after assholes who trashed motel rooms.

Of course he wasn't much better off, teaching snot-nosed kids on a day-to-day basis instead of selling his paintings. His hand brushed the bulge of the folded-up stationery in his pants pocket, the one with Georgia's phone number on it, and the bitterness disappeared as quickly as it surfaced.

"So tell me, buddy," he said to Johnny as he backed out of the lot and pulled into the street. "Did you get laid last night or what?"

Johnny stared straight ahead, his brow knitted as if pondering the question. He saw her in his mind's eye; a soft light and warmth shining from her face, concealing the darkness and pain he sensed underneath. The glow that seemed to surround her as they walked and talked for hours on end through the night. The feeling that he had known her before, that she was a part of him, and that they would be together now and forever.

"You really shouldn't talk about Chloe like that, Kenney," Johnny said suddenly, serious as a heart attack. "I don't expect you to understand. She's not that kind of girl. She's like no one you've ever known or no one you will ever know." He paused for a moment trying to find the right words. "She's different."

Twenty-seven

It was the hunger, welling up inside her and roiling in the very marrow of her bones, that had woken her initially. Chloe crawled out of the mound of corrupt earth piled high in the cellar of the Dearborn Street lair. The clumpy soil rolled off her porcelain skin like rainwater. The emptiness in her gut gnawed at her, nearly doubling her over in pain. She had never missed a feeding before, and despite the repeated warnings and lectures from Lizabet, she was unprepared for the distress it would cause in her body. A mewling whimper escaped her as she made her way toward the massive wooden doors of their sleep chamber. She hefted the heavy railroad tie from its struts, laying it down with a wooden thunk on the damp concrete. The cross-brace removed, she pushed open the door with a rusty squeak and shambled across the pitch-blackness of the basement toward the stairway. Her hands clutched at the screaming hollow emanating from her midsection.

The breaking light of late morning crept in over the tops of the high windows on the first floor, lending a fuzzy violet glow to Drew's sawhorse and plywood worktable sitting like a makeshift altar amidst the clutter of power tools and paint cans. This was to be the "showroom" for Cachtice Imports, the mock business that Chloe had thought up to launder the cash brought in by their calculated pilfering. It was a longtime dream of Lizabet's to secure a legitimate real-estate foothold and map a sound, long-term financial strategy. Chloe's natural business instincts proved to be invaluable in this regard.

Drew was only days away from securing the title to the property. As she ascended the stairwell to the second floor, fighting off the cramps in her gut, she couldn't help but note the amazing amount of work he had completed in just a few short weeks.

At the top of the landing, she could hear the labored breathing, weak but audible, through the door at the end of the hallway.

Good. She was still alive.

The girl's heartbeat intensified as Chloe entered the room, her anxiety triggering all manner of biochemical responses before she even looked up to see the vampire in the dim light stumbling toward her. Chloe could smell her fear, a sweaty, pungent scent, so easily recognized in the animal kingdom, but undetectable to humans and their inferior olfactory senses. It overpowered even the nefarious odor of death and human waste that hung so thickly in the dank air of the spacious but stuffy room.

A glimmer of faint hope lit up behind the terror in the girl's wide eyes as she watched the vampire approach, a sort of desperate relief washing over her upon seeing that it was not the older one who had come to visit her. Chloe allowed herself a brief, sad smile. Chained to a wall for two days and subjected to Lizabet's flights of perverse and sadistic fancy, the little street rat was still clinging to the prospect of living another day under the light of the sun. Amazing. At times like this she could almost feel pity for them.

With a gesture bordering on compassion, Chloe pressed her fingertip to the girl's gagged mouth, silencing the muffled protests as she silently inspected her naked torso for a suitable entry point. This one had been brought in late Friday morning; an afterthought as Lizabet made her way home in the waning hours of dawn, and although she had only been at the girl for a few hours, the mistress had left little in the way of unsullied flesh.

Chloe found a clean area, remarkably enough, just under the nape of the hooker's neck on her left shoulder blade. Driven by the maddening hunger, she hurriedly unfastened the restraint that held the girl's left wrist high over her head, allowing herself a clean shot at the trapezius.

The bite was swift and deadly accurate, catching the victim off guard so that she surrendered after the briefest of struggles, melting into death's embrace with an almost grateful resignation. Holding tight until the last drop was drained, Chloe released the body, leaving it to spin limply, still hanging from the wall by its right wrist like an off-kilter Christmas tree ornament. Satiated, but still slightly dizzy from the rush of the feed, she wiped her mouth and made her way downstairs, the stale smell of Drew Richards lingering in her nostrils. It had become apparent midway through the feeding that Drew had been at the girl without permission. She would have to talk to Lizabet and put a stop to that. They could not have him handling the food. It was repulsive.

In the cellar she stopped short of entering the cool sanctuary of the sleep chamber and glided over to the south wall toward the bank of blacked-out windows that faced Ontario Street. Without giving much thought as to why, she scratched a small fleck of the black enamel from the painted glass. She cautiously backed away from the narrow sliver of sunlight that shot through the din of the cellar.

She stood there for a long time, thinking of nothing while she contemplated the dusty needle of sunshine, fighting off the urge to touch it. What manner of being was she, she wondered, that something so natural, so delightful, could spell her doom. She felt, not for the first time, that there was something inherently wrong—something irregular—about her place in the grand scheme of things. Deep down she knew—despite all of Lizabet's pontificating about the natural order of things, and food chains, and existing on a higher plane, and divine birthrights—that she was an aberration. For all of Lizabet's disdain and hatred of the human race, she knew that even the mistress had been a mortal long ago.

And so had she.

But who?

Lizabet offered little in the way of explanation, saying only that Chloe had walked out of the woods on the night of the great storm and presented herself as an offering from the Master. It was not their place, she had scolded, to question the motives of the Dark One. The short time she had walked in the sunlight was merely a precursor to her true destiny: to assist the mistress in regaining her birthright and sit at her Left Hand when she ruled over the Kingdom of Man.

A somber melancholy welled up in her as she gazed pensively at the sunbeam and pondered the questions of her lost humanity. Was she, as Lizabet had told her, an outcast seeking refuge? An orphan of the Family of Man who chose to follow the Left-Hand Path and offered up her soul in exchange for the privilege to serve? What kind of life, however short, had she led under the rays of the sun? What kind of person was she? What kind *of food* did she like? Was it a gradual disillusionment or a sudden crisis that led her to abandon the earthly trappings of man and seek the higher plane of the Left-Hand Path? Who did she leave behind? Was there no one that mattered to her at all that she could just get up and walk away from it all? Did she *ever* have a family? Friends?

Did she have a lover?

She smiled an innocent girlish smile at the thought of Johnny Coltrane standing at the microphone bathed in the glow of a blue floodlight, his syrupy voice filling the auditorium, singing to the mindless, sweating throng but speaking only to her.

It was recognition that had flashed across his face in that fleeting, magical moment when their eyes had met. She had little doubt of that and even less in the way of an explanation. The connection was immediate and mutual, and when he had discovered her looking into his mind, he had paused only briefly before inviting her in. She knew beneath the laughter and swagger with which he carried himself that he was like her, a forsaken being cast adrift in a sea of uncertainty, searching for the defining elements of one's true self.

They had talked for hours after leaving that mad gathering at the motel. They strolled along Lake Shore Drive, and at Olive Park they had paused on the beach to watch the waves roll in, forming whitecaps on the inky surface as the wind picked up and tossed his long hair back, exposing the beauty of his boyish face. He bent to kiss her and she surrendered to it, forgetting for a moment what she was. She felt him recoil ever so slightly as their lips met, surprised, no doubt, by the icy resilience of her mouth before it melted into soft compliance upon contact with his warm, living flesh. Her body heat rose dramatically in just those few seconds, matching his 98.7 degrees exactly as the camouflaging aspects of her nature took over, aping his bodily characteristics like a predatory insect changing appearance to deceive its prey.

Knowing it could go no further without dire consequences, she imposed a minor charm, rendering him spellbound and clouding his thoughts, before releasing him from the heated kiss. She stood there for an instant, saddened by the confused and vacant look on his handsome face, angry with herself for letting things get this far. She reluctantly turned the bewitched singer in the direction of the LakeView Motel and disappeared into the shadows. She followed him from a safe distance to ensure his safe passage across the six lanes of traffic on Lake Shore Drive. She stayed with him as long as she could, waiting until the first light of day broke over the lake before making her way back to their lair. She darted through the sleepy streets and alleys faster than any human eye could see; a blur and a rush of wind to the scattered early risers and late-night vagabonds scattered across her path.

She had made it through the third-story window of the Dearborn Street sanctuary just as the last vestiges of dusk were drawn into the fireball rising out of the lake, burning away the morning haze and the few stubborn clouds lingering on the horizon.

Drew had been waiting for her in the cellar, a look of anxiety and impatience etched across his pimple-ravaged face. He opened the doors to the cool confines of the sleep chamber and closed them behind her as she snuggled deep into the reassuring embrace of the corrupt soil.

Lizabet, already asleep in her own mound piled high against the west wall, did not even stir as Chloe burrowed into the small mountain of earth, so grateful to be safe from the rays of the sun that she had forgotten to feed before laying herself down. Sleep had come immediately but was short-lived. Her vampiric bodily functions roared up in protest a few hours later, reminding her what she was and what it is she must do.

She remembered that pain now and backed away from the narrow shaft of sunlight pouring onto the floor and glided back to the cool refuge of the chamber, thinking about the ease and effortless grace with which she could move. The superiority of her kind, admittedly a permutation of the human form, was in fact a natural and progressive step up the evolutionary ladder and she was a fool to question the natural order of things. Her infatuation with the mortal had left her confused and pensive, clouding her thinking to the point where she had actually missed a feeding. What would she have done if the mistress had not kept a reserve supply on hand? Lay screaming and doubled over until nightfall? Such behavior was unacceptable and left her open to discovery, which in turn would only lead to her ruin. No, she decided, as she laid the heavy crossbeam over the thick wooden doors, it would not be wise to see Johnny, er, the mortal again.

She was asleep within minutes of boring deep into the mound of cool earth, dreaming of days spent laughing with Johnny Coltrane, walking together hand in hand, the warm, wonderful glow of sunlight on her face.

Twenty-eight

The voice, relentless and shrill, rattled in his skull. It cut through the pillow he had pulled over his head only moments ago in an effort to muffle the annoying shriek of the old woman pounding on his door.

"Vincenczo! I am not going to tell you again, if you do not get out of bed and come down for supper, I'm going to give it to the dog!"

Give it to the goddamn dog, old woman, he thought, pulling the covers over his head. See if I give a shit.

The voice again at the door—softer this time, the anger giving way to concern. "Vincenczo? Are you all right? Do you want me to call the doctor? Open up the door, Vincenczo, I want to take a look at you."

Realizing he would get no more sleep tonight, Vinnie the Razor pulled himself out from under the heap of blankets he had crawled under twelve hours ago and swung his legs over the side of the bed. "I'm up already!" he shouted defensively, unable to keep the contempt out of his voice, then added in a more soothing tone, "Uh—give me just a minute, Nan. I'll be right down."

"Honestly," she said through the door, her voice trailing down the hallway. "I've never seen anything like it. Out all night, sleep all day!"

Sitting on the edge of his bed, Vinnie ran his fingers through his thick mane of wavy black hair and took quick stock of himself. Jesus, he felt like shit. He was exhausted, but his limbs carried none of the heavy sluggishness usually associated with lack of sleep. In fact, his musculature throbbed with the vital hardihood one would feel after a good half hour at the gym and a few laps in the pool. He stood up and stretched in the exaggerated fashion of a cat waking after a long nap, enjoying the surprising vivacity coursing through his body. A dreamy smile crept onto his face as he closed his eyes and whispered the name without even realizing that he had spoken.

"Lizabet."

Her face, woven into the fabric of the strange, fragmented dreams that had plagued him throughout his deep sleep, sprang full-blown into his waking thoughts as he threw the robe over his shoulders and padded down the hallway to the bathroom. Standing over the toilet, he coaxed but a few drops from a bladder that should have been full after a long night spent drinking and an even longer day spent sleeping. With a curious shrug he flushed the toilet and bent low to the sink under the running faucet. He sucked the ice-cold tap water down in greedy, incessant gulps until it seemed his stomach could hold no more. He'd had hot pipes from excessive drinking more times than he would care to remember, but never anything this extreme. There was an inherent dryness throughout his body, almost as if all of the moisture had been drained from it, and his skin felt clammy and brittle to the touch.

Drained you dry, Vinnie, my boy!

The thought came from nowhere and spoke to him in a voice that was not his own, startling him for just a moment. Peering closer into the mirror, he pulled aside his robe and took notice of the haphazard pattern of scratches and bite marks spread out over his torso. Looking down to ensure his manhood was still intact, he noticed two rather deep puncture wounds high up on his left thigh, just inches from his genitals. He touched the wound gingerly, feeling no anger or revulsion, only a sense of wonder bordering on admiration. What an amazing woman, he thought. So wet and sticky. And cold. The whole experience was little more than a blur now, a fuzzy collage of wet kisses and pearl-white skin lost in a tangle of limbs and gnashing teeth. Closing his eyes, he could see her more clearly: the white face looming out of the pool of darkness; the wet red lips; the flash of the teeth.

"Hell of a night." He nodded absently to his pale reflection in the mirror before he turned to go. "One hell of a night."

Thor was standing at the foot of the stairs, delighted to see that his master had finally risen. The Lab greeted him enthusiastically, his tail thumping madly as he brushed up against his master's legs. Still groggy and unprepared for the high-spirited contact, Vinnie nearly tripped as he stepped off the last stair. He lashed out angrily at the dog, kicking the unsuspecting animal in the hindquarters.

"Goddamn dog! Stay the fuck outta my way!" he hissed, oblivious to the look of terror and shame on the animal's face as it slinked off into the corner with his head bowed low to the floor.

Nana had witnessed the whole exchange from the kitchen and was mortified.

"Vincenczo!" she gasped, barely able to believe her eyes and ears. "What in heaven's name is wrong with you?" She abandoned the meal frying on the stove and stormed down the narrow hallway toward him, waving her spatula. Bits of scrambled egg dangled precipitously from the edge of the utensil as she shook it angrily in his face. "How dare you use that kind of filthy language in this house! This is not one of your corner taverns, boy!" With that, she brought the spatula down hard, whacking the lanky guitar player across the shoulder. "Treating your dog like that! You should be ashamed of yourself!"

The sudden blow of the kitchen utensil crashed through the wall of hubris and contempt surrounding him, letting him see, with shocking clarity, the ugly nature of the mask that he wore. A rictus of shame and embarrassment worked its way across his face as the self-loathing welled up from deep inside him.

"I'm sorry, Nan," he said, hanging his head, unable to look his grandmother in the eye.

She narrowed her eyes and looked at him hard, the initial shock brought on by his behavior gone. She could see he did not look well at all.

"Are you all right, Vincenczo?" she asked, reaching up and putting her wrinkled palm against the cheek of his face, concerned by his pallor and the clammy texture of his skin. "Do you want me to call the doctor?"

"No, I'm fine, Nan," he lied, self-consciously pulling his robe tight across his marked chest. "I think maybe I'm coming down with a cold. I'll take some Tylenol and I'll be fine. Hey, boy," he said, calling out to Thor, eager to make amends, "come by Daddy. C'mon, Thor. . . ."

Thor emerged from behind the safe refuge of the sofa and hunkered out warily, the surprising sting of his master's outburst still fresh and immediate in his mind.

"C'mon, old boy," he urged as Nana left them to tend to his supper. "It's okay. Daddy's just a bit of an asshole."

Thor's tail wagged cautiously, testing the tension in the air before surrendering to his innate desire to please.

"Thatta boy," Vinnie said, patting him affectionately on his regal yellow head. "C'mon, let's go see what Nana's got cookin'."

The smell of ham sizzling in the frying pan amidst a pile of scrambled eggs laced with mozzarella cheese filled the kitchen and drifted out into the hallway. A queasy churning flip-flopped in his gut. Ignoring it, he kissed his grandmother on the cheek and pulled a carton of orange juice from the fridge. He sat down at the table where his lone place setting and a cup of fresh-brewed black coffee awaited him. Outside the window, the light was just starting to fade from the sky. Yes, he liked that.

"So—tell me about your night, Vincenczo," Nana said as she came up behind him, scooping a steaming pile of cheesy eggs and fried ham onto his plate. "You won, heh? I knew you would. That's a nice little group you boys have there. The music, I'm not so crazy about, but what do I know, heh?"

The band. He had almost forgotten all about the major coup that they had scored last night. "Not much to say, Nan," he said, fighting off nausea as the aroma of the food sitting in front of him wafted up into his nostrils. Usually his favorite breakfast after a long night, the sight and the smell of the heaping pile of ham and eggs were almost unbearable. "We came. We saw. We kicked a little ass," he said jokingly, backing away slightly from the food. "Looks like we might have a new gig, too. I gotta talk to Kenney and touch base with . . ." He blanched, unable to contain the nausea welling up from the pit of his stomach. He bolted up out of his chair and scrambled down the hall, barely making it to the bathroom, where he slammed the door shut behind him.

Dragana Navokovich sat at the kitchen table, staring at the untouched meal she had prepared for her grandson, and listened to the intermittent sounds of his retching coming from behind the bathroom door in the hallway. He was no angel, she knew, but this was not like him. The foul language. Throwing up like a schoolgirl after her first can of beer. Mistreating the dog like that! My goodness, she thought, getting up to clear the table. What on earth could have gotten into him?

Twenty-nine

Kenney Brandt was feeling the slightest bit of anxiety as he parked his shitty blue Maverick across the street from The Drop Zone and fingered the contract that was neatly folded in the inner pocket of his windbreaker. He'd gone over it with the proverbial fine-tooth comb earlier that evening after sleeping off the cruel hangover with a solid nine hours of sack time.

Almost a full day removed from the frenetic magic of last night's performance and the ensuing chaos of the party that followed, he found his recollections of the events surrealistic and detached, almost as if they had happened to someone else a long time ago. As if to lend credence to the developments, he pulled the crisply folded, multipage contract from his jacket and gave it a quick once-over by the dim light cast from the dashboard.

All in all, it could have been a lot worse. They were lucky Ruder didn't pants them when you think about how shit-faced they all were. The only hitch was the exclusivity clause, which pretty much stated that they were bound to Ruder and his corporation, Stardust Enterprises, for one year. Ruder had the right to drop them at anytime or pick up and extend the option for two more years if he so pleased. Furthermore, Stardust was entitled to thirty percent, right off the top, to any profits made from the sale of GloryDaze music or merchandise (merchandise!) while under the management and promotion of Stardust Enterprises—which, as far as he could figure, would only be a problem if they hit it big. Really not a bad problem to have when you consider that last week they were a garage band playing for beer money.

Maybe things were finally going to turn around for him. He had screwed up the courage to call Georgia earlier, unable to get the smiling face and the sweet smell of the beautiful waitress off his mind. They had talked for almost an hour. Turns out, she was only hustling drinks to pay her way through nursing school. She would be hanging up her apron for good upon graduation in June to pursue a career as a surgical nurse, hopefully in the trauma unit at Cook County Hospital. The conversation was light and breezy. They had both shared a sly, somewhat embarrassed laugh over their murky sexual encounter that really was no encounter at all, since he had passed out before anything of any consequence could happen. She had suggested that he could give it another shot if he cared to take her out on a proper date, and it just so happened she was free tomorrow evening after school.

Funny, the difference one night could make in your life.

He switched off the wipers and watched the light, intermittent rain bead up on his windshield. The hundreds of tiny droplets mirrored the buzzing yellow glow cast by the neon sign hanging over the entrance of his favorite watering hole. He had designed that sign, when his old friend first opened the small tavern a few years back, and he felt a certain amount of satisfaction every time he walked under it and through the doors, which was often. Looking at it now, he realized it was probably just a little too "busy." The words "Drop" and "Zone" shared the same letter "O," stylized to look like a splashing drop of beer, and it took a moment for the viewer to realize exactly what it was supposed to be. Other than that, it was pretty damn good, and you couldn't beat the price, which was free (although Tommy was more than generous about spotting Kenney beers on the house). Tommy was a few years older than Kenney, and although they had never really palled around much, they ran in the same circles and had known each other since they were boys, which counted for something. Tommy had given the band their first break, letting them gig there even before Vinnie came on board and made them a solid draw. Eventually the band's reputation grew and made the "Zone" the place to be on Friday nights.

Kenney cut the ignition and sat for a moment in the silence, listening to the light patter of the rain on the roof of the car. "Well, shit," he said aloud. "Did he think we were going to play there forever?"

Rather than fiddle with the damned bungee cord on the driver's side, Kenney Brandt crawled across the stick shift on the floor and let himself out the passenger side. Stepping into the light rain, he jogged across the street and paused for a moment in the doorway, rehearsing how he would tell Tommy that their days of playing at The Drop Zone for pocket change were history.

The joint was about half full, which was a pretty good crowd for a Sunday night. No doubt a result of the Blackhawks-Mapleleafs game being aired. He nodded to his friend as he made his way down the bar, greeting the few familiar faces scattered about, and found a quiet seat on the far end between a couple of empty stools.

"I understand congratulations are in order," Tommy said, wiping the bar and setting a cardboard coaster down in front of him. "Word is, you guys really lit it up last night. Budweiser?"

Kenney smiled nervously. "Yeah, thanks, Tommy. Good crowd tonight."

"Good drinking crowd," Tommy agreed. "Best thing I ever did, showing cable-TV sports. That and the live music on the weekends. But pretty soon you guys will be too big to swim in this little pond."

Sooner than you think, Kenney thought, pulling a new fifty-dollar bill from his wallet and laying it out on the bar next to his cigarettes. "Eh . . . yeah, that's what I wanted to talk to you about Tommy. We landed a big fish last night. A chance to play the Pharaoh Room at the Sphinx."

"Pharaoh Room, huh?" Tommy said, yanking a cold Bud from the freezer beneath the bar and sliding it in front of Kenney. "No shit. I hope you took it."

"Yeah, we took it," Kenney said, trying to get a read on Tommy's reaction. "It's a good move. A big step. We figure—"

"When do you start?" Tommy asked, cutting right to the chase.

Kenney squared himself up on his stool and looked his old friend in the eye.

"Friday."

"Friday!" Tommy exclaimed, somewhat taken aback by the finality of the single word. "Holy shit. You couldn't give me one week's notice?"

"I tried, Tommy, but this guy kind of put the screws to me," Kenney said, shaken by his friend's reaction. "He said he needed us in a pinch. His house band crapped out on him and he had to fill the slot right away. He said if we didn't want it, he was going to offer it to someone else. It was a onetime offer, we had to take it or leave it."

"Hey, fuck it. Don't worry about it," Tommy said, waving off Kenney's apology. "You just sort of caught me off guard. You guys were sendin' me to the fuckin' poorhouse anyway with all the beer you drank between sets."

The joke eased the tension between the two old friends, and Kenney let out a relieved laugh as he stuck a cigarette in his mouth and fished around in his jacket for a match. "Hey, thanks for being so cool about this, Tommy. I was scared you were gonna be pissed."

"Fuck that," Tommy said, reaching across the bar and lighting Kenney's smoke. "I'm happy for you guys. Now I can say I knew you when. The rest of 'em coming in tonight?"

"Yeah, they ought to be drifting in any minute now. I wanted to get here a little early and talk to you," Kenney replied, pushing the crisp fifty toward Tommy. "Hey, gimme a pack of Cheyenne Lights and give everyone in the house another round."

He had always wanted to do that.

Tommy feigned mild shock and clutched at his heart. "Whoa! I never thought I'd see the day!" He pulled the fifty off the bar and looked at it as if awestruck, still intent on busting Kenney's balls a little more before he let him off the hook. "Kenney Brandt buys one for the house! I think I read something in the Bible about this and the end of the world."

Dave and Johnny drifted in a short time later, and by the time the Blackhawks took to the ice for the start of the third period, Vinnie had stumbled in, not looking nearly as rested and refreshed as the rest of them appeared to be. The lazy charm and carefree attitude that he normally exuded was notably lacking. The guitar player made straight for the small round table in the back where his bandmates sat, barely acknowledging the salvo of greetings that were showered upon him whenever he walked in the door. Dave, in high spirits as usual, couldn't resist needling the lanky guitarist as he sat down and pulled the mirrored sunglasses from his face.

"Well, shit, look what the cat dragged in! Vinnie the Razor not looking real sharp tonight. Hey, Tommy," he yelled, not realizing the awful validity of his words, "get my friend here a beer quick. He looks like he needs to replenish his vital fluids."

"Make it a screwdriver, Tommy," Vinnie said. "Lots of juice and a tall glass."

"A screwdriver?" Dave asked incredulously. "What kind of pussy-ass drink is that? Since when do you drink anything besides beer?"

Vinnie, normally one to enjoy a lighthearted volley of ball-busting as much as the next guy, merely glared at the big drummer. A look of sheer hatred flashed in his eyes for just a moment and then was gone.

"All right, ladies, let's get down to business," Kenney said quickly, trying to cut the sudden, uncomfortable tension at the small table. "We've got a lot of ground to cover here. Now, I went over this page by page," he continued, pulling the contract from his pocket and spreading it out on the table for all of them to see, "and while it's a pretty good deal overall, it does have some drawbacks. Number one: We're bound to Barry Ruder and Stardust Enterprises for one year, with Stardust having the option of picking us up for another two at the end of that year if they so desire."

"And what," Dave asked, "if we so desire to tell them to fuck off?"

"Yeah," Johnny piped in, "like, what if something better comes along?"

"It's not that easy, guys. We don't have an escape clause. We're in bed with these guys for at least a year. Now on the flip side of that, we'll benefit from the heavy exposure of their promotions department. The Sphinx is a major club. You guys have all heard their spots on the radio, and being more or less the official house band, GloryDaze will become synonymous with the Sphinx and Stardust Enterprises." Kenney paused, letting that sink in. "In addition to the radio spots, they advertise heavily in the *Illinois Entertainer*, the *Reader*, and the weekend pull-outs of both the *Times* and the *Trib*. Now, let's say that within that one-year time span, we strike gold: record deal, tour offer, chartbusting single, whatever. Stardust handles that and takes thirty per—" He stopped dead in the middle of the glib tutorial dialogue he had been spinning. Monique and a friend of hers, a no-talent photographer known far and wide as Lauren the Bitch, were walking through the double doors.

"Uh-oh," Dave said to no one in particular.

Monique looked great as usual, and Kenney felt the familiar tug in his heart as the two women, turning heads in the synchronous manner of falling dominoes, made their way down the bar. They took their time, chatting it up with a few of the regulars before wandering up to Kenney's small table as if by pure chance.

"Hi, boys. Mind if we sit down?" Monique asked, pulling a stool from the bar and sliding it in between Dave and Johnny.

"There's an empty spot on my face here, Lauren honey, but you better hurry. It fills up quick," Dave said to Lauren as she searched for an empty bar stool.

"I'll have to take a pass on that, Dave. I draw the line on bestiality," Lauren quipped as she found a stool and dragged it across the floor.

"Well, my dog will be glad to hear that!" Dave said, taking a long swallow of beer and wiping the foam from his bearded face.

"Come on now, you two," Monique said, smiling at Kenney. "Let's play nice."

By the time eleven o'clock had rolled around, Lauren had relinquished her bar stool altogether and had found a more comfortable seat on Dave's lap. Apparently, four beers were just enough to blur her delineation of the species, Kenney thought with quiet disgust. Monique had all but abandoned her charade of why she had come here tonight and had cozied up to Vinnie, who despite his laconic manner seemed very willing to accept her obvious attempt at reconciliation.

Although the sting was lessened considerably by the mere presence of Georgia's phone number in his wallet,

Kenney still carried a torch for the beautiful sculptress that time alone had failed to extinguish. Unable to watch the spectacle unfolding before him any longer, he decided to call it a night. "Well," he said, checking his watch for effect, "six o'clock rolls around awful early. I'm gonna take off. I'll talk to you guys tomorrow."

"Still subbing, Kenney?" Lauren asked, knowing full well that he had yet to find a real job.

"Yeah," Kenney answered bitterly. "It pays the bills. We all don't have the luxury of going to college forever on Mommy and Daddy's money like some people."

That shut her up. Lauren came from a big-money Pittsburgh family and had aimlessly wandered the halls of the Chicago Institute for Artistic Study for four years before even declaring a major.

"Hey, can I catch a ride with you, Kenney?" Johnny asked quickly, realizing there would be little room in Dave's truck for him with Lauren the Bitch.

"Yeah, drink up," Kenney said, slightly aggravated that he would have to go so far out of his way now. "I'll talk to you guys later. Nice seeing you, Monique."

"You too, Kenney," she answered, briefly putting a few inches of space between her and Vinnie. "And congratulations—on last night I mean."

They laid in bed, sleeping the deep sleep that follows long and passionate lovemaking, completely unaware of the vampire watching outside the window, clinging like a spider to the wet bricks three stories above the sidewalk. They did not hear the beast undo the latch and enter the loft, gliding like a phantom across the cement floor toward the dressing table in the corner. Suppressing the urge to wake the whore and kill her where she lay, Lizabet Bazore pulled a single strand of hair from Monique's brush. She paused at the foot of their bed and glowered at the sight of the two lovers intertwined in the tangle of covers. With her long fingernail she scooped a drop of sweat that had settled in the small of Monique's back and placed it, together with the hair, into a small pill container she had snatched from the dresser. Capping the vial, she bent low over the prone body of Vincenczo Rosario, silently watching the steady rise and fall of his chest, the almost imperceptible beating of his heart. He twitched slightly, his face contorting into a tight grimace as her lips brushed feather-light across his own. The charmed perfume of lilac was barely able to camouflage the stench of death and decay that drifted up from the core of her being, where her soul had once been. The sheet stretched across the man's loins rose like a totem in response to the whispered kiss. The succubus saw this and smiled a horrible, smug smile, full of sharp teeth, before slipping out the window and disappearing into the night.

Thirty

Drew Richards was whistling a happy tune as he shuffled across the Dearborn Street Bridge. The people that he passed on the crowded walkway gave the squalid little man in the khaki-green army-surplus jacket a wide berth. They saw in his eyes the detached but obvious focus of the truly mad. He had had a very busy day indeed, what with running back and forth between City Hall and First National Bank and the closing at Knebloff and Rottman. It had taken him less than a month to tie up all the loose ends after securing the deed, using his easy access to the archives at the Cook County Recorder of Deeds office to circumvent the mountains of paperwork common to dealings with City Hall.

He thought old John McInerney would flat-out shit when he handed him that certified check for the back taxes: $275,883. Thank you very much.

Sure would like to meet that gal you're working for, Drew, he had said, sliding the deed across the counter. I could stand to meet a nice rich broad with all sorts of money to throw around.

No, I don't think you'd like to meet her, Johnny, you old fuck. I don't think you would like that at all.

He picked up his pace as the gabled roof of the vampire's lair came into view. He broke into a gallop across Ontario Street, the briefcase slapping against his thigh in his haste to deliver the news to the mistress. Reaching the entryway, he stood between the large stone pillars flanking the oak doors and fumbled for the keys in his pocket nearly dropping them before sliding the shiny new key into the lock and driving it home. He felt the initial resistance of the old tumblers give way and entered the building legally for the first time.

Viewing the vast foyer from this vantage point, he could, even in the fading light of the evening sky filtering in through the windows, see the jewel that lay hidden beneath the layers of old paint and years of neglect. He stood there a moment, looking around, imagining the place within a year's time, completely restored to its original glory. Now that the trivial legalities involved with securing the deed were out of the way, he vowed to devote his every waking hour to its restoration. He would never rest until he transformed the crumbling edifice into a palace, a temple worthy of housing his queen. Yes, that is why she had chosen this place. That is why she had chosen *him.*

Scurrying over to his worktable, he unhooked the halogen work light from the small generator and ran the extension cord over to the nearest outlet on the far wall. Nothing. Damn Con Ed, they had told him the electricity would be turned on by three o'clock. No matter. He would get by with the generator until tomorrow. Stripping off his coat, he set about preparing for a few hours of work before the mistress awoke. He was changing the circular belt on his power sander when he heard the most wonderful sound in the whole world, the silvery sound of her voice whispering his name.

He whirled around and there she was. She stood in the hallway beneath the main staircase, a shimmering angel framed by the vaulted archway.

"Drew," she said again, a hint of a smile in the corners of her red mouth. "Drew, darling, you have news for me?"

"Yes!" he almost shouted, so overcome with joy to see

her. "Yes, Mistress, great news! I can't wait to tell you—the most marvelous news!"

"Well, then," she said, "you must tell me, Drew." She glided over to the large high-backed chair against the west wall, away from the direct rays of the sun, and poured herself into it. "Crawl to me and tell me of your news."

Drew Richards dropped the sander and fell to his knees in the sawdust, his heart pounding in his ears as he thanked the heavens above for blessing him so. At last! A chance to truly serve! Barely able to control his rapid breathing, he swallowed hard and crawled on his hands and knees toward the vision of his queen, looming over him, smiling down at him from her throne.

"That's far enough," she snapped when he had reached the tips of her shiny black patent leather pumps. Slowly pulling the slit of her long gown to one side, she crossed her legs. Her dangling foot swung slowly back and forth in front of his lowered face. "Tell me, little man, have you secured the title of this dwelling, as you promised you would?"

"Yes," he croaked, choking back a moan. "Yes, it is just as we had discussed. Everything—everything is in order."

"Details," she demanded, nudging the side of his face with the pump. "Tell me everything." With agonizing deliberation and a breathy sigh expressed solely for his benefit, she uncrossed her long nyloned legs and planted her feet squarely on the floor on each side of his bowed head.

He tried to pull himself together, to speak clearly and succinctly. He tried to tell the mistress exactly what she wanted to hear in a timely and concise manner, but the glimpse he had stolen of the dark paradise nestled between the milky expanse of her parted thighs—that was too much for him to bear.

"An ac-ac-ac . . . the mu, mu, mu—balance! The ba-ba-ba . . ." He stammered, unable to stop the rapid-fire stutter even as it was clattering off his twisted tongue with the choppy cadence of a V-8 engine running on seven cylinders. The sharp and sudden crack of her hand across his face snapped his head violently to the side, bringing with it an explosion of electric snow, blinding him for just a moment. Ah yes, that was just what he needed. She knew. She always knew.

"The balance of the mortgage due," he continued, the words now flowing like the rhythmic exhaust note of a finely tuned motor, "along with a percentage of yearly real-estate taxes, will be drawn monthly from the Cachtice Imports corporate account at First National. You're entitled to a sizable income tax break at year's end if this property is listed as a business rather than a residential structure, so long as you fail to show a profit—a luxury you're privy to for your first five years. After that, you can expect to pay considerably more, but we'll cross that bridge when we come to it. Using the Social Security number of one, Charlene Scurlock—recently deceased—I managed, through some file pilfering at City Hall's Department of Records, and very creative computer programming, to give you an official identity. As far as the state of Illinois, the county of Cook, and the United States government are concerned, you are Lizabet Bazore, president and owner of Cachtice Imports, Social Security number, 391—"

"Enough," the vampire snapped, quite pleased with the meticulous efficiency of her loyal manservant. It was almost a shame she had to kill him, but he was, unfortunately, a victim of his own proficiency. He had performed his assigned tasks so well that she no longer had any use for him, and he was simply too repulsive and undesirable to keep around as a luxury. "You've done well, Drew," she cooed, spreading her legs just a little farther apart. "Come closer, my darling boy. I have a surprise for you."

Drew Richards raised his eyes from the floor and found himself surrounded by the serpentine curves of her shapely calves, the dark garden of forbidden fruit coming into focus beyond her kneecaps. Looking up, he could see the auburn thatch of pubic hair twinkling like a distant star, snug and inviting amid the taut white flesh of her thighs. As he inched closer, taking great care not to touch her in his haste, he could smell the thick perfume of lilac, so powerful it made his head swim.

"Yes," she laughed, bringing her feet up off the floor and draping them over his narrow shoulders, "know the essence of womanhood. Taste the nectar of the flower that gives rise to life itself." She crossed her ankles on his back and pulled him closer still. He could feel the scratchy fabric of her sheer nylons rubbing the sides of his face. Oh God, any second now he would explode.

"Ooh, not yet, little one," she laughed. "I am not ready. You are not a selfish lover, are you?"

Something like a moan rose up from deep inside him and the monster clamped her legs tight around his neck catching the sound in his throat as his windpipe closed shut. The revenant lifted the aromatic glamour spell, and the stench of a thousand rotting corpses assaulted his olfactory senses as he desperately tried to draw air into his lungs. Lizabet Bazore squealed with delight and increased the pressure on his neck. The mangy little man kicked and clawed at the floor in a spastic dance of death, spittle and blood dripping from his open mouth.

"Yes, I think I'm ready now," she stated matter-of-factly, watching his face turn from red to purple. Feeling her victim was on the verge of passing out, the vampire rolled her hips in the chair. Drew Richards's neck snapped like a pretzel stick, the click of the vertebrae cracking barely audible above her peals of laughter. "Now I quite enjoyed that! Was it good for you, too, darling?" she giggled. She opened her legs and let the body roll to the floor with a muffled thud.

Chloe's voice, angry and disbelieving, rose up from behind her and answered for the dead man on the floor. "What have you done now? Who will attend to the daylight matters? This was not part of the plan! You—"

"Silence!" the ancient one hissed without turning around. She had felt Chloe's presence before the young vampire had walked into the room and had prolonged the spectacle just long enough for her to see the fatal conclusion. "You will not question me," she said, rising from the chair so quickly no mortal eye could see. In a flash she was in the doorway, inches from Chloe's face, assertive, almost confrontational. "I will do *as I please* when it pleases *me.*" She softened slightly, the menacing edge less apparent but still present in her voice. "We no longer need his services. He had long outlived his usefulness, and that," she said, motioning toward the twisted corpse at the foot of the chair, "is what awaits those who cease to be of service and become a burden to me."

Chloe stood her ground but swallowed her anger. They had sparred over trivial matters in the past, but nothing that would induce anger or elicit a threat—and that was a threat, thinly veiled, but a threat nonetheless.

"Now," the old one said, brushing past Chloe, "make yourself useful and clean that up."

Thirty-one

Johnny Coltrane was struggling not to become airborne as the wind roared down the concrete canyon formed by the tall buildings flanking Jackson Boulevard. The gusts caught the broadside of the oversize portfolio he was carrying, creating a sail effect that made forward progress difficult, if not at times impossible. Hefting the cumbersome display case back down to earth with both hands, he forged ahead, cursing the blustery wind with every shambling step.

He was not in a good mood. There had been a critique tonight in his watercolor class and the reviews of his work were less than encouraging. He had expected as much from his peers, a shallow, arrogant bunch that wore the label of "artist" like a badge of superiority, even though they had yet to master even the most rudimentary drawing skills. The bashing from Professor Blaylock, though, a teacher whose work he admired and whose opinion he respected, was both unexpected and embarrassing. Calling his work—a highly detailed series of large still lifes—"heavy-handed and conceptually uninspired," was akin to ringing the dinner bell for the avant-garde students eager to attack his traditional rendering style as boring and "obsolete with the invention of the camera." The last comment, a snippy remark from a sneering punk-rocker with lots of purple hair and very little talent, infuriated him to no end. Just what the hell was that supposed to mean?

The advent of photography releases the artist from his basic obligation to be able to draw? Man, what bullshit! He couldn't wait until tomorrow night when purple-hair would put his work up on the wall, and he could expose *him* for the fraud he was.

Angry and disillusioned, Johnny strode with head down into the teeth of the howling wind. He was mentally sharpening his verbal ax in preparation for tomorrow night's critique when he looked up and saw her.

She was less than a block away, a glimmer of golden effervescence flickering like a perpetual flame. She was seemingly unaffected by the gale forces, save for the locks of silky hair lashing about her narrow shoulders. He had been thinking of nothing but her for the last two days, until the savaging of his paintings struck a nerve and rousted him from the idyllic funk he had been in since Sunday morning. Seeing her now, he felt an immediate and irrefutable calm bordering on bliss. The bitterness and anger pent up inside of him blew away like ashes from a distant fire, inconsequential and harmless.

She paused at the corner under the El platform, a pensive, almost sad smile hiding in the corners of her dazzling eyes.

"Forgive me, I could not stay away," he heard her say above the hellish racket of the train clamoring by overhead, although her lips did not move.

No never. Never stay away, he thought rushing across Wabash against the light, oblivious to the blare of the car horn. That thought coaxed her smile out of hiding, letting it fall full-blown onto a face clearly unaccustomed to such expressions of happiness. It lingered there on her lips like a lone fall rose in a winter landscape, beautiful, foreign, and ultimately doomed.

"I was praying I'd see you again," he said. He touched her arm, feeling the leather of her jacket between his fingers, substantial and real. "I was beginning to think I dreamed the whole thing up!"

"Be careful what you ask for," she teased, unable to resist aping the verse from their song "Thrush." "There's much that you don't know."

He laughed. "You can say that again. What are you doing here? Do you work in the Loop? How did you know where I was?" He suddenly realized he knew almost nothing about her in spite of the fact that they had talked for hours, taking Saturday night into Sunday morning and beyond.

"Is that your artwork?" she asked, motioning to the portfolio flapping against his leg. "I would love to see it."

He smiled. "Has anyone ever told you that you have an unusual flair for changing the subject?" He fingered the wallet in his back pocket, full of crisp twenties from his cut of the prize money, and eyed the flashing sign of the Exchequer Pub blinking behind her head. "Hey, what do you say we get out of this wind tunnel. You feel like grabbing a pizza and a couple of beers?"

She hedged, not wanting to go through the whole charade of dealing with their food—pushing it around on her plate, pretending not to be hungry. Her body, with its altered digestive system, no longer had the ability to break down or draw nutrients from solid food and would, she had discovered, consequently reject it if she tried for some reason to ingest it. "I dislike crowds," she said, frowning, then brightening. "Can we go back to your place?"

"Sure," he laughed, delighted with the suggestion. "I'll take you upstairs and show you my etchings."

"That was fun," Chloe said, pushing her way through the turnstile at the Ravenswood Armitage station. "What do you call that thing again?"

"It's called the 'El,' " Kenney said with a laugh. "Short for 'elevated train,' until, of course, it goes into the subway, then it's called, naturally enough, a subway train."

"I know what a subway train is," Chloe chirped. "I also know that *sub* is short for subterranean, which, naturally enough, you never stopped to consider."

He had to laugh again as they walked to the corner and turned up Kenmore Street. Funny, but he never did stop to consider that. "Most people wouldn't," he said, wondering how she knew he was one of them.

"I'm not like most people," she replied, a hint of melancholy in her voice now.

"Understatement of the year. Well," he announced, somewhat surprised to see that she had already turned and was making her way up his front steps, "here we are."

"It just looks like the kind of place where a fledgling artist-slash-musician would live," she explained, seeing the perplexed expression on his face. "Come on, I want to see those etchings."

"Okay," he said, unlocking the door and leading her up the stairway, "but I'm warning you, the maid hasn't been in yet this week."

The place was relatively neat for a young single guy living alone. The Coltrane household in Belvidere was modest but always spotless, right down to the crisp white doilies his mother would lay out on the polished wood tables and chair arms. He had always hated those doilies, but years of living under Anne Coltrane's roof had instilled in him an appreciation for sanitary surroundings that he found lacking in many of his fellow students living away from home for the first time. Jeez, some of them lived like animals.

"You have a nice place here, Johnny," she exclaimed, amused and oddly pleased by his penchant for neatness. His drawing table, a large, smooth slab of maple sitting at a seventy-five-degree angle atop a wide rectangular storage cabinet that served as its base, dominated most of the tiny living room. Drawings in various stages of completion were tacked to an expansive sheet of corkboard mounted on the wall behind the table, and a rickety wooden easel stood in the corner supporting a tall blank canvas. An old couch wearing a beige slipcover acted as a partition, separating the "studio" portion from the rest of the living room, leaving just enough space for another chair and a bookcase with a small television and stereo system crowded on top of its scarred surface. A hunk of particleboard laid over two metal milk crates, stuffed tight with albums, served as a makeshift coffee table upon which a dog-eared copy of the essential *History of Art* rested, along with a rather full ashtray. She stared at the half-empty pack of Cheyennes next to the ashtray, unable to comprehend the sudden sting of grief.

"Make yourself at home," he said, slipping the bulky portfolio behind the couch. "Can I get you anything? A beer? A can of pop? Here, let me take your coat."

"No, thank you," Chloe replied, slipping off her jacket and handing it to him. "I'm fine. This is such a charming little place you have here," she said, feeling a twinge of sadness. His modest but comfortable living quarters somehow gave a substance she preferred not to acknowledge to the faceless food supply out there, wandering through their short and inconsequential lives. For a moment she could not help but feel an unwelcome compassion for the plight of his kind. How many had fallen to her in her time? Thousands? How many more to come?

"Charming?" he yelled from the closet. "That's a new one. No one's ever called it charming before. Not that I get a lot of visitors."

"Oh, come now, Johnny Coltrane," she replied, looking at the work in progress on his drawing table. "A young handsome artist and budding rock and roll star?

I'm sure there is a steady flow of eager young women through these doors."

He laughed. "Actually, I guess I'm what you would call a little on the shy side. I certainly wouldn't classify myself as an artist just yet, *art student* maybe, and the whole rock and roll thing kind of took me by surprise. I mean, I've always had a pretty good voice and I could blow a decent harp. But aside from singing in the church choir back in Belvidere—well, shit, I could never imagine myself getting up and singing in front of all those people before I came to Chicago and met Kenney. My parents wouldn't believe it if they saw it! Besides," he said, grabbing a beer from the refrigerator, "I get kind of tongue-tied around girls, and the two or three I've had up here weren't nearly as pretty as you."

Hearing this pleased her more than it should have and she smiled like a schoolgirl, hating herself for it immediately. "That's very sweet of you to say, Johnny," Chloe said, staring at the collection of drawings tacked up on the corkboard behind his drawing table. "You have a very distinctive style. It reminds me of the work of Carlos Schwabe."

"Carlos Schwabe?" Johnny said, coming up behind her and setting a glass of ice water on the drawing table at her elbow. "For you—in case you're thirsty," he said, indicating the glass. "I don't believe I'm familiar with him."

"He was a member of the Symbolist movement—popular for a very brief time in Europe at the turn of the century. They were kind of buried underneath the sweeping success of the Impressionists and lost in the bleak functionalism that pervaded the arts after the First World War. Gauguin and Seurat waded briefly into Symbolist waters, but Moreau probably remains"—she stopped, a quizzical, almost distressed expression on her face—"the most well-known." She had no idea how she knew that or where the textbook-style synopsis of the Symbolist movement came from. Up until a moment ago she could not recall knowing or caring a thing about it.

Johnny was looking at her in amazement. "Wow," he exclaimed. "Someone really knows their art history. I didn't realize you were so well versed in obscure movements of nineteenth-century European art."

"Neither did I," she said with a halfhearted laugh. "Must have been something I read in a book a long time ago." She thought for a moment that she might cry. "But," she continued, eager to change the subject, "that is of little concern. We're here to look at your work and I must say I'm very impressed."

"Aaah, it's okay," Johnny said, taking a quick swallow of his beer. "The whole art scene has got me in kind of a funk right now, to tell you the truth. I look at all the money I'm spending on this education and I have to ask myself if I'm doing the right thing. I mean, back in my little town I was easily the best artist anyone could remember, but here I'm just another guy that can draw. I look at guys like my friend Kenney Brandt, the best artist I've ever met, and I see him substitute teaching to get by. Busting his hump trying to scarf up any measly little commission, taking shit from uppity gallery owners, who are only concerned with riding the next trend—man, I don't know. It's kind of scary."

He took another swallow of his beer, a good long one this time. "I've been loading up on graphics courses the last two semesters, sort of like a parachute to fall back on if I don't take the art world by storm—and it doesn't appear that I will. But then again, do I really want to spend my life designing fold-out brochures and doing key-line and paste-up? I don't think so."

She looked at him, saddened by the maelstrom of emotions and conflicts confronting him. She never realized *their* lives could be so complicated.

"But, hey . . . ," he said, seeing that he had cast a slight pall on the mood in the room, "I still have the band. If I become a rich and famous rock and roll star, I won't have to worry about selling out and wondering where my next paycheck is coming from. I won't have to worry about a thing."

"And you would like that?" Chloe asked innocently.

"Like it? Hell, yeah! I'd love it. Who wouldn't? It's the dream of every kid who's ever strapped a guitar over his shoulder. Unfortunately," he lamented, "there are about as many aspiring rock stars out there as there are starving artists. It's hard to catch a break. Ask any waiter."

"Why would I want to ask a waiter?" Chloe asked, puzzled.

"Because they're all waiting tables *waiting* for something to pop with their so-called 'real' careers," Johnny explained. "Nobody *wants* to be a waiter."

"I see," Chloe said. "And what would it take for you to catch this break?"

"Hard to say," Johnny said thoughtfully. "Being in the right place at the right time has a lot to do with it. Getting someone in the industry to listen to a demo tape—that's how we got the chance to play in the Battle of the Bands at the WhereHouse. Look what happened there—we got a good paying weekly gig at a top club, and best of all, I met you."

She smiled again. He could say the simplest, sweetest things with that beautiful voice and he was so pleasing to look at. How could she stay away? "Yes," she said a little sarcastically, "aren't you the lucky one?"

"Well, things do seem to be going my way lately," Johnny said. "I got lucky coming to Chicago and hooking up with Kenney. We form a band, our guitar player quits school, and Vinnie comes on board. Now, that was either pure luck or divine intervention. Of course my dad always said you make your own luck, but then is that really luck? I mean, I'm talking more like fate, you know? Like suppose I'm walking down the street tomorrow and a car jumps the curb and hits me. Wrong place, wrong time, right? Maybe. Or maybe it was just supposed to happen like that, maybe that was the fate laid out for me in some grand cosmic plan and there wasn't a damn thing I could do about it. Predestination they call it. Kind of scary, don't you think?"

"Yes," she said. "I know exactly what you mean and I can tell you from my own experience that we have little control over what fate holds in store. However, I like to think that we're given a predestined set of circumstances and allowed to make certain choices that can alter the course of events somewhat. I don't know why, but I take a little comfort in believing I have *some* control over my own destiny. But your lives are so short, Johnny. Why dwell on these things? Enjoy the time you have. Paint your pictures. Sing your songs."

"Yeah, I guess so," he said, puzzled. "What did you mean when you said 'your lives'? You said *your lives* are so short."

"Tell me," she said, changing the subject again, "this friend of yours—the guitar player, Vinnie. He is very important to you?"

"Important? Well, yeah. Without Vinnie we're just an average garage band making a lot of noise. We don't go anywhere without him. Why?"

"Let's just say I'm making one of those choices that will alter the course of events," she said, parting her wet lips and giving him a look that made his knees weak. "Come here, I want to give you a kiss."

Thirty-two

Vinnie the Razor stirred from his nap and stretched his long, well-toned arms high over his head, enjoying the sensual rush of blood flow into muscle tissue triggered by the mild exertion. Lying in bed, staring out his window at the new moon settling into the darkening sky, he felt a motivation to get out of bed and venture from the house—a drive that had been notably lacking through most of the daylight hours.

He hadn't gone to work today. The very thought of putting on those ridiculous scrubs and pushing that mop around the hospital was enough to make him ill. He knew Nana would put up a major bitch when she found out he was going out tonight after calling in sick at the hospital this morning. It was her friend Mrs. Borovich, who had gotten him the job, and how would it look if he got fired? You know his attendance record was nothing to brag about and blah, blah, blah. Well, he'd just have to file that in the "who gives a shit" pile along with the rest of her bitching and moaning. She was really starting to get on his nerves.

Rolling out of bed, he stepped lightly across the hardwood floor and pulled the little wooden cigar box down from the top shelf of his closet. Keeping his ears open for the sound of his grandmother coming up the steps, he tiptoed back to his bed and pulled a dime bag of Colombian Gold from the stash box and set about cleaning it.

Using a double-album cover as a plane, he deftly separated the seeds from the leafy plant. Tilting the cover at a forty-five-degree angle, he allowed the round seeds to roll down its surface, scooping the pot back up toward the top with the flat edge of his driver's license.

Satisfied with the end result, he dumped the seeds into the trash receptacle next to his bed and emptied the finished product back into the plastic sandwich bag. With the practiced skill of a seasoned pot smoker, he plucked a cigarette paper from the pack and rolled a joint, tight and perfect as any store-bought cigarette.

He sat at his half-open window and smoked the joint, letting his mind wander as he stared into the murky void of the night sky. She was out there somewhere. She was out there somewhere waiting for him, and all he had to do was venture out into the streets and she would find him. He knew that for certain.

He thought he would see her last night but she had only come to him in his dreams as he lay in bed with the other one, the whore Monique. Monique was nothing to him now, a brief dalliance in a moment of weakness. There would be no more instances like that without Lizabet there to share in the bounty. He took one more hit off the joint and wet the tip with his fingertips, dabbing it out completely on the windowsill before sticking the remaining half-joint back into his wooden stash box. He had tucked the box back up on the top shelf of his closet, out of his grandmother's prying reach, and was slipping into his favorite pair of blue jeans when he heard Thor's sudden and explosive barking from the kitchen below.

"Vincenczo!" Nana's voice called, frightened and shaky at the foot of the stairs. "Vincenczo!" she yelled, the alarm in her voice cutting through the clouds in his head and setting off the protective instincts reserved for loved ones in time of need. "Vincenczo, I think there's someone in the backyard!"

He rushed to the window and peered into the mottled shadows, trying to make out a discernible form, when he saw her. She was sitting, stretched out, across the wooden swing suspended from the overhang of his garage roof. Her white face, smiling up at him, bobbed in and out of his field of vision with the steady rhythm of a metronome before disappearing again under the eave of the garage with each lazy pass.

Lizabet.

He mouthed her name, mesmerized by the almost hypnotic oscillation of the porch swing, when suddenly it swung under the eaves and returned empty.

She was gone.

Taking the stairs two at a time, he bounded past his grandmother, tiny and frightened on the landing, and rushed to the back door.

"Vincenczo! What is it? What's wrong?" she asked over Thor's frantic and incessant barking, "Who is—"

"It's nothing, Nan," he said, unlocking the double dead bolts. "Nothing to be alarmed about. Don't worry, it's just . . ." He swung the door open and the vampire stood there, smiling at him, her white skin luminescent under the fuzzy glow of the porch light.

Thor let out with a harried wail and backed away from the door, snarling and baring his teeth. His nails clacked and slipped on the tile floor as he clawed for a foothold, bearing down into a defensive crouch in front of Nana Navokovich. He would die before he let the thing get any closer to her.

". . . a friend," Vinnie continued, opening the door wide and stepping aside.

He had let the beast into the house.

She stood there, ramrod straight, an exultant gleam in her eye as she surveyed the intimate surroundings of the homey little kitchen. Her frame relaxed visibly, falling into a more moderate, though somewhat still unnatural, attitude upon ascertaining that the dog was the only threat to her here.

"Nan," Vinnie began, as if introducing a school chum, "this is a friend of mine, Lizabet—Thor!" he yelled. "Stop it, boy! Go in the other room! Go on now! Get!"

"Perhaps it would be best," Lizabet said, reacting to the dog's distress, "if I waited outside. It appears that your . . . animal does not like me."

"Yes," Dragana said, looking the creature directly in the eye, "that's very strange. Thor likes everybody. That is most *unusual*. Maybe you had better wait outside."

The vampire smiled. Something had passed between the two of them. The old woman knew things. "A pleasure," she said before turning to go. "I shall see you again, I'm sure."

Dragana nodded and watched the woman back out of the room and close the door behind her. Thor, somewhat relaxed by her departure, stood his ground, alternately snarling and whining at the closed door.

"Vincenczo," Nana demanded, "who is that woman!" More of a demand than a question. "That is your *friend*? Where would you ever meet such a person? She looks too old for you. Where do you think you are going? Out? After not going to work today? I thought you were sick?"

"One question at a time, Nan," Vinnie said, tugging his cowboy boots on over his bare feet. He was in a hurry to be with *her*, and he had no time for the old woman's questions. "Yes, that's a friend of mine. And yes, I'm going out. I'm feeling much better now, thank you."

"I swear," she said, watching him hurry into a T-shirt and slip into his leather jacket, "sleep all day and go out all night. I've never seen anything like it. You're like a . . ." She stopped, unable to say the word.

"Don't wait up," he said curtly, slamming the door on her objections. He left without kissing her good-bye, something he had never done before. The sound of his footsteps clomping down the back steps led her to the window. She squinted into the darkness and saw the two of them disappear into the garage. A moment later, light poured from the little window cut into the side of the garage and she could see the porch swing, where the *thing* had sat smiling at her with its white face, still swaying in the walkway. The roar of his motorbike broke the terrible silence, and as she watched the bright cluster of red and amber running lights float down the alley and vanish from her sight, she felt a dread overtake her that had little to do with her fear of motorcycles.

"God be with him," she said, invoking the Lord's name in something other than anger for the first time since He took Vesna from her more than twenty years ago.

There was something foul about that woman, something unnatural. She knew of the old legends, but she would not allow herself to give voice to the thoughts clamoring in the back of her head. Knowing there would be no sleep for her this night, and because she could do little else, she padded to the refrigerator and hefted the gallon of milk from the top shelf, hoping a nice tall glass might calm an old lady's nerves.

"You saw it, too, old pup, didn't you?" she asked, patting the dog on the head as she sat down at the table. "Something not quite right about her, eh?" She took a sip from the tall glass, feeling the cold liquid pour over her gums and spit it back out, recoiling at the bitter taste.

"Oh—goodness," she gasped through her pursed lips. "How . . . ?" She had bought that gallon of milk at the Jewel just yesterday—double-checked the freshness date as she had always done and had a glass with her dinner this evening. Bringing the glass back up to her nose, she inhaled deeply just to make sure.

Sour.

With her hand shaking uncontrollably, she set the glass

back down on the table, her lips no longer able to suppress the word rattling off the back of her teeth.

"*Nosferatu.* . . ."

Thirty-three

"Faster!" she yelled in his ear, her laughter lost in the rush of wind blowing past her face. "Make it go faster!" The vampire, in all her supernatural aberrations, had never experienced the pure sensation of speed that she felt sitting atop the passenger perch of the Honda Super-Sport as it roared off the exit ramp of Interstate 55 and banked into the feeder lanes of northbound Lake Shore Drive.

Vinnie rolled the throttle on, bringing the motor into the meaty range of its power band, pushing the tachometer needle up toward its 9,500 rpm redline before backing off and power-shifting into fourth gear. The Honda screamed down the lakefront, rocketing past the somber Romanesque columns adorning Soldier Field and the picturesque beauty of Buckingham Fountain.

The traffic light at Jackson Boulevard was on the far end of yellow and turning to red when Vinnie toed the shift lever into fifth gear and grabbed the last handful of throttle left on the Honda's howling motor. Had they stopped, they may have turned and looked toward Columbus Boulevard in time to see Johnny Coltrane walking out of the Chicago Institute for Artistic Studies, but they blew through the light in a blur amidst a symphony of screeching brakes and honking horns. Vinnie's exhilaration turned to panic as he saw the stunted S-curve at Randolph hurtling toward him much sooner than he anticipated.

Vinnie downshifted and jumped on the brakes hard, using every possible inch of asphalt. He slid the bike across four lanes and nearly kissed the retaining wall that separated the oncoming traffic before bringing his speed down to an almost manageable seventy miles an hour. He leaned hard to his right, fighting to control the rear-end slide. The tire lost its grip and skittered across the asphalt like a flat rock over a smooth pond, flexing the machine's frame into a stomach-wrenching shudder that nearly pitched him off the bike. A shower of sparks poured out from beneath them as the right footpeg touched down, knocking the rear tire back down to earth. With a firm contact patch established, Vinnie wrenched the wayward missile out of its spin and into the mouth of the hard left dead ahead. He braked smoothly, finding an easy line through the tight sweeper and grabbed third gear on the way out. The front wheel inched off the ground as he dipped onto the Grand Avenue exit ramp and headed for River North.

"What a marvelous machine," Lizabet declared, climbing off the bike in front of the stone fortress on Dearborn Street. "I simply must have one. You will teach me to operate it."

Vinnie followed her up the stairs, nodding stupidly, still somewhat dazed from the near-death experience. "Uh, yeah, sure," he said, stepping across the threshold and stumbling after her in the darkness of the foyer. He nearly tripped over the bundle of rolled-up carpet that contained the lifeless body of Drew Richards. "Do you think you could turn—"

He felt a rush of air beside him and in an instant the room was awash in the glow of the hundreds of tiny light bulbs hanging like icicles from the massive chandelier in the middle of the room.

"How thoughtless of me," Lizabet said, smiling, standing next to him again. "I sometimes forget your eyesight leaves so much to be desired. We will certainly have to do something about that." She looked at the tall, angular guitar player, loving the way his dark curly hair fell over his broad shoulders. She could smell the heady scent of his olive skin. The urge to bite clean through it to the taut muscle underneath was almost overpowering. "Right now I can't figure out what to do with you."

"This place is unbelievable," Vinnie said, turning slowly and taking in the vast space. "I've seen it before but only from the outside. It's like a medieval castle."

"Yes, it is very comforting," Lizabet said. "You will excuse the disarray. I'm afraid my last worker proved inadequate and I had to . . . terminate him." She followed Vinnie's eyes to the rolled-up carpet. "So hard to find good help these days."

"I think this place used to be a nightclub," Vinnie said, his dull eyes brightening at the recollection. Was that a *body* rolled up in that carpet over there? Not that it mattered. He was with her now. *Now and forever.* "Look, you can see the marks on the floor where the bar used to be. Hey, maybe you should open up a club. We could be the house band." Anything to be closer to her.

"What an interesting idea," Lizabet said, pondering the thought of all that attractive young flesh milling about beneath her very roof. She imagined herself standing at the top of the stairs looking down at the sweaty throng. She could have her pick each night before closing the doors and sending the wretched souls home to their empty beds, only to come back again and again, offering themselves up as food for the gods. "Tell me, beautiful one, what would it take for such a thing to happen?"

"Money," Vinnie answered. "It would take a lot of money to turn this place into a top-shelf club." He thought for a moment. "When the band makes it big and we strike it rich, you can have it all. I'll give you everything," he declared, so desperate to please. "I only want to make you happy."

The vampire laughed, amused but genuinely touched by the mortal's misguided devotion. "That is a most generous offer, my sweet Adonis," she said, reaching out and stroking his cheek. "But I'm sure it would take much more revenue than your little band of musicians could ever generate."

"Oh no," Vinnie said. "There's big money to be made in rock and roll! Millions! The music business is a multibillion-dollar-a-year industry. It would only take one hit record for us to turn the corner. One platinum album and you could open up ten clubs!"

"Is that so?" she asked, her interest piqued. "Tell me more, Vincenczo Rosario."

"They live like royalty, the ones who make it big," he said excitedly. "Private jets, yachts, mansions . . . summer homes on the East Bank! The whole deal. We're almost there. I can feel it. We've got our own sound and we're building a following. One hit would put us over the top, I know it!"

"If what you say is true," she said, contemplating the fortune that would allow her to live in a manner more befitting her royal lineage, "then what is stopping you from making it so?"

"Well," he began, his enthusiasm tempered somewhat, "there's no guarantee. You need to find someone who will give you a shot. Someone in the industry willing to roll the dice and take a gamble on you. It takes a lot of time and money to record and promote an album. Talent and ambition don't always get it done. Sometimes you need a little luck."

"Luck is such an enigma to your kind, Vincenczo," she said, taking his hand and walking him across the foyer toward one of the narrow corridors branching out from the hub of the lobby. "You let it manipulate and shape your lives like pillars of sand yielding to the force of the wind. What you fail to see all around you are the tools to utilize those forces and make them work for you in much the same way a mariner harnesses the wind with a sail."

"Magic," he said, looking at her as if he had finally figured out the answer to some great riddle. "You're talking about magic. Witchcraft."

"It has many names and many interpretations," she explained as she led him down a dark hallway, the light from the chandelier fading with every step they took. "It has many practitioners throughout the world, but only a mere handful make the sacrifice needed to reap the full benefits of its power."

The door at the end of the hallway opened of its own accord as they approached. Inky blackness poured out from within, and with it came the faint smell of compost and decay. They crossed the threshold together and a thousand black candles came to life, illuminating the room in a warm, undulating bath of flickering yellow light.

Vinnie the Razor stood rooted in the doorway, scarcely able to believe his eyes. In the center of the room a pentagram was painted on the floor in what could only be blood and a large altar of black marble stood against the far wall underneath an upside-down cross. The walls were lined from floor to ceiling with shelving units stocked full with hundreds of glass jars of all shapes and sizes containing all the various tools of the sorceress's armory. Ri Ri bags and neat little bundles of St. John's Wort shared space with jars of robins' eyes and animal entrails floating lost and dismembered in formaldehyde. In one corner several larger jars housed the fetuses of a diverse but unidentifiable range of animals, including several that—no, they couldn't possibly be human. Pulling his eyes from the various bottled monstrosities, he looked to Lizabet, who had drawn a long ceremonial knife from a sheath on the wall.

"Take off your clothes, my darling," she said, smiling at him. "It is time to harness the wind."

Thirty-four

She could not recall how long she had been standing under the scalding jets of hot water before the pulsating spray gave up its torrid caress and turned to ice, jolting her from her benumbed tranquillity. Monique LeFlamme twisted the ersatz crystal handle all the way to the left, trying in vain to coax a few more gallons from the depleted hot water tank, but it would be hours before it would replenish itself and she could take yet another shower. This was her third of the day, and as she reached for her towel and patted herself down, she could only think that she could not wait to take another.

She had awoke late this morning to find Vinnie gone from her bed. No note, no kiss good-bye, only a rumpled pillow and his scent, stale and foreign—nothing like the wonderful smells she remembered, lingering on her sheets. She had felt none of the bitterness or resentment that would normally accompany such a rude departure, only relief that he was gone. She had hurried from the bed, stripped it clean and tossed the soiled sheets into the trash, knowing she could never sleep on them again without thinking of the strange turn their lovemaking had taken last night. While their sex had always bordered on rough, there was an underlying tenderness to it, maybe even love. But last night was unenjoyable—ugly, she would go so far to say. The scratching and the biting! My Lord, was he on something? He certainly wasn't himself.

Wrapping a second towel around herself, she stepped from the steamy bathroom and into the spartan studio, leaving perfect little footprints on the cold concrete floor.

She lived over a converted storefront on Halsted Street. The open space of the third-story loft was ideal for her large sculptures but lacked many of even the most basic creature comforts. There was no kitchen to speak of, only a hot plate next to the utility sink for the simple meals she occasionally prepared for herself. Her bed, positioned so that she could stare at her works in progress as she fell asleep, was pushed against the far wall next to a portable cedar closet, which, along with a lone dresser, housed her entire wardrobe. All in all, it was a far cry from the pampered lifestyle she had come to resent while growing up in Rochester, New York.

If Daddy could only see her now. He wouldn't of course. They had hardly spoken since she had announced she would not be attending the University of Rochester (Daddy's alma mater) after graduating from the Mount Assisi Academy for girls, opting instead for art school in Chicago, some eight hundred miles away.

Looking around now at the large, abstract, metal-and-wood fabrications, she felt for the first time a dissatisfaction with her work, a suspicion that it might very well be the slightest bit . . . pretentious? Was it all worth it? Living like this, in this hellhole of a neighborhood, in this shitty loft, all in the name of self-expression? Who was she kidding? It was all a sham. This whole art thing was a thinly disguised ruse, a slap in Daddy's face. The poor little rich girl off to the heart of the big city, trying to make a name for herself as a sculptress. It was all bullshit. She was a phony.

Walking among the pieces, she felt none of the smug contentment that used to bring her such peace—no attachment whatsoever to the complex structures that consumed her every waking hour. What had she seen when she had looked at these pieces before? Surely, only the selfish and arrogant musings of a self-inflated ego left unchecked and gone awry. She paused at her latest creation, a massive and imposing spherical half-moon wrought from a steel girder and copper sheeting, floating deceptively light and airy on a free-spinning base. At its core, organic shapes carved from walnut and sandstone bubbled up and spilled out over the sides, creating a stark contrast of form and texture. It was a striking piece and she had already received several very generous offers for it based only on her preparatory drawings. Looking at it now, she found fault with it from every angle and wondered how she could have ever created anything so god-awful ugly.

She let the towel drop from her torso, paying no mind to the chill in the room as she walked to her worktable and searched for a suitable tool among the clutter of acetylene tanks and welding gear. Lifting the long-handled cutting shears from beneath her welding mask, she strode resolutely back to the piece and went to work on the copper sheeting. She indiscriminately pared off large strips, letting them fall to the floor with a clang. Beads of perspiration formed on her naked body as she proceeded to hack away at the delicate carvings at the center of the work, intent on removing as much of the eyesore as possible. Stepping back, she considered it once again. Yes, not quite so ugly now, but look at her. She was dripping with sweat and she had just gotten out of the shower. Best to rinse off once again before she caught her death of cold. And besides, she still felt so *dirty* inside.

Still carrying the heavy cutting shears, she paused at the bathroom mirror and considered her reflection, startled to see the incongruities present in her own face. My goodness, had her nose always been that long? Her ears so large? Ugh! They looked like dinner plates. How could she not have seen that before? And just look at her breasts! Her nipples were far too large for one thing and wasn't that the most unsightly birthmark scarring the edge of her left areola? It was so obvious now. The fault lay not with her work, but with herself. (But hadn't she known that all along?) Her eyes darted back to her face, barely able to stand what she saw there, but how else was she to fix it?

Reaffirming her grip on the cutting shears with both hands, Monique LeFlamme slowly hefted the tool from her side until the cold steel rested against the soft smooth skin of her cheek. She closed her eyes for a moment, enjoying the hard caress, the stark contrast of the two surfaces before she pulled the handles wide and opened the sharp steel jaws.

She did not even realize she was crying.

Thirty-five

"It's gonna blow their minds," Johnny said, grinning madly and shaking his head. "Flat out blow their minds. I can't wait for them to get here."

"Gonna be sweet, Johnny my boy," Vinnie answered from his squatting position on the floor of his garage, where he was positioning the equipment for the evening's rehearsal. He walked off ten paces to Dave's drum kit and back again, inching the monitor forward about half a foot. "I'm kind of eager to hear it myself with the full accompaniment, but I gotta tell you, I already know what it's gonna sound like. It's been playing in my head all day."

"Yeah, I know what you mean," Johnny agreed. "I've never had lyrics come to me so easily before. It was almost like I had written the song in my sleep and it was just a matter of getting it down on paper before it faded away. The melody was just out of reach, like an old song you couldn't quite remember, but when you showed up—man, I just knew we had it pegged."

He had, in fact, been humming the tune without even realizing it as he had sat at his drawing table earlier that morning. He'd been scratching out the lyrics in a mad rush, desperate to squeeze the words from the tip of his pencil and capture them on paper when he had heard the growl of Vinnie's Honda from the street below. Johnny was not the least bit surprised by the unscheduled visit from his guitar player on a Tuesday morning when they both should have been elsewhere. Actually, he'd been expecting him.

Vinnie had looked up and flashed a knowing smile and a quick wave as he climbed off the bike, leaving no doubt in Johnny's mind that he had come to help him write *the* song. Johnny handed Vinnie the lyrics as he walked through the door and Vinnie was still reading them when he grabbed Johnny's six-string and began strumming out the melody. Johnny had pulled his Marine Band harmonica from his pocket and fell in right behind him, laying low at the breaks, nodding his head and slapping out the backbeat on his thighs as the guitar wizard fleshed it out and made it whole.

After two hours of making notes, minor rhythm changes, and some chorus adjustments, they had the song completely written, wrapped, and ready to play. Looking back on it now, only a few short hours later, Johnny could scarcely believe how effortless it had all been.

"You ever write a song like that before, Vinnie?" he asked, watching his friend throw a leg over the Honda parked in the middle of the garage. "I mean, so easy like that. Usually, it's such a struggle for me."

"Never had one come that easy, Johnny," Vinnie replied as he hefted the bike off its centerstand and paddled it over to the side, away from the band equipment. "You hear these stories of guys waking up and writing songs they've heard or sang in a dream—boom, fifteen minutes and they're done. Never happened to me, but I suppose it's common enough. I wrote 'Thrush' in about six hours, but that's just a head-banger—a filler—something to get the adrenaline pumping. This one, though . . . this one's got legs. I think it may be the one. It's far and away the best thing I've ever done."

Johnny nodded. "I know. I feel the same way. Like it's the culmination of my life's work or something. My opus."

Vinnie laughed. "Whoa, we're still relatively young, my

friend. Don't write yourself off just yet. There's plenty more where this one came from." Deep down, though, he had to wonder. Could he possibly ever write anything this good again? Vinnie cocked his head suddenly and motioned toward the side door of the garage. "They're here," he announced.

"You sure?" Johnny asked, peeking his head out the door into the empty backyard. "I think you're hearing things."

"I'm hearing things all right," Vinnie replied as he rummaged through his guitar case for the Fender's power cord. "I'm hearing things I've never heard before. It's like I can hear the leaves falling from the trees. Believe me, they're here."

Moments later, two car doors slammed and the sound of Dave Hannon's robust laughter filled the narrow gangway leading into the backyard. "Hey, bitches," the big man said, stepping into the garage with Kenney Brandt close behind. "What's all the fuss about? I hope you got a good reason for calling an early rehearsal. You cost me two hours of beauty sleep."

"You guys said you got a new song?" Kenney asked, looking around, surprised to see everything already set up and ready to go. "Hey, Johnny," he said, nodding hello to his friend. "Hey, Vinnie, what's up?"

"Hey, guys," Johnny said with a sly grin. "Hey, Kenney, how'd your date with that waitress go last night?"

Vinnie grunted as if too busy to acknowledge the greeting and handed photocopies of the song to Kenney and Dave. "Let's quit fucking around and get down to business," he said, strapping Thor's Hammer over his shoulder. "I want to get a feel for how this is gonna play in Peoria. Just follow me from A to G and watch Johnny for the break and chorus cues."

"Whatever you say, boss," Dave said a bit sarcastically as he settled in behind his drum kit. He threw a "what the fuck is his problem?" glance in Kenney's direction, but the methodical bass player was already studying the words and lyrics, a look of near astonishment on his face as he read the title aloud.

" 'Dancing with the Devil's Daughter.' You guys wrote this, this afternoon?" he asked, marveling at the hooks and catchy leads. It looked great. He couldn't wait to play it.

When it was over three and a half minutes later the four of them stood staring at each other in the deafening silence that followed.

"Goddamn!" Dave yelled, breaking the silence. "Goddamn, that was good! Better than sex!"

"Maybe better than any sex *you've* ever had," Vinnie said, laughing, the edge gone from his voice with the song fully realized. "Of course that's always been a solo act anyway. Let's run through it a few more times. Kenney, I want you to pick it up a bit after the first chorus—you were late on your lead-in. Dave, I want a cymbal roll right before we pick up tempo for the closing—maybe a double-pump on the bass drum. I won't know until I hear it. Other than that, I liked it. What do you guys think?"

"Wouldn't change a thing," Kenney said, shaking his head in awe. "I think it's fantastic. Where are we gonna place it in our set? I would imagine it's gotta be the closer."

Vinnie rubbed his chin thoughtfully. "Yeah, I definitely think we should wrap up with it. Leave them wanting more and all that. But I want to rework the order of the whole set for the Pharaoh Room. I think 'Ice Cream Headache' or 'Fever' would make a nice lead-in."

Johnny nodded. "Let's go with 'Ice Cream' first, and have 'Fever' lead into 'Dancing.' The bass fade-out at the end will make a nice segue into 'Dancing.' What do you think, Dave?"

"I think you should stop using words like 'segue,' "

Dave said with a straight face, "or I'll call all those farm boys back in Belvidere and tell them the big city turned you into a fag."

Kenney laughed and looked at Vinnie. "Whatever we decide, let's do it quick. I need to get a playlist into Ruder's hands by tomorrow night. The guy's been up my ass for two days now."

"Ouch," Dave said.

"Ruder will get his playlist when it's ready," Vinnie said. "What's happening on the promotions side?"

"He had some flyers printed up and he's got ads running in the *Illinois Entertainer* and the *Reader.* They both hit the stands on Thursday. He used the old pub photo, but he wants to get us over to his guy sometime soon and take some new shots."

"Good," Dave said, twirling his drumsticks. "That old one made me look fat."

"You are fat," Johnny said, jumping on the chance to needle the big drummer. "And you're a good twenty pounds heavier now from when that picture was taken. You might want to opt for just a head shot."

"I'll give you a head shot, you skinny little fuck," Dave said, feigning indignity. "I'll have you know that's twenty pounds of muscle. I—"

"Knock it off, you guys," Vinnie snapped. "We've only got two rehearsals until we open at the Pharaoh Room. We have to rework our set and add a few more covers. Now are we gonna play or are we gonna fuck around and play grab-ass all night?"

"He started it," Dave said, curling his lower lip in a mock pout.

Kenney shook his head and stifled a laugh. He had never seen the mercurial guitarist so uptight before, but he did have a point. They had a lot of work to do before Friday and precious little time to do it. Fingering the meaty strings of his bass, he dribbled out the opening

notes to "Fever" and shot a wink at his friend sitting behind the Pearl drum kit. "Vinnie's right. Let' get down
to it and we'll break halfway through for a couple of beers.
I'm buying."

They were well into the second hour of rehearsal, fine-
tuning their rowdy cover of "Needle and Pins," when Vinnie stopped suddenly as though frozen in time, his brow
knit in a combination of annoyance and surprise. He
mouthed her name before he turned around.

"Lauren?" he asked, breaking the sudden silence.

They all turned to see her standing in the doorway, her
face red and raw from crying. Dave groaned to himself,
at first thinking she had come for him. But he quickly
realized the look on her face had nothing to do with him
running out and never calling after Sunday's drunken
one-night stand. She looked like she might be in shock.

"Dead," she said, staring straight ahead. "She's dead."

Kenney felt a lump rise in his chest. Please don't let it
be who he thought it was.

"Blood," she muttered, dropping her eyes and staring
at the garage floor. "So much blood."

Kenney swallowed hard. She was talking about Monique.

"Who's dead, Lauren?" Kenney asked. "Who?"

"Monique. Isn't that who we're talking about?" she
asked, somewhat annoyed by the question. "I went over
there this morning to pick her up for school. When she
didn't answer the door, I let myself in. I have a key, you
know. She was my best friend."

Kenney did not know that. In their time together,
Monique had never spoken very highly of her.

"There was blood everywhere," she chirped up, intent
on painting a complete picture. "Blood. Pooled up in the
uneven swells of the floor, like dark puddles of liquid rust.
You know, it kind of smells like copper." Her eyes brightened for a moment. "Rusty copper!"

Eyes darted back and forth among the four musicians,

trading astonished glances, before finally landing on Vinnie, who only appeared to be growing more annoyed with the break in rehearsal.

"Just what the fuck are you talking about, you goofy bitch?" he suddenly asked her.

"She cut her nose off," Lauren answered, unperturbed by the insult. "She cut her own nose off. Other . . . parts, too. Self-inflicted. The police said that. I heard them. Look! I've still got blood on my shoes. How am I ever going to get that off? I don't want to touch it."

"Cold water soak with bleach and a short rinse with All-Temperature Cheer," Vinnie answered flatly. "Now if you don't mind, we're trying to wrap up a rehearsal here."

"Jesus, Vinnie, didn't you hear what she just said?" Kenney asked, floored by the guitar player's stone-cold indifference. "Monique is dead! Dead! Don't you even care?"

"Well, I don't see what good sitting around here pissing and moaning is going to do about it," Vinnie snorted. "It sure doesn't change the fact that we open the biggest gig of our lives on Friday night and we only have one more day of practice after tonight. Or maybe you think the whole world will just stop spinning because your precious Monique offed herself. Me, I'm going to get on with the business at hand and I suggest you do the same. Unless, of course, you don't share the commitment to this band that the rest of us do. If that's the case, just let me know, and I'll round up another bass player." He paused, then added with a snort, "It shouldn't be too hard."

"Hey, you're out of line, Vinnie," Dave said, rising up behind his drum kit. "Way out of line."

"Yeah, Vinnie," Johnny added nervously. "Kenney's committed to the band. Aren't you, Kenney? You—"

"Can it, Johnny," Kenney snapped, not realizing he had balled his hands into tight fists. All the jealousy, all the unspoken, pent-up resentment he had ever felt toward the easygoing, "I don't have a care in the world" guitar player welled up inside him like a hot stone. He hated his incredible, effortless talent and his Mediterranean good looks. He hated the way women threw themselves at him, and his shallow, simplistic outlook on life. He hated that he probably *could* find another bass player tomorrow. A better one at that.

"Rehearsal's over," he said, unclenching his fists. "If you want another bass player, go out and get one. See if I give a fuck. I don't like being around you lately anyway." He walked past the guitar player and unplugged his bass. "You've become quite the asshole ever since you hooked up with that spooky bitch Saturday night."

"Kenney goes, I go," Dave said, gathering up his gear. "This is bullshit."

Vinnie glowered, working his jaw as he tried to stifle his anger at the slight directed toward Lizabet. Johnny stood nervously, shuffling from side to side, not knowing whether to piss or go blind. Lauren the Bitch stood in the doorway, trembling, seemingly unaware of where she was or what she was doing there.

"I want to go home, "she said and she started to cry.

"You're right," Vinnie said finally, watching the band and its immediate success dissolve around him. This was not part of the plan. He reached out and stopped Kenney, putting one hand on his shoulder and offering him the other. "Hey, man, I was out of line. That was fucked up. I'm sorry." A part of him, buried deep inside, really meant it. He always liked Kenney. "We cool?"

Kenney took the hand and shook it, feeling a selfish sense of relief at being back in the band that he did not want to acknowledge. "We're cool," he said. "Let's call it a night, huh? Dave and I will give Lauren a ride home."

"Yeah, sure," Vinnie said, hiding his disappointment at cutting the rehearsal short. "We'll pick it up Thursday night, huh?"

"I want to go home," Lauren said, staring straight ahead.

"We'll take you home, Lauren," Kenney offered. "Right now. And you can tell us exactly what happened, okay?"

"Home? Home to Pittsburgh?" Lauren asked, her eyes lighting up. "By Mommy and Daddy? I don't want to stay here anymore."

"Eh, Pittsburgh's a long drive, honey," Dave said, slipping an arm around her tiny shoulders and leading her out the door and into the yard. "Let's start with getting you back to your apartment, okay?"

Kenney paused in the doorway as he turned to go. "We'll see if we can get anything else out of her and try to make some sense out of this. If I don't talk to you, I'll see you guys Thursday night, six o'clock."

"Try to make it five," Vinnie answered. "We lost an hour of practice tonight."

It was almost ten o'clock when Dave pulled up in front of Kenney's apartment, still shaking his head over the bizarre circumstances of Monique's death. They had managed to glean a few more details from Lauren's rambling, incomprehensible ranting by the time they had finally taken her home and put her to bed—aided in no small part by the prescription valium in her medicine cabinet. Apparently, a neighbor had called the police after hearing Lauren's screams upon discovering the mutilated body of her friend. Monique had been lying in a pool of blood in the center of the room—no signs of a struggle and naked as the day she was born, as if she had just lain down and gone to sleep. The police had kept Lauren there for a good part of the day, asking her a thousand questions over and over before finally bringing her home. Unable to stand being alone, she had driven around aimlessly before ending up at Vinnie's house simply because she had nowhere else to go.

"I got an uncle who's a cop," Dave said, breaking the comfortable silence as they pulled up to the curb. "Detective actually, works homicide in the Englewood District. He sees some pretty grisly stuff. I'll give him a call and see what he can tell me about this if you want. Speaking of which, don't be surprised if you should get a visit from one of Chicago's finest during the next couple of days. They're probably going to want to talk to anyone who knew her well."

"Lauren said they think it's a suicide," Kenney said, not believing it himself.

"I don't know, man," Dave replied. "How do you cut your own nose off? And all that other stuff. Jesus Christ, something ain't right. Something isn't right with this whole situation. And what's up with Vinnie? I've never seen him act like this before. You know he may have been the last one to see her alive. There's something rotten in the air. I gotta tell you, man, I'm a little spooked."

Kenney felt a chill race up his spine as he remembered the dream and the words his brother had spoken to him from the grave: *An evil wind is blowing your way.* He shuddered, thinking that a woman he may have loved, beautiful and alive only yesterday, was gone forever.

"You okay, bud?" Dave asked as they sat for a moment in the van. He lit up a Cheyenne and offered one to Kenney, who paused just a moment before taking it.

"I picked a hell of a week to quit smoking, huh?" he said, bending over and taking the light from Dave's Zippo.

Dave shook his big shaggy head and sighed. "Fuck it," he grunted, "you want to live forever?"

Kenney took a deep drag and exhaled, watching the smoke curl up and drift out the window into the cool night air. "Yeah," he said after giving it a little bit of thought. "Don't you?"

Thirty-six

"I want you to promise me you're going to keep an open mind before I show you this," Dave Hannon said, shielding the eclectic stack of books from Kenney's prying eyes as they walked up the back steps to his apartment. "Because if you don't, you're gonna think I'm nuts."

Kenney had just returned home from a particularly nerve-wracking assignment at St. Mary's Star of the Sea grammar school, surprised to see Dave waiting in his van in front of his apartment. The odd selection of reading material tucked under his friend's beefy arm only piqued his curiosity.

"My mind's always open, Dave," Kenney said, hurrying through the door. He immediately pulled a bottle of Tylenol down from the cabinet over his refrigerator. "And I already know you're nuts. You want a beer?"

"No—eh, fuck it. Gimme one," he answered. He watched Kenney chase a handful of Tylenol down with a long splash of Budweiser. "Rough day, huh? I'm surprised you could work after last night."

"Well, I couldn't sit around here all day thinking about it. Besides, there's nothing like a class full of whiny third-graders to take your mind off a mutilated ex-girlfriend," he deadpanned. "What's with all the spooky books?"

"I knocked off work early and went to the library," Dave said, laying the books down and spreading them out across the kitchen table. "There was something about Vinnie's new girlfriend that rattled me aside from her overall weirdness. I just couldn't shake it and then I realized it was her name—Lizabet Bazore. Check this out," he said, flipping through *The Book of Werewolves* to the chapter entitled "A Hungarian Bather in Blood."

"Look at the name, Kenney," he said, pounding his meaty finger down on the page. "Elizabeth Bathory! Sound familiar? I saw a special about her on TV a long time ago and it was one of those things that always stays with you, you know? She was a sixteenth-century Hungarian noblewoman who supposedly killed over six hundred young girls and bathed in their blood. She thought it was the key to eternal youth—that it would keep her young and beautiful forever—and that's not all. She was a practicing witch and a cannibal. Look," he said, sliding another book, *Erzsebet Bathory, The Bloody Countess,* across the table and opening it to a premarked page. "Tell me you don't see a resemblance," Dave said, pointing to a grayscale reproduction of the countess's fuzzy portrait.

Kenney leaned forward and examined the painting of the rather plain-looking woman. He gave her the benefit of the doubt and attributed her homeliness to the style of painting prevalent in sixteenth-century northern Europe—an unflattering blend of Late Gothic and the emerging Italian point of view. It would be a stretch to say she looked like the striking auburn-haired beauty that had Vinnie so enthralled. But there were some notable similarities, particularly around her eyes.

"Okay," Dave said, pulling the book away and flipping to the next page. "Maybe not so much with that one, but look at this."

This painting, from the nineteenth century, depicted a "typical torture scene" outside the countess's castle, wherein young female servants were being dragged into the snow by cackling hags, who poured freezing water onto their naked bodies. Sitting on a raised throne off to the right, Elizabeth Bathory sat laughing, obviously enjoying the spectacle unfolding for her benefit. Leaning in closer and looking at the tiny face thrown back at that particular angle, he had to admit that there was a definite resemblance.

"All right, so they look a little bit alike," Kenney said, taking a quick swallow off his Budweiser. "What's your point?"

"Come on, Kenney, you know what I'm getting at. What about the names? Elizabeth Bathory—Lizabet Bazore? And that business she said she runs. Cachtice Imports. That was the name of her castle, *Cachtice*, back in Transylvania—now modern-day Czechoslovakia."

Kenney looked at his friend across the table, unable to believe what the carpenter from Wrigleyville, a man he had known for almost five years, was saying. "Jesus Christ, Dave, you can't possibly be suggesting—"

"That they're one and the same? You bet your ass I am. Look, I asked you to keep an open mind about this, didn't I? You tell me there isn't something really spooky about that bitch. You know damn well there's something strange about her and that little blonde fox that hangs around with her, the one that's got Johnny walking around on cloud nine. Okay, I can see Johnny getting all gooey over a babe like that. They don't have pussy like that in cow town, but Vinnie doesn't act like that around women. He doesn't get pussy-whipped. It's the other way around. And what about Monique? She sleeps with Vinnie a day after he meets this broad and she winds up dead the next day? Cuts off her own *fucking nose?* Come on, man, something ain't right with those two. Look at the goddamn pictures, Kenney! Look at the names!"

Kenney Brandt pulled his glasses from his face and rubbed his temples in frustration, his logical mind unable to accept, for even a moment, what his friend was telling him.

"So what are you asking me to believe, Dave? That she's a four-hundred-year-old demon and she's fucking our guitar player? I'm sorry, man. What you're saying would make perfect sense—would actually be a neat and tidy explanation for some of the weird shit going on around here, if it wasn't for one simple thing. It's impossible."

"What about your dreams, Kenney?" Dave asked, catching him by surprise. "Anything out of the ordinary lately?"

"What are talking about?" Kenney asked, startled by the question. "What do you know about my dreams?"

"Just that I've been having some really fucking scary ones lately and I can tell by your reaction just now that you have, too. And you know what the funny thing is? I never remember my dreams, ever—except for the last couple of weeks, and now I can't forget them."

Kenney sat for a moment staring at the grainy portrait of Elizabeth Bathory, unable to pull his gaze from the haunting eyes when he heard Ronny's voice in his head for the second time in as many days.

"An evil so powerful it has survived for centuries, refusing to die. It walks the earth in human form. . . ."

He closed the book with a quick thump, spooked by the disturbing similarities between the two women that were starting to become more apparent with each passing moment.

"I don't know what you're talking about, Dave. My dreams are fine, and aside from the one I had the other night where my aunt Agnes chased me through the wading pool at Aqua Park with a giant inflatable penis, they're actually kind of boring. Okay, I'll admit, Vinnie's latest squeeze looks a little bit like this . . . this Blood Countess bitch from the sixteenth century, and he has been acting like a colossal asshole and there is definitely something very strange about Monique's death. But this theory of yours is . . . unacceptable. There *has* to be a logical explanation. You read way too much of this shit," he said, tapping the top of the book with his finger. "It's starting to cloud your judgment."

"Unacceptable, huh?" Dave said, a note of anger in his voice. "I'll tell you what's unacceptable. Your refusal to admit when you're full of shit, that's what's unacceptable. Now you can just sit here on your ass and bullshit all you want about logical explanations and all that other crap, when you know damn well there's nothing remotely logical about this. But not me. I'm going to do something about it."

"C'mon, Dave," Kenney said, watching the big man gather up his library books and head for the door. "I didn't mean anything by it. Come on, sit down. Let's have another beer and talk this over. Where you going?"

"I'm done talking, buddy. It just makes me sound crazy. I'm going over to Cachtice Imports and have me a look around. Here," he said, pausing at the door and handing the stack of books back to Kenney, "just do me a favor and take a look at these tonight, will you? I'll give you a call later on, let you know if I come across anything interesting over there."

Kenney Brandt followed his friend to the door, an unspoken and totally irrational fear gripping him as he watched the drummer lumber out onto the tiny landing and make his way down the weathered wooden stairs. For a moment he thought he might cry out and plead with Dave not to go, but that was ridiculous, and he caught himself as his friend's name barely escaped his lips. "Dave. . . ."

The brawny percussionist turned, surprised by the muted croak from the top of the stairs. "Yeah?" he asked, that goofy grin breaking in the corner of his mouth.

"Do me a favor," Kenney said, "and get out of there before the sun goes down."

Thirty-seven

A bolt of fuzzy static crackled through the oversize speaker cabinets mounted on the sidewalls of Dave Hannon's Econoline van as the skyscrapers of the Loop, looming up on his right, blocked the 50,000-watt signal of WDAI, the Rock of Chicago. The ass-end of the hard-rocking, commercial-free, ninety-minute afternoon drive melted into a harsh jumble of white noise that cut into Dave's last nerve like a switchblade knife. His decision to bypass the rush-hour traffic on I-55 and take Archer Avenue to Halsted Street and sneak around the downtown congestion had paid off handsomely until a broken-down semi at Madison cut traffic down to one lane. Impatient commuters jockeyed stubbornly for position around the halted vehicle, turning the smooth traffic flow into a jerky stop-and-go parade. He swore to himself and shut the radio all the way off, using the sudden, startling silence to collect his thoughts and reflect on the conversation that he had had with Kenney Brandt almost two hours ago.

"You read too much of this shit," Kenney had told him, sounding exactly like his father when he used to bitch and moan about his son's less than scholarly reading habits.

Fangoria and *Famous Monsters of Filmland* magazines had made up the brunt of Dave's library as a young boy, with a smattering of *Vampirella* comic books (which his father did not allow in the house), hidden in strategic spots throughout his bedroom. Young Dave's preoccupation with monsters and the supernatural was a cause to worry for his strict Irish-Catholic parents. When the youngster's natural athletic ability had begun to blossom early on, they did not hesitate to "encourage" him, seeing organized sports as a healthy alternative to spending hours locked in his room with "that nonsense."

"If you could only see me now, Dad," he laughed, inching along before finally reaching the corner at Grand Avenue and turning right. "Dave Hannon, fearless vampire hunter!" The laughter was short-lived as he noticed the long shadows cast by the setting sun behind him, stretching out and reaching toward the lake.

He had an hour, maybe an hour and a half tops, before the sun disappeared behind the endless expanse of factory-dotted prairie to his left, taking the calm and self-possession that accompanied the daylight hours with it. He stepped on the gas, swerving around a slow-moving Ford Crown Victoria in the left lane, paying no mind to the beating the potholed street was administering to his tires and suspension. Crossing the bridge, he took a left onto Dearborn and drifted into the right lane, slowing almost to a crawl. It had been years since he had been through this part of town: a dead zone between the bustling daytime activity of the Loop and the heady nightlife of Rush Street, populated, it seemed, only by those who appeared to be on their way somewhere else. Sitting at the stoplight on Ohio Street, he looked up and saw the medieval-looking turret peeking over the rooftops to his left a block ahead. Looks just like a castle, Vinnie had told him. Sure enough, as he crossed Ontario and pulled into the abandoned Shell station across the street from the stone fortress, he saw the tiny sign, carefully hand-lettered by the deceased Drew Richards, tucked unobtrusively into the corner of one of the large, empty black windows:

Coming Soon
Cachtice Imports

"Bingo," Dave said, switching off the ignition. He sat for a long moment staring at the imposing facade of the building. The stony tomblike countenance gave one the impression that whatever lay inside was long dead.

"Let's get it done, Dave," he said to himself, grabbing the small nylon satchel off the floor and swinging it over his shoulder. Inside were a vial of holy water he had siphoned from the sacristy at St. Gaul's, along with a pry bar and an assortment of small tools and lock picks borrowed from an unsavory friend.

He trotted casually across the street and walked up to the entrance, having no idea what he would do if someone were to answer the series of loud knocks he thumped onto the surface of the double oak doors. Relieved to find no one to answer his call, he strolled around to the back of the building, taking note of the blacked-out basement windows rising up from the sidewalk. Looking for a suitable entry point, he found his way around to the back gate, an evil-looking maw of wrought iron and dense foliage tucked into the imposing stone wall that ran the entire length of the courtyard. After waiting for the traffic to clear on Ontario Street, he gave a final look over his shoulder and tossed the nylon satchel up and over the top of the sharp teeth crowning the iron gate. In a minute he was scrambling up the no-nonsense ironwork and hoisting his 250-pound frame over the jagged spikes at the top with a neat acrobatic flip that was actually quite remarkable for a man his size. He landed feetfirst on the pebbled concrete on the other side and scooped up his bag. Using the wild overgrowth of the unchecked landscaping for cover, he scurried in a half-crouch to the far side of the crumbling courtyard. Satisfied his covert entry onto the grounds had gone undetected, he settled in under a

thicket and surveyed the west face of the building, evalu-
ating his options. The cellar door nestled in the small
cubbyhole at the bottom of the short flight of stairs was
tempting, but it was heavy and secured with a massive
padlock. The first bank of windows was accessible enough,
but their height would expose him to the sight lines from
the street and he didn't come this far to be arrested for
breaking and entering. He crept along the side of the
building to the north wall and discovered a narrow cavity
where the high stone barrier met the wall. There was just
enough room for him to maneuver his large frame in
between the cold stone planes. Using his body as a lever,
he planted his feet firmly against the building's exterior
and boosted himself, inch by inch, toward the second-
story window. Moments later he found himself standing
atop the broad, flat cap of the enclosure, less than a foot
from the target window. Concealed in part from the street
by the neighboring building, he raised himself up on his
tiptoes and peered over the sill into the darkness within.

The window frame was locked down tight with a spherical clasp and nailed shut for good measure with shiny,
new tenpenny nails. Swearing silently to himself, he pulled
the glass cutter from the nylon satchel and set about cutting a small, perfect hole in the pane. Pulling back the
sleeve of his jacket, he was able to squeeze his beefy hand
through the opening and undo the fastener, catching the
soft skin under his forearm on the deceivingly smooth
edge of the hole as he pulled it back out. He winced at
the sting as the salt from his sweat mixed with the blood
seeping from the superficial but painful cut and set about
prying open the windowsill.

A tortured groan preceded the popping of the nails as
the big carpenter made short work of Drew Richards's bur-
glarproofing. Moments later Dave was picking himself off
the dusty floor of the vampire's lair and fishing for the flashlight in his bag. The room was empty, save for a few rags

and some empty cardboard boxes piled into a corner against the wall. Opening the door with a long theatrical creak, he stepped into the hallway and clicked off the flashlight, slightly unnerved by the red glow suffusing the walls cast by the setting sun. Not knowing exactly what he was looking for, he made a quick room-by-room inspection of the second floor, finding nothing out of the ordinary, until he came upon the holding room at the end of the hall.

The room looked like an Irving Klaw–Betty Page photoshoot gone awry. Leather wrist restraints and handcuffs were mounted high on the wall, along with a large X-shaped wooden cross adorned with finishing nails protruding from strategic points along its length. A large stainless-steel examination table sat in the middle of the room, complete with blood gutters positioned over two five-gallon pails to collect the carnage.

"Jesus Christ . . . ," he whispered, gingerly sorting through a shallow bin housing an odd assortment of surgical tools and torture devices. Thumbscrews and heretic's forks lay next to scalpels, hemostats, and vacuum pumps—a bizarre accumulation of bloodletting mechanisms, flecked with gore and smelling of death. Blood splattered the walls, and the floor on which he stood was painted almost entirely in the dark crimson wrested from the poor souls who died here, screaming and begging for death to come and rescue them. Beads of sweat broke out on his forehead and Dave felt his lunch rising up in his throat as fascination turned to revulsion. He backed out of the room, unable to tear his eyes away from the chamber of horror. He closed the door with a soft click and made his way down the hall toward the stairway, taking the steps in a quick but quiet, staccato pump, not far removed from the conditioning drills repeated endlessly on countless football fields and sandlots throughout his athletic career.

He had seen quite enough. Bounding across the foyer to the front door, bathed in the soft light of the approaching dusk, his only concern was getting his story straight for the police. He unlocked the last of the long row of tumblers and dead bolts on the double oak doors and pushed, letting a tiny sliver of the fading Chicago daylight into the foyer before slamming it shut again with a start.

What was he doing? Did he really come this far so he could go to the police with a crazy story? Maybe even get arrested for breaking and entering? No, of course not, that would be silly. Oh no, he needed more proof before he could report anything.

The voice of reason, that soft, silvery voice in his head, told him exactly where he could find it.

The basement, Dave. Everything you need. Everything you could ever want or need is in the basement.

"Of course," he said, slowly and methodically relocking the series of latches and dead bolts. "We wouldn't want to leave without checking the basement first."

Crossing the lobby, he veered to his left, pausing just a moment before choosing the proper hallway and navigating his way to the back of the building. He found the cellar door tucked into a small antechamber in what might have once been a kitchen.

"Not so hard to find your way around here," he said to himself, almost whistling as he clicked on his flashlight and stepped down the stairs. "Not too hard at all."

At the foot of the stairs Dave swung his flashlight around in a long sweeping arc, catching sight of the heavy wooden doors of the sleep chamber just as the cellar door slammed shut tight above him. His bucolic state of mind vanished as suddenly as it had appeared, leaving the big drummer standing alone and bewildered in the silent darkness of the dank basement. My God, what was he doing down here? What on earth could have possibly possessed. . . .

Frantic, he turned the fading beam of his flashlight toward the south wall, drawn by the tiny sliver of dusk filtering in through the tiny hole Chloe Covington had scratched in the black paint only three days earlier. He was chipping away at the thick enamel in a desperate bid to let in more of the fading light when he heard, to his horror, the door of the sleep chamber opening behind him.

A heretofore unimaginable fear gripped his entire being, locking his muscles down and freezing him to the spot. He was actually too frightened to move or even breathe. His bladder released upon hearing the horrible little giggle that followed the sound of the heavy chamber door close with the familiar, leisurely thunk of wood rolling into wood.

The thing was right behind him.

Looking at him.

"Well, Mr. Hannon," she purred, the voice soft and enticing, "how very good of you to drop by, although I do wish you would have waited for an invitation."

Unable to resist the silky, almost musical tone, he swallowed the fear rising in his throat and turned to face the beast, bringing the flashlight around in a timid arc, framing her in the fuzzy, generated halo of electric light.

He had never seen anything so beautiful in all his life.

Vampirella. Morticia Addams. Simone Simon in *Cat People*. Barbara Steele in *Curse of the Crimson Altar*. She was all that and more. All the dark, raven-haired sirens from the late-night *Creature Features* movies and the horror comics that made his loins ache so as a child. A weak moan welled up inside him and she laughed, a true, haughty laugh, mocking and full of disdain. It made him want her even more and he felt his cock grow hard, straining against the pants he had wet only moments before.

"So predictable," she said, smiling as she walked around him in a lazy circle. "So common." She paused and ran her finger down the length of his muscled arm. "So strong . . . and yet so weak. You were quite foolish to come here, Dave Hannon, to my house. Meddling in my affairs. Disturbing my sleep. Now you will tell me," she said, plucking the flashlight from his hand, "all that you know of me and how you came to know it." With a casual sweep of her left hand, the naked bulb dangling from the rafter behind her came to life, throwing the room into a stark jumble of harsh light and dark shadows. "Behold," she said, passing her left hand slowly across her face, "what it is that you came here to see and prayed you would not."

The muffled screams coming from within the cold flagstones sent a shiver up the young street hustler's spine as he walked past the "castle" on Ontario and headed east toward Clark Street where the "chickenhawks"—the old men who paid so dearly for his services—prowled. My goodness, he thought, trying to make light of the horrible cries as he crossed Ontario against the light and ran across to the other side of the street. Someone's playing awful rough in there tonight, awful rough indeed.

Thirty-eight

Kenney Brandt pulled the fresh pack of Cheyennes from the visor of his Maverick and contemplated the tightly wrapped package for a long moment before giving in. He pulled back the thin red cellophane stripe and methodically peeled back the tiny square of tinfoil, savoring the aroma of the sweet Virginia tobacco under his nose. Kenney loved the smell of a fresh pack of cigarettes. He loved all the little rituals involved with smoking: the first one of the day; lighting up after a good meal; sitting in your car waiting for a friend to come home so you can talk to him about vampires infesting your band.

He thumped the pack against the heel of his hand, extracted the first of twenty, and popped it in his mouth. He held it there, enjoying the familiar feel of the fragrant cylinder between his lips. Watching for Johnny's train on the El tracks two blocks up, he drummed his hand absentmindedly on the steering wheel and dwelled on the day's events, lighting the Cheyenne only as his mind drifted back to his conversation with Mrs. Navokovich less than an hour ago.

He had gone there hoping to find Dave, after not hearing from him or being able to trace him anywhere since their conversation earlier that afternoon. When Vinnie's grandmother answered the door, he could tell by the look on her face that the old gal wasn't in her usual high spirits.

"Kenneth!" she said, her wrinkled face breaking into

a smile as she peeked through the screen door. "So good to see you, young man. Come in, please—Thor! Get down. Let the boy in now!"

"Hello, Nan," Kenney greeted with a smile. "Hey, Thor. How's the boy, huh?" He squeezed through the doorway, patting the yellow lab on the head and playfully cuffing his face as the dog circled around him, wagging his tail.

"I'm sorry, Kenneth. You have to excuse him, please. He's happy to see you. I'm afraid Vincenczo doesn't have much time for him anymore."

"That's okay," Kenney said, following the old woman into the living room. "I'm a dog lover from way back. I used to have a black Lab when I was a kid. Great dogs, they—"

"Yes, I remember," she said. "Smokey was his name. Hit by a car you told me. Terrible thing."

Kenney shook his head, marveling at the old gal's memory. She had to be just a few years younger than Moses, but she was still as sharp as a tack.

"Not quite that old, Kenneth," she said, turning around and facing him with a sly grin. "Please," she said, motioning to the couch, "sit down. Would you like some tea?"

"Uh, no, thank you," Kenney replied, a little flustered. Had he spoken out loud? Jeez, he'd have to watch that. "Is Vinnie home? I was wondering if maybe he heard from Dave."

"Vincenczo has not been home for some time now," she said sadly. "Even when he is here, he is somewhere else."

Kenney raised an eyebrow at that one. She saw it, too, the person who knew him longer than anyone. Changed his shit-up diapers, for crying out loud. He tried to shrug it off with a smile, but she would have none of it.

"Sit," she said curtly, and this time he did as he was told, out of respect and admiration for the old girl. It could not have been a picnic raising a wild-ass like Vinnie the Razor all by herself.

"Vincenczo left on his motorbike less than an hour ago," she said, taking a seat in her chair across from him. A tea cart was positioned at her elbow and as she talked she prepared a cup for him along with the one that already sat steaming on the coffee table before her. "I fear he is going out to see that woman again. You know the one of which I speak?" She looked him in the eye, gauging his reaction. "Sugar? Or maybe some honey?" she asked, pouring his tea.

"Uh, yes," Kenney replied, unsure as to which question he was answering.

"I'm glad it was you who came, Kenneth," she said, placing the teacup on a saucer and handing it over the table to him. He reached across and took the rattling cup from her somewhat unsteady hand. "You are the sensible one out of the whole group. I can tell. Those other boys are nice enough. Johnny, the shy one, and David—he's a wild one, but you—you have a good heart and a strong mind. My Vincenczo, he's a good boy, too. He likes to have his fun—maybe too much fun sometimes, but he's always been a good boy." The old woman paused for a moment, her eyes distant and lost, as if recalling someone or something from long ago; then, just as suddenly, she was back, focused, a bitter tone in her voice. "Until now," she said. "That is not my Vincenczo who sleeps in that bed upstairs all day with the blinds drawn . . . picking away at the food I prepare for him—pushing it around on his plate like it was poison. Staying out all hours of the night doing God knows what and sneaking back into my house before the sun rises. That is not my Vincenczo, and that woman—that woman is not of this earth."

"Well, he certainly hasn't been himself lately," Kenney said, recalling Vinnie's bizarre reaction to the news of

Monique's death. I bet the old gal would shit if she heard about that, he thought, taking a sip of the hot green tea.

"My condolences to you on the death of your friend," Dragana said suddenly. "Terrible thing. Such a lovely young girl."

"Eh, thank you," Kenney said sheepishly, choking back the tea in his windpipe. Caught him off guard again.

"Tell me all you know of this woman, Kenneth," she said, a note of almost pitiful desperation in her voice. "I need to know. Where did he meet her? Does she travel alone? Have you ever seen her in the light of day?"

"I'm sorry, Mrs. Navoko—Nana," he corrected himself, putting his teacup down on the saucer. "I don't know much about her. She was at a party Saturday night after the Battle of the Bands and he met her there. There's a girl, a younger girl, closer to our age, nineteen, twenty, maybe, who was there with her. She hooked up with Johnny. She seems nice." He took another sip of the tea, pleasantly surprised by how good it tasted. "That's about all I can tell you about her. She really doesn't talk to anyone but Vinnie. Not what I would call a real friendly type, but I wouldn't worry too much if I were you. She probably—"

"She is not of this earth!" Dragana cried out suddenly as if she could no longer contain it.

"Excuse me?" Kenney asked, a little startled.

"Nosferatu . . . ," the old woman whispered. "She is undead. *Wampyr!*"

Christ, Kenney thought, not her, too.

"Who else knows?" Dragana asked suddenly, leaning forward and cupping his hand. "Who else knows of the beast?"

"David—Dave," Kenney snorted, shaking his head, "seems to think she may be a witch or something. He has some half-baked idea that she's this Blood Countess of

Europe from the sixteenth century. Elizabeth something or other. But you can't—"

"Erzsebet Bathory . . . ," the old woman croaked, her eyes suddenly wide and frightened.

Kenney thought for a moment that she might keel over right on the spot.

"Nan?" he asked, leaning closer. "Nan, listen to me. There is no such thing as vampires. It's nothing but old folklore and silly superstitions. All this talk of demons and the undead—I've got to admit, it even had me going there for a while but if you—"

"Quiet, boy!" she snapped. "There are things in this world you know absolutely nothing of. Do you think these 'silly superstitions,' as you call them, just rise up out of the thin air? That they have no basis in reality? Let me tell you, evil—*real evil*—is more than the irresistible urge that clouds the mind of the child molester or the rage that engulfs the disgruntled postal worker who decides his world would be a better place if all those around him were dead. Real evil, the work of the Dark One, is everywhere in the world and it cannot be explained away by your psychiatrists and your lawyers and your scientists!

"It manifests itself in a weak soul, creating monsters that prey on the meek and the unsuspecting. Sometimes it is an isolated incident. Charles Manson. Richard Speck. There are times, however, when evil has risen up and spread like a plague, leaving the whole world to gasp at the depth of its horror. The Spanish Inquisition. Adolph Hitler and the Third Reich. Evil is a real entity, Kenneth, a cancer born from the seed of the Dark One and it does not die merely because the body that carried it ceases to draw breath." She paused, leaving Kenney Brandt staring at her as though she had grown a second head.

"I have seen these things, Kenneth, and if you open your eyes, you will see them, too. Do not be blind to the things that lurk in the shadows, or they will destroy you if they have the chance. My Vincenczo—there is still hope for him, but it fades with the rising of each moon if what I fear is true. Your friend David—you tell him to stay as far away from that creature as possible. If she is indeed the countess, he is in great danger if she knows of his suspicions. She will read his thoughts just as I can sometimes read yours."

Kenney Brandt put his tea down and considered the old woman for a moment before speaking. "Dave was going over to her shop this afternoon after he got done talking to me. He said he was going to snoop around a little. Some old building up north. I'm not sure where it is."

Dragana lowered her eyes as one would at hearing of a friend being diagnosed with terminal cancer. She made the sign of the cross, a reflex action come to life, after twenty years of bitterness and resentment. "I'm sorry," she said, pushing herself up and out of her chair. She shuffled across the floor toward the china cabinet, rummaging through the top drawer a moment before returning with a St. Christopher medal, which she pressed into Kenney's hand.

"Take this with you," she said, indicating it was time for him to go. "Keep it on your person at all times. It will protect you from the curse of the beast."

"I'm not Catholic," Kenney said, staring at the medal dangling from the fine silver chain. "I mean, I was, but I don't practice anymore."

"It matters little what you *practice,*" she said sternly. "Only what you believe. Please take it and let your faith protect you. Watch over my Vincenczo," she said, leading him to the door. "Keep him away from this creature until his soul can grow strong again and he can rebuff her advances. It is his only hope now."

Kenney stopped at the door, trying to maintain some semblance of composure while sorting through the conflicting jumble of thoughts and emotions clamoring around in his head. "Vinnie will be fine," he said as gently as possible, not knowing if there was anything wrong with the guitar player a good kick in the ass wouldn't cure. "Don't worry, I promise I'll watch out for him. And just to give you some peace of mind, I'll call you as soon as I hear from Dave."

She clutched his hand as he turned to go, the grip of her bony claw surprisingly strong. "Kenneth," she said gently, "do not lose heart, but there is a possibility you may never hear from your friend David again." She gave his hand a pat and turned away, disappearing into the shadows as the door closed, leaving him alone with her parting words on the front stoop.

Looking back on it now, in the safety of his car he had to admit that the conversation had really spooked him. He took a deep drag off the Cheyenne and exhaled, watching the smoke curl and roll lazily out the Maverick's window. He thought, not for the first time, that there was a lot more to Vinnie's grandmother than Old World charm and her flair for cooking. No, she *knew* things.

The hairs on the back of his neck stood as though electrified.

Right behind him.

Their eyes met in the rearview mirror and her face broke into a horrible grin, relishing the terror she saw on his face. The long canines protruding from her black lips, stained with the fresh blood of Dave Hannon, glistened wet and sticky as the grin gave way to mad, braying laughter.

He did not hear his own scream as he twisted around, kicking at the seat in a mindless scramble to push himself out of the car, only to be foiled by the thick length of rubber tubing that caught the door in midswing. Struggling to right himself, he clawed frantically at the broken door as the vampire's insane laughter rang in his ears. He turned one last time to see the face that would spell his doom.

There was no one there.

The backseat was empty and the only sound breaking the silence on the quiet street was the fading thunder of the departing El train roaring away from the Armitage station two blocks up. His heart was beating like a trip-hammer. He straightened himself out and picked the burning Cheyenne cigarette off the floor mat, noting that it had burned all the way down to the speckled filter. "Holy shit . . . ," he muttered, pitching the hot butt out the window. "Holy hot shit!"

Must have dozed off a little there, Kenney old boy, he thought, turning around and giving the empty backseat a good long look. He turned to see Johnny walking toward him, his oversize portfolio bumping against his hip. More relieved than he would care to admit, Kenney flashed his lights on, drawing a wave of recognition from the singer before undoing the bothersome rubber tie-down and stepping into the empty street. Still somewhat edgy, Kenney shot a final glance into the empty backseat and strolled over to Johnny's front stoop, hoping his friend would see no lingering signs of distress on his face.

"Hey, wild man," Johnny said, genuinely glad to see him. "What brings you to this neck of the woods? You bring beer?"

Kenney held his arms up in the air, indicating his empty hands. "Sorry, chief," he said, suddenly wishing he had stopped for a twelve-pack. A cold beer would taste real good right about now.

"You dog-ass," Johnny laughed, fishing for his keys. "That's okay, I think I may have a few stray brews floatin' around the back of the fridge."

"Critique tonight?" Kenney asked, indicating the over-size portfolio as he followed his friend up the stairs.

"No, had mine Monday," Johnny snorted. "Don't ask

me how it went. This is just some work I'm bringing home from the office. So, what's up?" he asked, unlocking the door and tossing his coat on the ratty brown couch. "You look like you're about to shit a chicken."

"What? A guy can't stop by just to bullshit?" Kenney asked, laughing at the rural colloquialism. "Actually, there is something I want to talk to you about," he said opening the refrigerator door and peering inside, "but I need a beer first."

It wasn't hard to find. The refrigerator was empty except for a nearly depleted package of American cheese, a carton of eggs, and three Budweisers.

"I think I can see 'em way in the back over here behind the caviar and the roast duck," Kenney said, tossing one to Johnny.

"Very funny," Johnny replied, catching the long heave with one hand and putting the beer down on the table to settle. "You're a funny guy. Hey, I thought you were going out with Georgia tonight?"

"She had to work," Kenney said, popping open his beer and taking a long swallow. "Last-minute type of thing. She switched with another girl at the WhereHouse so she can come and see us play Friday night at the Sphinx."

"You really like her, huh?" Johnny asked, patiently waiting for his beer to settle.

"What's not to like?" Kenney replied. "Yeah, she's a doll. Smart too. I gotta wonder what she's doing with me. I think I'm way out of my league here."

"Bullshit," Johnny said, rapping his knuckle on top of the beer can, which opened with with a hiss. "You got a lot going for you, dude. It was just a matter of time before you met up with the right chick. Someone not quite so flighty, wrapped up in herself, and fucked up." He paused, regretting the indirect slight at Monique. He never cared for her or the way she treated Kenney, but he didn't want to speak ill of the dead. "Sorry, man," he said, bowing his head. "I didn't mean nothin' by that."

"Don't worry about it," Kenney said, shaking his head. "Unreal, huh? Hey, I have to ask you, man—what did you think of the way Vinnie reacted when he heard the news?"

"I gotta admit, that was kind of fucked up, but I think he was caught up in the rehearsal. That whole opening-night thing, you know? He's always been real intense like that."

"Well, he's wrapped up in something," Kenney said. He took a seat at the drawing table, absentmindedly flipping through Johnny's sketchbook as he spoke. "But I think it has a lot more to do with his new girlfriend. I want to ask you something, Johnny, not that it's any of my business—but what's the connection between her and Chloe?"

Johnny took a sip of his beer and looked intently at his friend. "Actually, I think they're cousins or something. From what I can tell, she sort of looks after Chloe since the death of her parents. They must have died when she was real young. She doesn't remember them at all. I guess Lizabet's got some big money—owns some shop on Dearborn Street just outside the Loop."

"Yeah, I know," Kenney said. "That's what I wanted to talk to you about. Dave went over there this afternoon to check the place out."

"Dave?" Johnny asked, sounding slightly agitated. "What the fuck for?"

Kenney sighed and put his beer down, searching for the right words. "Johnny, don't you notice anything strange about her? The way she acts? The way she *looks* at people?"

"Yeah, I guess she's a little out there," Johnny replied. "But no weirder than some of the chicks we go to school with—a little older maybe."

"Well, Dave seems to think she's a *lot* older," Kenney said. "About four hundred years to be exact."

Johnny looked at his friend. "What the fuck you talkin' about, Kenney?"

Kenney decided to just let it all out in the open. "He thinks she's a vampire, Johnny. From the sixteenth century—Elizabeth Bathory, the Blood Countess of Europe. A real-life monster. I was reading some of the stuff he left at my place. She made Vlad the Impaler look like freaking Mr. Rogers."

"A vampire, huh?" Johnny said, scratching his chin thoughtfully. "Well, how about that? Hey, did I tell you what happened at the critique Monday night? That little douche bag, Kevin Garret, called my work *pretentious*. Can you believe the nerve of that uppity little fuck? I felt like—"

"Johnny!" Kenney interrupted. "Didn't you hear what I just said? Dave is convinced that this woman is some bloodthirsty monarch from the Middle Ages, risen from the dead, and I've got to admit, it's a little creepy. They have almost exactly the same names—Elizabeth Bathory, Lizabet Bazore. Get it?"

"Yeah, that's kind of close," Johnny said. "But so what? My name is Johnny Coltrane, but that doesn't mean I'm a black jazzman, back from the dead, intent on wreaking havoc on the world with my decadent rock and roll."

Kenney had to smile. The kid was making a hell of a lot more sense than he was at the moment. "He's not the only one," he said, hedging a little. "I popped in on Vinnie's grandmother tonight and she's convinced of it, too. And that was before I even mentioned anything about Dave."

Johnny laughed. "Mrs. Navokovich thinks any woman who wants her little *Vincenczo* is a monster." He pronounced it Veen-*chen*-zo, just like she did, drawing a smile from Kenney, who was finally starting to feel a little more at ease.

"Yeah, I guess you're right. Fuckin' had me going there for a while, though," he said, remembering the face in his rearview mirror. "Man, I thought I was starting to lose it. That's what I get for listening to Dave."

Johnny shook his head. "What did he hope to prove by going to the shop downtown?"

"That he's an asshole with an overactive imagination," Kenney laughed, thinking of the big drummer snooping around like an overgrown Sherlock Holmes. "But we all knew that. I don't know. He was supposed to call me and he never got back to me. Probably holed up in some bar he discovered down there. Hey," he said suddenly, stopping in midflip as he looked through Johnny's sketchbook, "nice work! Did she sit for you?"

"What are you talking about?" Johnny asked, picking up his beer and ambling over to the table.

"This portrait of Chloe," Kenney said, looking down in admiration. "It's rough, but it's very good. You really managed to capture her essence."

"I never drew Chloe," Johnny said, struck silent by the image of the dream angel staring up at him from the open page. "Holy shit," he mumbled. "I didn't even realize . . . this is the drawing of the angel from a dream I had a few weeks ago. Wow, it looks just like her."

"It is her," Kenney said, unblinking.

He thought he was going to be sick.

Thirty-nine

Kenney Brandt trudged up the back steps to his apartment with the six-pack of Buds tucked under his arm, wishing he had opted for something stronger to bring home. He had swung by The Drop Zone one last time before calling it a night. Dave wasn't there. Hadn't been there all night, as a matter of fact, Tommy had told him, which was a little strange considering it was tournament night and Dave's dart team had forfeited its seed in the standings by his absence.

Wasn't like Dave to miss a dart tournament, Tommy had said, more than a little disgusted, seeing as he was Dave's partner.

Wasn't like Johnny to draw dead-on portraits of his girlfriends three weeks before he met them, either, Kenney thought as he fumbled the key out of his pocket. Wasn't like Monique to cut her nose off and . . .

The door was open.

He stood, staring at the tiny sliver of air lining the door-jamb, listening intently for the sounds of an intruder but hearing only the rapid pounding of his own heart. Cursing the loud crinkle of the brown paper bag in the still night air, he set the beer down at his feet and slowly pushed the door open. His body quivered with the tension wrought from the struggle between cowardice and courage that grips a man upon entering a life-threatening situation. He stood in the dark apartment for a long moment,

his ears cocked for any sound at all before reaching over
and flipping on the kitchen light. His presence now clearly
established, he grabbed a cutlery knife from the drawer
and made a quick but thorough, room-by-room search
that yielded nothing but the quirky feeling that something
was amiss. Satisfied that he was alone, he returned to the
kitchen and snatched his beer from the back stoop, looking around nervously before double-locking the door behind him. He opened a beer and retraced his steps
through the apartment, noting with no small measure of
distress, the subtle but distinct disarray of his personal
belongings. His album collection, which was carefully
crated in alphabetical order, had been rifled through, and
although many were out of place, he could find none
missing. The knickknacks on the shelf above the stereo
had been moved about, their displacement made all the
more obvious by the telltale islands of clean in the thin
layer of dust where they had originally stood. Feeling
strangely embarrassed by his less than perfect housekeep-
ing skills, he rearranged the small ceramic elephant, re-
planting the tiny pachyderm's legs in the four small
perfect rings so that his raised trunk faced the door as
before.

"Have to get a maid in here," he said aloud, trying to
make light of the situation and calm his own nerves. Puzzled, he took a deep drink and looked around the living
room. It was obvious someone or something had been in
his apartment, but he could find nothing missing. His
camera sat untouched in plain sight on the coffee table
as well as his rather expensive stereo equipment and his
bass. A recheck of his bedroom revealed the same subtle
degree of disturbance, but again, nothing was missing. He
almost picked up the phone to call the police but thought
better of it after playing the conversation over in his head.

*"Hello officer. Could you send a car over here please? Someone
broke into my apartment and rearranged all my knickknacks.*

There is no sign of forced entry and nothing is missing but my album collection is in disarray. You'll have someone over right away? Thank you."

He grabbed another beer and headed into the studio, where he did his best thinking. Kenney sat down in front of the large landscape that he had been working on, taking in the familiar and comforting smells of linseed oil and turpentine. The second panel was nearly complete and as he sat looking, making mental notes and observations, he had to fight off the temptation to roll up his sleeves and apply another coat of glaze to the foreground trees. He had more than a few beers in him and he had made a rule a long time ago to never touch his work when he was buzzed. He knew that what looked good at two in the morning—when you're high—would, more than likely, look like shit when you woke up the next day. Had he given in and sat down to work, he would have noticed immediately what it was that the intruder had taken from his apartment.

Instead, he drained his beer and decided to call it a night. Mentally exhausted and knowing there was little he could do about the unnerving condition of his apartment at one in the morning, he double-checked the locks and slipped into his bed. He hoped the new dawn would offer a fresh perspective and shed some light on the strange occurrences of the last few days.

He was asleep within minutes, unaware of the hulking figure of Dave Hannon staring up at his window from the alley below.

A murderous hatred consumed the drummer as he stood there in the shadows, squeezing Kenney Brandt's number 9 Robert Simmons glazing brush in his meaty fist. The parting words of the mistress swirled through his clouded mind.

Bring me something personal—something he cherishes, she had told him after the kiss. Only then can I guarantee that he will do us no harm.

Ah, yes, the kiss. Of course. Everything was so much clearer after the kiss.

Kenney Brandt was an insignificant, meager talent, riding their coattails to the big time. A trivial, pathetic little man, intent on basking in their glory and pilfering the fortune that awaited them. His services were no longer needed. The mistress would guide them to the Promised Land.

He had offered to kill him for her—begged her, in fact, but she declined.

All in good time, she said. All in good time.

They were going to have some fun with him first.

Kenney Brandt moaned aloud in his sleep.

The fluttering under his eyelids twitched in harmony with the banging in his subconscious as his cognitive mind loosened its grip on the harrowing events of the day and plunged him into the deep abyss of the dream state. He found himself walking through a large, dimly lit factory, surrounded by mammoth, two-story-high whirring turbines which were spitting electric fire from their copper-wire guts. The shriek of the humming engines was not enough to drown out the steady, mesmerizing beat of the distant drumming, growing louder with every step he took. He quickened his pace, mindful of the sparks jumping across the cold concrete floor, desperate to escape the looming shadows of the doomsday machine rattling and buzzing all around him. The door to the control room fell into view just up ahead. He knew that if he could reach it, he could save them all. Find the switch. Power the whole thing down and stop the madness, stop the destruction before they killed themselves and all would be lost forever.

A metallic crash of cymbals exploded in the back of his skull as his hand closed on the knob. He twisted hard, almost pulling the door from the hinges, unable to stop the scream rising up in his throat.

Dave sat there on a simple wooden stool, pounding away at the control panel surrounding him, the delicate equipment disintegrating under the heavy blows of the human bones he held in his clenched fists. He was long dead, this old friend of his, gray and cadaverous and smelling of the grave. Black drool poured from the corner of his slack mouth and pus oozed from the ragged wound in his neck, where his throat had been torn open. His powerful arms flailed about haphazardly as if controlled by some unseen puppeteer. His head snapped up at the intrusion, teetering on the loose hinges of his broken neck.

A glimmer of recognition shot life into the drummer's dead eyes as he looked at Kenney and smiled.

Kenney woke and tumbled from his bed, unable to hear his own screams over the pounding inside his head. Scrambling up off the floor, he looked about the room in lost desperation, clutching his throbbing temples, trying to quell the violent tremors pulsing through his skull.

His head was going to explode.

He careened across the room and pulled open the closet door, fishing madly through his jacket pockets for the one thing that might save him. *It was there!*

A shower of loose change, car keys, and gum wrappers spilled out onto the floor as he pulled the fine silver chain from the pocket and clutched the St. Christopher medal to his forehead with both hands. The pain subsided, slowly at first, then disappeared in a hasty flourish.

Tears of relief trickled down his face, culminating in a racking sob as he dropped, naked, to his knees on the floor, swept up in the undeniable reaffirmation of the faith he had forsaken so long ago. Shame quickly gave way to absolution, but the rapture was cut short by the

realization—the certainty, he had dared not acknowledge.

It was true.

All of it.

Forty

"Compliments of the gentleman," the young bartender said, nodding his head toward the end of the bar. He wiped the condensation from the mahogany surface of the bar with a hand towel and set the long-stemmed glasses down with a wet clink.

"Thank you . . . *Steve,*" Lizabet purred, glancing at the neat name tag on his crisp white shirt. Her fingertips grazed the top of his hand as he pulled it away, sending a delicious tingle up his arm.

Steve was tall, blond, and blessed with movie-star good looks. He tended bar at Sweetwater, one of the more elegant watering holes lining the nightclub strip along Rush Street. Women of all shapes and sizes were available to him on a ridiculously steady basis, but now he was grinning like a shy schoolboy. He had been absolutely smitten by the exotic brunette from the moment she had walked (glided?) through the door with the little blonde dish. He wasn't the only one to notice them. Four glasses of wine, sent by admiring gentlemen, sat on the bar, backing up the nearly full drinks they had ordered when they sat down over an hour ago.

"You will let me know when he arrives, won't you Steve?" the brunette asked with a toothy smile. "I would so hate to miss him after waiting so long."

"Yes, ma'am!" Steve beamed, happy to be of service. "I'll let you know the moment Mr. DeMarco gets here."

"Thank you, dear boy," Lizabet said, releasing him to tend to the rest of the neglected patrons clamoring for his attention in the crowded nightclub.

"We'll just have to refuse the next one," Chloe said, indicating the drinks lined up three deep in front of them. She raised a glass and nodded her acknowledgment at the grinning businessman with the receding hairline who had sent them the latest round. It was amazing what fools they could be at times.

"Yes, it's all starting to make me very thirsty," Lizabet said, staring at the glasses brimming with the dark-red wine. "If Mr. DeMarco doesn't get here shortly, I may have to make a quick meal out of our yummy little friend tending bar. I know DeMarco has a piece of this place. I read an article about him in _Crain's Chicago Business_. He has his hand in quite a few—"

"Hey, there!"

Lizabet turned, appalled by the interruption.

A middle-aged man in the early stages of male-pattern baldness stood behind her, sucking in his gut and nervously adjusting the collar of his turtleneck.

"Bruce," he said, flashing a new smile full of expensive and recent dental work. "Bruce McFadden. How you ladies doin' tonight?"

Lizabet stared at him, incredulous that he would interrupt her while she was speaking. Chloe could not help but smile at the almost comical look of astonishment on the ancient vampire's face. She spoke up quickly, trying to quell any potential violence that might ensue.

"We're doing fine, Bruce," Chloe said politely. "But as you can see, we're right in the middle of something here and not really looking for any company at the moment."

Bruce ignored the brush-off and pressed on. "I hate these joints, don't you? _Meat_ markets is all they are. It must be hell for a couple of gorgeous ladies like you two.

Me? I just come here to unwind after work. I'm in advertising. Talk about *stress*. Let me tell you—"

"I would really prefer you wouldn't," Chloe said, growing impatient. "Like I said, we're really not looking for any company right now."

McFadden looked at her, puzzled, intent on clearing up the misunderstanding. "I don't think you realize," he said, motioning to the bar, *"I bought you those drinks. You smiled at me. That was me."*

"Oh? That was you?" Chloe asked. "I'm so sorry. You must excuse us. We're new to this. I didn't realize that gave you the right to walk over here uninvited and interrupt our conversation."

"Fuck off, Bruce," Lizabet said. "Fuck off now."

"Hey, hey," Bruce said, turning to Lizabet. "There's no reason to get nasty here. I was just thinking it would be nice if we could have a few drinks and talk—get to know one another a little better. Let me tell you a little bit about myself first, and if you don't like what you hear, then I will fuck off. In fact—"

"No, Bruce McFadden," Lizabet sneered, "let *me* tell you a little bit about yourself first, and if you don't like it, *then* you can fuck off." She paused for a moment, looking intently at him, then continued. "You're an assistant copy editor at a major advertising agency. A very small fish in a large bowl. Your superiors and your coworkers regard you as an embarrassment because you've been holding down an entry-level job for fifteen years due to the fact that you've never shown the potential or initiative to reach the next level. You fancy yourself a writer. You dream of writing a novel you will never start, and being rich and famous, but that will never happen. In fact, the single greatest moment you will ever know is long in the past. You were only a child, Bruce, twelve years old, playing a game called football. Do you remember?"

Bruce McFadden had the look of a man who had just

been kicked in the nuts and was torn between trying to walk it off or just drop to his knees and be done with it. All the color had drained from his face and his lower lip twitched uncontrollably, making speech impossible. He could only nod.

The crowd around them had grown silent, halting their late-night patter to eavesdrop on the train wreck that was Bruce McFadden's life derailing before their very eyes.

"Yes," Lizabet continued, enjoying herself now, "of course you do. Hardly a day goes by that you don't think about it. Your team was down by six points and your opponent was getting ready to score in the final moments and put the game away for good when you picked up a *fumble* and raced ninety-nine yards down the sideline for the winning *touchdown*. Your teammates mobbed you and carried you off the field on their shoulders while all the parents cheered and the coach shook your hand and gave you the game ball. Covet that memory, Bruce McFadden. Cherish that feeling of joy you felt running toward glory and the elation you felt riding the shoulders of your teammates. Remember it, because I can promise you, even if you live to be a thousand years old, you will never, ever, approach a moment so shining and glorious as that day again. It was, and always will be, the single greatest moment of your inconsequential and trifling life. Would you like me to continue?"

Bruce McFadden wanted to say no. He wanted to beg— to plead with her to stop, but it was all he could do to clutch the Manhattan in his trembling fist and keep his knees from buckling underneath him. A few people in the crowd turned away, unable to watch the humiliation and the degradation a moment longer.

"Very well, then," Lizabet laughed. "You married, not for love, but out of fear of spending your life alone. Your neglect and selfishness drove your wife into the arms of another *woman,* and your children are a disappointment—underachievers and lacking the ambition and drive it takes to be a success in school. No fault of their own, Bruce. They were never given the guidance or direction a proper father would—"

"Stop," McFadden croaked, finally finding his voice. "Please stop."

"Are you quite ready to fuck off now, Bruce?" Lizabet asked, her voice dripping with mock compassion. "Or shall we get into the questionable masturbatory habits you conduct with—"

A womanish scream preceded the crash of Bruce McFadden's drink falling to the floor. He pushed through the crowd and scrambled blindly toward the door away from the shame, away from the humiliation, away from the devil-woman that had stolen the secrets of his very soul.

Lizabet casually turned back to the bar, an almost childish giggle escaped her lips.

"My, that was fun," she said. "And I didn't even have to soil my hands on his loathsome carcass. I really should do that more often."

Chloe said nothing. Something about the inherent and unnecessary cruelty of the act rubbed her the wrong way.

"Is there a problem, child?" Lizabet asked, immediately sensing the younger vampire's cold reaction.

"No problem," Chloe replied. "It just seemed rather pointless. He was about to leave."

"He was lucky to leave with his throat intact," Lizabet hissed. "The next one will not be so fortunate. I did not come here tonight to subject myself to the clumsy come-ons and pathetic meanderings of the great unwashed. The very thought that that braying jackass would dare to approach me! It would serve you well, young one, to remember that your place among these swarming cretins is not beside them but above them. Far above them. I do hope, for your sake, you are not losing sight of that."

"I'm well aware of the natural order of things," Chloe said with just a trace of sarcasm. "You taught me very well."

"Did I now?" Lizabet asked, looking hard at her young charge.

Yes, she supposed she did. The child had ventured farther down the Left-Hand Path and learned more of the Dark Craft in nearly twenty years than even the most skilled practitioners could master in a century. Her appetite for knowledge surpassed even her thirst for lifeblood. It was not uncommon for Lizabet to rise and find the child already up, poring over the old books and delving deep into the secrets of sorcery. She had been a fool not to notice that the child's burgeoning sense of independence was getting out of hand. Lizabet looked at her beautiful creation, feeling a pang of trepidation, for the first time.

The creamy, perfect skin, the white-hot mane of luxurious blond hair. And those eyes, those beautiful, amazing golden eyes. She really was a creature for the ages.

It would be a shame to have to destroy her.

It might not come down to that, though. Aside from being such an apt pupil, the child had been a wonderful companion, providing her with invaluable insight into the mores and customs of twentieth-century America. She knew the fortune they had accumulated thus far was due, in no small part, to the girl's sly business savvy. She would need her at her side if this venture into the music industry was to bear fruit.

There's big money to be made in rock and roll, the guitar player had told her. Millions—and the ones who make it big live like royalty. Royalty. Yes, she rather liked the sound of that.

She had heard the music. Simple, but powerful and engaging, driven by the raw vitality, the unbridled energy, of a young and thriving life force. She had seen the crowd that night, worked up to a fever pitch, clamoring for more, drunk on the excitement, mesmerized by the infectious rhythms pouring from Vincenczo and his little band of musicians.

They would have their hit record. She had seen to that, as had Chloe, but it would take more. It would take sound management and skillful promotion from an industry insider, someone with a solid foothold in the business who could open the right doors, push the right buttons, and clear their way to the top. There was far too much money at stake here for . . .

"Excuse me. . . ."

Steve the bartender was at her elbow. She looked up, somewhat annoyed by the interruption.

"I'm sorry," he said timidly. "But you wanted to know the moment Mr. DeMarco arrived. That's him over there, coming down the stairs. He must have been upstairs with Mr. Pearlman. I didn't see him come in. I'm sorry, I—"

"Thank you, Steve," Lizabet said as she turned with Chloe to look at the dapper gentleman descending the spiral staircase nestled behind the expanse of mirrors surrounding the dance floor.

A gold pinkie ring glittered on the manicured hand skipping along the chrome handrail, a trademark of the man *Chicago Magazine* called ". . . a dynamic new force in the recording industry, creating a buzz in the heartland not heard since the early days of Motown."

Paul DeMarco founded the "bold and flourishing" Green Iguana record label two years ago, backed by the deep pockets of the Chicago mob. His father, Tony "the Beak" DeMarco, controlled the video poker concession for the entire Midwest region, taking in a fat sixty percent off the top of every machine in every bar from Mount Pleasant, Illinois, to Fon du Lac, Wisconsin. Armed with a keen eye for talent and a genuine love of music, "little Paulie" signed an obscure pool of talent from the local blues clubs that he loved to frequent and packaged their music into a slick and tidy album for the mainstream market. Sales for *Chicago Sings the Blues* went through the roof, and in less than six months Green Iguana Music had grown from a storefront money-laundering operation into a legitimate record label.

He made his way through the crowded nightclub and was almost to the front door when Lizabet stepped in front of him, sliding past his two "assistants," Mike and Tommy, as if they were no more than wisps of smoke in a mirror. Paul DeMarco had seen them come and go in his time, but his eyes grew wide at the sight of the fiery vision spilling out of the tight cocktail dress.

"Good evening, Mr. DeMarco," she said with a winsome smile. "My name is Lizabet Bazore and I have a business proposition that you want to discuss with me."

Forty-one

"Page sixty-eight," Vinnie Rosario said without looking up as he threaded a new E string over the fret board of Thor's Hammer. "Upper left."

Johnny Coltrane flipped excitedly through the oversize pages of the *Illinois Entertainer.* Sitting sidesaddle atop Vinnie's motorcycle, he stopped abruptly and stared at the quarter-page ad.

"The Sphinx, Chicago's premier nightspot. Three bars. Live music. Appearing this Friday and Saturday in the Pharaoh Room, GloryDaze." Johnny slid off the bike and slowly paced around the garage as he continued to read. "Featuring Vinnie 'the Razor' Rosario, guitar virtuoso." He cocked an eyebrow at Vinnie and smiled.

"Hey, don't look at me," Vinnie protested. "I just play guitar. I don't have nothin' to do with writing ad copy. That's all Barry Ruder's doing. I guess he figured I had some name recognition."

"Hey, I'm just fuckin' with you man," Johnny laughed. "Hey, look, they even got a picture of all of us." He paused, then added quickly, "Not just you."

"Asshole." Vinnie smiled, twisting the E string down tight. "I wonder what's keeping Dave and Kenney. We got to go through the whole set tonight and it's almost seven o'clock. They should have been here over a half hour ago. It's not like them to be late for rehearsal. I think I'll give Dave a call and see what—"

"Don't bother."

They turned to see Kenney Brandt standing in the doorway, his face hard and expressionless.

"It's about time," Vinnie said, keeping his eyes on the doorway as Kenney entered and looked around the garage. "Where's Dave?"

"Why don't you tell me?" Kenney asked, staring at the drum kit sitting vacant at the back of the garage. "Or maybe we should ask your girlfriend. Of course, we'll have to wait until the sun goes down to—"

"What are you talking about?" Vinnie asked, rising up off the folding chair.

"Your girlfriend, Vinnie," Kenney said, stepping into the garage. "You know, the one who runs an import store with no merchandise. The one you've never seen in the light of day."

"You're way out of line, teacher," Vinnie said, walking over and standing just inches from the bass player. "You best step back a little bit and start making sense."

"Hey, come on, guys, let's settle down," Johnny said, fearing they would come to blows. "Jeez, Kenney, what's gotten into you?"

"I think we should be more concerned with what's gotten into Vinnie," Kenney replied, refusing to be intimidated. He looked into the pallid face of the guitar player glaring back at him, into the dark circles under his vacant, bloodshot eyes. "When was the last time you ate something and didn't feel like throwing up, Vinnie? When was the last time you actually slept through the night? When was," he asked, looking at the Honda parked in the corner, "the last time you took off on your bike just to feel the sun on your face? You used to like that, didn't you?"

Vinnie stood silent, unable to answer the questions he never thought to ask himself. "Fuck this," he said finally, squaring himself up. "You got something to say, I suggest you come out and say it."

Kenney paused for a moment, knowing he had gone too far to back down now. "She's not human, Vinnie—not for the last four hundred years anyway."

"Oh Christ," Johnny wailed in exasperation. "Not this again!"

"She's a vampire, Vinnie," Kenney continued, ignoring the singer. "A vampire! And I'm not the only one who knows. Nan's convinced of it, and Dave too. He went over to her place yesterday to check it out. I haven't seen or heard from him since. I think he's dead. I think she caught him snooping around over there and I think she killed him."

"She killed me all right."

They turned to see Dave Hannon's bearlike frame crowding the narrow side doorway. He was somewhat disheveled but very much alive.

"Knocked three grand off my initial bid," Dave said, casually stepping over the threshold. "That's one tough negotiator, Vinnie," he continued with a sick smile. "You're gonna have a hard time flingin' your usual bullshit at her."

Kenney's initial relief at seeing his friend alive was tempered somewhat by the uneasy feeling that all was not well with the big carpenter. His movements and mannerisms were stiff and stunted, lacking his usual grace and natural athleticism.

"What happened, Dave?" Kenney asked. "What the hell happened over there? I tried to get in touch with you all day. You should have called. I was—"

"She offered me a job," Dave said, answering Kenney and ignoring him at the same time. "I'm going to rehab her entire building. The last guy she had bailed out on her. It's a seventeen-thousand-dollar gig. I wanted twenty, but like I said—"

"Dave!" Kenney yelped, growing infuriated. "What about the books? What about the Blood Countess of

Europe? The whole vampire thing you pitched to me yesterday? Don't stand there and act like it never happened!"

"Oh that . . . ," Dave said, turning and looking at him with an offhand sneer. "Yeah, I guess I let my imagination get the best of me. My parents were right. I read too much of that nonsense. Clouds my judgment. Makes me talk a lot of goofy shit sometimes. I can't believe I actually had you believing it. You should be smarter than that, being a teacher and all."

"There, it's settled," Johnny said eagerly. "Can we all unclench our assholes and get back to work now? You guys are starting to freak me out here."

Vinnie looked at Kenney, then Dave. "What about it, Hardy Boys? Are you two junior detectives ready to rehearse, or are we gonna stand around and talk more shit?"

"Fuck that. I'm ready to rock," Dave said, leering back at Vinnie.

"Oh, and remind me," Vinnie added, "to kick your ass later on for trying to move in on my woman."

"I'll make a note of it," Dave said.

Kenney shook his head in frustration, torn between feeling like a complete horse's ass and the overwhelming relief he felt at seeing his friend alive. Looking at him standing next to Vinnie with that stupid grin on his face, he found himself questioning the cavalier attitude the rowdy drummer had suddenly adopted. It was hard to believe this was the same man who had pleaded with him so passionately only yesterday to drop his inhibitions and believe the impossible.

"Yeah, let's go," Kenney said finally, watching Dave stroll past him toward his drum kit. He looked at Vinnie strapping his guitar over his shoulder and walked over to the flamboyant musician and offered his hand. "Hey, man, I'm sorry about all that. I kind of freaked out a little. I was worried about Dave."

Vinnie looked up, ignoring the hand. "Fuck that, man. It's not important, only the music matters. Let's just get to work, we got a lot of ground to cover."

Kenney nodded and began to slink away, when he felt Vinnie's hand on his shoulder.

"Hey," he said, flashing that easy smile, and for just a moment the old Vinnie was back. "Rich and famous, rock and roll stars, remember?"

"Yeah," Kenney said. "I remember." But it seemed so long ago.

Slipping his bass guitar over his shoulder, Kenney ambled back and plugged into the amp behind Dave's drum kit, taking a moment while Vinnie and Johnny adjusted the monitors. He looked up to see Dave glaring at him over the bank of snares positioned at his right elbow.

"Dave," he said softly, coming out of his crouch and looking into the vacant eyes of his friend. "Are you sure you're okay?"

"What the fuck is it with you?" Dave spit back defensively. "Can't you just let it go? We got a rehearsal to get through here."

"Just worried about you, that's all," Kenney said, surprised by the nastiness of the response. "But I guess that doesn't matter."

"Only the music matters," Dave said, staring straight ahead. "And the riches it will bring."

. . . *and the riches it will bring?* Who the hell talks like that, Kenney thought.

Four-hundred-year-old vampires, that's who.

Christ, maybe he *was* going nuts.

"All right, ladies," Vinnie announced, making no pretense as to who was running the show. "Let's take it from the top of the first set and then we'll polish up 'Devil's Daughter.' I want it shining like the fucking Hope Diamond when we drop it on that crowd tomorrow night."

They were well into their second go-round of "Dancing

with the Devil's Daughter," when Vinnie stopped suddenly. "Whoa, hold it!" he bellowed, "Hold on guys—break!"

"What's wrong?" Kenney asked, puzzled. "That was great. Why are we—"

"Quiet!" Vinnie snapped, his eyes searching but looking at nothing. He stood there, his head cocked toward the partially open overhead door. Then a smug, dopey smile of relief broke across his face and he announced, "She's here."

Kenney looked at Dave, alarmed, but not surprised by the vacant, hopeful stare on the drummer's face. He followed Johnny's eyes toward the door and saw the headlight beams breaking on the neighbor's garbage cans before he heard the tires crunching on the loose gravel at the mouth of the alley. Vinnie was already hoisting open the overhead door when the front end of the limousine rolled into view. Long, dark, shiny, and black as the night that surrounded it.

Its back door opened. A red stiletto pump emerged. Lizabet Bazore climbed out from the limo and stood on the cement apron of the doorway. She sparkled like a Roman candle on the Fourth of July. A sumptuous mink stole was draped over her naked white shoulders, protecting them from a chill that she could not feel. Moonlight glittered off the elegant pearl necklace and the clusters of diamonds adorning her fingers and wrists. She paused a moment, striking a pose to burn into the retinas of all who watched.

"Excuse me," she said coyly. "I didn't mean to interrupt your little practice, but I was wondering if you could play a song for my friend here. This is Paul DeMarco," she said, moving aside and allowing the superbly tailored gentleman to step from the limousine, "president of Green Iguana Music. I have been going on and on about your wonderful band. I fear I may have chewed his ear completely off. I do hope he's still in the mood to listen."

"Nonsense," DeMarco said, pausing to pull a strand of lint from the sleeve of his custom-made suit. He flicked it into the stiff breeze with an exaggerated gesture of annoyance and gallantly offered his hand to Chloe as she stepped from the lush interior of the limousine.

Chloe nodded her thanks to the mobster-turned-record-producer. With her gold eyes blazing, she smiled a demure and shy hello to Johnny Coltrane.

"Always looking for new talent, and your friend Ms. Bazore has been so persuasive I couldn't resist," DeMarco continued, giving the four musicians a quick once-over. "Good-looking bunch of boys—never hurts. Image counts for a good thirty-five percent of sales in the mainstream market. You must be Vinnie," he said, eyeballing the stunned guitar slinger.

"I am sorry," Lizabet said, with undisguised pride, "Paul DeMarco, Vincenczo Rosario. And this," she said, almost as an afterthought, "is Johnny Coltrane on lead vocals and my new friend, Dave Harmon, percussionist."

Kenney Brandt stepped up as his bandmates shook hands with the dynamic promoter. He was too overwhelmed by the sight of Paul DeMarco standing in Vinnie's garage to be intimidated by Lizabet's obvious snub. "Kenney Brandt," he said, offering his hand. "I play bass and sort of handle the business end of things around here."

DeMarco shook his hand, shooting a quizzical look at Lizabet, who refused to acknowledge the resolute bassist. "Really?" he said with a snort. "Well, if you guys are half as good as I've been led to believe, I'll be lifting that burden from your shoulders. Let's hear what you fellas got," he said, checking his watch. "I don't have all night."

"The song, Vincenczo," Lizabet said as the band dispersed and settled back into position. "You know which one."

Vinnie nodded and looked to Johnny, his jaw set and his eyes burning. Johnny pulled himself away from Chloe after a gentle squeeze of her cold hand and took his spot behind the microphone. With a quick look to ensure that Dave was firmly ensconced behind his drum kit, Vinnie the Razor toed the pedal at his feet and wrenched the opening chords of "Dancing with the Devil's Daughter" from the neck of his Stratocaster.

When it was over and the electronic hum of the last notes faded into the night air, Paul DeMarco wore a stunned expression. A bit later a bemused grin spread over his stony features, followed by laughter.

"Solid gold," he said, shaking his head. "Solid fucking gold!" He turned to Vinnie. "How long you guys been lying on this? How does an audience react to it? Has anyone else heard it?"

"It's brand-new," Vinnie said. "We were gonna unveil it tomorrow at the end of our first set." He paused, a note of pride in his voice. "We're playing the Pharaoh Room at the Sphinx."

Paul DeMarco ran two fused fingers thoughtfully along the side of his jaw, a gesture passed on from his father. "The Pharaoh Room. Good room. Good money crowd, twenty-three through thirty-five, lower-middle to lower-upper class. A few high rollers. Excellent demographics. We'll see how they like it, but after that, I want to get you guys into the studio and get this down on tape. After a little airplay, we'll go on the road and barnstorm—coast to coast. I think I may be able to get you in as an opener on a big-name bill. If not, we'll go solo and play some smaller venues just to get the ball rolling."

"You mean like a tour?" Johnny asked wide-eyed. "We're gonna go on tour? Holy shit! Man, I can't believe it! Hey, guys, GloryDaze is going on tour!"

"Eh, we may have a problem there," Kenney said, stepping up and addressing DeMarco. "We're under contract with Barry Ruder and Stardust Enterprises for at least a year and he has an option to tack on two more if he wants. We all signed on the dotted line. I don't think he'll let us out of it."

DeMarco paused and looked at Kenney Brandt as if noticing him for the first time. He cocked an eyebrow at Lizabet, who stood glaring at the bass player, making no effort to conceal her distaste.

"Uh, that's right, Mr. DeMarco," Johnny piped up almost apologetically. "Kenney went over it with a fine-tooth comb. He says we—"

"I'll handle Barry Ruder," DeMarco said. "You boys just concentrate on the music." He looked at Kenney for confirmation. "You don't have a problem with that, do you, Karl?"

"Kenney. No, I don't have a problem with that at all, Mr. DeMarco," Kenney replied, sensing he was being squeezed out. "In fact, if there's anything I can do to help with the transition, I'll be glad to lend—"

"There isn't going to be any fucking transition," DeMarco snapped. "Anything you signed with Barry Ruder is null and void as far as I'm concerned and that's all that matters. *Capisce?*"

Kenney nodded and said nothing. He knew who Paul DeMarco was and where he came from.

"Good," DeMarco said, checking his temper. "Enough unpleasant talk about business, let's celebrate." He looked around the garage at the four musicians. "When you're done rehearsing, why don't you boys let me show you a night on the town?"

"Rehearsal's over," Vinnie said, nodding toward Lizabet and Chloe, who were standing by the open door of the limo.

Johnny, twitching like an overgrown kid, looked to Kenney.

"Yeah, I think we can do that," Kenney said with a laugh. "Unless, of course, you guys object." Dave was already unplugging equipment and Vinnie was busy locking down the garage.

They filed into the limousine one by one: Chloe, then Johnny on one side and Dave, Vinnie, and Lizabet on the other. DeMarco slid in next to Johnny, leaving Kenney standing awkwardly on the cement apron.

"C'mon, Kenney," Johnny said, leaning forward and scooting himself over against the opposite window. "There's plenty of room."

"Yes, Kenney," Lizabet said, looking up at him. "Don't be left out in the cold. You can sit next to me. Come join us."

Kenney's head was swimming with talk of a record deal and airplay and a coast-to-coast tour. He had forgotten all about vampires and sixteenth-century blood countesses and was thinking that maybe Vinnie's girlfriend wasn't so bad. She had gotten Paul DeMarco to listen to their song and now here she was, willing to sacrifice her own comfort just so he could ride with them. Besides, she had such a lovely voice. How could he refuse?

No, he had to go. His hand rested on the doorsill and he bent to step into the opulent interior, when he suddenly froze.

She was smiling at him.

His heart stopped for a moment as his eyes locked on the horribly long canines, glistening, wet, and bone-white. Their sharp points pressed like tiny daggers into the soft pink bed of her lower lip. The smile grew wider still, pulling his gaze up to her eyes, brimming with their own cruel and taunting laughter. He jumped back, barely able to stifle the gasp rising in his throat, and pulled his hand from the shiny steel door of the limousine.

"I'll take a pass!" he mumbled. "I gotta get up early tomorrow. You guys go on ahead. I'll be all right. Go on. . . ."

"You sure, Kenney?" Johnny asked, leaning forward, obviously concerned about his friend's sudden and quirky change of heart.

"Yeah, really," Kenney replied, managing somehow to close the door and step back away from the *thing* grinning at him. "Don't worry about me. I'll see you guys tomorrow night."

"Fuck 'em," Dave said coldly. "He said he don't wanna go."

"All right, man," Johnny chirped. "Your choice, your funeral."

DeMarco rapped his knuckles twice on the smoked glass partition, signaling his driver to take off. Lizabet's tinted window powered up in its frame before stopping suddenly.

"Oh, Kenney," the *thing* said to him, peering over the dark glass, "I do hope you'll be bringing that delicious girlfriend of yours tomorrow night—the barmaid? I am *so* looking forward to getting to know her better."

She smiled again and this time he almost did scream. God, couldn't the rest of them see it? She cast one final, hateful glance his way before the window glided up past her face and the limousine hitched into gear. He stood alone in the alley, trembling in the dim light of the new moon, and watched the taillights grow smaller as the black Lincoln motored silently down the alley to the end of the block. It wasn't until the brake lights flashed once and the long car disappeared around the corner, that the fear overtook him and dropped him to his knees.

Forty-two

Kenney Brandt stared at the telephone for a long time before he picked it up and dialed Georgia's number, a number he had already committed to memory after only three calls. He was ready to hang up after the tenth ring, almost relieved that he could put it off a bit longer, when he heard her voice, breathy and hurried on the other end.

"Hello?"

"Hey, there, it's Kenney," he said, the thrill of hearing her voice tempered by what he had to say. "I was just about to hang up. I didn't think you were home."

"I was in the shower, silly boy," she laughed. "I'm sitting here dripping wet with a towel wrapped around me and it's very cold in this kitchen, if you know what I mean."

He winced at the thought of her large, perfect nipples, erect and straining against the fabric of the bath towel. "You're killing me," he said. "I wish I was there to help you towel off."

"There'll be plenty of time for that tonight, Mr. Brandt," she scolded. "After the show. I saw the ad in the *Reader* and I showed it to all my friends at school. They called me a shameless groupie."

He bit down hard on his lip. She wasn't making this any easier on him. "Yeah, eh, look, I wanted to talk to you about that. I don't know if you should come tonight."

There was a long pause on the other end.

"What are you talking about, Kenney?"

"I don't know," he continued lamely. "I mean, what if it doesn't go well? What if we bomb? I don't want you to see that. How 'bout I swing by your place after the show and—"

"Bullshit," she said. "You guys are going to be great. This is a big night for you, Kenney, and I want to be there. I took off work for this. I bought a new outfit. Wait till you see it."

"I don't think you understand," Kenney said, not realizing how tough this was actually going to be. "You can't come tonight. It's not a good idea, trust me."

"Trust you? I don't even know what you're talking about!" she said, growing angry now. "You better come clean with me right now, Kenney Brandt!"

Well, it's like this, he thought. It's not safe for you to come because Vinnie's girlfriend is a four-hundred-year-old blood-drinking demon and she made an offhand reference about you last night that I'm not completely comfortable with. I would really prefer that you stay away from the Sphinx tonight because I don't want her to kill you.

He swallowed hard, forcing the words from his throat. "Look, Georgia, maybe this whole thing, me and you—maybe it isn't such a good idea right now. There's going to be an awful lot of women hanging around after the show and if you're there—"

"You bastard!" she seethed, unable to believe her ears. "I thought you were a nice guy! I thought you were different!"

"Georgia, look—"

"Fuck you!" she cried, then the inevitable click and the cold, empty hum of the dial tone buzzed in his ear.

"Damn it!" he hissed, squeezing the phone so hard his knuckles turned white. Trembling, he carefully hung up the phone and walked to his bedroom, knowing full well that he had just chased a beautiful and remarkable woman from his life forever. He sat on his bed and rubbed his temples trying to erase the image of Georgia standing in her kitchen, smelling sweet, fresh out of the shower, crying and cursing his very existence.

Better that than what happened to Monique.

"And that was the easy part . . . ," he muttered. He reached under the bed and pulled out the length of wood that he had sharpened to a point earlier that afternoon. Kenney rolled the chair leg around in his hand, hefting it, feeling its weight. He wasn't sure if he would be able to do it when the time came. But he knew this game of cat and mouse could not go on much longer, and if he was going down, he was determined to go down swinging.

He dressed quickly, with none of the primping and fawning normally associated with his pregig ritual, taking time only to slip the makeshift stake into his cowboy boot and loosely secure it to his calf with a ribbon of masking tape. Pulling the leg of his jeans over the top of his boot, he walked around the room once, making sure the weapon was unnoticeable. Satisfied, he stopped in front of his dresser and draped the St. Christopher medal over his head, letting the medallion hang outside his shirt, in plain view. Pausing in front of the mirror, he stared at his face for a long moment, looking deep into his own eyes, as if for the first time. He wondered if the man looking back at him had the courage to face what lay ahead.

"Better get going, Kenney," he said to his reflection. "Big night tonight."

The steady drizzle that had fallen through most of the afternoon had blown out over the lake, allowing Kenney the luxury of opening his window as he made his way across town. The interior of the Maverick was musty, and he welcomed the clean smell of the air after a good long rain—one of the simple pleasures of life he usually take for granted. He switched on his stereo, then turned it off, preferring to be alone with his thoughts and the soothing hum of his tires on the wet street. He found a tight spot a few doors down from the front entrance of the Sphinx and backed the old Maverick in, ignoring the tortured whine of the clutch as he angled for position. The sun was just starting to drop below the horizon and he sat for a moment looking at the purpling of the sky behind the Chicago skyline. This, along with sunrise, was his favorite time of the day. To his landscape painter's eye, there was nothing more thrilling than the drama of a changing sky, and as he walked toward the tomblike doors of the Sphinx with his bass under his arm, he lingered, wondering if it would be the last time he would see it.

A flyer hung in the ticket window announcing the festivities and talent lineup for the week. Bold type trumpeted the arrival of Foghat and Wet Willie to the main room, The Hall of Kings, next Thursday. Almost obscured by a poorly drawn cartoon camel proclaiming Wednesday's "Hump Day" drink specials, a small banner welcomed "local favorites" GloryDaze to their exclusive engagement in the Pharaoh Room every Friday and Saturday. He stooped and stared at the glossy 8"x 10" publicity photo of the youthful renegades. Taken only a few months ago, they all looked so much younger for some reason.

"Pretty good, heh?"

Barry Ruder had emerged from the entryway, nodding his head and holding the door open for Kenney with one arm.

"Pretty good, heh?" he repeated. "Best I could do on such short notice. Best I could do. We'll get a new ad for next weekend. I'll line you guys up for a new shoot with my photographer. He's good—my brother-in-law—a pain in the ass, but a good photographer."

"Looks fine, Mr. Ruder," Kenney said, stepping inside and shaking the little man's hand. "Looks just fine."

"Barry! Call me Barry!" he scolded as he led the younger man down the hall and into the foyer. "Where's the rest of the boys? You got the playlist?"

"They'll be along shortly," Kenney replied, reaching into his jacket and handing Ruder a crisply folded sheet of paper.

Kenney had spoken to Johnny earlier that afternoon. They had stayed out with DeMarco well into dawn and Johnny didn't wake up until almost three o'clock, having no recollection of how he had gotten home. Big surprise there, Kenney thought bitterly as he looked around at the grand interior of the old building.

He was impressed. He had only been inside once before and the memory was foggy at best, seeing as it was his last stop that night. The main floor, which housed the Hall of Kings, a grill, and three separate bars, was flanked by two sweeping staircases that led up to a second floor, looking down on the main level, giving the partyers a bird's-eye view of the action on the dance floor. A huge, circular, stained-glass window, framed in neon, depicting Egypt's famed Sphinx, loomed above the concourse, flanked by two small bars nestled into the landings at the top of each stairway. If people-watching wasn't your thing, you could play pool or darts in one of the game rooms, or watch satellite TV on any number of screens built into the walls.

"What's this one, 'Dancing with the Devil's Daughter'? I don't believe I'm familiar with that one," Ruder asked, scanning the playlist as he walked him down the hall. Busboys hustled back and forth with racks of bar glasses and cases of beer while bartenders and waitresses sorted their change and counted their banks.

"That's our new song," Kenney shouted over the hum of the industrial vacuum cleaner. "You'll love it," he said, staring straight ahead. "Trust me, everyone does."

"Sure, sure, we'll give it a go. Love the new stuff," Ruder chirped, stopping in front of a huge sliding door that took up most of what appeared to be the back wall. It was sprayed with a thin layer of cement, as were the walls and supporting pillars, to look like weathered stone in keeping with the ancient Egyptian motif. The words PHARAOH ROOM were sandblasted into the cornice above the door in classic Roman script. It reminded Kenney of the lettering on a headstone.

"You like that?" Ruder asked, following Kenney's eyes. "My sister's kid did that. He works for a monument company—you know, grave markers. Talented kid, he can sandblast a rose out of a hunk of marble in about twenty minutes—uses a template. It's a union job. I know some people in the Local. Ah . . . ," he said, fumbling with the handle behind the door, "here we go." He hefted up the latch with a clang of iron and slid the massive door back on its rollers, walking it all the way back to the adjoining wall.

Kenney stood in the gaping threshold, squinting into the shadowy interior of the hidden chamber. Ruder switched on the houselights, giving him his first look at the last room they would ever play. "Holy shit," he whispered.

"Nice room, eh?" Ruder asked, pleased with the youngster's reaction.

It was a bit smaller than he had imagined, and not quite as polished as the rest of the joint, but acoustically superior to the main hall. The floor, which was probably the building's true foundation, was recessed, almost three feet lower from where they now stood, and the walls were lined with sheets of thick, sound-absorbing tile. The stage at the back of the room was first-rate, fitted with deck lighting and girdled by scaffolding that housed spots and color lamps. It jutted about fifteen feet out onto the floor at its crown, giving the performers ample space for moving about. Stacks of amplifiers flanked both sides, and monitors were already strategically placed at various spots on the polished wooden surface. The area surrounding the stage was open, but tables and chairs dotted the perimeter and aluminum bleachers folded down from the opposing walls. A well-equipped bar was nestled into a cranny to his immediate left, and large iron tubs waiting to be filled with beer and ice were scattered about the floor.

"Let's light a fire under it here, people!" Ruder snapped to a pair of busboys struggling past them down the short flight of stairs with an unwieldy keg of beer. "We open in two hours! Two hours! Jeez, try to get good help nowadays. Everyone wants money, but no one wants to work. Come on," he said, walking Kenney backstage, "you can get set up. I'll send the rest of your guys back when they get here."

With the most recent crumpled butt still smoldering in the ashtray beside him, Kenney pulled the pack of Cheyennes from his pocket and carefully extracted the last one. Funny habit, smoking, he thought as he straightened the bent cigarette. Coffin nails, Ronny had called them. Ronny had never smoked and he was always on him to quit. Ronny could never understand why a perfectly sane person would stick a tube of poison in their mouth and light it on fire—unless, of course, they had a death wish.

A death wish, is that what this was? He looked down at his feet dangling over the side of the stage, well aware of the sharpened chair leg rubbing against his calf. He had thought, many times that afternoon, of running, of packing up everything he owned and hightailing it out of town. Move to another state—hell, another country.

What, then, spend the rest of his life looking over his shoulder? Sleeping with a night-light on? Wondering when he would wake up and find that *thing* standing at the edge of his bed grinning at him? No, this had to end, and it had to end tonight, one way or the other.

He was halfway through the last cigarette that he would ever smoke, when Johnny Coltrane ambled into the room carrying a snare drum from Dave's kit under each arm.

"Hey," Johnny called out to Kenney as he looked around the room, "I thought you quit."

Poor bastard, Kenney thought, he has no idea.

"Tomorrow," Kenney replied, looking at the cigarette. "Too much already on tonight's agenda without having to worry about nicotine fits."

Johnny looked at him. For just a moment it was like it was before, the wide-eyed country boy and his big-city mentor, *friends*, in the most sincere form of the word.

"I know what you mean," Johnny said. "Shit, would you have believed any of this last week?"

"There's a lot I wouldn't have believed last week," Kenney replied grimly, taking one of the snares from Johnny. "Where's Vinnie?"

"Helping Dave unload out front," Johnny said, hopping up onto the stage. "We're in a no-parking zone. You get a chance to talk to Ruder? About DeMarco, I mean."

"That's not my department, Johnny," Kenney said abruptly. "I'm not managing the band anymore, remember?"

"Hey," Johnny said, noticing the bitterness in his friend's voice. "What the fuck is bothering you, Kenney? You still don't believe all that shit you were talking last night, do you? I mean, come on, man, let it go."

"Let it go and give us a hand with the gear."

They turned to see Vinnie the Razor standing in the doorway, surveying the room. His guitar case dangled from his left hand like a sheathed saber and his stance was even more confident than usual—cocky, almost confrontational. Black leather pants replaced the weathered Levi's he always wore. His torso was adorned with a new vest, still black, but embellished with a large pentagram on the back and the Mark of the Beast over his left breast. Dave lumbered past him wordlessly, loaded down with the bulk of his drum kit.

"We got a dry-ice machine and some new lighting," Vinnie continued. "Let's get it in here and do a couple of quick run-throughs." He paused and looked around the room again, a bemused smile on his handsome face. "We're gonna' blow the walls off this fuckin' place tonight."

Forty-three

"DeMarco's out front talkin' to Ruder," Johnny said, stepping inside the tiny cubicle that served as the back-stage dressing room. "And Barry doesn't look too happy. I don't think they're hitting it off real well."

Vinnie looked up, squinting through the smoke wafting up from the cigarette dangling from his mouth. "No?" he deadpanned. "How can you tell?"

"He made me pay for this beer!" Johnny said, out-raged. He hoisted the icy bottle of Budweiser as evidence. "The first two I had were on the house, but not this one. He stopped talking to DeMarco when he saw me by the bar and signaled to the bartender. 'No more on the house for him, Angela,' he yells to her, then gets right back into it with DeMarco. So fuck it. I had to pay for it. Three bucks! I saw Chloe out front, too, and Lizabet."

"I know," Vinnie said, casually rubbing a final coat of polish into his guitar's weathered body. "They got here about ten minutes ago."

Kenney stood up. He had been sitting just a few feet away from Dave in the cramped quarters and the tension was starting to get the better of him. The big man had not spoken to him all night, except for a brief, business-like exchange during the sound check.

"Where you going?" Vinnie asked, rising up with him. "We're on in five."

"I know," Kenney said nervously. "I gotta take a piss."

He swallowed hard and looked at the lean guitarist standing in front of the door. "It can't wait," he said, trying not to sound like a student seeking permission from a study-hall monitor.

"Hey," Vinnie said, with a sly smile, "if you gotta go, you gotta go." He stepped away from the door, allowing the bass player to squeeze by.

"Ain't that the truth," Kenney said, brushing past him, noticing for the first time the welt on his chest, almost concealed by the leather vest. It was an upside-down cross carved into his left pec, starting at his armpit and ending just above his nipple. Her mark. She had branded him like a prize bull, he thought as he stepped through the curtain and ambled down the short stairwell onto the crowded floor.

The place had filled up quickly in the two hours since their sound check and the room was buzzing with anticipation and alcohol-fueled high spirits. The crowd milled about, doubling up on drinks and settling into position in preparation for the show, due to start in just a few minutes. He took an indirect route to the bathroom and was scanning the room for any sign of DeMarco or Lizabet, when he almost walked right into Chloe standing in his path.

"You must leave tonight," she said matter-of-factly. "Right after the show. I can buy you some time, but not much. You know she means to kill you."

He said nothing for a long moment. So taken was he by the sudden and startling appearance of the dazzling revenant that it was all he could do to keep from staring. He saw her then as Johnny saw her—an exquisite woman-child with skin like liquid porcelain, barely able to contain the light and energy emanating from within.

"I know," he said finally. He saw then what he had suspected all along; she was one, too, but she was different somehow, and she meant him no harm. What kind of bond existed between her and Lizabet? It certainly wasn't friendship. He doubted Lizabet's death would be nothing short of liberating for this creature.

"Don't be a fool," she said, reading his thoughts. "You cannot kill her. The world is not so small that you could not hide from her in your short lifetime. She has other kingdoms to conquer. With the passage of time and some luck, she may forget you even exist."

"Why do you stay?" he asked, seeing the underlying sadness in Chloe's face, and then a flash of alarm as her eyes darted over his shoulder.

He turned to look, searching the faces in the crowd.

"There's nothing there, Kenney," Lizabet whispered in his ear, mocking the chiding tone his mother would take when he woke her up after a bad dream. *Now go back to bed and quit being such a scaredy-cat.*

He spun around and Chloe was gone, leaving him alone with the unseen demon's whisper still wet in his ear. He pressed through the crowd, eager to be away from the claustrophobic tangle of arms and legs that surrounded him. My God, he must have been out of his mind to think he could possibly pull this off. She could be standing right behind him—clinging to him like a shadow and he would never see her, never even know she was there, until . . . until it was too late. Panic overtook him and he bolted into the bathroom, pushing his way past several patrons. He threw open a stall, interrupting a young man rolling a joint.

"Hey, what the fuck, man, I'm busy here!" the pothead bellowed, rising up off the toilet seat. "Get your own—"

"I'm gonna be sick," Kenney said. "Get out, unless you want to watch."

"Fuckin' asshole." He quickly gathered up his stash and scrambled out of the stall before the sorry-looking bastard in the granny glasses could throw up all over him.

Kenney closed the door and braced himself against the

cubicle wall, fighting off the nausea and vertigo that threatened to drop him to his knees. Reaching down, he fingered the St. Christopher medal dangling from his neck, finding a small measure of inner strength from the shiny talisman. As the panic gradually subsided, he realized that he did indeed have to relieve himself, and in doing so, he found a quirky comfort in the normalcy of the simple act. He walked out of the stall, indifferent to the angry stares of the few men still waiting in line as he headed toward the door.

"Stage fright," he quipped, managing a weak smile. "Gets me every time." He stopped at the sink and splashed cold water on his face, washing away the icy sweat that had crystallized on his forehead. Looking at his face in the graffiti-covered mirror, he realized with a sudden and tranquil certainty that he was not afraid to die. Funny thing, but the events of the last couple of days, for all their horror and tragedy, had reaffirmed his lost faith and restored his belief in the afterlife. No, he thought, toweling himself off, there are things far worse than death.

The boys were waiting for him outside the makeshift dressing room when he returned.

"What the fuck," Johnny said, handing him his bass guitar. "We were getting ready to start without you. I thought maybe you were getting cold feet."

"Not me," Kenney said, strapping the instrument over his shoulder. "I'm ready to rock." He glanced at Vinnie, who nodded and motioned to the grip to cue the lights for the intro. Dave and Johnny filed out through the curtain, leaving Vinnie and Kenney alone for a moment.

"It doesn't have to be like this," Vinnie said suddenly. "I can talk to her. You can be a part of this."

"No," Kenney said, silently acknowledging that this would be the last time that they would all play together. "No, I can't—I won't—be a part of this. This is my last dance. I want you to know," he added, looking his friend in the eye, "it's been a real pleasure playing with you."

"Same here," Vinnie replied, nodding solemnly, pulling the curtain aside. "C'mon, let's give 'em something to talk about in the morning."

Kenney took his place in the background on the darkened stage and discreetly plugged into the stack of amplifiers to Dave's right. The drummer, usually grinning and warming up the skins with a few well-placed thumps at this point, merely stared straight ahead, his gaze seeming to burn a hole in the back of Johnny's head. The muted, expectant rumbling of the crowd was the only noise as Johnny stepped up to the mike and glanced back at his rhythm section. Kenney took his cue and coaxed an ambling backbeat from the bass as Johnny launched his intro.

"Good evenin', everybody," he began as the stage floods came up and the crowd settled in. "And welcome to the Pharaoh Room. We're gonna ease into this with somethin' a little cool, a little funky, while you all find your seats." He paused and pulled the harmonica from his shirt pocket, letting Dave, then Vinnie pick up on Kenney's beat. "But after that, I ain't makin' no promises, so hang on tight."

The well-orchestrated sampling of old blues standards bought the crowd's immediate respect. The slick interplay of Johnny's syrupy voice and Vinnie's searing leads served notice that this was no ordinary garage band. Feeling totally at ease with his role as front man, Johnny took a short bow and basked in the enthusiastic applause before prepping the audience for the next round. "Thank you," he said, spotting Chloe sitting with Lizabet and DeMarco at a choice table to the left of the stage. "We're gonna sneak in a little heavy metal here, written by the maestro himself, our lead guitarist, Vinnie 'the Razor' Rosario. This is called 'Thrush.' "

They followed up the bombastic "Thrush" with a cover of "Needles and Pins" before letting Vinnie showcase his wizardry with "Ice Cream Headache." Kenney lay back, dour and watchful, as the young axeman wrapped up the blistering solo. The crowd rose to its feet, perhaps realizing they had just been treated to an early peek at rock and roll's newest guitar hero.

"Vinnie Rosario, lead guitar!" Johnny bellowed into the mike, eliciting another burst of applause from the adoring throng. Vinnie stood steely-eyed in the lone spotlight and raised his fist in the air in deference to the ovation, grimly biding his time. He was looking ahead, toward the end of the set, waiting for *the song*. The song that would bring the house down.

The room was filled past capacity, and more people were bottlenecked at the entrance pushing to get in, by the time the earthy closing notes of "Fever" melted into the eerie opening of "Dancing with the Devil's Daughter." Dry-ice smoke filtered across the darkened stage. Vinnie the Razor stood bathed in the soft glow of a green spotlight and tore a G off the third string at the twelfth fret, letting the harmonic note fill the room before bending it a full step up to A. Johnny stepped up to the mike, pulling the wet ringlets of hair away from his sweaty face, and stepped lightly onto the haunting, wide, vibrato resonating off the guitar strings.

Vinnie shifted in the middle of the phrase into a smooth, ascending run, connecting the notes with a seamless finger slide up the Strat's long fret board before Johnny pounced back on.

Climbing a wall of notes, the Razor pulled off a bone-crushing, two-and-a-half step overbend. He brought the open G note all the way up to C and hooked into a scintillating unison bend, producing a unique chorusing effect. The double note cut through the rhythm section like a laser through thick fog, and Johnny caught the tail of the hard lead as the song moved into second gear, his voice now a tortured wail.

The crowd came to its feet, driven into a foot-stomping frenzy by the thundering power chords resonating from Thor's Hammer. Johnny tore the mouth harp from his shirt pocket and blew a frenzied, clattering accompaniment that skipped over the hell-bent pounding of Dave's drumming and Kenney's rock-steady bass line. The Razor ripped a barrage of dizzying salvos from the Stratocaster before shifting gears one final time with a nifty series of open G double pull-offs, bringing the runaway tempo crashing into a wall of gut-wrenching funk. Johnny wailed the closing verse, his voice a mournful testament to despair and heartache, the soulful timbre seeming to slide right off the shuddering strings of Vinnie's guitar.

Paul DeMarco sat expressionless, watching the pandemonium break around him. The bleachers on the far walls shook and rattled with the rhythmic crashing of stomping feet. A mob mentality gripped the assemblage, whipped into a rowdy lather by the infectious beat and catchy hooks of the hard-pounding anthem.

Johnny raised his fists triumphantly over his head as Vinnie slammed the fat closing riffs home and handed off to Dave, who finished it up with a raucous flurry of calculated and controlled demolition. Several tables overturned and one fight broke out as people pressed toward the stage, pumped by adrenaline and the cowardly bravado that infuses a faceless mob. Johnny walked the length of the stage, bowing and pointing to his bandmates, soaking up the adulation, waiting for a lull in the din before grabbing the microphone.

"Okay, people," he shouted, "we're gonna take five, so let's all settle down here. We don't want no one getting hurt. We're GloryDaze and we'll be back after a short break. Remember to tip your waitresses and—"

A shirtless woman broke past security and brought the

wispy singer down with a textbook tackle, thrusting and grinding herself against him as he struggled to break free from the obscene clinch.

Chloe looked on in horror, amazed at the base display of lust, as Vinnie and a stagehand pulled the moaning groupie off the startled farm boy from Belvidere. Paul DeMarco could not suppress a wide grin as he rose from the table and took Lizabet's cold hand.

"Come on," he said. "We have business with Barry Ruder."

Forty-four

"You gotta be out of your fucking mind if you think I'm just going to hand those boys over to you," Barry Ruder said to the stocky gangster and the feral bitch on his arm. "You don't scare me. I know people. I got muscle, too. I didn't get where I am today by being some fuckin' choirboy!"

"Where you are today," DeMarco sneered, looking around the cramped office, "is way out of your league. This band is too big to be playing bars and nightclubs, even glorified shitholes like this one. Miss Bazore is now managing the band and she feels that their best interests would be better served elsewhere. Green Iguana Music can provide the proper handling and exposure for a band of this caliber, and you . . . ," Demarco paused for effect, ". . . can go back to counting fucking swizzle sticks and watering down your top-shelf booze. I made you a fair and reasonable offer to buy out the remainder of that horseshit contract you conned those kids into signing and you insult me with your veiled threats and innuendos. Now I'm going to ask you one more time to reconsider this very fair and reasonable offer. . . ."

"Fuck your offer!" Ruder blurted out, his tongue a step ahead of his brain. "You Guinea cocksucker! I was scouting talent when you were still wetting your goddamn bed! I came from nothing. *Nothing!* I built this all by myself. I didn't have it fucking handed to me like you. I—" he stopped, realizing too late that he had gone too far.

Paul DeMarco bit down hard on his lip, trying to control his rage. It had been years since he had struck a man in anger, and the legal ramifications of that beating and the medical expenses that he had incurred from the punk's ensuing coma were still lingering. Remembering the words of his therapist, he silently began to count to ten—to take a step back, when Lizabet, amused, but growing impatient with the whole ordeal, decided to have some fun.

"Is that right, Paul?" she asked, turning to him with a look of mock surprise. "A bed-wetting cocksucker? My goodness, perhaps I would be better off with Mr. Ruder after all."

Johnny Coltrane worked his slight frame through the crowd, searching for Chloe among the shifting swell of bodies streaming onto the main floor, his progress impeded by the well-wishers and fans eager to shake his hand or share a brief word.

"Great fuckin' show, man. You guys wail!"

"Thank you. Excuse me."

"Dude, you all right? That chick really got a piece of you up there."

"Can you sign this? Do you have a pen?"

"Uh, no, sorry. Excuse me, I'm trying to find some—"

"How about these?" A top-heavy redhead, waving a felt-tip pen, stepped in front of him and pulled her blouse open, exposing the spacious writing surface lying beneath. "Ooh, I know," she squealed. "Sign my bra! That way I can keep it forever!"

"Uh, sure . . . okay," Johnny blushed, unable to resist someone so resourceful. He was scrawling, *Thanks for your support—Johnny Coltrane,* across the industrial-strength

Maidenform when he thought he saw Lizabet disappear into a hallway at the top of the stairs.

"There's room on there for your phone number, too," the redhead purred, pushing her bountiful attributes against his hand.

"There's room on there for my life story," Johnny laughed, capping the marker and handing it back to her. "But no time. I'll see you around."

"You can count on it!" she called out to him. He disappeared into the crowd and headed for the closer of the two winding staircases that flanked the east and west walls.

Johnny dashed up the wide stairwell and elbowed his way past the people jockeying for position at the bar on the second-floor landing. Walking along the concourse that overlooked the main floor, he took a moment and peered over the oak rail, delighted with the pandemonium generated by their set. The overflow crowd from the Pharaoh Room had rushed the three bars in the Hall of Kings during the intermission, eager to load up on drinks before GloryDaze started their next set.

Maybe they'd come back and play the Hall of Kings after they hit it big, he thought, just for old time's sake. He came upon the small bank of offices tucked into the hallway between the game room and the bar. Johnny looked around, unsure of where they may have gone, when he heard Lizabet's laughter ringing out from behind the door at the far end of the hall.

He knocked once and entered, making the last mistake of his life.

Barry Ruder lay slumped in his chair behind his desk, his face an unrecognizable bloody pulp of smashed teeth and broken bone. Lizabet Bazore was sprawled across his lap, lustily licking the blood off the man's ruined face. Paul DeMarco stood off to the side, hunched over, trying to catch his breath, apparently exhausted after administering the savage beating. Lizabet looked up, startled from her blood stupor, and Johnny saw her as she truly was. He saw the horrible, sharp white teeth glistening like enamel daggers in the bloodstained mouth.

"Ohh . . . ," he moaned, the sound catching in his throat. He bolted down the hallway, sensing the vampire's pursuit but too terrified to turn and look. He sprinted past the game room, feeling her hot breath now on his neck. The claw came down and snared his shoulder just as he reached the landing of the far stairwell. He spun around and lashed out, struggling to break free. With one last burst of adrenaline, he tore himself from the icy grip of the beast.

Johnny teetered on the landing for one long moment before his momentum pitched him headlong down the long sweeping stairway.

The fall, a violent, pinwheeling tangle of arms and legs, stunned onlookers with the horrifically long time it took for his body to finally come to rest at the bottom of the stairs. To Johnny, it was over in a flash, a blur of pain and surreal images, but not so quick that he didn't have time to realize the exact moment his back broke. He fell into a sea of darkness and felt his body gradually rising to the surface before he opened his eyes and saw the face of the golden angel looking down on him.

Chloe Covington had almost given up on trying to locate Johnny Coltrane among the sea of humanity milling about the main floor when she picked up the faint electrical charge of his brain waves coming from above. She had honed in on the signal and was casually working her way through the press of bodies toward the stairs when the sudden and violent spike in his alpha rhythms alerted her that something was terribly wrong. She looked up just in time to see Johnny's mad dash down the concourse with Lizabet giving chase and closing rapidly.

She had witnessed the whole event from her vantage point at the base of the stairs. An immobilizing wave of unreality washed over her as Johnny tumbled down the stairs and crashed through the musty barriers of her chemically altered psyche. Memories, fragmented and cloudy, came rushing through the open floodgates. By the time he had landed at her feet in a twisted heap, exactly as her mother had done nearly twenty years earlier, she remembered it all—everything: her mother and father arguing at the top of the stairs; the drive to Duke Hospital in Clinton's Cadillac; the storm; the old woman in the cabin; waking up and finding herself . . .

The sheer horror of what had befallen her manifested itself in a long plaintive cry to heaven that shook the very rafters of the old building with its sorrow and its rage. Tears of blood streamed from her golden eyes as she knelt and cradled the broken singer in her arms. She looked into his eyes and saw the life in them slipping away, a sight she was all too familiar with. He struggled to speak, forcing the words past the pain squeezing his collapsed lung.

"Shhhh," she whispered, pulling him close. "Don't try to talk, my darling. You'll only make it worse. You know that I can hear your thoughts. Save your strength, our time is short but you must know that I love you. You must carry that with—"

Take me with you!

"Johnny, Johnny . . . ," she cried, blinking the crimson veil of tears from her eyes, "you don't know what you ask! You don't want this. You must know there are things far worse than death!"

An eternity without you? Nothing could be worse than that. . . .

"I cannot," she whispered, trying to convince herself. "I will not."

He pulled her closer, his breath hot and short in her ear. "You and I, Chloe, together . . . forever. . . ."

She gathered him in, covering his face with soft kisses. Dimly aware of the gunshots in the distance, she pondered the unthinkable.

Paul DeMarco leaned over the railing and stared in mute disbelief at the scene unfolding on the main floor below him, unable to believe everything could go so wrong, so quickly. "You crazy bitch!" he said suddenly to Lizabet standing next to him at the rail. "You crazy fucking bitch! You just killed the golden fucking goose! Don't you realize—"

The vampire turned and showed the gangster her true face, the manifestation of over four hundred years of unfathomable depravity, twisted into a death mask of evil incarnate. His scream was cut short by the volley of gunfire that ripped through his torso, propelling him over the rail in a bloody, lifeless free-fall into the gathering below.

Lizabet wheeled around and saw the crowd parting like the Red Sea for Barry Ruder, screaming and waving his chrome-plated Beretta. A bullet tore into her skull above her right eye, shearing away a generous portion of the preternatural flesh and bone. The muzzle of the gun flashed two more times and she felt the lead projectiles strike her chest, pass through the mutated tissue of her lungs, and spin harmlessly out her back. The silver-dollar-size exit holes shrank to pinpoints, then closed completely even as she reached up and dug into the shattered bone of her eye socket and pulled the bullet from her skull. She stared at it, red with blood. (Her blood!) The novelty of being shot for the first time gave way to anger.

"Son of a filthy whore!" she seethed, tossing the slug aside. "It will take weeks for this to heal!"

Grinning madly, she advanced on the backpedaling nightclub manager as he tried in vain to squeeze another round from the Beretta's empty clip, the glass bowl lamps protruding from the wall exploding in conjunction with her every step. The crowd streamed down the stairways in a frantic stampede, trampling the slow and the weak, spilling over the railings in their haste to flee from the demon who walked like a human.

Barry Ruder tried to run but found to his horror that he was frozen to the spot where he stood, his limbs now serving a higher power. His ears began to grow hot and he dropped the gun, clutching at them as if to contain the tremendous pressure building inside his skull. The vibration started as a quiet hum, swelling until a thousand hornets filled his head, rattling his teeth loose and forcing his bulging eyes from their sockets. His ravaged face twitched and contorted, pulsating like a tuning fork just before his head exploded, splashing the walls with gore and blood.

The headless body of Barry Ruder wavered for a moment, did a crazy two-step and toppled over backward, sending Lizabet into gales of mad laughter. Half-crazed by the smell of blood in the air, she turned to see Vinnie ascending the stairway, struggling against the flow of the frantic exodus. He froze on the landing when he saw her there—saw the true face of the beast he had lain with.

"Darling," she said, extending her arms to him, "come to me. Come to my side."

The look of revulsion and horror on the guitar player's face slowly melted away. He took a few rambling, uncertain steps in her direction, then paused before shuffling forward with the blank conviction of a sleepwalker.

"Yes, that's it, beautiful one," she beckoned. "Come to me now and we will leave all this behind. We will start anew, just you and I. Come with me and you will be forever young, forever beautiful. We will rule together, we will—"

"To hell with you, bitch."

She whirled around, so engrossed in her enchantment of the guitar player that she did not have time to fend off the blow. Kenney Brandt brought the length of sharpened wood down in a high arc and buried it in her chest cavity.

Kenney could barely hear his own manic shouting over the unearthly screams that welled up from within the beast as they dropped to the floor, fighting for control of the stake protruding from her rib cage. Calling upon all his strength, he hung on while she bucked and kicked beneath him, howling and gnashing her teeth.

"This is for Johnny!" he screamed, pulling the stake out and bringing it down again with all his might, directly into her breastplate, prompting a projectile geyser of blood that covered his face and torso. "And this is for Monique!" he shouted, putting all his weight down on the stake, pushing it to the hilt. "And this—"

The blow to the back of his head knocked him clear off the howling specter and onto the brink of unconsciousness. He blinked through the fuzziness and the blood just in time to see Dave Hannon's meaty fist coming in for another landing across the bridge of his nose. A shower of electric stars poured over his face like acid, blinding him to the left hook that landed flush on his jaw. The fury and frequency of the punches raining down from the bigger man rendered him limp and helpless, and when he caught a flash of Vinnie standing over him with his guitar raised high over his head, he closed his eyes and waited for the end.

Although he had not seen the fall, the sight that awaited him when he reached the top of the stairs told Vinnie everything he needed to know about Johnny Coltrane's death.

He saw Lizabet conducting Barry Ruder's macabre dance of death. He saw the pain and fear on the little man's trembling face just before his head exploded from the inside out and he toppled over—finally, mercifully dead. He saw the corruption and depravity that lay beneath the smooth white mask of unearthly beauty on his dark lover's face, red with the blood pouring from the gunshot wound. He saw all this and he wanted her still.

Turmoil gave way to a sad inner peace when she beckoned to him and he answered the call with the listless resignation of the truly damned. He moved toward her, oblivious to the chaos and carnage all around him, too numb to notice or care that Kenney Brandt was rounding the landing at the opposite stairway, poised and ready to strike.

Vinnie felt the first blow in his own chest, a symbiotic thud that dropped him to his knees. The stranglehold that the sorceress had on Vinnie's soul slipped with every devastating strike of the sharpened chair leg into Lizabet's black heart, allowing the stifled vestiges of his humanity to regain a foothold in his psyche. The spectacle of Kenney Brandt's savage beating at the hands of Dave Hannon touched a nerve long numbed by the poisonous blood feeding the neurons in his oxygen-starved brain. Instinct took precedent over his muddled intellect and he raised his guitar high, bringing it down hard across the back of Dave Hannon's head.

Dave crumpled forward, dazed by the blow, and staggered to his feet with all the cognizance of a rabid dog. He glared at the guitar player circling warily around him, unable to comprehend the treason perpetuated by one of the Chosen. Fueled by a fresh hatred, the big carpenter lowered his head in a blind charge, intent on tearing the betrayer limb from limb. The shrieking howls of his mistress filled his ears just before the stained-glass window exploded in a shower of lethal color and his world went black.

Cradling the lifeless body of Johnny Coltrane in her arms, Chloe methodically ascended the stairway, never taking her eyes off Lizabet as the demon whirled about the concourse, screeching and struggling to pull the stake from her chest. Chloe reached the landing and gently laid the broken singer in the corner, planting a kiss on his cold forehead. Struggling to contain the whirlwind of emotions roiling inside her, she turned to face the monster who had stripped her of her humanity and had transformed her into an aberration in the face of God and nature.

Their eyes met for the briefest of moments, long enough for the mistress to see the hatred lit by the fire of truth blazing in her disciple's face. The heavy veil of deceit had been lifted and the beast stood there like a debunked faith healer, confounded and exposed, stripped naked of the power of deception. A glimmer of true fear flashed through Lizabet's dark eyes before she rose up into the air with one final, unearthly shriek and hurtled through the stained-glass window above the concourse in a crystal hail of wrought iron and colored glass.

Chloe charged through Dave Hannon's blind bull rush, sending the former linebacker crashing into the wall like a rag doll. She arrived a second too late at the spot where her antagonist had stood bleeding to death only a moment before. She cursed herself for misjudging the old one's power, knowing after all these years that such a mistake could prove fatal. Undaunted, she pulled the semiconscious Kenney Brandt to his feet and led him over to the corner where Johnny lay at rest.

"This was your friend," she said. "See that no more harm comes to his body."

An almost nauseating grief welled up inside the bass player's chest as he looked at the boyish face of the small-town kid he had taken under his wing nearly three years ago. The singer's eyes were closed and his mouth bore the slightest hint of a smile. He looked like he was asleep, perhaps in the middle of a pleasant dream. Kenney pursed is lips, fighting off the oncoming tears, the words croaking from his tight throat, halfway between a plea and a testament. "You will finish her. . . ."

"The nightmare ends tonight," Chloe said soberly. "For all of us. I will stake the monster so deep into the core of the earth that hell will choke on her carcass till judgment Day."

"Use this."

Vinnie the Razor stood there, his eyes clear and full of conviction. He held the broken neck of Thor's Hammer at arm's length, offering it to Chloe, like Merlin presenting Excalibur to King Arthur. "It's pure maple," he said in a way of explanation. "It won't reach the earth's core, but it's plenty long enough to get the job done."

Chloe very nearly smiled as she examined the Stratocaster's smooth rounded neck, feeling the tangible weight of the thing in her hands. She nodded her thanks and looked to the shattered window high above their heads, filled now with the strobing blue lights and frantic wails of police sirens.

She turned, allowing herself a final somber look at the prone body of Johnny Coltrane and then she jumped straight up, perching briefly on the rounded sill before dropping into the night sky.

Forty-five

The rage and indignation that had masked the severity of her wound thawed with each shambling step the monster took, giving new life to the excruciating pain in her chest. Lizabet Bazore ducked into a driveway, out of the light drizzle, searching for refuge from the pursuit that was as sure to follow as the rising of the sun. Chloe would come for her, she knew, as soon as she emptied her body of tears for the boy. That was only part of it, though.

Chloe knew the truth.

What triggered the revelation she could not imagine, but it mattered little now. She had to get underground, and quickly. The wound to her chest was near catastrophic, missing her heart by mere inches. She cursed her carelessness. The thought that she had allowed one so weak—one that she hated so—to inflict such damage did little to lessen the excruciating pain of the projectile grating against her rib cage. Bracing herself against the damp brick, she bore down, gripping the stake with her ungainly claws and wrenched it free with a wet plop. The wooden thunk of the chair leg clattering to the ground jarred her from the lethargy brought on by the loss of blood. She scrambled to her feet, the thought of waking in this alley to a burning sun, shocking her system into action.

Scanning the rooftops overhead, she clung to the shadows, making her way to the mouth of the alley before dashing across the street. A speeding Dodge Charger braked to a skid on the wet pavement narrowly missing her before careening onto the curb and striking a light-post. She paused at the corner, unsure of her next move, when she felt the vibration coming up through her toes from the metal grating beneath her feet. The rumbling grew steadily louder, almost deafening. She watched in fascination as the subway train passed right beneath her feet, a blur of clacking metal and maddening noise.

"Hey, lady, what the fuck is the matter with—"

She whirled and caught the driver of the Charger with her left hand, slicing his jugular with one deft strike. He dropped to the ground, clutching stupidly at his throat, trying to stem the flow of blood.

A scream rose up from a woman passing by with her boyfriend, drawing more people to the small gathering that was building a safe distance away from the bloodied woman on the corner. Regretting that she could not stop to feed and replenish herself, Lizabet knelt down. With the last of her strength she tore the metal grating free from the sidewalk and tossed it aside. As the last subway car hurtled by, she dropped like a stone into the tunnel below, leaving her signature chaos on the street above.

She picked her way along the dank interior of the tunnel, leaning against the arcing curves of the cement wall for support. She rounded a long bend, pleased that the light from above had disappeared altogether, the only illumination coming from the spotty lighting lining the top third of the cylindrical passageway. The hard cement upon which the tracks lay made digging out of the question, but she knew that there was soft earth to be found somewhere in the subterranean labyrinth. She could smell it, just as she could smell the rats long before she could see them scurrying across the tracks in the darkness. The scent grew stronger as she traveled deeper into the tunnel, following her keen nose until she came upon the nondescript steel door nestled into the tunnel wall. She pressed her face to the cold surface, delighted to hear the distant but telltale trickle of running water. She knew that soft earth could not be far behind. A wave of relief coursed through her damaged frame as she thought of the warm embrace of the earth and the comfort and strength it would provide. She would settle in for a long sleep. She would heal. She would grow strong again and then she would come back and kill them all. That last thought brought a smile to her face as she reached down and turned the heavy iron handle.

She heard the roar before she saw the blinding flash of golden light that knocked her senseless the instant she opened the door. The impact propelled the wounded vampire into the opposite wall, buckling the reinforced concrete before tossing her semiconscious onto the steel tracking. Her first thought upon waking was that she had somehow stepped into the path of a train, a comforting notion compared to the stark reality that greeted the dazed griffin when she opened her eyes.

Chloe stood there, looming over her limp body, like a shining archangel in the murky gloom of the tunnel. Her face bore no expression, but her eyes blazed with the conviction and fury of a battle-weary crusader sensing the conclusion of a long and bloody campaign.

"Did you ever think it would end this way, monster?" she asked finally, breaking the silence. "Or in your twisted vision of grandeur, did you think you could actually rule in a world lit by a sun unable to tolerate one so loathsome and foul?"

Lizabet coughed, clearing the blood collecting in her windpipe. "One such as yourself, child?" she reminded her young disciple with a sneer. "Know full well what you are, and that it is of my doing. It is my blood that gives you life."

"Why didn't you just kill me?" Chloe whispered in despair. "You stole my life and denied me the dignity of death. And now from my endless nights of darkness, you took my one ray of sunlight, the last warm link to the thing I used to be."

She raised the splintered guitar neck high over her head. "I want you to remember this moment for all eternity. I want my name on your lips as they are dragging you screaming through the gates of hell."

Lizabet Bazore smiled, sensing the high voltage coursing through the length of steel just inches from her head. "Not by your hand, child," she cackled. "You'll never have the satisfaction." With the last of her strength, the ancient one rolled over and clamped onto the live third rail with both hands.

A scream rode on the trail of smoke that billowed from her black lips as six hundred volts of electricity surged through the demon to the grounded steel tracks over which she lay. Her body bucked and shuddered under the strain of the mounting amperage, crackling and burning from the inside out. Staring defiantly at her would-be executioner, she grasped the hot rail tighter still, fusing the roasted skin of her claws to the track bed like melted plastic. Her eyeballs rattled and popped from their sockets, but the smile on her charred face remained, the sharp teeth backlit by the yellow flames rising up in her throat.

In the horrible moment of silence that preceded the explosion, Chloe realized, a full second too late, what the creature had done. She nearly recovered in time, bringing the guitar neck down in a desperate but futile arc, swinging through the blinding flash point.

The concussion of the blast knocked Chloe off her feet and rattled windows in the world above for a three-block radius. When she opened her eyes again, she was flat on her back some twenty yards from the epicenter of the detonation, blinking into the darkness like a child waking from a fitful dream. She gathered herself up, letting her preternatural eyes adjust to the absence of light in the man-made cavern. A noxious green cloud wafted up from the smoldering traces of ash scattered about the twisted rails at ground zero, leaving an electric stench in the dank air of the tunnel. She toed indifferently at the scant remains; unable to dispel the frustration she felt at being stripped of her own personal stamp on the monster's destruction. The beast had taunted her, laughed at her, right up until the very end; denying her, even in victory, the spoils of vindication.

With one last symbolic but empty gesture, she drove the neck of the Fender Stratocaster into the dormant rubble, leaving only that token monument to mark the end of Lizabet Bazore's four-hundred-year reign of terror. An aching emptiness gnawed at her corrupted soul as she turned and walked wordlessly toward the distant lights of the boarding platform, refusing to yield to the oncoming tears.

Forty-six

Kenney Brandt sat in his piece-of-shit blue Maverick outside All Saints' Cemetery sixty miles northwest of Chicago, watching the last of the day's light disappear behind the trees on the horizon. He pulled the *Sun-Times* from the small stack of newspapers on the seat next to him and switched on the dome-light, flipping through the serrated edges until he came upon the story, a short column on page 16.

Cops Sound Final Note on Rock and Roll Tragedy

By James McGee
Staff Reporter

In what police are calling a business deal gone bad, three people are dead and seventeen were injured in Friday night's double homicide/riot at the Sphinx, the trendy Superior Street nightclub. A power struggle over rights to the band GloryDaze, an up-and-coming rock group, led to the confrontation between the club's manager, Barry Ruder, and Paul DeMarco, president of the Green Iguana record label and reputed mobster, that left both men dead. Angry words apparently escalated into an exchange of gunfire that sent club patrons scrambling for the exits. Johnny Coltrane, lead singer for the band, was killed in the ensuing stampede that sent seventeen people, including the band's drummer, Dave Hannon, to local hospitals with varying degrees of injury. Police are ruling out the existence of the so-called mystery woman that some eyewitnesses claim killed Mr. Ruder, dismissing their accounts of the incident as hallucinatory and drug induced.

Kenney bit his lip and folded the paper neatly in half, his hand trembling slightly as his thoughts drifted back to the funeral earlier that day. He had never met Johnny's parents before and he was touched when they had told him that Johnny had spoken highly and often of him. They were still numb of course; wearing the haggard mask of devastation and loss that comes only with the death of a son or daughter. He knew that look well.

He swallowed back the lump rising in his throat and climbed over the seat out the passenger door, ignoring the pain in his bruised ribs. It was near dark now and strangely quiet as he walked along the iron fence that surrounded the graveyard. He found a spot, not too far from the Coltrane family plot where the bars had been pried open, and he squeezed his wiry frame through, grateful he didn't have to climb over the top in his somewhat brittle condition.

Walking through the valley of stone, he could not help but admire some of the elaborate and beautiful statuary marking the graves of the more well-to-do dearly departed. He thought of Barry Ruder's nephew sitting in his monument factory, sandblasting stenciled roses from blocks of marble, and frowned.

Doesn't really matter how fancy the wrapping is, he thought as he came upon Johnny's fresh grave. Time wears on and the memory withers, like the flowers placed on a grave with less frequency each passing year. With the passing of a few mere generations it's as though you never existed at all.

"Your thoughts are quite cryptic for one so young, Kenney Brandt."

Her voice kissed his ear like a summer breeze.

"An eternal pessimist, I guess," he replied without turning around. He knew that she would come, once the sun was down. "I never was the type to sugarcoat things."

"It's not as final as you may imagine," she said, stepping up and standing beside him. "Try to think of it as another plane, another level of existence. If we have learned anything from all of this, it's that life does not end with death."

He turned and looked at her now, struck again by the simple but elegant beauty of her face. It was as if one of the exquisite marble angels had stepped off its grave marker and stood before him dressed in blue jeans and a black leather jacket. A sad, sympathetic smile danced in the corners of her golden eyes as she looked up at him.

"I always suspected that," Kenney replied. "Even after my falling-out with my faith, I never really quit believing . . . or hoping."

They stood in awkward silence for a long moment.

"I hate to cause you any more pain," she said, searching for the right words, "but I have to ask you about the . . . condition . . . of your friends."

Kenney shook his head. "Vinnie's holding up pretty well, considering. He wanted to come to the service today, but he gets sick if he's out in the sun too long. Can't hold down any food, throws up a lot."

"That should pass with time," Chloe said thoughtfully. "How long is anyone's guess. He was still in the first stage. It all depends on the level of pollution in his blood. Transfusions would speed the healing process, but I would be more concerned with his state of mind."

"And Dave?" Kenney asked bitterly, thinking of his

friend ranting and raving on the fifth floor of Barclay Hospital. "What about his state of mind? He almost bit the finger clean off an orderly yesterday when they tried to feed him. They've got him strapped to a fucking gurney like a wild animal. I need you to tell me *that* will pass. I need you to tell me he'll be okay. It's all in his blood, right?"

Chloe shook her head, remembering the drummer's screams that had roused her from her sleep the night he had broken into the house on Dearborn Street and stumbled into hell.

"It's different. She brought him to the brink of madness and dangled him over the edge. His actual infection is minimal, the true corruption lies in his brain."

Kenney let the words sink in. Dave Hannon was insane. "Is there anything . . ."

"I can do nothing for him," she replied. "I'm sorry. But modern medicine being what it is, who knows? There is still hope, however slim."

Kenney lowered his head, knowing as she did, that there was *no* hope. He gazed at the fresh mound of overturned earth at his feet, unable to believe Johnny was really gone.

She reached up and touched his cheek, an innocent but highly personal gesture that conveyed to him just how close their shared love for the fallen singer had brought them. "Go home, Kenney," she said. "Do not let this destroy you, too. Lose yourself in your painting. Live the rest of your life. He would have wanted it that way. Quit trying to carry the weight of the world on your shoulders."

He nodded, realizing she wanted her time alone with him. "And what will you do?" he asked. "Where will you go now?"

"I think," she said, as if pondering the question for the first time, "I may go home."